STAY

BY EMILY GOODWIN

EMILY GOODWIN

STAY
©2014 by Emily Goodwin

This is a work of fiction. Names, characters, businesses, places, events, and incidents are either the products of the author's imagination or used in a fictitious manner. Any resemblance to actual persons, living or dead, or actual events or places is purely coincidental.

Other Books by Emily Goodwin

Contagious
Deathly Contagious
Contagious Chaos
The Truth is Contagious

Unbound
Reaper
Moonlight

Beyond the Sea

Stay
All I Need

Never Say Never

Outside the Lines

First Comes Love
Then Come Marriage

One of Many

Jailbait
Jailbreak

To Lori, Lindsay, and Elyse, the real ladies behind
Contagious Reads book blog. You all rock.

AUTHOR NOTE

STAY is about the very real issue of human trafficking. While writing this book, I spoke with two FBI agents on the issue and did a lot of research, wanting to keep the details as realistic as possible.

One thing I hope you understand is that fear controls the victims. There may be times that seem ideal for escaping or calling for help that are not taken because the fear of getting hurt or having loved ones hurt is so deep.

Human trafficking is a real issue. It happens everywhere, even quiet, 'safe' little towns like the one I live in. The more I researched, the more horrified I became. There are *more* slaves today than there were 100 years ago. The average age of sex trafficked victims is 13-14. Trafficking victims have a life expectancy of two years. 100,000 to 300,000 people are trafficking in the United States every year. Girls as young as five have been forced into child prostitution. Every thirty seconds, someone becomes a victim of human trafficking.

I didn't set out to raise awareness or to be preachy about the issue of trafficking, but I do hope you can take away the fact that this isn't an issue that should be ignored. There is only a supply of slaves because there is a demand.

STAY

EMILY GOODWIN

CHAPTER 1

Just one more chapter. I rolled my eyes and closed the book, smiling at the lie I had repeatedly told myself. It was almost four in the morning, but pulling the almost all-nighter was worth it to finish the latest book in one of my favorite fantasy series. My eyes burned and begged to be closed. I rested the book against my chest and thought about the cliffhanger ending, sorting through my mixed emotions of anger and excitement.

I turned my bedside light off and rolled over, feeling slightly sad that I had read through the book so quickly. I closed my eyes and tried to shut off my mind; I had to get up in just over three hours and I had a long day ahead of me. The cheerful chirping of birds outside my window was as unwelcome as the muted glow of dawn that filtered in through the sheer purple curtains.

My thoughts were still tangled with dragons and Rangers dressed in black furs when I finally drifted to sleep, only to be rudely awoken by the blaring alarm clock. *Ugh, not yet.*

I rolled over and slapped the snooze button—twice—before I forced myself out of bed. I dragged my feet as I crossed my room, stumbling into the bathroom to begin the time consuming ritual of making myself look halfway presentable.

I turned on the shower and inspected myself in the mirror as the water warmed up. Circles clung under my eyes, and my shoulder length brown hair was a tangled mess around my face.

Whatever.

I waved my hand at my sloppy reflection. It wasn't anything

a shower and a little makeup couldn't fix.

Tired, I stayed in the shower too long, enjoying the steamy hot water. I got out, dried my hair and put on the least amount of makeup that was socially acceptable for an outing with my friends.

"Addie?" Arianna, my younger sister, called from across the hall.

"Yeah?" I answered and bent down to pet Scarlet and Rhett, my German Shepherds who were sleeping on a pile of dirty laundry I had thrown on the floor.

"Can you help me do my makeup? I keep messing it up," Arianna replied, sounding annoyed.

"Sure, come here." I told her. It took every ounce of self-control I had not to laugh when she walked into my room. Black eyeliner was smeared across her face, and eye shadow powdered her cheeks just under her eyes. I brought her into the small bathroom that was attached to my room and put the lid down on the toilet for her to sit on.

"Hold still," I told her while I cleaned up her face. Ari looked a lot like me: high cheekbones and green eyes with a nose that was a hair too straight, and cheeks that caused dimples to form when we smiled. I lightly dusted her eyelids with shadow and drew a very thin line of black liner over her top lashes. "There," I said when I was done.

"Thanks." She looked in the mirror. "I wish I was good at doing makeup." She wrinkled her nose.

"I wasn't good at makeup when I was thirteen. And you're good at doing hair," I reminded her with a smile. "Speaking of, I need to dry mine."

"Hurry up!" She scuttled out of the bathroom. "Don't make us late!"

I rolled my eyes and ran a brush through my hair. Lynn would make us late. Lynn-time was generally a half hour behind real-time, hence why I told her to meet us at my parent's house at nine when I really wanted to leave at nine-thirty. And, like I predicted, I was done, ready, and waiting by the time my best friend arrived.

I grabbed my purse, double-checked that I had my cell phone, and led the way to the door. "Bye Dad!" I called before

I opened the garage door.

"Are you leaving?" Dad asked from inside his office.

"Yeah." The floor creaked as Dad walked down the hall. He hugged Arianna and me goodbye. "Drive safe and call me when you get there. And have fun at whatever you're going to."

"The Pride Parade." I smiled.

"Yeah, that." He and shook his head. "You kids are getting too liberal," he mused.

I jingled my keys. "And you are too old fashioned," I countered. "Besides, you like Matt. Don't you want me to go support him?"

Dad nodded. "I do like him. He's a good kid. You're going to his house after the parade, correct?"

"Yup," I replied. "And yes, his parents are home." I rolled my eyes. "Good thing because it's not like I spent a whole year living on my own at college or anything."

Dad ignored the snark. "Watch out for your sister and don't be out too late. Have fun. And call me when you get there."

"We will," I promised. "Love you!" I hurried out the door and unlocked my car. I rolled down the windows and cranked the air conditioning before we all piled in.

"Are you and Dillon gonna double date with me and Luke tomorrow?" Lynn asked as she raked her fingers through her wet hair.

"Maybe." I'd have to come up with some real excuse. Saying I wanted to stay in to finish a book had been my reason for skipping out on a double date the weekend before.

"Maybe?" Lynn echoed. "Try not to die from excitement, Addie."

"I'll try and contain myself."

"Oh come on! Just give Dillon a chance. It would be so perfect if you dated my boyfriend's best friend!"

"I know," I agreed. "And this will be the *third* chance I've given him." Dillon was a nice guy. He was outgoing, like Lynn and Luke, and attractive. But he didn't like books and said reading was boring. It would never work between us.

"You could at least use him for the night," Lynn added. "You know what happens after the third date."

I considered it for a second then shook my head. "I can't do that to him … or me. I have higher standards for myself than that."

"Your loss," she said with a shrug and threw her blonde hair over her shoulder. "If I wasn't with Luke, I'd tap that."

I laughed. "You're so full of shit, Lynn."

She looked at me innocently then laughed too.

"What are you talking about?" Arianna piped up from the back seat. "What happens on the third date? I think I know. Isn't that when you—"

"Nothing happens," I interrupted. Ari was too young for this. "Nothing fun."

"You have an odd definition of 'fun,'" Lynn teased. I glared at her.

"Are you talking about boys?" Ari asked, suddenly more interested. "You know Addie secretly hopes to find some Prince Charming type of guy, like in one of her books."

"It's not so secret," Lynn said with a laugh.

"So," I said, changing the subject to our planned trip to Wizard World in Chicago later in the summer. I hated talking about my relationships—or lack there of—with Lynn. It made me depressed, and it wasn't that I wasn't looking. Honestly, I felt like there would never be anyone right for me. Maybe I *was* holding out for my knight in shining armor and didn't want to admit it to myself. "We need to decide on a theme for our costumes ASAP. Batman characters or Disney princesses? Personally, I'd go with Batman." We talked about our costumes and the rest of the fun stuff we had planned for the summer, making the long drive to the city go by quickly.

We parked and got out, taking a few minutes to fix our hair. I grabbed my cell phone and called Dad as we shuffled into the flow of people headed toward the parade.

"Matt said to meet him at the end," Lynn informed us. "And," she continued, scrolling through her text messages, "it ends on Mackinoff Drive. So let's go a block before that. We can still see the parade and then easily find him."

"Good idea," I affirmed and let her lead the way. The further we got from the heart of the festival, the more run-down the buildings became. The street sides were hardly occupied so far down; we easily found a spot and sat down on a bench while we waited. I stretched my long legs out, wanting to soak up as much sun as possible before I was beach-bound tomorrow for Lynn's family's annual Memorial Day cook out. Next to Lynn, who went to the tanning salon four times a week, I was ghostly pale. I had intended on going tanning a few times with her, but I had spent my 'fun money' allowance on books. I pushed my sunglasses low on my nose, trying to avoid an awkward tan line.

I saw a blur of black out of the corner of my eye. It was moving fast and headed right toward the street that ran perpendicular to the one we were on. It wasn't blocked off for the parade. I whipped my head around to see a girl race into the street, jumping off the sidewalk with such haste that she didn't take the time to see if the coast was clear.

A horn blared and tires squealed as a car slammed on its breaks. *Holy shit.* My heart skipped a beat. The car missed her by just a foot. It wasn't going fast being so close to the parade route, but it was fast enough to cause some damage.

"Did you see that?" Lynn stood and put her hand to her face, shading her eyes. "That was close. Dumbass isn't looking where's she's going."

"I think she's crying." I narrowed my eyes, watching her race across the street. She kept her head down and her arms wrapped around her chest. It was odd to see her in a long sleeved sweater in eighty-degree weather. When she was parallel to us, she whirled around, looking behind her as if she was scared of being followed. Whatever she saw made her pick up the pace. She dodged behind a building and out of sight. My eyes lingered in her direction, waiting to see if anyone else would accompany her down the alley.

I shook my head and turned back to Lynn and my sister, making lazy conversation and enjoying the sun. I was hot by the time the distant music and cheering from the parade floated down the block, and I had already drained my water bottle. I stood, told Arianna and Lynn I'd be right back, and dashed across the street to use the bathroom. I pushed my way through the crowded coffee shop and impatiently waited in line for the single stall bathroom.

When I was done, I left the ladies room and held my purse close to my body, prepared to side-step my way through the crowded cafe once again. But then I saw the back door. I looked at the crowded cafe and decided I'd rather go through the alley than wade my way through all the people. I put my hand on the knob and twisted, hoping an emergency alarm wouldn't sound. Luckily it didn't, and I emerged into the alley behind the coffee shop.

Then I saw her, the crying girl who almost got hit by a car, slumped over next to a dumpster. I froze, unsure of what to do. I knew it wasn't any of my business. She probably didn't want to be bothered anyway. But then I noticed the blood.

My heart pounded and my breath rushed out of me. "Are you okay?" I asked, my voice meek. I doubted the crying girl even heard me. I swallowed and asked again.

Slowly, she lifted her head, revealing a black eye and a fat lip. "Go," she croaked and wiped her bloody nose.

"Oh my God," I blurted and assumed she had been mugged. "I'll help you," I said and started to move in her direction. "I'll call the police." Just then, someone walked down the alley. I jerked my head up, heart racing. The young man slowed his gait when he saw me. Despite my fear, I couldn't help but notice his extreme attractiveness. A black t-shirt stretched over his broad shoulders, tight enough to show off his muscular chest and arms. The perfect amount of stubble covered his face from his defined cheekbones to his strong jaw. Carefully tousled hair fell just above his beautiful blue eyes.

"Help!" I said. "I...I think she's been mugged." I shook my head, hands shaking. " I don't know what happened but she's bleeding. She needs help!"

Another guy stopped short, staying behind the guy with the blue eyes. He was tall and robust with a head full of wavy, black hair that fell an inch below his ears. His eyes were a dark chocolate brown, and his full lips were pulled into a frown. His dark eyes flicked from me, to the girl, and then to the guy in front of him. They widened with fear, and he opened his mouth as if in warning when Blue Eyes elbowed him in the ribs.

"It's okay," Blue Eyes said and held up his hands, flashing me a smile. "I'm going to help her, don't worry." He took a step forward, and the crying girl picked up a handful of gravel and sprang to her feet.

"Go!" she yelled and threw it at Blue Eyes. His handsome face twisted into something hateful, and he lunged forward with alarming speed. His hands struck the girl on the shoulders, shoving her back into the dumpster. Her head hit, resounding against the metal, and she slid back down onto the ground. My fear turned into terror. Those guys weren't going to help her. They were the ones who hurt her.

My pulse rose, and I scrambled to stick my hand into my purse, feeling around for my phone. I whirled around at the same time in a desperate attempt to get back inside the safety of the crowded coffee shop and call the police. I diverted my eyes when I felt the familiar rectangle of my phone, needing to look at the screen to unlock it.

I put my phone to my ear and reached for the door handle. My fingers graced the worn knob when he grabbed my wrist. His nails dug into my flesh as he jerked me forward. My feet caught on themselves and I toppled over, cutting my knees on the dirty alley ground. The phone flew from my grip and clattered on the pavement.

I caught a glimpse of the guy with the dark hair holding onto the crying girl. His body was rigid and his brown eyes were opened wide as he watched my struggle. The muffled voice of the 911 operator floated into the air.

"Help!" I screamed.

Blue Eyes kicked me in the side, causing me to fall flat on my face. Music from the parade began to grow louder. "Help me!" I called again. My cries were drowned out by the roaring cheers coming from the crowd. I stretched out my arm, frantically slapping at the ground in a desperate attempt to reach my phone. Bits of glass and tiny pieces of asphalt stuck to my palm. I drew my legs up underneath me and pushed myself forward and away from Blue Eyes. I planted my feet on the ground and sprang up, only to be knocked down again.

Blue Eyes laughed and walked around me. His intense eyes met mine before his foot came crashing down on my phone. The case cracked from the force. The screen shattered and little rhinestones popped off and rolled away. He stomped on it once more before picking up the broken device and throwing it into the dumpster.

Little droplets of blood pooled around the torn skin on my hands. Blue Eyes stepped over to me again, though when he kicked me, I grabbed his ankle and pulled. I imagined he'd fall, we'd struggle, and I'd get away.

But he was strong, so much stronger than me. He yanked his foot up and out of my grasp. Grit fell from his shoes onto my face and into my eyes. Involuntarily blinking, I recoiled. I pressed my blood-covered hands onto the hot pavement and pushed myself up. I opened my watering eyes. My vision was blurry. Then something struck my head, right above my left eye. The clanging of cymbals echoed from the street. The sun was suddenly sickeningly hot. An instant wave of dizziness coursed through me. Gravel crunched under the soles of Blue Eyes' shoes. The last thing I remembered was his fist making contact with my face.

CHAPTER 2

Something slammed shut above me, clicking into place. The noise brought me back to consciousness, waking me up into an instant panic. My eyes flew open and my breath came out in ragged huffs. I was lying on my side, and it was dark. Too dark to see anything. My heart hammered with fear, and I felt like I was going to get sick. Beads of sweat rolled down my face and the hard surface I was lying on hurt my hip. Where the hell was I? What was going on?

Rough carpet rubbed against my cheek, irritating my skin. I reached up above me, stretching my stiff arm. My hand hit the ceiling. I pressed my palm against it. It was solid. I pushed, straining my muscles. The air was hot and stale. *No.* This wasn't happening, it couldn't be happening. *This isn't real,* I told myself. I was in the trunk of a car. I flipped over onto my back and began banging on the roof of the trunk.

"Help!" I pushed against the roof. I balled my hands into fists and pounded. Frantic, I banged on the roof until my hands hurt. "Please, help me!" There had to be a way out. I rolled back onto my side and began to madly search for a release. I reached out in front of me, feeling for the metal latch. "Please," I cried. "Somebody, help me!"

My fingers fastened around something hard. My eyes widened, and I sucked in a deep breath. Was it the trunk release? There was no way to tell, but I pulled it back anyway. Nothing happened. I curled my fingers around it and yanked it back with all my strength. My sweaty hands slipped off the little piece of metal and flew back. The top of my hand hit the roof of the trunk. White pain webbed across the bones in my hand, tingling along my fingers. I cradled my hand against my body, waiting for the sting to pass.

I was going to die. I knew it. I would swelter and die in this trunk. I kicked my legs against the side of the trunk and screamed. *Oh, God.* I would suffocate. The air was going to run out, and I was going to suffocate and die. It would be a slow horrible death. I swallowed a sob and clamped my mouth shut. I needed to save the little oxygen I had left.

As soon as I was still, I heard muffled voices coming from outside the car. My muscles ached as I struggled to keep calm while everything inside of me wanted to scream for help. Whoever was outside the car would have heard me, and they hadn't helped me. And they wouldn't. They had to be the two guys who put me in here. I moved my trembling hands over my mouth, pressing then against my lips to silence my chattering teeth. Hot tears silently rolled down my face, soaking the rough carpet beneath me. I moved to the end of the trunk, pressing my ear to the side to listen.

"Bitch saw the whole thing and called the cops. What the hell was I supposed to do?" he spoke. I recognized his voice right away. Terror turned my blood cold, and his face flashed through my mind. Eyes as blue as the summer sky. High cheekbones covered in day-old stubble. Tousled brown hair and full lips. I had been so taken aback by his good looks that I hadn't suspected him of being anything but helpful. I was so fucking dumb.

"You could have left her," a deep voice responded. I had yet to hear him speak but I was certain that voice belonged to the man with the dark eyes. "There's no way she could have turned us in."

"And that's a risk you're willing to take? I don't think Nate would be too happy with that."

"N-no," he nervously stammered. "But bringing her with? She'll slow us down. W-we could have..." he trailed off. "There are other ways."

The guy with the blue eyes laughed. "Other ways?" His

voice got louder as he leaned on the car. "You're a fucking idiot, Jackson. Killing her on the street is too obvious and messy."

Killing her on the street? A painful stab of horror pierced my heart. What kind of people were they? Cold fear crept over me at a dizzying rate. They wanted to kill me? Fuck the lack of oxygen. I needed out. Now. I pushed off the side of the trunk and started kicking, blindly aiming for the brake lights.

"Help me!" I screamed as loud as I could. "Help! Get me out of here! Help!"

Someone hit the car. "Shut up, you stupid whore!" Blue Eyes yelled. "No one can hear you!" he taunted. Panting, I became still. I sucked in a gulp of hot air. Nausea twisted in the pit of my stomach. How far was I from the city? What kind of a place were we in? It had to be secluded if no one could hear me screaming. Then again, he could be lying.

I took in another breath, coughing from the hot air, and screamed. I extended my arms and desperately clawed at the top of the trunk.

Blue Eyes hit the car again, though this time he began rocking it. "I said SHUT THE FUCK UP!" he screamed.

"Zane!" the guy called Jackson yelled. "Stop it!"

Zane must have taken his hands off the car, for it suddenly stopped moving. I heard shoes scuffle on loose gravel. I took in a ragged breath and listened. "Don't tell me what to do, you worthless piece of shit!" Then I heard the sound of a fist smacking flesh. A second later someone huffed in pain.

"This is your mess," Jackson muttered before making a strangled noise of pain. "If you hadn't roughed up Phoebe in the alley this all could have been avoided!"

"Goddamn it!" Zane started. "I swear to God I'm going to—" he cut off when a phone rang. I swallowed hard and realized that I was shaking uncontrollably. I pulled my arms to my chest. I couldn't see a way out of this. I was stuck in the trunk. Zane and Jackson were not going to let me out in time. I was going to die.

More gravel crunched as Zane walked away, his voice fading. "Yes, sir. We ran into a complication. It's been taken care of. We are picking her up now. Yes, sir, we will."

I thought of the girl in the alley. What did they want from

her? And why were they so mad at her? I remembered the look in Jackson's eyes before I hit the ground. He was angry, so angry, as if having to deal with me was the last thing he wanted to do. My thoughts switched to Lynn and my sister. What was going through their minds? Had they come looking for me? Did they assume I wandered off and would be back? Fear audibly bubbled in my stomach, and I hoped that they were okay. They were smart, both of them. It wouldn't take long before they realized I was missing. The police would be looking for me soon. And they'd find me. They'd have to. Everything was going to be okay.

Suddenly the trunk opened. I was momentarily stunned by the bright sunlight. I gulped in a breath of fresh air. Blinking in the harsh light, adrenaline surged through me. I pushed myself up, prepared to make a mad run for it, but someone grabbed my arms.

"Going somewhere?" Zane sneered. His fingers dug into my skin. He smiled and twisted my flesh.

"Get off me!" I screamed and struggled. I turned my body to the side and twisted my arm, breaking free from his grasp. I curled my fingers into a fist and hit him as hard as I could in the temple. My blow was strong, but not strong enough. The pain it caused only fueled his rage.

In a swift movement he brought his hand back and smacked me across the face. Hurt stung the corner of my eye. Still, I didn't give up. I wrapped my fingers around his wrist and pressed my nails into his skin before dragging them down. He grunted in pain and head butted me. My ears rang, and I felt disoriented. He grabbed my shoulders and pushed me down.

My arms buckled and I fell back into the trunk. I pushed myself back up, but Zane was right there, reaching for me. I opened my mouth to scream as his fingers wrapped around my neck. My voice died and my throat burned as he tightened his grip. My pulse pounded against his fingers. I brought my hands up and grasped his arms in a desperate attempt to break away. I squeezed my hands around his forearms, which were tight with hard muscle.

My vision blurred, and I lost the strength in my hands. My arms flopped down to my sides, the back of my hands smacking against the car. My body shuddered, and I strained for a breath

I couldn't take. The blurriness darkened. My eyes darted to Jackson. He was standing a few yards back. His arms were tightly crossed across his chest and his dark eyes conveyed nothing but pure rage. I hated him for just standing there, watching. I knew he would not help me.

Just when I thought I was about to pass out, Zane released one hand and reached behind him, pulling a needle from his back pocket. He used his teeth to pull the cap off and jammed it into my arm.

The liquid burned as it absorbed into my muscle. Still unable to breathe, the noise that tried to come from my throat was pathetic and weak. Zane let go of my neck and moved his hands to my arms, pinning them to my side. He kept his blue eyes locked on mine.

My legs began to feel heavy and my movements slowed. Zane chuckled and let me go. He tipped his head and ran his fingers down my arm, stopping at my wrist. His skin was soft and smooth, and his touch was deliberately gentle. He circled his thumb over the palm of my hand in slow movements. With his other hand, he fingered the hem of my tank top for a few seconds before slipping his hand under it. His eyes closed when he slowly dragged his hand up over my stomach.

Hot tears fell from the corners of my eyes. His skin against mine was revolting. Black dots clouded my fuzzy vision. His fingertips reached the base of my bra and he hesitated, enjoying the buildup he was creating for himself. He pushed his hand up, groaning when his fingers curled around my breast. Unable to scream, a muted whimper escaped my lips. I fought against my heavy eyelids. Zane licked his lips and pinched my nipple in between his index finger and thumb.

My eyes shut. I was so tired and weak. I tried opening my eyes again and failed. The last thing I remembered was Jackson's voice, though I couldn't recall what he had said. His deep brown eyes flashed before me until the vision faded. And then he was just a voice in the dark.

CHAPTER 3

The next time I woke up, I was lying on a cement floor. Everything was dark again. My body hurt, though I wasn't sure why. I pulled my legs up and rested my head on my knees. And then the memories came rushing back at a dizzying rate.

The parade. I could still hear the distant beating of drums and cheering. The sun was still warm on my skin, and I could still smell Lynn's perfume.

I cried out and doubled over when a throbbing pain shot through my head. My hands smacked against the gritty floor. My cheeks burned and my body went rigid as I retched.

The girl in the alley. Why had I stopped to help her? Her despairing face flashed into my mind. If only I had recognized the fear in her eyes, maybe I could have gotten away. I shook my head. *No*. It wasn't her fault. She didn't kidnap me. She didn't inject me with something that made me black out.

It was those two guys. Zane, with the clear blue eyes, and Jackson, with his dark wavy hair hiding his face. It was their fault. They did this. They took me, forced me into a car trunk, and drugged me. And now I had no idea where I was. Fear sunk its claws into me. I squeezed my eyes shut. This wasn't happening. This was a dream, a horrible dream. And I would wake up any second.

Oh, God. I straightened up when the memory of Zane groping me pushed its way into my consciousness. I knew he had fondled my breasts. I was still awake for that. What had he done once I was out? I began crying uncontrollably at the thought.

I shook my head. I had to keep it together. I forced out a shaky breath and moved my hand to my waist. My fingers went numb and I fumbled with the button on my shorts. Finally, I popped them open and yanked down the zipper. My heart was beating so fast I could hear it pounding in my head. A lump of vomit burned in my throat. I pushed my fingers inside the shorts.

I was still wearing my underwear. A tiny bit of relief washed over me. And then I realized that I felt no pain between my legs. I had not been raped. My shoulders relaxed just a hair. I zipped up my shorts and looked around in the dark.

My heart fluttered when I saw soft light outlining a door. My breath rushed in and out of me and my body trembled. I put my hands out in front of me and took a tentative step forward. I slid my shoes along the floor, afraid of tripping over something, until I reached the door. I ran my hands up the splintering wood until they found the doorknob, which was covered in peeling paint.

"Hello?" I croaked, my throat dry. Though I already knew it was a feeble attempt at best, I twisted the knob. It turned. A desperate surge of hope flowed through me. I moved my wrist, waiting for the click. But it never came. The knob was loose. It moved in a complete circle but did nothing to open the door. I pushed against it and discovered a deadbolt lock on the opposite side. "Hello," I spoke again a little louder, afraid of who might answer.

A sliver of light poured in through an old fashioned keyhole. I leaned forward and peered through it. I was fairly certain I was in a basement from the musty smell. Cots with blankets neatly folded at the foot were lined up along the wall across from the little room I was in. A card table and four folding chairs were in the center of the room. A stack of papers and a tipped over plastic cup sat on its surface.

The scent of unwashed hair, body odor, and urine hung heavy in the air. I sniffled back tears and turned my head. Something dark flashed in front of me. Startled, I sharply inhaled and leaned away from the door. My heart pounded in my ears. I forced myself to take a breath and move my face to the keyhole once more. A green eye stared back at me. My heart skipped a beat and my nerves prickled down my spine. I pushed myself away, landing on my butt.

I looked at the door. "Hello?" I whispered. "Help me, please," I blurted. Whoever was outside the door tapped the knob. "Please," I begged. "Help me."

"I can't," a heavily accented female voice whispered back. "I sorry," she went on. "You try to help me and you get taken. So sorry." Emotion weighed on her tone. She sniffled as if she was crying.

"Just let me out," I pleaded. "Please!" My voice broke and I started crying. "I just want to go home. Please!"

She got up, shuffling her feet. I flew back to the door only to see a trail of black hair as she turned and ran. I heard her run up a set of stairs and a door slam shut. Then everything was quiet again. I sank back down to the floor and put my head in my hands, biting my lip to curb my tears.

My body was numb, yet it screamed in pain. I clamped a hand over my left bicep where the needle had driven into my skin and rubbed at the dull ache. My head throbbed, and the rest of me was sore all over, no doubt from being jostled around in a car trunk for God knows how long.

I scrambled to my feet and wrapped my hands around the rusty doorknob. I rattled it and shoved against the door. When it didn't so much as budge, I stood back and kicked at it until my foot grew sore.

Panting, I drew back and stretched my hands out, half afraid of what I might find. The room I was in was no bigger than a closet. All four walls were cement. The ceiling was too high for me to reach. Not knowing what else to do, I sat in the middle of the room, hugging my knees to my chest, and waited.

And waited.

And waited some more. The pale light that filtered in from under the door was turning gold. I had to go to the bathroom, bad. I moved to the keyhole and watched, hoping somebody, anybody, would come back down the stairs. My stomach grumbled, though I was so sick with fear I doubted I could eat if a feast was laid out in front of me. I sat with my back against the door and nervously fiddled with my necklace. I closed my fingers around the silver heart and gently pulled on it. Arianna wore one identical to mine, except her center stone was a different color. Mine sported a diamond, while hers had a less fancy pearl. They were our birthstones, and the necklaces had been given to us by our parents on our thirteenth birthdays. Arianna had just gotten hers last year.

I watched the light disappear from the outline of the door as the sun set. I was trapped. I felt like I was suffocating, like the walls of the tiny room were closing in on me. Silence rang in my ears. Being choked made my throat burn on each exhale, and swallowing was like daggers dragging down my esophagus. I desperately wanted a glass of water, but just thinking of water reminded me of how badly I needed to urinate. I squeezed my legs shut and pulled on the door knob again, trying to break it loose until my bladder protested in pain, forcing me to get up and move to the farthest corner of the small room, pull down my pants and squat on the floor.

Feeling ashamed and humiliated, I went back to the door, focusing on removing the doorknob. I wrapped both hands around it and pulled again for good measure. Something cracked, sparking a tiny flame of hope. I pulled again, and the base of the knob loosened.

I yanked it back and jammed my fingers into the splintery hole and twisted a screw. Half of the knob clattered to the ground outside the door. I froze, holding my breath. But no one came. I pulled the other end toward me, feeling a sense of satisfaction when the rust covered oval fell into my hands. I quickly fiddled with the only screw I had managed to salvage and stuck it in my back pocket.

I ran my fingers around the knob, envisioning it in my hand, since I couldn't actually see it in the dark. I held it tightly, imagining using it to hit Zane or Jackson in the face if I ever saw them again. I held on to that vision of attacking my attackers, replaying it in my mind, over and over. The fear of not knowing what was going to happen to me ate away at my stomach. Bile burned in my throat but I had nothing to come up.

Why did they take me? What did they want? If they were going to kill me, why hadn't they done so already? The fact that

I was still alive brought on more terror. What were they going to do to me? I thought about the girl in the alley. What happened to her? Was she the person they were going back for?

I twisted the knob over and over in my hands and rested my head against the door. I closed my eyes and then opened them, feeling too vulnerable. I shook my head at the thought. It was too dark to see anything anyway. Even though I had explored the tiny closet, I couldn't let go of the fear that someone was in there with me. Images of villains from horror movies flashed through my mind, but they all fell short when I remembered Zane's pretty blue eyes. They were so captivating, so beautiful, but held back animalistic rage.

A door opened and slammed shut above me. Muffled voices floated through vents in the floor. I pushed myself up on my knees, the concrete biting at my bones, and pressed my ear to the hole where the doorknob used to be. Not knowing who was above me was terrifying. Was it Zane and Jackson again? Maybe Zane was coming to finish what he had started. My teeth chattered as I tried not to cry.

I knelt down and peered out the small hole where the doorknob used to be. Something crawled across my neck. My hand flew up, slapping my skin and squishing a spider. I hated spiders. In a panic, I flicked my hand away from me. A shiver went up my back and I felt like bugs were crawling all over my body. I ran my hands through my hair, expecting to find it full of insects.

"God, please help me," I prayed. "I'm sorry I didn't go to church yesterday. Or the week before that…and the week before that one too…and every Sunday that I was at school. Please, let me get out of here alive."

Footfalls came from the stairs. I ducked down, away from the keyhole. My fingers tightened on the knob and my legs ached with anticipation as I played out the plan of attack in my mind.

"He asked for you, girl," a female voice spoke. The lights flicked on. "You must've made an impression on him." She had a thick Brooklyn accent, which was out of place in Iowa.

Whomever she was talking to laughed. "I'm telling you, Rochelle, after what I did for him tonight he will *always* be asking for me."

"What did you do?" Rochelle asked. I silently rose up and peered out of the hole. Two females sat on one of the small cots. The girl who was called Rochelle had her back to me. She was wearing a backless dress, something so revealing I would never be allowed to leave the house in. She brought her legs up under her and I caught a glimpse of her four-inch, hot pink stilettos. "Come on, girl, tell me!" she urged and flicked her black hair behind her back. A dozen gold bangles jingled on her wrist.

"Well," the other girl started and kicked off her platform shoes. "He made me … " she trailed off, her voice faltering. Then she leaned forward and whispered something to Rochelle. When she leaned back, I saw her face and was shocked at how young she looked. She was pretty: strawberry blonde hair that fell in perfect ringlets around her flawless face and striking blue eyes. I guessed her only to be the same age as Arianna.

Rochelle laughed. "You better have charged more for that."

The redhead smiled and nodded. I was suddenly aware of just how fast my heart was beating. I pressed a hand over my chest, scared they would hear the pounding. My breath came and left my lungs, but I felt like I was getting no oxygen. Part of me didn't understand what they were talking about. That part of me didn't *want* to understand what they were talking about.

"Nate likes me, right?" she meekly asked Rochelle.

"Of course he does," Rochelle promised her. "I think Nate will be—" she abruptly cut off when the redhead grabbed her arm. "What the hell, Lily?"

Lily shook her head and held a finger to her lips. Her eyes were focused on the closet door.

"Shit," Rochelle swore. "What the hell happened to the door?"

"Is there someone in there?" Lily asked, her tone teetering on fear and excitement. "Hey, anyone in there?"

I opened my mouth but nothing came out. I took a breath and tried again. "Help me," I croaked.

Lily screamed and Rochelle grabbed her wrist. "No. Leave it alone. Zane will fill us in about her in the morning."

Lily's blue eyes widened and terror pulled down her cheeks. Then she closed her eyes and shook her head, snapping back into the smiling girl she was just seconds ago. "Okay. I'm, like, really tired anyway."

"I'll say," Rochelle said with a laugh.

My body trembled. They were just going to leave me? No. No, they couldn't. They wouldn't. I stuck my fingers through the hole and banged on the door.

"Help me, please!" I cried. Panic rose. I couldn't stand being in the dark a minute longer. I jiggled the door. "Let me out!"

"Ignore her," Rochelle instructed Lily. I couldn't believe what I was hearing. What the hell was wrong with her? I was a human being. Trapped in a closet. And she wanted young Lily to ignore me? I pressed my face against the door, crying.

"But why is she in the closet?" Lily asked, shooting Rochelle a dubious look.

"Please!" I tried again. "You have to help me. You know it's wrong!"

"I don't know," Rochelle said loudly over my cries for help. "She must have done something wrong. Do you want to mess with that?"

"No!" I screamed. "I didn't do anything wrong. Please," I begged. "Please!" I sunk to my knees, bawling. I hiccuped a sob and forced myself up. I put my face to the hole and looked out. Lily's eyes moved to the door, and I caught her eye. "Lily!" I cried. "Help me, please!" She held my gaze for a second, staring into me before flicking her eyes to Rochelle. She bit her lip and shook her head. I sniffled at my runny nose. Was she trying to tell me something about Rochelle? Lily ran a hand over her hair and turned her attention back to Rochelle. "Is she going to keep this up, like, all night? I can't sleep."

Rochelle cast a halfhearted look in my direction and shrugged. "Doubt it."

"Please!" I tried again. "I just want to go home. Please! Help me!" I collapsed against the door and cried until my eyes swelled.

Rochelle and Lily ignored me and undressed. I made myself get up again and look through the hole. Lily looked at me and then quickly away. She pulled her shirt over her head and looked again. Her eyebrows pushed together and she bit her lip, looking conflicted. Then she moved out of my line of sight.

They got into their beds after turning the light off. Like a thousand dark hands, absolute terror grabbed me and pulled me down. My hand slid off the door, and a sliver of wood shoved its way under the skin on my ring finger. I almost didn't feel the sting of the splinter. "Please!" I called again and broke down in tears.

I collapsed against the door, hitting it with the knob while sobs hiccupped out of me. "Please," I cried. "How can you just leave me?" I asked, though I knew my words came out incoherently masked by sobs. "I didn't do anything wrong."

And I didn't. I did the right thing. I was here because I was trying to help someone. But then again, no good deed goes unpunished.

CHAPTER 4

"Get up," a gruff voice spoke. Something jabbed me in the side. My eyes flew open, and my hands scraped on the concrete floor in my haste to scramble to my feet. Fear made its way deep into my heart. I hadn't been in a deep enough sleep to forget where I was or what had happened. I had, however, been out of it just long enough for Zane to take the doorknob from my hands.

The closet door was open, and weak sunlight filtered through a small basement window. Zane stood in front of me, blue eyes narrowed. I looked at him, trembling. He took a step forward, and I flinched. Was he going to choke me again? I crossed my arms tightly over my chest and backed into the wall. I clenched my jaw to keep my lip from quivering.

Don't cry. Not now. Not in front of him.

"Go upstairs," Zane ordered. "Nate wants to see you." I wanted to know who Nate was and what he wanted with me. Zane jerked toward me, and I flinched away again. He snickered at my trepidation. I took a deep breath and tried to force away any visible fear, not wanting to give him the satisfaction of seeing my obvious terror. Jackson stood back but kept his eyes on me. His quiet distance was unnerving.

"Now," Zane added pointedly and jabbed my shoulder.

I stepped past him and hesitated, looking around the dingy basement. The card table was several feet in front of the closet, and the row of cots was just beyond that. Jackson tipped his head.

"This way," he said softly and turned, leading the way upstairs. I blinked away the tears that threatened to spill down my cheeks. Jackson moved slowly, his muscular body stiff as if he was sore.

The stairs were wooden and worn in the middle from use. There was a splintering railing and only a single, uncovered light bulb above us, offering a minimal yellow glow. Jackson opened the door at the landing and moved to the side to let me pass. Zane slammed it shut when he exited the basement. There were multiple locks on it.

On their own accord, my hands began to tremble. I balled them into fists, digging my nails into my skin. We had emerged from the basement into a large kitchen. The walls were painted a soft yellow and the white cabinets and stainless steel appliances were new. The granite counter tops were gleaming, and there wasn't a crumb or streak of dirt on the polished hardwood floors. There was a bowl of fruit on the center of a light oak table in the breakfast nook, which had large, four pane windows. Pale yellow flowers had been hand stitched onto the valance.

The sound of chirping birds was carried in on the breeze through an open window. I quickly stole a glance outside and saw nothing but a neatly manicured lawn that stretched for about an acre, then gave way to a forest full of thick trees with dark leaves. Jackson picked up his pace and walked out of the kitchen, through a formal dining room, and into a living room. Both rooms were decorated in such a way that they reminded me of something out of a magazine. Everything was spotless and organized, leaving me to wonder if anyone actually lived here.

"There she is," a middle aged man said and stood from the couch. He was wearing khaki pants and a blue polo shirt that matched his eyes. His smile was warm, and his dark blonde hair was painstakingly styled around his handsome face. Jackson turned his head down, staring at the floor, and stepped to the side. He crossed his arms and pulled them close to his tense body.

The man, who I assumed was Nate, moved close to me. His eyes darted up and down my body several times before they settled on my face. He put his hand on my chin and tipped my head to the left. I immediately flinched. Zane took a quick step forward, holding out his arms as if anticipating a fight.

"Shhh," Nate soothed. The tears I had been holding back rolled down my cheeks. He used his thumb to wipe them away. I recoiled at his touch. "You shouldn't have hit her," Nate scolded Zane. "This is going to take time to heal. And time costs me." Nate's hand slowly trailed down from my face to my neck, sweeping across my collarbone and then down towards my breasts.

I didn't even think about it; my arm came up, and my fist made contact with Nate's face. Heart hammering, I spun and took two steps before Zane grabbed my arms. He yanked them down and pulled me back, knocking me off my feet. I crumpled to the floor but continued to fight, struggling to free my arms. I threw my head back and hit him below the waist. He let out a grunt of pain. I twisted and pulled my right arm out of his hold.

Planting the soles of my shoes on the ground, I sprang up and hit Zane as hard as I could in the stomach. He responded by yanking my left arm back, and I screamed as I was pulled to the floor. He brought his foot up and kicked me in the side.

"Get her up," Nate sternly ordered.

Zane kicked me once more in the back, his blow smacking into my kidney before he knelt down and hoisted me to my feet. I was crying and I hated it. I took a deep, sniffling breath and glared at Nate.

"You're not going to get away with this!" I threatened. "My family knows I'm missing. They will come looking for me!"

Zane pulled my arms back, looping his arms around my elbows. I wiggled my shoulders but was unable to break free. Nate moved forward again and grabbed the front of my shirt with both hands. In one swift movement, he ripped it open. Several buttons popped off and bounced on the dark, wooden floor. Then he pulled down my tank top and slid his hands over my breasts.

"Don't touch me!" I yelled and kicked at Nate.

Zane jerked me back. He slid his leg through mine and hooked it around my ankle, putting me off balance.

"She's old," Nate noted, looking past me to Zane.

"Nineteen, according to her license. But the older ones do better on the street," Zane pointed out.

"Yes," Nate agreed and moved his hands down to my stomach. "But someone could recognize her. The girl is right. People will be looking."

"She could do well in the club," Zane blurted, desperate to please Nate. "She's tall and thin. She'd fit right in."

"And pretty. Very pretty." Nate's words slid out of him like oil. His hands moved to my thighs. "And possibly an athlete. She would look good on stage." He squeezed my muscles and then let me go. "But you do not seem to grasp the concept of being recognized. I'm not risking my business."

My heart raced and my stomach churned. Club? Streets? What the fuck were these guys into? I knew deep down, but I didn't want to admit it.

"I told him there were other options," Jackson spoke for the first time since the basement. "But he didn't listen."

"Nobody asked you, Jackson," Zane spat.

"He's right," Nate said. Zane's grip on me tightened in unspoken anger.

"It's your fault," Zane snarled at Jackson. "You can't even handle looking after one measly girl. She fucking ran away! You're a worthless piece of shit!"

"Enough," Nate calmly spoke. "She's here. We have to deal with it, one way or another."

Sweat dripped down my back as I witnessed the exchange. I was drowning, slowly sinking below dark, icy water. Only I was stuck in my body and in this room. Stuck with three men who inspected me like a horse at an auction and thought of me as nothing more than a body to profit from.

"What else do you know?" Nate asked Zane, sounding bored with me already.

"Her name is Adeline Miller. Parents own an art gallery where her mom teaches painting classes. She's in school to be a nurse, has a younger sister named Arianna, two dogs that she trains and shows, and runs some blog called *Contagious Reads*. It's about books."

"Very good," Nate praised. His charming face twisted into a sadistic smile when he took in my horror and confusion.

"Teenagers," he sighed, "never listen to the warnings about the dangers of social networking. You're all so willing to post every single mundane detail about your pathetic lives." He spun around and rubbed his forehead. Sitting heavily on the couch, he stared at me. "Do you know where you are?"

I shook my head.

"Good." He tipped his head and ran his eyes over me again. His brow furrowed like he saw something that wasn't pleasing to him. "Are you a virgin?" he asked causally.

I opened my mouth but didn't know what to say. I hadn't been a virgin for several years, but they wouldn't be able to tell, would they? I mentally debated whether or not being a virgin would act in my favor.

"Well?" Nate asked.

"I can find out." Zane moved one of his hands down to my waist and into my pants, slipping his fingers into my underwear. With no hesitation he shoved a finger inside me. I cried out in pain as his skin stuck to me, feeling like skin was tearing off. He dug his nails into me, laughing.

"No!" I shouted. "I'm not. I'm not a virgin."

Zane shoved his finger deeper. I screamed again. Pain shot through me, choking me. Tears ran down my face.

"She's not lying," he said and removed his hand.

Nate sighed. "Too bad. Older virgins are so hard to come by these days." He wistfully shook his head. "It's pretty simple here. Follow the rules and you won't get hurt. Break the rules … " he trailed off with a sickening chuckle. "Well, you'll just have to see for yourself now, deary." He waved his hand in the air. "Take her downstairs. Feed her. I'll figure out what to do with her later."

My gut twisted and my head swam in a cloud of black terror. If Zane didn't have a painful grip on my arms, my knees would have buckled. Nothing felt real as I was ushered back into the basement. I was floating above my body, barely able to feel Zane's rough hands on my skin. My mind didn't want to accept that this was my new reality. There was a slight ringing in my ears and my eyes just wouldn't focus.

Zane turned me around and placed his hands on my shoulders, shoving me into a sitting position onto a thin mattress. The cot creaked under my weight, and the screw in my back pocket bit at my skin. Pain still burned between my legs. I folded my arms against myself, just then realizing that my shirt was still pulled down. I fixed it, keeping my eyes on Zane. Why was he just standing there? I was crippled with terror. A little voice screamed at me to jump up, grab my screw, and shove it in Zane's eye. But another voice told me to lie down, close my eyes, and think of something else. This was all too much for my mind to handle.

Before I could choose which voice to listen to, Jackson loudly stomped down the stairs, holding a tray with food. His eyes met mine and he offered a slight sympathetic smile that I wanted to slap right off of his stubble-covered face. He set the food down on an overturned milk carton and backed away before turning and trudging up the stairs. My stomach grumbled when I looked at the sandwich. I knew I needed to eat.

Suddenly Zane knelt down to my level and pushed my knees open with his hands. His body jerked forward as he moved onto me, pinning me onto the bed, his legs between mine. Panic flooded through me and I manically struggled to get away. My hands pressed into his shoulders. I tried to bend my knees but couldn't. Zane was too heavy.

"Get off!" I shouted. "Get off me!" Knowing he was too strong to shove away, I let my hands drop and I frantically tried to turn over and crawl to freedom. The metal springs of the cot protested under our weight. Zane pressed his torso against mine, grinding his hips into me. His face moved to my neck, hot breath warming my skin as he panted. My fingers tangled around the tattered quilt as I tried to pull away. Zane walked his fingers up my leg and wrapped them around my thigh. My heart pounded with desperation and fear. Tears spilled from the corners of my eyes and I screamed.

"Keep struggling, girl," Zane spoke, his voice smooth and seductive. "I like feeling you squirm underneath me." He pressed himself in between my legs, rubbing his erection against me.

My fear twisted into disgusted rage. My hand flew up and made contact with his face. Momentarily stunned, Zane's muscles went slack. I grabbed a metal bar at the head of the bed and heaved my body up. I curled my legs and kneed him in the stomach.

"Fucking cunt!" he swore and grabbed a handful of my hair. He harshly flipped me over and pressed my face into the mattress. "Don't you ever put your hands on me again! Got it? You do what you're told." He gave my head one final shove into the thin mattress before getting up. He looked down at me and laughed.

I scrambled up, my fingers curled into fists. *Don't cry.* My chest rapidly rose and fell, and I struggled to not hyperventilate. Zane's piercing blue eyes burned into me. He let out a breath and smiled before biting his lip and shaking his head. He crossed his arms, flexing his muscles.

Slowly, he turned and walked away, taking the stairs two at a time. I heard the door slam shut and the locks slide into place. A dry sob escaped from my tightly closed lips. My ears began to ring and I felt like I was going to pass out. I sunk back onto the bed, rocking back and forth as everything began to sink in.

I had been kidnapped, and had no idea where I even was.

CHAPTER 5

This is a dream, I told myself. *A horrible, horrible dream.*

"Wake up," I whispered. "Wake up!" I removed my hands and looked around me. Several hours had passed since Zane locked me down here. I was still in the basement. Trapped. Alone. Not even attempting to put an end to my noisy tears, I shakily rose from the bed.

The basement was considerably smaller than the house. It had either been boarded up to make a small, confined area, or the house had a large addition. The ceiling was low, and the foundation along the small, barred window was crumbling. Six beds were crowded together along one wall. They were nothing more than wire cots with thin mattress pads and faded blankets that smelled like they desperately needed to be washed. Each bed had a single pillow covered with a dingy pillowcase, and nothing distinguished one bed from another.

Across the room was the closet I had been stuffed in. Next to that was a long table. A large mirror hung above it, and a row of single, exposed light bulbs popped out of the wall. I walked over to it and ran my finger over a flat iron. The cord was cracked and frayed from being wound around the styling tool so often. I picked up a pot of eye shadow from a cluttered mess of makeup. Silver powder colored my fingers. I dropped it back onto the table where it rolled to the back, bumping into a crooked line of glass perfume bottles.

I stepped to the side and pulled back a slimy shower curtain of a single stall shower that was next to the vanity. Rings of yellow circled the drain, and brown and green mildew clung to the walls. There was a toilet beyond that, made private only by sheets hanging from the ceiling.

I walked to the other side of the room, stopping in front of a rack of clothing. They smelled like a mixture of perfume, laundry detergent, and sweat. I wrinkled my nose and coughed. My hands trembled as I leafed through the revealing clothing. The clothes were organized by color, ending with an array of slutty costumes. My stomach flip-flopped when my fingers touched the smooth satin of a black French maid uniform. Stilettos and tall platform shoes were haphazardly piled beneath the clothes.

I slowly walked to the end of the rack and stopped in front of an old dresser. The top drawer stuck, and I had to tug hard to open it. It was full of lacy bras and panties. I owned stuff like that, but rarely wore it since it wasn't comfortable. The other two drawers were full of pajamas, socks, and all sorts of tights. I sifted through the assorted colors of fishnet stockings before closing the drawer.

Across from the dresser were the stairs. I gazed longingly at them, knowing that they could ascend me into freedom. I swallowed back a sob and sat down on the bed again. I turned my attention to the food Jackson had brought me. There were two peanut butter and jelly sandwiches, a one serving-sized carton of milk, two water bottles, and an apple. It was enough to last a day. I guessed he wasn't going to bring me anything else until tomorrow. I didn't want to eat it. Somehow it felt wrong, as if they had an advantage over me. But I knew that not eating would make me weak, and I was hungry. I picked up the shiny red apple and took a small bite, chewing slowly.

The floor creaked above me. I jumped and a tingle of fear slid down my back. I swallowed the piece of apple. It scraped like nails against my sore throat. My eyes flicked to the ceiling. Dusty cobwebs decorated the old wooden beams. Whoever was above me shuffled their feet as they moved throughout the house. A pipe rattled when a faucet turned on.

I took another bite of the apple. How could they just go on with their lives as if it was perfectly normal to have a prisoner in the basement? I closed my eyes and braced for the pain when I swallowed. I set the apple down and slowly crept up the worn stairs. The wooden planks creaked under my weight.

The door had no locks to pick on this side. The door was covered in scratch marks dotted with dark brown stains. I put my fingers on the marks. It was a perfect match. My eyes bulged and my stomach dropped. Someone had clawed at the door until their fingers bled. My head swam and I swayed. I grasped the rough railing to keep from tumbling down the stairs.

I turned and moved one foot. I knew I was walking down the stairs, though physically I couldn't feel it. I was floating again, feet above my body watching it all happen. But it was happening, really happening. I was trapped in this forsaken basement, and I had no idea how to get out.

CHAPTER 6

The basement door creaked open. I was lying on a cot, curled up in a little ball with my back to the stairs. I didn't bother to turn when I heard the footsteps. It had been the same thing for the last several days. Sometime in the late afternoon, Jackson brought me food and two water bottles. He would set it on the table in the center of the room, stand by the base of the stairs for a few awkward seconds looking at me, as if he was waiting for me to speak, and then turn and slowly walk back upstairs.

And then I'd be alone.

I wondered where Rochelle and Lily had gone, and I spent a lot of time thinking about the dark haired girl from the alley. Sometimes I felt sorry for her. Other times I was mad at her. If she had crossed the street a few seconds earlier, maybe I wouldn't have seen her. Maybe I never would have seen her and tried to help. Anger at her built up in me, and I wanted to know what she did to make Zane mad. I wanted to yell at her and tell her that if she hadn't pissed him off, I wouldn't be here.

But then I'd remind myself that she was just as innocent as I was. Or at least I believed she was. The possibility that I had put myself in danger to help someone undeserving wasn't a thought I could handle.

"Adeline?" Jackson said softly. His voice was deep and soothing. I hated it. "Adeline?" he repeated when I didn't so much as flinch. "Are you awake?"

"Technically," I mumbled. "But I feel like I'm in a nightmare."

He shuffled his feet and said something under his breath that I couldn't quite hear. I thought he might have agreed with me, but I wasn't sure and I didn't care enough to ask.

"I brought you a plate with hot food. You might want to eat it now. I don't think barbecue chicken or mashed potatoes would be good cold." He didn't move. Was he waiting for me to thank him? The last thing I planned on doing was showing him gratitude. Though, I preferred him to Zane. While Jackson's creeper staring was unnerving, he never so much as laid a finger on me.

I pushed myself up and looked behind me. Jackson was still standing near the table. He tipped his head down when my eyes met his face, his dark hair falling over his brown eyes in an attempt to hide the bruise on his cheek.

"What happened?" I asked. Would whoever hit Jackson come for me next? I took my eyes off him, moving them to the plate. My mouth watered at the smell of the chicken. After several days of nothing but peanut butter and jelly sandwiches, apples, and cereal bars, the plate full of chicken and potatoes looked divine. The metal springs creaked when I moved off the bed. My dirty hair was pulled up in a messy bun, and I was still wearing the same clothes that I was when I was taken.

"Nothing," he blurted. Red tinged his cheeks.

"Right," I retorted. "I hate when *nothing* gives me black eyes."

My heart skipped a beat in fear when he sharply turned his head to me. I grabbed the plate and moved to the other end of the table, putting the cheap metal and plastic between us. He didn't completely terrify me, but I didn't feel comfortable enough to sit when he was standing in the same room.

"I got hit," he explained.

"No shit," I said back and shoved a spoonful of mashed potatoes into my mouth. They were homemade, and were just as delicious as they smelled.

His lips pulled down in a frown and he inspected the ground. He looked so dejected it caused guilt to flicker through me. I mentally shook my head and ate another heaping spoonful of potatoes, not caring that it burned my tongue. Jackson didn't deserve my pity.

He took a step back and looked at me, his dark eyes empty. He just shook his head and went back upstairs. I refused to let myself read into it while I quickly finished the rest of the potatoes. I devoured the chicken just as quickly. I set the peanut butter sandwich and apple aside, saving them for later, and drank half of a water bottle.

I went to the bathroom and used the shower to wash my hands and face, since I was too scared to strip down and actually shower, and lay back in the bed. After a few minutes of feeling like I was going to waste away, I got up and began pacing. My body was still sore from the trunk ride, and the bruises on my face were taking their time to fade.

I carefully stretched out my arms and then bent over. My stiff muscles ached as I reached for the ground. I stood back up and reached above me. The pull on my back felt wonderful and painful at the same time. I had never been into yoga; it seemed boring and lame. I did my stretches before and after I ran but left it at that.

I went back to the cot closest to the stairs. I had claimed it as my own, though I had the feeling many girls had laid down to rest on that miserable cot. I pulled the screw out from my back pocket and rolled it back and forth between my fingers.

The sound of the deadbolt shooting back startled me. I hurried to stash the screw and laid back down, not caring to look at Jackson when he came down to get my dishes. But the chitchat of female voices caused me to sit straight up. My fingers pressed into the mattress, and my eyes stayed glued to the base of the stairs.

Heels clomped on each wooden plank. I wasn't familiar enough to recall their voices, but I was sure the Brooklyn accent belonged to Rochelle. She stopped mid-sentence when she saw me, her foot hovering above the last stair. The dark-haired girl from the alley bumped into her, causing Rochelle to stumble. Her foot planted on the ground with a click, and she wobbled before the five-inch, black patent leather stiletto tipped to the side. I watched her ankle twist as she fell. On instinct, I rose, wanting to help her. The dark haired girl got there first and extended a hand.

Rochelle leaned forward, her fingers wrapping around her

ankle. "Ah!" she cried and pulled off her shoe. "Fucking hell!"

"Are you all right?" I meekly asked, standing so close to the cot it brushed against the back of my legs.

Rochelle looked at me and scowled, as if it was my fault she fell. She removed her shoes and allowed the dark-haired girl to pull her to her feet.

"I'll be fine," she grumbled and took a step, immediately crying out in pain. She hobbled to the cot next to me and flopped down.

"You should elevate it," I whispered. "And ice would be ideal."

The dark-haired girl eyed me curiously, guilt flashing across her face as she took a pillow from another cot and stuck it under Rochelle's ankle. She whisked around the cot and flew up the stairs, returning a minute later with a bag filled with ice. Lily, the young redhead, was behind her. She slowly approached me.

"Hi," she spoke. "I'm Lily."

"Addie," I said, struggling to find my voice.

"This is Rochelle and Phuong. We call her Phoebe. She doesn't speak English very well."

"Nice to meet you," I blurted, the manners my mother instilled in me coming out on their own accord. "I don't know why I'm here," I told them.

Lily bit her lip and looked at Rochelle. A life of hard times and too much responsibility masked her young innocence. Her blue eyes were clouded with fear and shame, and the self-doubt was apparent in her sagging shoulders. She crossed boney arms and offered me a small smile.

"Phoebe told us that you tried to stop Zane from hurting her, and he brought you back."

I nodded. "What's going to happen to me?"

Lily's brow pushed together. "The same thing that happens to us," she spoke, her voice nothing but a hollow whisper.

I swallowed hard, pushing my pounding heart back into place. "And what is that?" The icy words spilled out of my mouth.

"Sit," she said and motioned to the bed.

My legs bent, and I sank down onto the mattress.

"Nate finds us clients and we take care of them," she

said gently and put her hand on mine. Everything about this felt wrong, from the way someone younger than my sister was comforting me to the way she sugarcoated being a sex slave.

"And if we don't?"

"You don't, you die," Phoebe said harshly in a heavily accented voice.

"Pheebs!" Rochelle scolded.

"No!" she retorted and rose from Rochelle's cot. "She need to hear truth! They make us have sex, all kinds. I sorry you here," she continued. "Here is hell."

Her words hung in the air and nobody spoke. Lily picked at the frayed hem of the tribal-print skirt she was wearing, and Rochelle clenched her jaw and moved her eyes to the floor, looking almost as if Phoebe's words were offensive.

"How did you get here?" I quietly asked.

Lily twisted her red hair between her fingers. "I started doing *things* for money. I was out on the street a few nights a week. I didn't charge much. Then I met Zane, and he said he could get me like twice what I was making if I worked with him." She yanked on her ponytail and shook her head. "And he did. But it didn't last long. He started taking it. Then I, like, got into some trouble with my stepdad and got kicked out. I didn't have anywhere to go, so I called Zane, and I've been here ever since."

"How old are you?"

"I just turned fourteen."

"Aren't your parents looking for you?" I blurted.

Lily's innocent eyes flashed like blue glass. "We're not all lucky enough to have nice families like you," she spat.

"Sorry."

"Nah, it's not your fault," she recovered. "My mom has too many issues and my stepdad likes to drink. And cheat. And hit. I've, like, run away so many times they probably figured that's what happened."

"Do you want to go home?" I asked gently.

She shrugged. "What do I have to go home to?" Her eyes glossed over and she stood up, making a big deal of stacking the cards and pushing the chairs into the table.

"What about you?" I asked Phoebe.

"I want to come to United States," she stated. "Thought I got modeling job. Nate pay for everything, even got me visa." She shook her head. "I don't think visa real."

"It's not all bad like this," I felt compelled to tell her.

"I know. Bad parts and bad people where I'm from too." She gave me a small, pressed smile. "It's been six months. Lily here almost year. Rochelle even longer. Other girls come and go. We don't know why we stay."

"Rochelle says it's because the clients like us, like regulars. I've seen the same girls in the clubs. They just don't live in one of Nate's houses," Lily explained.

"Clubs?" I inquired.

Phoebe nodded. "Dance clubs, strip clubs, whatever they called. Less touching when work there. I like it better."

"Until they get you backstage," Lily added ruefully.

"Does it end?" I whispered, asking a question I already knew the answer to.

"Not well," Phoebe answered just as quietly.

"There has to be a way," I pressed.

Phoebe shook her head. "I try. Many times. And no."

I ground my teeth and forced back tears, refusing to believe that I was never leaving this place. "People are looking for me," I said suddenly, my voice too full of hope. "When they find me, you will be found too."

"*If* they find you," Lily corrected. She pressed her full lips together and shook her head, causing red ringlets to fall into her eyes. "Why would they even think to look here?"

"I don't even know where we are," I blurted.

"Somewhere near Des Moines," Phoebe told me. "But out in country."

"There is nothing around this house," Lily went on. "For miles, literally. It's like a century old farmhouse, restored, obviously. I think the land is, like, historical or something. Nobody does anything to it." She shrugged and then yawned. "I'm *so* tired," she mumbled and pushed herself off the bed. She kicked off her heels and stretched her feet before moving to another cot and pulling back the covers. "Addie," she said softly. "I wish I had something to say to make this better, but I don't." She gave me a sympathetic smile and got into her bed.

EMILY GOODWIN

"What's going to happen to me?" I asked.

Lily looked at Rochelle, who shook her head. "I don't know," Rochelle spoke. "Girls like you haven't been here before. Nobody looked for us." Her brown eyes narrowed so slightly I almost didn't see it. With a huff, she rolled over, wincing when she moved her foot. Phoebe got up and went to another cot as well. She wrapped a blanket around her shoulders and leaned against the wall. Beneath the layers and layers of makeup that was applied to her face, I could see the dark circles that pulled down on her eyes. Just what had they been forced to do for the last three days?

CHAPTER 7

Later that day, when the sun began to glow a reddish haze, the basement door opened. Zane clunked down the stairs.

"Time for work, ladies," he announced.

I glared at him then glanced back at Phoebe. The screw in my back pocket poked at my butt uncomfortably. Maybe with her help we could get away.

"What the hell is this?" he demanded when he saw the pillow underneath Rochelle's ankle. He snatched it up and grabbed her foot.

She woke up crying out in pain. Phoebe shot up and Lily cowered under her blankets. "I tripped," Rochelle mumbled, biting back tears. "But it's fine. I can still work tonight." She pushed herself up and moved toward Zane.

"Get up," he said, his voice level.

My stomach twisted as I watched Rochelle struggle to her feet. There was something desperate in her eyes, something more than wanting his approval so that he wouldn't hurt her. She looked at him with admiration and awe. She wanted to please him, not for her safety, but for her happiness. Zane put his hand on her arm, steadying her. Rochelle melted into his touch.

He looked into her eyes and slowly licked his lips. "Can you walk?"

Her head bobbed up and down. "Mh-hm," she quipped in high-pitched agreement. She took a step and faltered. Zane caught her, bringing her body close to his. He smiled when she thanked him but quickly cast his eyes away, the smile instantly fading.

"Come with me," he ordered.

"She shouldn't put weight on it," I said softly, scared of Zane.

"Nate needs to see this," he said in a condescending tone.

"Then have him come here," I spat back, surprised at the venom in my voice.

Zane snaked his arm around Rochelle and sneered at me. "Don't tell me what to do, cunt."

"Don't call me that, asshole," I retorted and was again surprised at how easily the insult rolled off my tongue.

"Addie, stop," Rochelle whispered. "I'm fine." She clung onto Zane. "Come on, let's go." I unclenched my fists and watch them disappear up the stairs.

"You shouldn't make him mad," Lily warned. "He *is* an asshole. A really. Big. Asshole," she said slowly. "One who doesn't like to get insulted."

I swallowed my fear. "I don't care."

"You should care," Phoebe spoke. "I used to not care. I tired of getting hurt."

Lily folded her blanket down. "He's leaves you alone if you leave him alone and do what you're told," she said. "Most of the time, at least."

I ran my hands over my face, and that weird feeling of not really being in my body began to take over. I stared at a brown stain on the faded yellow quilt on my bed until my vision went blurry. I knew Lily and Phoebe had gotten up and were moving around, but I didn't know what they were doing. I couldn't bring myself to move to look at them. I didn't want to acknowledge anything around me. If I didn't see it, then maybe it wasn't real.

"Adeline," Zane's called in a deep voice, startling me. I tipped my head up and looked into his beautiful blue eyes and was immediately sucked out of my unrealistic reverie. "You're filling in for Rochelle tonight."

My mouth opened but no sound came out. Suddenly I wasn't able to breathe. My chest tightened and the peanut butter sandwich I recently ate rose in my throat. Zane laughed and walked away, leaving Rochelle to hobble to the bed unassisted.

"I only got one tonight," Rochelle said as if to comfort me.

"Sometimes you have more than one?" I somehow managed to squeak out.

"Most of the time," she replied casually.

"I won't do it," I said definitely and shook my head. "I won't. I won't."

"You have to," Rochelle said.

"No, I don't. They can't make me. I refuse."

"Just do it, Addie." Lily's voice came from across the room. "I don't want to see you get hurt."

"They won't hurt me that much. I heard Nate say that they prefer us to look pretty."

Lily frowned and looked at Phoebe. "Addie," she said slowly. "He *will* hurt you. He tie you down and *make* you work."

"No," I cried and ran my hands through my hair, stopping to dig my nails into my scalp. "No. No, no, no!"

"She's freaking out." Rochelle sighed. "Get me a Xanax."

"No have," Phoebe replied. She pulled her shirt over her head and traded the pink bra she was wearing for one made of see-through black lace. Then she opened up the dresser drawer and rooted around until she found a pill bottle. "But have this." She tossed the little orange bottle to Rochelle. Without looking at the label, Rochelle pressed and twisted off the cap. She stuck one pill in her mouth and held out another.

"Take this," she told me. I clamped my mouth shut and shook my head. I had never seen, let alone done drugs before in my life. "Addie, it will help." She held out her hand, and I shook my head again. For good measure, I crossed my arms and looked away. "Fine," she sighed. "Suit yourself. I won't force you."

"Thank you," I said and let my body relax just a little.

"You're welcome," she replied and leaned closer to me. Suddenly, she pitched forward, pinched my arm, and popped the pill into my mouth when I cried out in pain. She pressed her hand over my lips and held me close to her. The pill dissolved almost immediately.

"Now you'll really thank me," she said and tightened her grip. She was surprisingly strong, and I wasn't able to fight her off until the pill was nearly gone.

I spit out what I could on the floor. "What the hell?" I shouted.

"I hate seeing people get their ass beat," she told me. "It'll take a while to kick in. You need to shower. I'll do your hair and makeup. Get up." When I didn't move, she grabbed my wrist and gave me a shake. "Addie! Come on! You're going to regret this."

"Yes," I said when I moved my feet to the floor. "I will."

In a haze, I got up and moved to the shower. I turned on the water and waited. I had no clothes to change into, no towel, and soon I would have no dignity.

"Here," Lily said and pulled an unfolded towel from a basket that was stashed under the make-shift vanity table. "The water, like, never warms up, either," she advised. "It's best, like, to get in and get it over with. Oh," she said suddenly and turned around. She pulled a package of disposable razors from the bottom of the towel basket. At least it was unopened. "Make sure the only hair on your body is on your head."

I nodded, feeling devoid of emotions. Was it from the drugs? Or was the situation too much for my mind to handle?

"And," she continued, bending over again and rooting though a box under the sink. "You need to take one of these. Everyday."

Immediately, I recognized the little yellow plastic container. I took it from her and opened it. I stared at the little pills and didn't hesitate to pop the birth control pill into my mouth, swallowing it dry. I stepped out of my filthy shorts and pulled my shirt over my head. I moved behind the slimy shower curtain and took off the rest of my clothes, dropping them on the cement floor. I took the razor, my fingers barely grasping it, and stepped into the freezing water.

It stunned me at first, sending a wave of shock and awareness through my mind. A few seconds later, the drugs pushed all logic away and I just stood there, letting the cold water pelt down on me. Soon my body was as physically as numb as it was emotionally. Feeling like someone set me on autopilot, I began washing my hair.

I nicked my legs more than once, since I was shivering nonstop. I watched the blood swirl down the yellow stained drain. Teeth chattering, I tipped my head and stared, wishing I could disappear down the drain as well.

"Addie?" Lily's voice spoke from outside the curtain. "You okay in there? It's been a while. You have to be freezing."

I slowly blinked and shook myself. I turned the water off and pulled back the curtain just far enough to grab the towel. I wrapped it around my goosebump-covered torso and walked back to my cot, water dripping on the floor. Dirt and grit stuck to my wet feet. Normally, that would have grossed me out, but what was a little dirt compared to what was going to happen to me?

Phoebe and Lily exchanged sorrowful looks. Phoebe came up behind me and gently towel dried my hair. I just sat there, completely still except for the shivering.

"Here," Lily offered and held out a robe.

Holding the towel up with one hand, I snaked my arms through the crushed velvet robe and tied it around myself.

"I don't get your tattoos," she said and tipped her head.

"Theban," I simplified and looked at the squiggly characters that surrounded a triple moon symbol my left shoulder blade. "It's an old alphabet. It's from a book."

"Oh." Lily nodded. "What about that one? It's a circle inside a triangle with a line through it?"

"From another book," I summed up, looking at the tattoo on my wrist. I had one more tattoo on my left side. I parted the robe to show her. "Get this one?"

"Nope. 'To infinity'," she read. "Don't get it."

"'And beyond'," Phoebe finished. "I like *Toy Story*. Who has other half?"

"My best friend, Lynn," I told her, my voice hollow.

"You must miss her," Lily said quietly. I bit my lip and nodded. Lily looked at me for a few seconds, her blue eyes flashing with emotions. She closed them, shook her head, and put on a small smile. "Rochelle will do your makeup," she said. I nodded and rose from the cot and made my way over to the makeshift vanity. Rochelle was leaning on the counter, keeping the weight off of her injured ankle. I sat on a rickety stool and faced the mirror.

It was the first time I had allowed myself to look at my face since I'd been taken. I had bruises on my face from being hit by Nate and Zane. My right eye was swollen a little on the outside. I knew I had bruises on my body, both from being beaten and from the trunk ride to wherever the hell we were.

"You have nice skin," Rochelle told me. "It'll be easy to work with." She said it in such a way that it wasn't a compliment. Before she started on my makeup, she brushed and blow dried my hair and set it in curlers. Then she spun me around so that I couldn't see in the mirror anymore.

I flinched from the cold liquid foundation she smeared over my cheeks. If I had such nice skin, why did she feel the need to cover it all up? I rarely wore makeup at home. If I did, I focused mainly on my eyes, having fun playing with different colors of eye shadow and liners. I hated the way foundation felt caked onto my face.

"There," she said, sounding satisfied. She had been working on me for what had to be at least half an hour. She took the curlers out of my hair, and after a while of fluffing and spraying enough hair spray to eat away a layer of the O-zone, she leaned back and pressed a smile, nodding as she admired her work.

I turned and looked in the mirror. My eyes were heavily outlined in silver and black. The bruises were gone, though my right eye still looked tender. Red blush on my cheeks made it look like I was permanently embarrassed, and the dark red lipstick was just … trashy. My hair was teased and was inches away from my head. It was coated in so much hair spray that it barely moved with me. Big, wavy curls cascaded around my face.

Suddenly, a smile cracked my face, and a snort of laughter escaped my lips.

"What?" Rochelle demanded.

I shook my head, the humor in my grossly stereotyped appearance quickly fading. Rochelle glared at me for a moment longer before waving me away. She hobbled to the rack of clothing and skimmed through the section of lingerie. She pulled a short, silky nightgown from its hanger. It was dark purple, with black lace outlining the top and bottom. My stomach churned when my fingers touched the shiny material.

"You'll need this," she mumbled and tossed me a push-up bra. "Your boobs are on the small side." She shook her head and sighed. "Whatever. I'll make it work. You should gain some weight."

I held my arms close to my body, feeling very self-conscious. I was thin due to an over-active thyroid. Over the years, I had tried different medications but was unable to find something with a good balance so I just stopped taking the pills. I always had eaten more than enough, but I just couldn't keep the weight on. It had been one of my number one pet peeves to be told I was lucky I was thin. I had a medical condition that took a toll on my body and my health. How lucky is that?

"Tonight you have Travis," Rochelle began explaining. "Give him a good show. He likes to watch."

My stomach clenched and the sting of sour vomit bubbled in my throat. I felt like my head was being shoved into a bucket of dirty water, and no matter how hard I struggled, I couldn't get out, couldn't take a breath.

"I don't know any good shows," I mumbled.

"What?" Rochelle asked and wrinkled her nose. "Well, you do now," she went on, widening her eyes and giving me the girl-you're-crazy stare. She shook her head and sighed. "Just follow his lead, do what he wants, and you'll be fine."

Nerves audibly grumbled through my intestines. I feared something was going to come out one end or the other. Yet I just stood there, my mind wanting to shut down and refuse to process what was going to happen. There was no way around it.

I was going to go upstairs. I was going to go into a room with a sick and twisted man who would force me to have sex with him.

Or I could refuse.

And that would get me severely beaten, if not killed. For a few seconds, dying seemed better than getting raped. I shook my head at the thought. I wasn't going to give up. Today might not be my day for escaping, but it *would* come. It had to.

CHAPTER 8

When I emerged from the basement, I saw Jackson sitting at the island counter in the kitchen, blotting a napkin to a freshly cut lip. He smiled slightly when he saw me, his eyes flicking over my barely covered body before quickly looking at the ground. The beginning of a bruise circled his left eye. His body stiffened when I walked past, and that look of sorrowful disgust took over his face.

Zane was in the living room. Lily let go of my hand and hurried away, reminding me of a dog being greeted by its owner with a rolled up newspaper. His clear blue eyes slowly traced every inch of my body. He stood from the couch and motioned for me to come near. I slowly shook my head.

His face twitched and he strode over and slapped me. He grabbed my shoulders and pushed me up against the wall. "Learn your place," he whispered with his lips inches from mine. His breath smelled like peppermint and was hot on my skin. Tears streaked down my face, no doubt messing up the raccoon-style makeup Rochelle had done for me. "It's unattractive when you cry," he leered. "Travis doesn't like criers. Jim, however," he said with a smirk, "he likes the fear." A deep, throaty laugh bubbled from his mouth.

A buzzer echoed through the room, and Zane snapped his head to the front of the house. A few seconds later, headlights filled the living room. He grabbed my wrist and twisted my skin. "Get upstairs." He pushed me forward and I stumbled into the dark oak staircase, my bare feet skidding uncomfortably on the polished hard wood. "First door on the right," he instructed.

It took every ounce of energy I had to pick up my legs and walk to the top of the stairs. Like the rest of the house, the second level was decorated immaculately. The bedroom was no exception, though a mirror hung over the bed, and metal links were screwed into the wall.

My hands shook uncontrollably as I sank onto the mattress. Scented candles had been lit and scattered on the dresser. The powerful smell of cinnamon only added to the nausea. Candlelight flickered off the soft grey walls. The furniture was all white, as was the love seat across from the bed, the decorative frame around the mirror above the dresser, and the curtains. The bedspread boasted an intricate design of loops and swirls; the material was shiny and was different shades of grey.

I noticed screws above the metal links, and there was a faint outline of a perfect square around each one as if pictures normally hung in their place. I ground my teeth and let my head droop. A strange, foreign, drugged up part of my brain thought that lying in the bed sounded like a good idea. I was, after all, tired.

"No," I said aloud. I wasn't tired. I was drugged. I blinked and shook my head, trying to cast off the fog. It didn't work, and the brilliant idea to hide popped into my head. I pushed myself off the bed and sank to my knees, prepared to duck under the bed. I flattened myself to the floor and shimmied a few inches before I froze in fear.

The scream died in my throat. I pushed myself up and away so fast that I hit my head against the metal frame. Sobering pain jolted through me and I swallowed a gulp of air. Wide eyed, I moved away from the naked body that lay face down on the floor. Blonde hair spilled over her ivory skin. I scooted myself back and bumped into the dresser, knocking over a candle. The hot wax spilled across the dresser's surface and splashed onto me. Tears bit at the corner of my eyes and I dove away, madly wiping the burning liquid off my skin.

Panting, I hugged my knees to my chest. I squeezed my eyes closed and thought about how little sense it made to hide a body under a bed. And then I wondered why the room didn't smell like decay. Slowly, I lay back down on the floor and peered under the bed.

The girl's body was rigid and her skin was tight. Too tight. I narrowed my eyes and moved my hand toward her. My fingers barely graced her arm when I realized she was a doll. A giant, life-sized, very realistic doll.

Sick.

I recoiled from the sex toy, feeling like I needed to wash my hands from just touching it. I wiped my fingers on the bedspread when the thought occurred to me. I flattened myself again and stuck my arms under the bed. I took a hold of the doll and yanked her out, surprised by how heavy it was. I hooked my arms under its armpits and hoisted it up onto the bed, struggling just a bit.

I hopped up on the bed and straddled the doll, fixing its hair and smoothing out the leather bra it was wearing. Then the door swung open.

"Oh!" a man said. "Warming up?"

My heart stopped beating, and my blood turned to ice. Red-hot fear coursed painfully through my frozen body. I looked over at the man I assumed was Travis. He was tall and overweight with a balding head of blonde hair. He was clean-shaven and tan and was wearing a brown suit with a moss green button up underneath, giving the impression that he was a businessman who just got off work.

He removed his suit jacket and smiled hungrily. "I like what I'm seeing," he practically cooed. "Keep going." He took off his collared shirt, revealing a well-done, yet creepy, tattoo on his neck of a black widow spider with vivid red eyes. I stared at it for a second, thinking it looked very out of place on someone dressed as professionally as him. He unbuckled his belt and stuck his hand down his pants, moaning as he rubbed himself. My stomach lurched, and I didn't move; my fingers were still pressed against the doll's silicon breasts. "Keep going," he grumbled.

Transfixed in horror, it took me another second to look away. I heard his pants unzip and slide to the floor. Tears splashed onto the doll's pasty skin. My breathing quickened as panic took over. The mattress sunk down as Travis got in the bed. He slipped one arm around me and pressed himself against me.

He smelled like body odor and fast food, and his breathing was hot and heavy on my neck. Another tear rolled down my face. I sucked in a sob, lip quivering. His hand moved from my stomach to between my legs. He pressed down hard and moved his fingers painfully fast, while still stroking himself. He grabbed my hand and yanked it back, forcing my fingers to wrap about his erection.

And then I threw up.

He shoved me forward, causing me to slip in my own vomit. "What the fuck?" he yelled. My body retched again. "What's wrong with you?" He hurried off the bed and glared at me. "I specifically asked for no sick ones!"

"The rash is gone, so I thought I was better," I blurted. My heart pounded and my head throbbed, though my stomach felt a tiny bit better.

His face wrinkled in disgust and he picked up his boxers. Hopping on one foot while he yanked them up, Travis snarled at me. "I didn't pay for *this*."

I just shook my head and looked at the vomit-covered doll. I wiped my hands on the bedspread and then wiped my mouth with my hand. Travis stormed out of the room, slamming the door shut behind him. I didn't know what to do. Was he going to come back? I thought about making a run for it. Maybe the front door was unlocked since the house had clients in it. My foggy mind created the image of a perfectly manicured lawn for me to run through.

The springy, green grass would be covered in cool dew, and my bare feet would slip as I sprinted to the road. I'd have to climb over a fence that I was sure was stationed at the end of the driveway, and gravel and bits of broken pavement would jab into my heels as I made a desperate dash down the dark road. I would see headlights, and I'd run into the middle of the street, waving my arms like a crazy person. The car would pull over and I'd get in. We'd go straight to the police station, and everything would be okay.

The door opened. I wasn't escaping, not today.

"What's going on?" Zane demanded, his blue eyes narrowed with anger.

I swallowed hard and wished for a glass of water to wash the taste of barf from my mouth. My eyes flicked to the doll, then back to Zane. "I got sick," I stated flatly.

"Why?" he demanded as if I did it on purpose.

"Rochelle gave me something," I blurted, my mind still too hazy to make much sense of anything. "It made me sick."

"What did she give you?"

"A little white pill."

Zane's face relaxed. He leaned against the door and crossed his arms. He really was good looking, and the black t-shirt he had on was tight across his chest, showing off his firm muscles. "Come here," he said, his voice gentle.

A bubble of nerves popped inside me as I slid my feet off the bed and padded across the hardwood floor. I stopped in front of him.

Zane gently tucked a loose curl behind my ear. "Get some sleep," he whispered, his eyes locking with mine.

I wasn't sure if it was the drugs, but I thought I saw something almost gentle in his gaze. Zane took my hand in his, softly rubbing my palm with his thumb. It took me by surprise. Then I shook myself. Even drugged, it wasn't going to work on me. I snatched my hand back.

Zane's face darkened. His shoulders tensed, and he leaned forward, narrowing his eyes. I wobbled but held my ground. With a huff, Zane stormed past me, disappearing down the hall. I exited the room to find Jackson waiting in the hall, his eyes cast to the floor. He looked up at me for a split second before holding out his hand, beckoning me forward. I clung onto the railing as I wobbled down the stairs. Travis was in the living room, still only in his boxers, with a scowl on his face.

"Pathetic," he said when he saw Jackson escorting me through the room.

I stopped in my tracks. "Me, pathetic?" I raised my eyebrows. "Says the guy who has to pay to get laid."

Jackson gave me a slight push to get me walking again. He loudly cleared his throat, covering up a snort of laughter. "You shouldn't talk like that," he whispered when we walked into the kitchen. "You'll get yourself hurt."

I spun around and stared at him. "I don't care." I twisted

back around, bare feet squeaking on the cold tile floor. The lie cut into me and my eyes twitched as I fought the tears.

Don't cry.

I did care. In fact, I cared a hell of a lot, and I hated myself because of it. I cared about my body and myself. I cared about my safety. I cared enough to feel my constantly racing heart and painfully tense muscles.

And I had cared about helping a crying stranger in an alley just a few days ago.

CHAPTER 9

A puff of steam rose from the curling iron as Rochelle unwound my hair. She took a step back and blasted the tendril with hairspray. Three days had passed since I had been taken upstairs to fill in for Rochelle. I hadn't left the basement since.

"There." She set the curling iron down and gently fluffed the curls. "You almost look hot."

I moved my head up and down and stared into my green eyes in the vanity mirror. I should have been offended by her backhanded compliment. But I wasn't. All I could think about was the next client. *My* next client. I stiffly moved off the stool and went back to the cot.

I turned to Lily. "It's in the woods?"

"Yeah." She pulled a dark blue dress off a hanger and held it up to herself. "Like five miles away. It's *such* a long walk."

Phoebe shook her head. "It not that far."

Lily pressed her full lips together. "Well, it *feels* that far. I hate walking through the woods in heels."

I chewed on my lip. "Why is it hidden in the woods?"

"Some people are paranoid," Lily explained. "They like don't want their cars seen at the house, so Nate put a trailer in the woods." She shrugged and put the blue dress back, trading it for a low cut, black sequined tank top.

"How do they get there?"

"I don't know." She went to the dresser. "They're already there when I get there." She extracted a neon green push-up bra. "There are plenty of toys in the cabinets above the bed. Use them," she suggested.

My head moved up and down but nothing actually processed in my mind. I slowly blinked, trying to rid myself of the residual dull headache that had clung onto me since I woke up. I flattened my sweaty palms on the tight shorts I was wearing. The fabric was stiff and itchy, and the waist was a size too small. It dug into me every time I took a breath.

Along with doing my hair and makeup, Rochelle had dressed me again. She picked out a pair of white, tight shorts and a midriff-showing black tank top with a pair of over the knee, black high-heeled boots to complete my 'outfit,' but no matter how hard she tried, she couldn't get her size seven shoes to fit my big feet. She gave up and tossed my sneakers at me, saying it didn't matter since I was going to take my clothes off anyway. My makeup was layered on to the point where I could scrape it off with my fingernails. I resisted the urge to wipe it off with my hands.

My heart skipped a beat when the deadbolt shot back. All four of us looked when the basement door opened, waiting to see who would emerge at the bottom of the stairs. I counted each heavy footstep that reverberated off the wooden steps. Jackson stopped at the base.

"Adeline." His eyes landed on me. I knew that was my cue to get up, but I couldn't move. I just sat there, perfectly still, yet internally screaming. "Adeline?" he repeated.

Someone moved behind me. I startled when a hand landed on my back.

"Go," Phoebe whispered. "I no want you get hurt."

I nodded again, thinking she meant Jackson would hurt me, and looked at Jackson. I didn't want to get hurt just as much as I didn't want to go to the trailer. I knew I had to, one way or the other, and I'd rather walk than be dragged. My legs shook. I pushed my shoulders back, trying to hide the fear, and crossed the basement.

We excited the house from the family room, emerging onto a large patio. Lights in an in-ground pool gave off a murky glow beneath the crystal clear water. Wicker lounge chairs with fluffy, red cushions surrounded an outdoor bar, and a built-in fireplace and grill occupied each corner of the patio. Like the rest of the house, it seemed to have been cut and pasted out of a *Better Homes and Garden* magazine. Though it was still early in the season, red and white flowers spilled over stone planters, leaving me to believe that someone had spent a lot of time and money having this place landscaped, manicured, and groomed to perfection.

But why?

My eyes swept the lawn. The entire thing was lined with a tall white iron fence. I knew right away that I wouldn't be able to climb it fast enough to get away. I was outside ... so close to freedom. I had to do something. I was out of the basement—out of the *house*. The open air and distant buzzing of crickets reminded me that there were other people out there. Other people who could help me. My shoes scuffed the cement patio around the pool as I slowed. I looked at the surrounding land. There was nothing, absolutely nothing but untended land around the yard. I felt trapped all over again.

"Could you take any longer?" The sound of Zane's voice sent a jolt through me.

I ground my teeth and pulled my arms close to my body. Zane was standing off to the side, concealed by shadows. He gracefully pushed off the shed he was leaning on. "Hurry the fuck up, you slow-ass whore."

"Don't touch me," I said through gritted teeth when Zane grabbed my arm, yanking me forward. I pulled my arm back, trying to break his hold. I wasn't strong enough. All I ended up doing was causing the first layer of skin to twist and tear.

Zane laughed and jumped in front of me. His fingers tightened on my arm, the pain biting into me until I was sure blood pooled under the half moon marks left by his fingernails.

"I like it when you fight," he groaned. With his free hand, he reached up and took a fist full of my hair and stepped closer, brushing his waist against mine. Jackson turned around, face blank. He didn't care what happened to me.

Then Zane let me go. He laughed and turned his back to me, purposely flashing the silver gun tucked into his pants. My heart was in my throat. Nerves tingled throughout my body, and my teeth chattered.

"Come on," Zane ordered and paced ahead.

I looked at the ground, blinking back tears. Jackson waited until I was a few feet in front of him to follow. The invisible wall of the cage closed in on me. I was sandwiched between Zane and Jackson. Their body heat suffocated me. Mixed with the humid air, it was nauseating.

We crossed the yard and stopped by a gate. Jackson dug a key from his pocket and unlocked it. He pushed it open and stepped aside. Zane took a hold of my arm again, forcing me to walk close to him. A gravel path cut into the forest, which started just several feet from the white fence.

The gate slammed shut behind us. A useless sense of hope fluttered through me. I wasn't fenced in. I *could* run away.

And get shot.

There was nothing I could do. There was no escape. I felt like I was walking to the end of a plank, precariously hanging over shark-infested water. When I jumped, sharp teeth would rip into me and the cold water would steal my breath away. The monsters would take everything from me, leaving me shivering and naked in the water. The only difference was that tonight I would be pulled from the icy darkness and forced to do it again. There would be no release from death, only pain.

Thinking of a plan of escape, I closed my eyes and continued to move forward, my pace subconsciously slowing down. Lily had said that Jackson and Zane would go back to the house while I worked. I had to run then. What other choice did I have?

Zane jerked me forward. The toe of my shoe caught on the uneven path and I stumbled and tripped.

"Seriously?" Zane huffed under his breath.

My throat tightened with fear and I blinked back tears. Zane scuffed his shoe, sending a cloud of dusty dirt into my face. I coughed and turned my head. He stepped away, laughing.

Jackson stopped next to me and extended a hand. I traced my eyes up from his fingers. He had a bruise just below his elbow in the shape of a large handprint, as if someone had grabbed him and twisted his skin. Did he do Nate's dirty work and that was why he was always injured? Maybe he collected unpaid money and got in a lot of fights. The black t-shirt he wore was faded and worn, and his dark eyes glazed over, hiding back his emotions. The emptiness on his face frightened me.

Ignoring his offer, I put my hands on the ground and pushed myself up. Jackson's eyebrows pushed together and he studied a vine of poison ivy that twisted around a maple tree. He stepped away from me and bit his bottom lip. Zane grabbed my arm and pulled me forward again. I didn't fight him. Really, the sooner I got into the trailer, the sooner I could put my plan into action. I took a deep breath and tried to steady myself.

Just like Lily said, it felt like we were miles away from the farmhouse by the time we reached what was called 'the trailer.' Really, it was a brand new RV, and it must have cost a lot of money. Yellow light spilled from slats in the mini blinds. An old blue Cadillac was parked behind it.

Zane kept a painful hold of my arm as Jackson knocked on the door. The blood drained from my face. It was as if I was waiting to see the face of my executioner, but he wouldn't kill all of me. Only part of me would die and I would be forced to carry the black and festering hole with me for the rest of my life. It would be a constant reminder of what was painfully taken from me.

Just seconds later, the door opened revealing a tall man with shoulder-length brown hair squished beneath a straw fedora. He wore a dark blue Hawaiian print button up over a white undershirt. He looked to be around my father's age. Wrinkles formed around his gray eyes when he smiled, taking in the sight of me.

"I can take it from here, boys," he spoke, his words slurring together. He beamed at me, his teeth crooked and yellow, and took a swig of something from a silver flask. I felt like I was going to throw up again.

Jackson's shoulder's sagged and he backed off of the RV steps before turning and trudging down the path. Zane stood to the side, his sky-blue eyes dark in the fading sunlight. His full lips curved into a twisted smile, and he backed away.

The man in the trailer extended a hand as if he expected me to take it. I held my arms close to my body and didn't move. The man let out a gritty huff and heaved his large frame down the first metal step and snatched my wrist. He gruffly yanked me up the stairs and slammed the RV door behind us, flicking the lock into place.

The walls closed in on me. I rapidly sucked in air, making myself dizzy. I didn't know what to do. A large man stood between the door and me. How was I supposed to leave? My eyes widened in terror and my hands began trembling. I pressed them against my thighs to keep them steady. I needed to hold it together if I wanted to escape.

The man didn't even move into the small bedroom. He just turned around and put both hands on my shoulders before pushing me down onto my knees. Little pieces of gravel littered the carpet and dug into my flesh. He unzipped his pants, exposing himself, and leaned back, putting his hands on his hips. I clenched my jaw. Vomit burned in my throat but I was too horrified to look away.

I was above my body again, seeing this all play out. I forced my eyes closed. *Keep it together.* It was all happening too soon. Zane and Jackson were too close. I opened my eyes and was back in my body. I took a breath to calm myself.

"Never seen a cock this big before?" he asked with a throaty laugh.

I wanted to tell him that his junk was nothing impressive, and he smelled like he hadn't washed his balls in days. I froze, not knowing what to do. My heart was racing and my fingers trembled. I wanted to spring up, hit him in the face, and run. That wouldn't work. I swallowed hard and took in a ragged breath, smiling up at the man. I needed a plan, I needed to buy time.

"Before we get started," I managed to say with minimal shaking of my voice. "Let me put on a show for you."

The man's eyes narrowed before he tipped his head up and nodded. I scrambled up and away, resisting the urge to pat my back pocket just to be sure the rusty screw was still in place. I walked as seductively as I could into the section of the RV that housed a cramped bed and knelt on the mattress.

I had to play it up, even though I was screaming inside. I blinked, then cast a coy smile over my shoulder and opened the cabinet, pretending like I knew exactly what I was looking for. My trembling hands knocked over a very realistic, and very large, flesh-colored dildo. My eyes widened as I looked it over and I slowly shook my head as terror and dread crept over me. These toys were in here for a reason … the same reason I was in here.

"Ready for me yet?" His gritty voice made me jump, and I knocked over a row of colorful vibrators. I sank onto the bed and swallowed hard.

"Uh … " My eyes flicked to the curtained window. Nervous sweat rolled between my cleavage. I swallowed hard.

The man plopped down on the bed. His pants were still undone. He let out a deep sigh, his hot, smelly breath wafting into my face. I turned my head and closed my eyes.

"Hey," he said suddenly. "Put one of those on."

I opened my eyes to see him pointing at a rack of lingerie and slutty costumes. I sprang up and tripped over my own feet. I internally winced at my timorous movements. I walked around the bed. The man slapped my ass when I moved in front of him. My shoulders stiffened. I clenched my jaw shut and kept walking until I was in front of the costumes.

"Who do you want me to be?" I blurted too fast. I smiled again, trying to keep up the façade that I was going to do exactly what I was told. I ran my fingers over the clothes, ignoring the white stains on the fabric. I randomly pulled out a Little Red Riding Hood outfit.

The man shook his head, his smile broadening. I picked another at random—a red, skintight body suit with a devil's horns headband. Another head shake. I grabbed a frilly, pink, Shirley Temple style dress and held it up to my body. The man nodded and groaned, his excitement physically apparent. I flashed one more coy smile before backing out of the room, pulling the curtain that separated the bedroom from the rest of the RV.

I threw the dress on the ground and took a few tentative steps toward the trailer door, looking outside. It was finally dark outside. I apprehensively reached out, my fingers shaking, and pulled back the blinds. The forest was alive with insects; their chirping and buzzing filled the humid night air. I cast a nervous glance behind me and unlocked the door. I swallowed my pounding heart and leapt down the metal stairs.

CHAPTER 10

My feet softly landed on the soft, powder-dry dirt. I froze, expecting Zane or Jackson to come rushing forward. I pulled the screw from my pocket and closed my fist around it so that the pointy end stuck out in between my index and middle finger. I raced around the RV to the old, blue Cadillac. My fingers bent under the handle. I pulled and the door opened.

Holy shit, yes!

My heart hammered. I ducked inside, landing on the driver's seat. I put my hands on the steering wheel and looked at the ignition. There were no keys.

Son of a bitch.

I hit the steering wheel, angry with myself. I should have looked inside the RV for his keys. But I didn't. I screamed in frustration. I madly opened the glove box and pulled down the visors. I was wasting time.

The smell of body odor and cigarette smoke inside the old Caddy suffocated me. I needed out. I needed to leave. The interior door handle was sticky, but I didn't have time to grimace at the mystery substance. I wrapped my fingers around it and pushed the door open.

I moved out of the car and looked at the RV. I could see the man's large silhouette moving behind the pulled curtains in the small bedroom. I put one hand on the doorframe and bent inside, ready to pop the hood and try my best to damage the engine when the RV creaked. I didn't want the man to drive away and find Zane. Or follow me down the road… if I made it that far.

Adrenaline surged through me, pricking every nerve in my body. I jumped away from the car, consternation pulling me into irrational darkness. I spun around and took off, sprinting down the dirt driveway. It had to lead to a road. It just had to. And once on the road, I would run into a car, and that car would take me to safety, just like I imagined.

"Hey!" the man yelled from behind me. "Where the hell do you think you're going? I can see you, bitch!"

Keys jingled, and the door slammed. I jumped off the dirt road and crashed into the trees, feet catching on tangles of weeds and uneven earth. I threw my hands out in front of me to catch myself. Low hanging branches hit my face, tearing open the skin on my cheeks.

I cried out when my knees hit the ground, tree limbs and roots biting into my flesh. I pushed myself up and blindly ran forward, not realizing how much noise I was making until I was several yards into the forest. I came to a sudden halt and put my hand over my mouth, trying to quiet my rapid breath.

Red-hot fear radiated off of me and hung in the thick air, cloaking my body in a sticky reminder of the danger I was in. I pressed my back against a tree and closed my eyes, trying to force out a slow, steady breath. Around me, the wildlife was blind to the horrors and went on with its usual night routine. Something whizzed past me and landed in my hair. Too worried about my life to freak out, I calmly batted the insect away.

Moonlight filtered through the thick vegetation, casting dark and eerie shadows off the trees. With my hands still pressed against my lips, I looked around, unsure of exactly where I had run from. *I made a straight line off the driveway, right?* Branches snapped behind me, and I jumped, making an irritating squeaking noise I winced and scooted my feet back until my heels protested against the roots of the tree. The underbrush crunched under someone's feet from only a few yards away. I edged around the thick tree trunk and put my shaking hands on the bark.

I counted to three and pushed off. Bits of sap pulled at my hair and stuck to my hands. Ignoring it, I dropped to the ground and out of sight. Slowly, I lifted my right hand and left knee simultaneously and moved forward. Something squirmed under my hand and I recoiled; my elbow hit a tangle of weeds that trembled from my touch.

"Shit!" I mouthed and battled against the urge to give up and sprint away. I put my hand back down and moved, only to repeat the slow process two more times before freezing.

"Yeah, the bitch escaped," the man's gruff voice carried through the humid air. I could see the glow of a cell phone only feet away. My heart plummeted to the ground, beating so fast and loud that he had to be able to hear it. "I chased her down the driveway, but the whore went into the woods. I didn't pay for this," he angrily spat. "Bring me another and find your own cunt-ass bitch!"

My eyes finally focused on his large shape. He turned around, swatting at bugs. His shoulders were tense, and his free hand curled into a fist. He lowered his phone from his ear and slammed this thumb onto the screen.

"Un-fucking-believable," he mumbled before shoving the phone into his pocket. He pulled something else out and put it close to his face.

The sudden brightness of the cigarette lighter blinded me. I flattened myself on the ground and closed my eyes, the shape of the flame burned into my retinas. The stench of smoke wafted slowly through the thick air, mixing with the scent of the man's overpowering cologne.

I peered through dew-covered leaves and watched the red end of his cigarette glow as he took a drag, then disappear from view when he turned around. Gravel crunched under his feet as he walked up the driveway. I let out my breath and crept forward, not daring to get up. When the nasty smell of cigarette smoke was gone, I painstakingly crawled on my hands and knees to hide behind the fat trunk of an oak tree. I pushed myself up and took off again, putting what I had hoped was yards between us before I darted onto the driveway again.

I didn't dare turn around. I just ran. Chest heaving for air, I ignored the pain and pressed forward. This was my chance. I was going to get away. And then I'd send the cops back here and smile when they arrested the sick, twisted men who occupied the house. The girls would be rescued too, of course, and everyone would be all right.

My heart fluttered when the tall black gate came into view. I skidded to a stop, realizing that I was so winded I couldn't breathe. On its own accord, my body doubled over as my lungs begged for air. Gasping, I put my hands on my knees and took a shaky breath. I tried to slowly let it out and failed. Close to hyperventilating, I gasped for air, which only made me panic more.

Hold it together, I told myself. I squeezed my eyes shut and just thought about breathing. A few seconds later, I was able to stand up. Still wheezing, I put my hands on the gate and pushed. The hinges screamed into the night.

I stumbled over the small indentation between the driveway and the road, falling on my hands and knees. Pain bit at the peeled-off skin. I pushed myself up and cradled my hands against my abdomen, glancing down at the rawness of my palms. Blood dripped down my left knee, and it stung every time I took a step.

Limping, I scrambled down the street. Wispy clouds rolled over the moon. A barbed wire fence hung from decaying wooden posts, lining a long-forgotten field. A dead oak tree was directly across from me, its spider web of bare branches reaching toward the night sky. An owl sat at the top; only its shadowy outline was visible in the dark.

The gates creaked behind me. I whirled around, hands held out to my sides, ready for a fight. White fear tingled down my spine, and my heart beat so fast it hurt. The wind blew and the gates groaned again. I let out a breath and felt my shoulders relax the slightest bit. It was only the wind.

I walked into the middle of the road and stopped. I looked at the woods and then at the field, knowing that I had to pick one to run through. Being in the street was too obvious. Deciding that the over-grown field was better than being anywhere near Nate's property, I crossed the street and carefully wrapped a bloody hand around the rusted barbed wire.

Bits of metal flaked off on my fingers. I pulled the sagging wire up and ducked down. Carefully, I stepped through. Then the owl took off, its wings flapping ominously in the silent darkness of the night. I froze, wondering if its absence was due to my presence or if something else had startled it. I lowered my head and squeezed through the wire. My hair caught on the blunt barbs. I grabbed my curls and yanked them free, leaving several strands blowing in the night.

And then I saw it, the thing that made the owl leave. I scrambled back through the fence with less grace and scraped my back. The cut instantly burned, and I was happy I had given in and gotten a tetanus shot like my mom suggested after I cut myself on broken picture frame in the gallery last summer.

"Hey!" I shouted and waved my arms. I tried to run towards the yellow glow of headlights but faltered with each step. "Hey! Stop!" I screamed though I knew the car was still too far away. Suddenly afraid that I gave away my location and Zane or Jackson would burst through the gate and tackle me to the ground, I pressed forward, wincing with each step.

The pain increased with my speed but I didn't care. I was so close. I was getting away. A manic laugh bubbled from my throat, and I waved my arms over my head once more. The car was approaching fast. I didn't want them to miss me. I limped into the middle of the road. "Help!"

Tires squealed. I stood rooted in the spot and watched the vehicle fishtail as the driver slammed on the brakes. They were stopping; they had seen me! But they hadn't seen me soon enough. My eyes widened and I made a move to jump out of the way.

But I was too late. The front end of the car made contact with my body. I fell forward, leaving bloody handprints on the hood. The car came to a stop and I tumbled back. I hadn't been hit hard, but I lost my footing and tripped as I backed away, falling and landing on my back. My head hit the pavement, and a wave of nausea rolled over me instantly.

The bright lights from the car only added to my blurry vision. I felt everything in the next few seconds. The heat from the engine. The sticky warmth of the pavement. The rocks underneath me. Every scrape, cut, and bruise on my body screamed in pain. I tried to sit up.

"Holy fucking shit!" The driver frantically spoke. "You came outta nowhere!"

I moaned as the pain in my head began to throb. I reached out, my hand slapping the bumper as I attempted to get up. "Police," I mumbled, not wanting to be taken to a hospital. "Take me," I breathed.

"Don't move. I'm calling 911!" the guy told me. His voice was familiar. My eyes fluttered closed. I felt his presence as he moved over to me. "Just don't—" he suddenly cut off. "Hey!" he said in surprised. "Shit," he swore again. I heard a rustled of fabric as he knelt down. "*Sh-iii-t,*" he said once more, this time drawing out the word.

"Police," I tried again, mustering up the strength to open my eyes. The fuzzy outline of a young man leaned over me. One hand went under my shoulders and the other snaked under my back. With a grunt, he hoisted me up and held me against him.

"Everything's gonna be okay," he soothed, sending chills through me. He turned, and a bout of dizziness passed over me. My ears rang. I knew I was going to lose consciousness. And something wasn't right. My face was pressed against the man's neck. I lifted my head up and forced my eyes open just long enough to see the glowing red eyes of a black widow spider.

CHAPTER 11

I woke up in agony. Every inch of my body hurt and my arms and legs felt too heavy to move. The indiscernible hum of hushed voices filled the air, stopping when I groaned and sat up. My arms and legs didn't just *feel* heavy, they were heavy. And that was because they were weighed down with thick chains. Panic flashed through me, and I jolted up, instantly regretting the fast movements.

I was chained to my cot in the basement.

Lily and Phoebe were sitting on the cot next to mine. Tears streaked through the bronzer on Lily's young face and Phoebe's eyes, which were hidden behind bright blue colored contacts, held back a terror that bit at my soul. Rochelle sat at the table in the center of the room, flipping through a deck of cards while looking incredibly bored.

"You shouldn't have done that," she scolded. "Zane was out *all night* looking for you," she said in such a way that made it seem like he was searching for me out of fear for my own well-being. I blinked, my fuzzy vision finally focusing, and saw that her jaw was set and her dark eyes narrowed. "What the hell were you thinking?"

"I was thinking," I began, rage fueling the fire behind my raspy voice. "That I was going to get the hell out of here and get someone to help the rest of you escape."

Lily whimpered, and Phoebe put her arm around her. "You so close," Phoebe whispered.

My mind flashed to the run through the woods and my escape to the road. My stomach twisted as I recalled being knocked over by the car, harshly landing on the pavement, and being scooped up by the only person in the entire world who recognized me for what I was supposed to become. Fear and horror rippled through me, and I wondered what Travis had done to me when I was unconscious. I couldn't think about that. I couldn't handle it.

The basement door opened and slammed shut. Feet plodded down the wooden steps. I lifted my head up as far as I could and felt pain ripple down my spine.

"Good, she's awake." Nate's voice was smooth. "Unchain her," he said. Jackson shuffled his feet as he hesitantly walked over. The entire left side of his face was spotted with dark purple bruises, and there were five fresh, clean cuts fresh on his right forearm. All were the same length and equally spaced from each other, but each got deeper as they went up his arm.

His movements were stiff, leaving me to believe there was more damage done to his body than I could see. His dark eyes flashed to mine for a millisecond, but that was all the time I needed to see his terror and pity. He stuck a key in the locks that held back my arms. He pocketed the padlocks and gently unwrapped the heavy links from my wrists. His eyes met mine again, though this time they pleaded for me to shut up and stay still. Next, he got up and walked around the bed, releasing the metal from around my ankles.

"Sit up," Nate ordered. He sat on the cot next to mine and smiled as he eyed me up and down. He had a yellow folder next to him, and he drummed his neatly manicured nails on it. Zane stood behind him with his arms crossed. Even he had a fist sized bruise under his right eye.

"I'm impressed," Nate started. "I'm very impressed with your efforts, but this has to stop."

I clenched my jaw and dug my nails into the mattress. Inside, I was shaking with fear. But I'd be damned to let Nate know that. I narrowed my eyes to keep from crying.

"You don't want to become more trouble than you're worth," Nate continued. He dramatically sighed and opened the folder, withdrawing several photographs and handing them to me. The ink hadn't completely dried; it felt sticky under my fingers.

My breath caught in my chest, and a whimper escaped my lips when I stared down at the pages. The smiling face of my little sister looked up at me. In a horrified trance, I flipped through the pictures. The next photo was of Lynn, then my parents, then Ari again with the dogs. The last image was printed straight from Google Earth, and my house was circled in red ink.

"Try anything again and I cannot promise their safety," Nate spoke calmly. He stood and yanked the photos from my clammy fingers, smearing the ink. I was too weighted down with fear to react. "Leave her. No food or water until tomorrow. If she tries to escape, put her back in the closet."

Lily, who was pressed against a wall next to Phoebe, tried to step forward. Phoebe took a hold of her wrist and pulled her back, quickly shaking her head. Rochelle crossed her arms and glared at me for another few seconds before getting up and limping over to Zane. She gently touched the bruise on his face. He snarled at her and pushed her away. Not having her normal balance, Rochelle stumbled and fell, her knees smacking against the concrete floor.

Crying out in pain, she spun herself around and crawled after Zane. With one hand outstretched, she called to him.

"Wait!"

Nate had already ascended the stairs. Jackson stood at the base of the stairs with his arms tightly crossed, looking like he might get sick. Zane turned, cold eyes flashing at Rochelle.

"Later," he said with no emotion. "I'll come back later."

Her whole body relaxed and a wide smile took over her face. "I'll be waiting," she cooed and used a chair to pull herself to her feet.

Zane turned, snapped his fingers at Jackson to follow, and stomped up the stairs. I heard the multiple locks click into place.

I let out a shaky breath and lowered my head. The adrenaline and terror were slowly leaving my body, letting the full extent of the agony my body was in register in my brain. Wincing, I moved so that my back was resting against the thin pillow. I closed my eyes, and hot tears rolled down my cheeks. It stung. I carefully reached up and felt several tiny tears in my skin, no doubt acquired from running through the darkened forest.

I turned my hands over and saw that my palms and been completely torn from the asphalt, as were my knees and my right side and hip. My head throbbed, and I was uncomfortably hot, making me wonder what would happen if my wounds became infected.

I heard the metallic squeak of the shower turning on. Phoebe moved around near it but didn't get in. And then it shut off. She came over to the cot, carrying several wet rags and a bottle of rubbing alcohol.

"Me help." She knelt down next to the cot. "This hurt," she warned. I closed my eyes and gobbled the old quilt into my fists. Phoebe gingerly ran the wet washcloth over my face. I whimpered but remained still. She worked her way down, cleaning the dried blood and mud from my skin. Then she blotted every scratch with alcohol. I turned my head to the side and bit the inside of my cheek in an attempt to distract myself from the pain of cleaning my wounds.

"There." Phoebe stood. "You want pain pill?"

"Sure." Why not? Why should I suffer any more than I already was?

Phoebe went to the dresser and returned with an orange pill bottle. She dumped the contents out in the cot. It was full of different types of pills varying in size, shape, and color. She pursed her lips as she thought, sorting through the medication.

"I think this right one." She picked out a large white pill. "Lily, get water."

I took the pill from Phoebe. "Thank you," I told her.

"You so close." She squeezed her eyes shut for a moment. "So close to freedom."

"I'm sorry."

"No." Her head whipped back and forth. "No apologize. So close to freedom is hope. We do it again."

"Yeah. Uh … next time. Next time we'll have a plan."

"Yes. We come up with good plan, and we get out." Her head tipped up and to the side as she spoke. She didn't believe a word she was saying. And at that moment, neither did I.

CHAPTER 12

Echoing booms woke me up. My eyes flitted across the dark basement to one of the small, rectangular windows. It was too dark to actually see it, but I knew the general location. Another boom rattled the house. Thunder. The loud noises had to be thunder.

I let my shoulders relax, and then I heard it again. My body went rigid. Bombs, it sounded like bombs. And then a faint, colorful glow illuminated the window.

"Oh," I said out loud. "Fireworks." Without warning, emotion bubbled through me and I started crying. There was one main reason for fireworks in the summer, and that meant we were four days into July. Four days into July meant that I had been held captive for over a month.

And I was still locked in the basement. I hadn't been put to work. In fact, I had been left alone most of this time. I didn't know where the girls were whisked off too. When they came back, they were only here for a few hours to rest before they went out again. They were constantly working, treated like objects with no traces of human needs or emotions.

I knew it was Nate's attempt to break my spirit. Being alone in this dark hole was enough to make me go mad. I was constantly scared, and now I was lonely. There were times when I had gone days without seeing the girls but I refused to let it break me. I was alone, but I wasn't forgotten. I wouldn't be forgotten. I held onto every ounce of hope I had with no intentions of letting it go.

I always made an effort to get up and move around the basement, keeping my muscles loose and ready to sprint out of here at a moment's notice. Lily and Phoebe helped keep that hope alive. Like me, Phoebe dreamed of running away. Lily hid from the emotions of her painful past by being unusually upbeat and cheerful for someone in our situation. Outside of this hell-hole, I wouldn't have gone out of my way to be friends with either of the girls. But in here, I cared about them. After all, we were all each other had.

More fireworks exploded, masking the sound of the basement door opening. It startled me when Jackson pulled the string, turning on the light.

"Sorry," he said quietly.

His dark wavy hair was wet and pushed back from his face. I blinked in the harsh light and looked at him, realizing for the first time that his eyes were shaped like almonds and lined with thick, dark lashes. I looked away, not wanting to acknowledge I found his dark eyes captivating.

"I brought you food," he told me and slowly approached the cot.

My stomach grumbled with hunger as I looked over the tray. It was always some sort of variation of a cheap school lunch. Today it was turkey sandwiches, fruit cups, milk, yogurt, and cereal bars.

Jackson put the tray on the table and looked at me. He had never tried to so much as touch me, but being alone with him unnerved me. There was nothing stopping him if he ever decided to do, well, anything to me.

"Thanks," I said automatically. "What's going on out there?" I pulled my arms close to me and glanced at the small window.

"Fourth of July party." He pointed behind him. "The pool is on the other side of the house, so I guess you can't hear the music."

"Oh, right." I looked at the turkey sandwich and then back at Jackson. *The pool, right.* No wonder his hair was wet. He had been swimming and partying and watching fireworks. I wanted to be angry with him. I wanted to throw the tray across the room and tell him what an awful person he was. Then I caught his gaze again, and he hit me with a pitying stare.

No.

I wasn't going to be like Rochelle, who had a textbook case of Stockholm syndrome. Maybe Jackson really did feel bad for me, but it didn't make him any better than Nate or Zane. A small part of my brain nagged at me, reminding me of the cuts and bruises that frequently decorated Jackson's face. I shook my head, dismissing the issue all together. Whatever happened to Jackson was his business, not mine. Besides, he lived upstairs with Nate and Zane, working with them. He was one of them, and I couldn't let my guard down, not if I ever wanted to get out.

"Well," he started and pulled on a lose string along the hem of his shirt. "Can I get you anything else?"

Was he serious? I shot Jackson the most incredulous stare I could manage. "Get me the fuck out of here," I said with my mouthful.

He recoiled from my words. "S-sorry," he stuttered. "Bad question." His cheeks turned bright red, and he took a small step backwards.

"Jackson!" a male voice boomed from upstairs. "What the hell is taking so long? We're out of beer!" Zane yelled.

Jackson's body tensed and he whirled around and scurried up the stairs. I stared at the spot where he had been standing and tried to hang onto the anger. It wouldn't be long before the emotions slipped away and I was left feeling empty again.

I finished my food and paced around the basement, thankful Jackson left the light on. Feeling restless, I dragged a chair over to the small rectangular window and put my hands on the ledge. Dusty spider webs crackled and caught on my fingertips. I jerked back and flicked my hand. The webs were old and void of spiders, but it still grossed me out. I couldn't see anything except the distant glow of lights and the occasional bright explosion of fireworks. When my heels started to painfully scream at me, I hopped down from the chair, shock stinging my ankles. My eyes closed as the pain radiated up into my calves. I bent down and pressed my fingers into the muscle, slowly massaging it out.

I pulled my shoulders back and took a breath. I wanted to scream and throw shit and watch it break. I pressed my hands onto my eyes and screamed in frustration.

Something clattered to the floor above me. I removed my hands and blinked. My vision was cloudy with dark spots from the pressure of my hands. I shook my head, huffed, and sank down on my cot. The air was humid and sticky, yet I shivered. I pulled the quilt over my bare arms, the rough fabric itching my skin. I closed my eyes and prayed for the safety of my family and friends.

I couldn't remember the last thing I had said to my mother before I was taken. I had seen her the night before the Pride Parade. I was sitting on the porch, deep into my book. She came home late from teaching a class at the gallery and was startled to see me huddled under a thin blanket, swatting mosquitoes and squinting in the yellow porch light with my book just inches from my face. She told me to come inside and talk with her. I said I would when I reached the end of the chapter I was on. Four chapters later and by the time I was sick of getting eaten alive by flying bloodsuckers, she had already gone to bed. The guilt was like acid in my stomach.

I angrily wiped away tears and lay down, curling my legs up to my chest. The grand finale of the firework show boomed and flashed with fury in the night sky. Scarlet hated fireworks, and I hated that I wasn't there to comfort my dog. The tears began to fall faster. I squeezed my eyes shut so tight they hurt, and I cried myself to sleep.

Heels clomped down the basement stairs, pulling me from the gray sleep I drifted in and out of all day. Lily and Phoebe trudged over, collapsing on their cots. I pushed myself up and rubbed the sleep out of my eyes, glad the girls were back.

"Are you okay?" I looked at Lily, who was walking as if she was sore.

"Define okay," she grumbled. "I got the shit fucked out of me."

My heart fluttered, and abhorrence flooded my veins. Heat rushed to my cheeks, speckling them with red. "Where were you?"

"Yacht party," Phoebe said.

"Yacht party?" I echoed. "We're in Iowa."

"It was just a big houseboat," Lily corrected. "On a lake a few hours from here. Nothing spectacular." She used her feet to push off her yellow heels and lay down. "It was hot, the lake smelled like fish, and the boat's air conditioning stopped working like halfway through our trip."

"So many people," Phoebe complained. "Nonstop work."

Horrified and at a loss for words, I looked at Phoebe. The thought of being stuck on a boat in the middle of a lake with multiple clients made me sick to my stomach. Would I eventually be forced to do the same thing? Phoebe began unclipping hair extensions. I noticed she was wearing false eyelashes as well. "Where is Rochelle?"

"With Zane," Lily mumbled.

"What?" I leaned back with shock.

"They're kind of a thing," she explained.

"No," Phoebe interjected. "He use her."

"Not all the time." Lily yawned. "He says he likes her."

"And I can say a lot of things," Phoebe spat. "Doesn't mean true."

"Whatever." Lily flipped her hand in the air. "He can be sweet sometimes. Plus, he's hot. She's lucky."

Phoebe looked at me and shook her head. "She don't get it," she mouthed to me.

I nodded in agreement, knowing there was nothing sweet about Zane.

"I'm tired," she said with a yawn. "Go to sleep now."

My eyebrows pushed together and I looked at Lily. What the hell would make her think Zane was sweet? I couldn't refute the fact that he was hot. He had a smile that could literally charm the pants off of almost every woman he met. Zane was nothing but a cold-hearted psychopath.

The basement door opened, bumping into the wall. The scent of his cologne made my skin crawl. *Think of the devil, and he shall appear.* Looking sleek and sexy dressed in all black, Zane slid around the corner. His tantalizing, blue eyes flitted around the room and settled on me.

"Hello, Adeline," he said, his voice smooth and deep, making me want to puke. He flashed a smile. I glowered at him, waiting for his eyes to turn back as he revealed himself as the demon he really was. "Time for work."

"Work?" I asked, my voice dying in my throat. I had stepped backwards off of a sharp cliff and was falling down, down, down, ripping through frozen clouds. Sharp icicles tore into my flesh. "It's the afternoon," I blurted.

Zane laughed. "So?" He moved with cat-like grace across the floor. "Get dressed. Nothing too flashy. You're going into the city."

"I am?" Something other than fear ran through me. I wasn't sure just what city he was referring to, but there was one thing all cities had in common: people. Lots and lots of people. This was my chance! All I had to do was run, scream, or make a scene and someone would come to my aid. But would I be putting my family at risk? No, I had to try, right? I could get to the police before Zane or Nate could get to my house.

I stood and dizzily walked over to the clothes. I randomly grabbed a garment and pulled it from a hanger. I didn't care what I looked like. What I cared about was coming up with a plan of attack. Or escape. Or whatever the hell would get me away from Zane.

I turned away from Zane and pulled the long sleeved t-shirt I was wearing over my head, trading it for a white dress. I put it on backwards. The tag tickled my neck. I twisted it again and straightened the hem before taking off my pajama pants.

Zane impatiently drummed his fingers on the chipping drywall that encased the stairwell. I turned around and hesitantly walked to him. His eyes trailed up and down my body. He frowned and then shrugged.

"Good enough," he mumbled and went up the stairs.

My pulse fluttered through me. I cast a glance behind me. *I'll save you too*, I thought to Phoebe and Lily. My hand shook when I extended it. I wrapped my fingers around the splintering railing and put my foot on the first step. This was it. My chance. Finally, I would be free.

I blinked from the bright, natural light that streamed into the kitchen. The windows were open, and a soft breeze blew through the large room. I stopped in my tracks and breathed it in. I hadn't left the basement since my failed attempt at running away. The fresh air felt wonderful.

Zane grabbed my wrist and yanked me forward. "Come on," he grumbled. My bare feet stuck to the tile and I skidded forward. Zane halted and looked down. "Where are your shoes?"

"I don't know," I said honestly. They were removed the night Travis hit me with his car and I hadn't seen them since.

"Don't move," he said gruffly and stormed off.

Once he exited the room, I ran through the kitchen to the backdoor. I put my hand on the knob and twisted it unsuccessfully before I noticed the electronic keypad. My parents had a similar one installed on the front door of their house, though theirs was wired to a security system company and allowed my parents to lock and unlock the door with an app on their phones.

I ran my fingers over the smooth keypad and felt my chance of getting out slip away. I stared at the numbers and felt compelled to try a random combination. I extended my index finger and stopped in fear of setting off an alarm. Logic jolted my brain, and I ran back to where Zane had left me not a moment too soon.

"Here," he said and tossed my shoes at me.

I bent down and put them on. The shoes had been new. Now they were stained with mud from running through the forest. Several drops of blood spotted the toe of the right shoe.

"Hurry the fuck up." He pushed me.

Already off balance from leaning over, I tumbled to the ground. A sickening crunch vibrated in my knee as the bone rolled against the hard floor. I scrambled up and stuck my feet in my shoes. I could lace them in the car.

Nerves began to bubble in my stomach when I stood. Zane grabbed my wrist and dragged me into the foyer. He stopped at the front door, using his body to block the keypad that this door also boasted. I counted four short beeps followed by one long beep and assumed that I needed a combination with four numbers to get out. I tried to come up with the number of possibilities that left me with, but came up empty handed. Math was never my strong point, but I knew it was a lot, a whole fucking lot.

We exited through the dark oak door onto a covered porch that ran the length of the farmhouse. Two white rocking chairs were angled around a little white round table. Baskets of red flowers hung in between each post on the porch, and a terra cotta pot of tiny yellow flowers sat on the first step down.

My pace slowed as I took it all in. The picture-perfectness of it all was unnerving. White and purple petunias followed the cobblestone path around the house and to the driveway. I had just noticed Jackson, who was shirtless and pulling up weeds by the mailbox, when Zane whirled around.

"Do you try to be this fucking slow?" He was right in my face, reaching for my wrist. I snatched my arm back just in time avoiding his touch.

"Keep your hands off me." I narrowed my eyes, but my voice quivered more than I would have liked.

Zane only laughed and reached into his pocket, pulling out car keys. He turned back around and pressed a button, unlocking a brand new black Camaro. He opened the passenger door for me, and for a split second, I thought he was being polite before I realized he was making sure I got in the car and didn't book it as soon as his ass hit the driver's seat.

I clenched my jaw and got inside. Hot, stale air choked me. Zane slammed the door shut and hurried around to the other side. My hands shook as I reached for the seatbelt. The metal was hot and hurt my fingers when I touched it. Zane slid into his seat with grace. He opened the windows and turned up the air before turning on the radio to a local alternative station. I hated that he liked the same kind of music that I did.

Jackson straightened up when the engine revved, and we made our way down the long driveway. Jackson wiped sweat from his forehead, pushing his long hair back behind his ears. My eyes darted past him to the mailbox, trying to see the address of this forsaken place. I leaned forward to get a better look.

"Like what you see?" Zane snickered.

"What?" I replied automatically. "Oh." He thought I was checking out Jackson, who was surprisingly fit and tan. I gave my head a slight shake, not caring what Zane thought. I leaned back in the seat and nervously picked at my cuticles, trying to pay as much attention as possible to the landmarks and street names that we passed as we made our way into the city. I would need to know them when I sent the police to save the other girls.

CHAPTER 13

The skin around my fingernails was almost raw by the time Zane pulled into the back lot of an apartment complex that looked like it had seen its prime thirty years ago. People milled about, soaking up the hot, July sun. The sight of anyone other than my forced roommates caused hope to blossom in my heart. A smile subconsciously tugged at the corners of my lips, and I just knew *someone* would be able to help me. I put my hand on the door handle, reminding myself not to appear excited, or Zane would get suspicious.

"Oh, Adeline," he said, his voice calm and low. The hair on the back of my neck prickled. "Does your dad ever take the Chevelle out of the garage? A nice classic like that deserves to be showed off."

A painful chill ran through my body. "H-how?" I stuttered, my head slowly shaking from side to side.

Zane flashed me a perfect smile, revealing his straight, white teeth. He cut the engine and hit the lock. My breath quickened as panic rose. My dad hadn't taken the '72 Chevelle out of the garage in years. He *couldn't,* since it didn't have an engine. It was his project that was put on the back burner when he and my mother opened the new gallery. I was falling again, faster and faster, until I plummeted into darkness. My ears rang. I swayed in my seat, suddenly lightheaded. There was only one way Zane would have known about the car.

"It's a shame your mom neglected her rose bushes this

summer. They must really miss you." His face remained expressionless, but there was pleasure in his eyes. He was enjoying every minute of this.

"You ... you've been to my house," I finally said. The ringing got louder.

Zane's blue eyes flashed and he smiled once more. "Your sister ... what's her name ... Arianna, right? She's pretty. She looks a lot like you but with gold highlights. You almost can't see them. But when the sun hits her just the right way, they sparkle."

Anger shot through me at the sound of my sister's name. I twisted in my seat, my fingers curling into fists. "If you touch her—"

"You'll what?" Zane cut me off. "Hit me? Spit on me?" he laughed. "I won't have to touch her if you behave," he reminded me. "It's funny how fast I can get someone to your house."

"What?" I spoke, my voice barely louder than a whisper. *No.* He was lying. He had to be lying.

He laughed, deep and throaty, reminding me of a wild animal. "You think it's just us?" He leaned in close so that he was only inches away from me. "Nate's well connected. Don't you ever forget that. Fuck up once and all it will take is one phone call." He bit his lip and smiled. His teeth were perfectly straight and unnaturally white. "We *own* you, and there is nothing you can do about it."

He laughed, his breath hot on my face. He pushed my hair back behind my ear and trailed his fingers down my neck and across my chest. "Just be a good girl, Adeline," he whispered. "And you'll have nothing to worry about. Listen to me and no one gets hurt." He tipped his head to the side and softened his face. He held my gaze, waiting for me to break and agree with him, to beg him not to hurt my family.

Instead, I slapped him.

It flipped a switch. Zane moved so fast that it was just a blur. He dove over the center console and grabbed my shoulders. He shoved me back against the seat. Black storm clouds covered his sky-blue eyes. Psychotic rage twisted his face into something horrible.

Then he stopped. With a snarl he pulled back and looked outside. The windows were tinted, but if anyone was close enough, they could see the exchange, and that would call attention to us. *Maybe I should slap Zane again.*

He jerked his body back and threw open the door. He stiffly exited the car. I let out a breath, my hands flying to my chest. *Holy shit.* Zane opened my door, still huffing. He reached into the car and wrapped his fingers around my wrist. My skin prickled under his touch. I yanked my arm back, half expecting to see my flesh charred and black from his touch. He grabbed me with his other hand and yanked me out.

My feet scuffed against the pavement. *You think it's just us?* He had been to my house. He had fucking been to my house. *You think it's just us?* Just *how* many people could he have working for him? I swallowed my pounding heart and shuffled past a windowless red van.

Nervous sweat rolled down my back, amplified by the beating sun. A group of kids screamed and laughed as they ran through a sprinkler in the parking lot. A few teenage boys huddled in the limited shade of a broken umbrella on a picnic table. Weeds grew in almost every crack in the sidewalk. Ants scurried around a popsicle stick. Zane went out of his way to stomp on them.

He pushed open the handprint-covered glass door to the front of the apartment complex. The lobby wasn't air-conditioned, and it reeked of body odor, water damage, and smoke. Zane pulled me up a flight of rose-colored carpeted stairs.

Everything began to feel surreal again as my mind checked out, unable to process what was going to happen. The muscles in my arms went slack as we walked down a hall. Zane stopped at a door at the end of the hall. He pounded on it, stepped back, and waited. It only took a few seconds for it to open.

A man stepped out. He appeared to be in his late twenties and was only about an inch taller than me. His wavy, blonde hair was oily and matted to his forehead. He had dark hazel eyes that slid up and down my body. I grimaced when he smiled, recoiling at his missing teeth. The few he had left were yellow. The skin around his nose and mouth was raw and red. The fact that this guy was most likely high from huffing household cleaners scared me.

"Got the money?" Zane asked, getting right to business.

"Yup. Here 'ya go." The guy dug a wad of cash out of his pocket. Zane smoothed out the twenties and counted it twice.

"One hour," Zane said and shoved me forward into the cruddy apartment before he spun around and casually walked down the hall.

The guy brushed past me and closed the door. I wrapped my arms around myself and fought back tears. Zane made it very clear that my family would pay for my misbehavior. I could risk myself, but I wasn't going to risk them. I couldn't.

The guy sniffled and wiped his runny nose with the back of his hand. He tipped his head, motioning for me to follow him. He unbuttoned his baggy jeans as he walked through the living room. I stepped over fast food wrappers and followed, my throat tightening with each step.

Halfway to the bedroom, I stopped, my foot hovering mid-step in the air. "No," I whispered to myself. I wasn't going to give up just yet. I still had faith I could make it to the police in time. I still believed Zane was lying. I took a deep breath, turned around, and sprinted to the door. My fingers fumbled with the lock.

"Hey," the guy started and made a move to race after me. I was faster. I threw the door back and froze.

No. I had come this far only to be stopped ... again.

Zane was standing in the doorway with his arms on either side of the frame. He laughed when he saw the horrified shock on my face.

"I knew you'd try and leave," he taunted. He put his hands on my shoulders and turned me around. "You'll pay for that." He shoved me inside and closed the door behind us. "You like 'em tied up?" Zane asked the customer.

The guy—my client—chuckled and nodded. Zane reached behind him and retrieved a set of handcuffs. Light reflected off the metal. Brown, crusted blood speckled the rims.

"No!" I yelled and fought against Zane. "No!" I tightened my arms and tried to twist away. He was going to handcuff me, and I wouldn't be able to get away. Panic choked me. I screamed. My head throbbed from the blood rush.

"Where do you want her?" Zane asked and grabbed the

back of my neck, tightly wrapping his fingers around me.

The guy pointed behind him, and Zane thrust me forward, forcing me down the hall. I straightened my legs and locked my knees, refusing to walk any further. Tears splashed to the floor. I brought my head back, hoping to hit Zane in the nose, but all it did was crunch my spine. Zane brought his knee up, hitting me in the tailbone. My knees buckled, and he forced me forward and into the bedroom.

Zane hoisted me up onto the bed and straddled me. The mattress was lumpy and smelled like stale cigarettes. He forced my arms over my head and locked the handcuffs to a wooden headboard. He slowly moved his body down, pressing himself against my pelvis and showing that manhandling me aroused him.

"You be a good girl," Zane whispered. He put his lips just an inch above mine, his breath hot in my face. Then he tipped his head and licked me, trailing his tongue up my neck. He laughed and moved off of me. He tossed the keys to the handcuffs to the client. "One hour," Zane reminded him and left. I heard the apartment door slam shut. The guy unzipped his pants and crawled onto the bed.

It was going to happen. There was no escape. No throwing up on a life-size doll, no running into the forest. Horrible things were going to happen to me, and I was forced to let them, forced to stay.

"You're a pretty thing," the guy said and crawled onto the bed. I clenched my legs together, breathing so fast with fear I was near hyperventilating.

"Don't touch me!" I screamed. "Don't fucking touch me!" Tears streamed down the sides of my face.

The guy pulled his pants down, kicking them off his ankles. He stuck his hand inside his boxers, rubbing his erection. He groaned, running his eyes up and down my body. Slowly, he pulled his hand out of his boxers, took them off, and moved down on all fours, holding himself up over top of me.

He put his hands on my knees. I jerked my legs to the side, breaking his hold. "Don't touch me!" I screamed.

He took hold of me again, pressing his legs over mine to keep them still. I thrashed around, madly pulling on the

STAY

handcuffs. If I could just break free, I'd grab something and smash him upside the head. Then I'd tie him up and get the hell out of here.

His fingers hooked around the elastic band of my underwear. He smiled and pulled them down. He gobbled them up and stuck them to his face, inhaling deeply. I wanted to throw up. Instead, I bent my legs up and kicked him in the stomach.

His breath left him in a whoosh. He tossed the underwear on the floor and moved back over me. "You like it rough, cunt? Huh?" He slapped me. "I'll show you rough."

Tears bit at my eyes and my cheek stung. I turned my head away, rattling the handcuffs. He got on his knees and grabbed my legs, trying to pry them open. I screamed. My pulse thumped in my neck, and my ears rang. I was dizzy, terrified, and my vision threatened to go black as my brain checked out, unable to handle this.

Please, God, no. This wasn't going to happen. I would get away. I had to! I pulled on the handcuffs, the metal cutting into my skin. Frantic, I twisted around, thrashing my legs against him. Fear suffocated me. Hot tears burned in my eyes. *No... no...*this wasn't happening.

His fingers dug into my skin as he tried again to pry my legs open. I couldn't breathe. Black dots floated in front of me. The ringing grew louder and louder. My chest painfully tightened, holding back my pounding heart. He wedged his knee between my thighs, forcing my legs open. I pulled on the handcuffs and screamed.

"You gonna scream for me, baby?" he asked and moved over me. He put his hands on the bed and forced his torso down on mine. "No one will care, princess." His breath was hot in my face.

He reached one hand down and widened my legs, putting a finger inside of me. He pulled his hand back and stuck his finger in his mouth.

"Mmhhh," he moaned, closing his eyes. "I can taste your innocence. I want more."

He reached down, taking hold of himself, and shoved himself inside of me. Horrible, searing pain shot through me. Completely dry, I felt my skin stick as he pushed further in. It was going to rip off. At least the blood would keep me from tearing even more. I screamed, hysterical from the fear and pain. The bed creaked and slammed against the wall as he thrust back and forth, jamming himself into me.

My arms jerked overhead as I pulled against the handcuffs. He moved back and thrust forward again, harder than before. And each thrust hurt just as bad as the one before. He grabbed my legs and lifted them up, shoving himself so deep inside it felt like daggers pushing into my stomach. Only I wasn't going to bleed to death. He would finish, and I would get up. And then it would happen again. I cried out in pain.

"Stop!" I screamed. He kept moving, grunting with each thrust. Sweat rolled down his forehead, dripping off the greasy hair that stuck to his face, and splashed onto me.

Suddenly, he pushed my legs apart, pushing them onto the mattress. I screamed as my muscles threatened to snap from the over stretch. With one final grunt he finished, heaving his body down onto mine. His weight on top of me made it hard to breathe. I turned my head to the side, gasping for air. His opened his mouth, moaning. His head pressed against my chest and he let out a growl.

Finally, he stopped moving. My body trembled. An echo rang in my ears, as if I was about to pass out. I wished I would. I didn't want to be conscious and able to think or process. I didn't want to understand what had happened. I wanted to crawl into a hole and die.

He collapsed onto me, panting. I squeezed my eyes shut, thinking about my house. I wanted to be there so desperately that I swore I could smell the lavender scented candles my mother was always burning.

He pushed off of me and stretched his hands over his head, letting out a satisfied breath. Then he got off the bed, picking his pants up from the floor. He stumbled into them and left the room.

My dress was pushed up to my chest. Everything inside of me hurt, and I was still handcuffed to the bed. I had never let anyone finish inside me before, not even Mateo, a previous long-term boyfriend. And there it was, dripping down my leg and onto the mattress.

And just like that, he had robbed me of my innocence. It was gone, never to come back. And I would never be the same.

CHAPTER 14

Tears blurred by eyes as I pushed myself up off the bed. I wrapped my fingers around my wrist, gently covering the lines of red, raw skin. A chill ran through me as I looked around the messy room for my underwear.

I took one step and doubled over. Searing pain burned between my legs, going up into my stomach. The palms of my hands pressed into my thighs. Open mouthed, I cried and gasped for air. Black dots speckled my vision. The world spun, and my arms flew out to keep from falling.

But I had already fallen. Down, deep down into blackness, miles below the surface. I couldn't breathe. Did I even want to breathe? I could sink into the darkness and it would all be over.

No. There was a way out.

I straightened up and took another step away from the bed. The burning shot through me all the way up into my chest. I clenched my jaw and bent over, the movements amplifying the pain, and grabbed my underwear.

I cried out when I lifted one foot off the ground and stuck it through the leg of the underwear. I made no attempt to hold back the tears that streamed in rivers down my face. I cast an angry glare at the door. How could that monster get off on my pain? How could he keep going when I screamed and cried and tried to get away?

My trembling fingers slipped and the waistband of the panties snapped against my skin. I straightened the dress and ran my hands over my hair. I kept my legs apart and walked out of the bedroom, dizziness setting in with a vengeance. I felt so violated, so helpless, so *dirty*. I wanted to scrub every surface of my body until my skin peeled off, though I doubted even that would make me feel better.

I let myself out of the apartment, expecting to see Zane. Instead, Jackson stood slumped against the wall. His head rested against his shoulder and his arms were loosely crossed against his chest. He pushed off the wall when the door closed behind me and took a step in my direction. The color drained from his face and his eyes opened wide. One of his hands flew up as if he was going to touch me, but he stopped himself and just stood there with his hand awkwardly in the air.

I brushed away tears and pressed my chin into my chest. Jackson averted his eyes to the ground and tipped his head forward, causing his messy black hair to fall into his face. His hand dropped to his side and he took a small step toward the stairs, pausing to see if I would follow. I pressed my arms to my sides and obeyed, following Jackson through the hall, down the stairs, and out of the apartment building.

My eyes closed when we stepped into the sun. I walked blindly, concentrating on how red the back of my eyelids were. Part of me wanted to think about what had just happened. Another part knew I couldn't process it just yet.

"Careful," Jackson said when I reached the curb. I slit my eyes open and stared at the pavement, watching Jackson's feet move. His worn out work boots were covered in mud. I slowly brought my eyes up, unable to see all that well from the bright light, and noticed that his jeans were dirty as well. Then I remembered seeing him pulling weeds. Why did he pick me up when Zane was already in this part of town?

Jackson stopped beside an old, white Trail Blazer and opened the passenger door for me. I lifted my leg to step in and felt shooting pain deep inside me, causing me to flinch. I closed my eyes and inhaled sharply. I could feel Jackson's eyes on my back. My face crinkled as I silently sobbed and I got into the SUV.

It was dark by the time we arrived back at the farmhouse. I walked in front of Jackson and went straight to the basement. Jackson's voice sounded muffled as he spoke, telling us that he would bring food down in a few minutes.

"Addie?" Phoebe gently spoke.

I was still standing at the base of the stairs. She rose from the card table where she was sitting with Lily and Rochelle and walked over, gently putting her hand on mine. I flinched from the touch, the feeling of skin on skin sending a horrible memory to flash in my mind.

"Shhh," she soothed and moved to my side. "Let get you out of clothes."

I knew I nodded in agreement, but I hadn't fully processed what she was saying. I allowed her to lead me to the cot and sit me down. I kept my eyes on the floor, my sight blurring with tears. I heard a metallic squeak as the shower turned on.

"Wash," she said and extended her hand.

Shaking, I reached out for her. Her fingers laced through mine. Her grip was strong and reassuring. Not feeling like I was in my body, I got up and went to the shower. Phoebe held up a towel to allow me to undress in privacy. I stepped into the icy water, physically waking up my body. Emotion balled in my stomach, and I doubled over, sobbing. It had happened. All the pain, all the fear had really happened. Something had been ripped out of me, leaving a burning dead hole in my heart. And I would never get it back. What happened could never be undone.

I wasn't sure how long I cried. I was shivering so hard my body hurt. Phoebe reached into the shower and turned off the water. Without looking at me, she stuck a towel in. I wrapped it around myself and straightened up, my hysterical crying turning into hiccups.

Still shivering, I made my way to the cots. My knees buckled and I fell onto the thin mattress. I clutched onto the towel and rocked back and forth. Water dripped from my soaking hair, splashing onto goosebump-covered skin.

"You cold." Phoebe gently lowered herself onto the cot and

held up a robe.

I lifted heavy arms and stuck them through the sleeves. She pulled the robe up around my shoulders and brought the front together before tying it tightly at the waist. Phoebe moved around the bed and picked up my discarded towel. Then she gently gathered my hair in her hand and rubbed it with the towel.

"I'm sorry, Addie." She blinked away tears. "I'm so, so sorry."

My head moved up and down. I tried to look at Phoebe and let her know it was going to be all right. But I couldn't. The edges of the hollow pit inside of me were frozen, so cold it hurt. I didn't want to feel anything. Not the searing pain from my delicate flesh being ripped off, not the terror that grasped me. And I didn't want to think about what my life had become. I brought my knees to my chest and fell onto my side.

Phoebe gingerly put her hand on my shoulder. Sobbing, I reached up and took her hand. She gently ran her hand over my hair.

"It be okay someday. Not now, not soon, but someday. We leave. Both of us. We have to," she promised, her voice low so only I could hear. "Somehow, we find way."

I sniffled and nodded, swallowing a sob. I took a ragged breath and wiped my nose with my hand. The skin under my eyes hurt from crying so hard. I sat up.

"We will."

The basement door floor open so suddenly, I jumped. Two sets of feet clomped down the stairs. Remembering that Jackson said he would be back with food, the sight of Zane and Nate took me by surprise.

Lily and Rochelle quickly stood from the table, looking shocked to see Nate. Lily's eyes latched onto him, following him across the basement. Rochelle ran a hand over her hair and smoothed out her skirt. She pushed her shoulders back and lifted her head, smiling at him.

"Adeline, Adeline, Adeline," Nate said, exhaling heavily and shaking his head. "What are we to do with you?" He gave me a warm smile as he continued over. I tried to read him: his posture was relaxed and his face soft. To anyone else, Nate would appear calm. But I knew better. He wouldn't come down for nothing.

He made a tiny nodding motion to Zane, who stepped next to the cot. He reached down and grabbed my arm, yanking me to my feet.

"Stop!" Phoebe yelled.

Still disoriented, I didn't pull against Zane's grip. He was right in front of me, his eyes sparkling as he yanked me off the cot with ease. My feet refused to work right, and I stumbled. Zane stuck his arms under mine and dragged me over to Nate. Lily whimpered and moved behind Rochelle. Zane turned me around so my back was to his front. He hooked his arms through my elbows and held me tightly against him.

Nate rubbed his temples, sighing dramatically. "I have a reputation to uphold. I *always* have the best girls." His eyes narrowed. "You're making me look bad, and I don't like to look bad." He smiled again, and something sadistic flashed across his face. He frowned, giving me a look of disappointment. He pushed his hand into a pocket of his designer pants and pulled out a shiny metal lighter and a lone cigarette. The house never smelled like smoke. I was sure Nate either wasn't a smoker or didn't smoke indoors.

He lit the cigarette, took a long drag, then, without warning, pressed the butt into the skin inside my arm, right above my elbow. I cried out in pain, arching my back and trying to break free from Zane's hold. Nate moved his hand back, but my skin still burned. He put the cigarette to his lips once more before dropping it to the ground and stepping on it.

He wiped his hands on pristinely pressed herringbone cotton pants and slapped me across the face. I whimpered and closed my eyes, fighting back tears. He put his face just inches from mine.

"Do *not* make me look bad," he said through clenched teeth. He exhaled, straightened up, and moved away. "Pink looks pretty on you." He eyed Rochelle, his demeanor calm again.

Her hands flew to her top, smoothing it against her flat stomach. "Thanks," she cooed. Her gaze moved from Nate to Zane, waiting for him to compliment her as well.

Zane tightened his arms and gave me a hard shake before letting me go. I tumbled forward, catching myself at the last minute. Nate turned and walked up the stairs with Zane at his heels.

The tears I had been holding back spilled and ran down my cheeks. I pressed my hand over the burn and flinched. My heart was beating so fast, my entire body shook. My eyes darted to my arm, and I carefully moved my hand. My stomach twisted at the sight of my charred skin.

In a daze, I moved back to my cot and sank down. I heard the shower turn on, and a moment later, Phoebe laid a cold washcloth on top of the burn. It was as if my body was suddenly on autopilot; I stuck my feet under the old quilt and rested my head on the flat, thin pillow. Holding the washcloth over the burn, I closed my eyes and tried to think about nothing.

Angry voices floated through the air ducts but were too muffled to make out what was being shouted. The yelling went on for a few minutes before something hit the floor with a heavy thud, making me jump.

My eyes flew open, and I thought I saw the guy from the apartment standing in the shadows. I pressed my eyelids shut again and swallowed my pounding heart. Prickly sweat broke out across my body. I couldn't think about him, not now, not yet. Instead, I thought about my dogs. It was a simple thought, one my overloaded brain could handle. I replayed a single memory of playing ball with Scarlet a few days before I was taken over and over in my mind. The sun was dodging clouds. There was a slight breeze. Lynn lay behind me on the deck in her bikini, even though I was chilled in shorts and a sweatshirt. She was obsessed with the sun. Then we went inside, joining the rest of my family around the dining room table. We talked and laughed as we passed around platters of food.

The basement door creaked open. The vision of home disappeared when I opened my eyes. I knew it was Jackson by the hesitance in his footfalls. I pulled the blankets up close to my eyes, as if that would protect me. I peered out at him to see that he was carrying a tray of our dinner. A fresh cut bled through the front of his t-shirt and he had another black eye.

"Thanks," Phoebe told him and took the tray. She said something else, too quiet for me to hear that caused Jackson to give her a tiny smile and shake my head. She reached out, gently touching his chest. He looked down at the blood and frowned. I moved the blanket down. Was she concerned about him?

Jackson looked behind him as if he was nervous someone might be there, and returned his attention to Phoebe. She asked him something and I heard him respond by saying that he didn't know. He shuffled his feet, muttered goodbye, and went back up the stairs.

Phoebe brought me a peanut butter sandwich. I had no appetite, no desire to eat. She sat on the edge of the bed and broke off a tiny piece, holding it up to my mouth.

"Eat. You need strength."

"I have none left," I confessed. And I didn't. Not at that moment, not after what had happened.

"Addie, you need it to leave," she whispered.

And I knew she was right. I pushed myself up and took the torn off bit of sandwich and forced myself to eat it. My throat was so dry and the sticky peanut butter wasn't helping. I got out of bed, the burn throbbing as I moved, and went to the table to get a water bottle.

It still hurt to walk. The pain between my legs was a constant reminder. My spine tingled with repugnance. How many times would it happen again before we escaped?

I moved back to my cot and ate the rest of the bland dinner. I was exhausted. Physically, I had been through a lot. But my mind sought sleep for another reason; I wouldn't have to think or process. I could escape into a dream … or a nightmare.

CHAPTER 15

Halloween used to be my favorite holiday. I loved wearing costumes, and I loved that it became socially acceptable to obsess over anything and everything paranormal. Most of all, I loved putting together a zombie-themed book giveaway on my blog. Gorging myself on bags of bite-sized chocolates was always a plus too. Seeing groups of kids in their costumes running through down town Des Moines on that All Hollow's Eve only made me sad.

I hadn't been so close to home since the Pride Parade. Seeing the familiar buildings sparked something inside of me, something that I had buried deep and was scared to bring to the surface. Zane slammed on the brakes, narrowly avoiding a gaggle of school-age children who ran out into the street.

"Dumbass motherfuckers!" he yelled, rolling down the window. "You're lucky I didn't want to dent the hood!"

I sighed and caught a glimpse of myself in the window's reflection. I was dressed as a slutty witch, my costume complete with sparkly purple false eyelashes and claw-like fake nails. Zane revved the engine and flipped off a mom who yelled at him for being reckless around her children.

I didn't even realize it was Halloween until Rochelle handed me the costume. I had been put to work almost every day since Zane forced me into that rundown apartment and handcuffed me to the bed. I lost count of the number of times I'd been raped. Each time was just as terrifying and demeaning as the first. And it happened day after day, night after night, in a horrific never ending cycle of abuse.

Since I attempted to escape more than once, Nate thought I was too much of a liability to allow outside the farmhouse. So everyday, I was dragged upstairs and forced into the guest room. Most of the time I was tied to the bed, not even allowed up to use the bathroom between clients. We were nothing but objects, living sex dolls. I wasn't seen as human anymore, just an item to be bought and used.

Phoebe was sick. She hadn't been feeling well for the last few days, not that Nate cared. He still made her work. She had woken up this morning *looking* sick, really sick. It made me nervous she had something worse than a flu bug. When Zane came downstairs to get her that evening, he recoiled at her appearance, saying she was too nasty to be seen in public.

He decided I was taking her place. I just sat there, staring at him while my mind whirled with the possibilities of escaping yet again. A small spark of hope warmed inside me. Maybe it would work this time…maybe. Then Zane picked up a stiletto and hit me hard in the leg with the heel, over and over until my thigh bled. I got up and got dressed after that.

And here we were, pulling into the back of some sort of industrial building with not a soul in sight. I was the entertainment of some sort of party. He cut the engine and got out. I wasn't supposed to get out of the car until he opened my door. I sat and waited, then followed him to a windowless, steel door.

He knocked three times and stood back. It took a full minute for the door to swing open. An overweight middle-aged man dressed as Mario scanned me up and down before he opened his wallet.

"This will get you three hours," Zane stated and recounted the money. "I don't care what you do to her in that time."

"Sweet!" Mario exclaimed. He eyed me again, though this time a puzzled look settled on his face. "Hey!" he said suddenly. "Y-you're that girl!" he stuttered. "That missing girl!" he took my arm and yanked me toward him. "Adeline," he spoke my name.

"Yes!" I said. "It's me!"

Zane grabbed my other arm and pulled. "She doesn't know

what she's talking about."

"Yeah she does," the guy argued. "Her face has been plastered all over the news." He pulled on me again, stretching my arm uncomfortably. He laughed. "You're fucked," he said to Zane. "You know what I'll get for turning her in? There's a reward for her return *and* a reward for turning in the guys who took her."

Zane's face tightened and his grip on me faltered.

"I'll tell you what," the guy dressed as Mario went on. "You pay me double the reward money, and I won't say a thing."

"Yeah," Zane said slowly. Panic flashed in his sky-blue eyes. He swallowed hard, and little beads of sweat broke out across his forehead. His hand fell from my arm and he purposely raked his fingernails against my skin. "About that..." he started and ran his hand through his hair. I almost didn't notice his other hand moving behind his back. I took a sharp breath and stepped closer to Mario.

Zane cast his eyes to the ground, looking defeated. Mario smiled and tightened his hold on my arm. Then Zane laughed, sending a jolt of fear and nausea through my entire body. I saw his muscles flex a millisecond before he whipped his arm around, shoving a gun in Mario's face.

"Get your motherfucking hands off the bitch," he said through clenched teeth.

Mario let me go and held his hands up. "Hey now. I-I don't need the money t-that bad," he stuttered, his eyes fixed on the end of the 1911 in Zane's hands.

Stuck in between a life-size, womanizing video game character and Zane, who was his own breed of evil, I just stood there, unmoving. Mario took a tentative step back. Zane lurched forward and grabbed the guy's blue overalls.

"Get in the car, Adeline," Zane ordered.

"I paid for that!" the guy blurted.

Zane jammed the gun into his chest. I scurried past him, my five-inch heels clacking along the pavement. I ran as fast as the ridiculous footwear allowed and skidded to a stop, my hands smacking into the hood of the Camaro. My heart was pounding, and I felt hot with fear despite the chilly fall night.

A gunshot rang behind me, echoing throughout the empty

parking lot. My heart was like a jackhammer in my chest, beating so fast it was painful.

Holy. Fucking. Shit. Did he really shoot him? My eyes went wide with terror and I was too scared to turn around to see if Zane had killed someone in cold blood. My breath clouded the shiny metal hood.

"Get in the goddamn car!" Zane's voice came from behind me. Fear made me incapable of moving. Zane's heavy footfalls reverberated off the brick building. "I said get in the motherfucking car!" he yelled. He was right behind me. His hand snapped around my neck, fingers digging into my skin. I cried out in pain and stumbled back. He thrust me forward toward the door. "What part of get in the car don't you understand?"

I grabbed the handle. "It's locked, Dipshit," I blurted.

I could feel his body tense as he leaned on me. My breath fogged the window. Zane's rage hummed in the night air. He growled as he exhaled, released me, and dug the keys from his pocket.

He unlocked and opened the door and shoved me in. Unable to keep my balance in the tall heels, my ankle buckled, and I fell. Zane kicked me.

"Get in!" he shouted.

I pulled myself up, my fingernails biting into the black and orange leather seat. I scrambled in, pulling my legs up quickly as Zane slammed the door. He stomped around and heaved into the driver's side and brought the engine to life. He hit the steering wheel three times then laid on the horn before revving the engine. I huddled against the door, terrified of Zane now more than ever.

He spun the car around and tore out of the parking lot, going the opposite direction we had come from.

"Where are we going?" I stammered, assuming he was going to take me back to the farmhouse.

"Shut up, cunt," he retorted.

I turned and faced him, taking in the wild aggression that twisted his face. His eyes darted off the road and at me, noticing my staring.

"What the fuck do you want?" he snarled.

Afraid of him, I bit the inside of my cheek and wrapped

my arms around myself. Forgetting that I was wearing pointed acrylic nails, I flinched from the pain of scratching myself.

I moved closer to the window, keeping my face close to the tinted glass in hopes of someone else spotting me. My breath came out in loud whooshes and my teeth chattered together from fear. Zane zoomed down the streets, running more than one red light in his haste to get wherever we were going. Nate's words from months ago haunted me. Was I more trouble than I was worth? What would happen to me if I was?

CHAPTER 16

Despite my fear, there was something calming about being in the familiar setting of Des Moines. My parent's gallery was on the edge of the town, and our house wasn't too far beyond that. My heart swelled when I thought of my family. I was so close it hurt.

Zane stomped on the gas to plow through a yellow light. His reckless driving was going to get me killed ... or save me. My eyes widened with hope. If he got pulled over, it all would end. I peered over at the speedometer; he was going ten over the limit. He glanced at me, following my eyes to the dash. He realized how fast he was going and let off the gas.

The hope in me died. Expecting him to make a wise-ass remark, a threat, or even reach over and hit me, I leaned back in the seat and waited. But he did nothing.

Time passed slowly, but I dreaded our destination. The more I thought about the implications of being recognized, the more I was certain I was going to die. I wondered how he would do it. Would it be fast, like an execution? That didn't seem to be Zane's style. There were so many ways to kill somebody. My gut twisted as I thought of the possibilities.

The Camaro lurched to a stop in a familiar alley. I had been there before, I just couldn't place my exact location in the dark.

"Stay here," he growled and cut the engine. Zane scrambled out of the car, ran around to my side, and yanked open the door. "Open your mouth and I'll break your fingers," he threatened.

"One at a time."

I clenched my jaw and nodded. He took hold of my arm and jerked me forward, feet teetering in the stupid heels. The stench of old food lingered in the air and I held my breath when we passed the dumpster.

Zane fumbled with his keys, trying to separate them with one hand. Giving up, he pushed me forward and picked out the right key. I noticed the writing on the door right as he stuck it into the lock.

THE DISH was engraved in gold on a small plaque. I froze when I saw it. I had been here before, just last year. The upscale restaurant opened several years ago and my mom was dying to eat there, but we never got around to it until her birthday last winter. When my dad got the bill and realized the cost of our meal could have bought him another piece at the gallery, he swore he would never go back.

The Dish was a nice, fancy place to eat along one of the more historic streets in downtown Des Moines. Why was Zane taking me here?

"Keep your mouth shut," he reminded me and looked around the alley before pushing open the door.

My heart was still racing. I flicked my eyes to Zane, terrified and so angry at him at the same time. We stepped into a brightly lit break room. Coats and purses hung on the wall next to the time clock. Zane pulled me close and wrapped his arm around me, making it look like we were an affectionate couple. Keeping me smashed into his side, we crossed the narrow room and stepped into an even narrower hall. Just then, a waitress, dressed in all black, rounded the corner.

Zane pushed me up against the wall. His pelvis pressed into mine and his chest flattened my breasts. His cologne instantly suffocated me, and I hated that I found the scent pleasant. He tucked one hand behind the small of my back and put the other on my cheek. Then he kissed me, his lips soft and gently against mine. He slipped his tongue in my mouth and pushed his hips against me, rubbing back and forth ever so slightly. I felt the large bulge in his jeans grow. He was getting off on this.

Abhorrence churned my stomach. I wanted to puke right then and there, but I only held my breath and waited until it was over. I was getting good at that.

"Ugh," the blonde waitress sighed. "Zane," she spoke, her tone heavy with annoyance. My heart skipped a beat. She knew him? "Don't waste your time, honey." She continued walking and I realized she was talking to me. "This boy might be good at the game, but trust me when I say he's a *player*," she huffed and flipped her hair over her shoulder.

Once she disappeared into the break room, Zane took his lips off mine. He slowly moved his face back and gently traced his fingers down my cheek. I turned my head, not wanting to look at him. He slipped his fingers behind my ear and ground his hips against me. My detestation for him was turning into anger.

"I like the way you taste," he whispered, his breath hot on my neck. "Adeline," he said, drawing out my name in the most seductive manner. His lips pressed against my neck, sucking at my skin. He moved his mouth up and his tongue found my ear. "It makes me want more," he groaned.

"Suck a dick," I spat and pushed him away.

Zane only held on tighter. "That's your job," he said. He took his hand off of my face and grabbed my wrist. He laughed and pushed off the wall, making sure the coast was clear before he dragged me into an office.

"It's in excellent condition," Nate's voice came from behind a tall, leather chair. My anger turned back into fear. What was Nate doing here? "And can easily be rezoned for business. But I must be honest with you, Phil, I did get another offer just this morning."

Zane closed the door. Nate casually spun the chair around. Shock then rage covered his face when he saw me.

"Listen, something just came up. I'm going to have to call you back," he spat into the phone before slamming it down. He put both hands on the dark oak desk. "What is going on?"

"We have a problem," Zane began. His eyebrows were pushed slightly together and he stood with his legs apart.

"You're damn right we have a problem," Nate said and stood up. "I told you never to bring the girls here. Let alone *her*. You have one minute to explain," he said calmly.

I wished he would yell; the way he kept himself so collected was so creepy. It was like the calm before a storm, and I had no idea how damaging the winds would be.

"The Asian is sick. I had her fill in," he said, motioning toward me with his head. "Full-service party," he added and took the wad of cash from his pocket. "But one of the clients recognized her."

"And what do you mean by that?" Nate asked, the skin around his eyes tightening.

"He knew who she was, knew she was missing. He wanted the reward money for turning her in."

"And I trust you took care of it?" Nate asked. A vein on his forehead was becoming visible. I watched it pulsate, feeling his anger growing with each heartbeat. He was going to explode soon, unleashing hurricane winds upon us.

"Of course," Zane said. Standing in front of Nate, he looked boyish and vulnerable. And I still hated his fucking guts.

"Good." Nate's phone rang and he turned to pick it up. "We will figure out the rest of this mess tonight," he said and smiled ever so slightly. His eyes narrowed and he shot Zane a look that said *this is all your fault*. "Go."

Zane opened the office door, looked around and pulled me out. The blonde waitress was sitting in the break room, but was too busy scrolling through Facebook on her phone to even steal a glance at my face. Zane slammed the door and stepped into the alley. The city was alive on this holiday night and I wanted so desperately to call out for help and run away.

But something might happen to my sister, or Lynn, or my parents. I was close, but Nate and Zane had people even closer. I silently got into the car, my head spinning. Did Nate own The Dish? If he did, it made me sick to think that my family ate a very expensive meal there and put money into Nate's pocket. The talk of rezoning and offers made it sound like he sold real estate too, in addition to an underground sex business.

It dawned on me that people would wonder how he had so much money if he didn't have a legitimate job, and the fact that he was ambitious enough to run not only one but two real businesses scared me. Nate loved money and he would do anything to get it. Now I was certain he would think I was more trouble than I was worth.

I hugged my chest and shivered. I had been too wrapped up in anger and fear to realize that I was cold. My slutty costume left a lot of skin open to the chilly fall air. I looked at the dial for the heater and debated on reaching out and turning it on. I turned the radio on once, and Zane pulled over and hit me. Deciding against it, I huddled down in the seat, closed my eyes, and waited until we arrived back at the farmhouse.

Zane exited first, going around the car as he always did to pull me out. Not needing direction from him, I opened my door and slowly walked down the cobblestone path and onto the front porch. I stood to the side so that Zane could punch in the code to open the door. I stepped into the foyer and removed my shoes from my aching feet

Jackson sat on the living room couch, feet propped up on the coffee table, reading. My nostrils flared as I gave him a jealous stare. He looked up from the book, dark eyes flitting from me to Zane, and pushed his eyebrows together in question.

Zane slammed the door so hard a picture fell off the wall and clattered to the floor. Shattered glass scattered on the dark hard wood floors.

"Clean it up," he spat and glared at Jackson before storming up the stairs.

"Everything okay?" Jackson asked and dog-eared a page in his book, making me cringe.

"When will you learn to stop asking me that?" I retorted and walked through the living room. Tears stung my eyes and I shook my head. I swallowed my emotions and went into the kitchen. To my surprise, the basement door was unlocked and open. I hesitated, looking at the open door as if it was some sort of trick. For months, this door was kept under lock and key and here it was, wide open. Something was wrong.

Fearing something had happened to Phoebe, I pushed past my fear and placed a bare foot on the first step. Dirt and grit stuck to my heel and the wood creaked under my weight. My heart began to beat faster with each step I took.

I finally reached the bottom, the hard, cold concrete familiar on my feet. I reached out in front of me and felt around for the thin white string to pull to turn on the light. I tangled it around my fingers and pulled, bathing the basement in a yellow glow.

"Addie?" Phoebe asked and sat up, blinking. I let out a breath and nodded. "What wrong?" She pushed herself off the cot. "You back too soon."

"Someone saw me," I told her and moved to my cot, which was next to hers.

"Lots of people see us," she replied, confused.

I shook my head. "No, I mean someone saw me and knew who I was. They knew I was kidnapped."

Phoebe's eyes widened, and she almost smiled before she shook her head. "How you come back here?"

"Zane ... Zane killed him," I spat.

Her face blanked. Then shock brought up her eyebrows. "Kill?"

I swallowed and pressed my hands over my chest. "Yeah. He just shot him. Right there." I moved my hands to my face, pressing my cold fingers on my cheeks. "It was like he panicked."

"Wow. Kill is messy," she said. "Maybe he get caught."

That hadn't even occurred to me. "That would be wonderful."

"We can hope."

I let out a breath. "And I do." Phoebe gave me a halfhearted smile. "How are you feeling?" I asked her, feeling bad for not addressing it right away.

She shrugged and held out her hands, revealing reddish brown spots. "Doesn't hurt," she assured me when she saw the concern on my face. "But I have headache and bumps here." She pointed under her chin and on the back of her neck.

"Your lymph nodes are swollen," I told her and she gave me a puzzled look. "It means you're sick and your body is fighting an infection."

"Oh," she said and nodded. "I feel okay other than headache," she said. "Just tired."

"Get some rest," I told her. She nodded, pulled the blanket around her shoulders, and lay back down. I began to get that disorienting floating feeling where my mind tried to escape reality. I longed for a book to get lost in, to worry about someone else's problems and forget about my own.

I got off the cot and tip-toed over to the dresser, trading the witch costume for a pair of pink pajama pants and an oversized white t-shirt, and hurried back to my cot. The basement wasn't heated. I dreaded the winter. If it was cold in here in October, it could only get worse. I curled up in the fetal position and wrapped the thin quilt over my body.

Worry about Phoebe competed with the fear and disappointment that swam in my head. I knew she wouldn't get any sort of medical care. She would get better. She had to. I didn't want to see her suffer just as much as I didn't want her to leave me.

Hot tears dripped down the corners of my eyes. A bubble of sadness began to form in my stomach and tears dripped down the corners of my eyes. I had been recognized. I was so close to being saved *again*, and the chance had slipped right through my fingers. I wiped my eyes and sighed.

Was part of me happy Zane had shot Mario? I didn't want to be glad about anyone's death, well, anyone who wasn't Nate or Zane. Did he—the guy dressed like Mario—deserve to die? He knew who I was, knew I had been kidnapped. He could have brought me in, saved me. I would have promised not to tell that he bought me for a party. He would have saved me *and* gotten the reward money.

But no, he wanted more. He was a greedy, horny bastard. Yes. I was glad he was dead. I didn't feel bad about that.

The bubble popped when I thought of the agony my mother must be feeling. A sob escaped my lips. I turned my head into my pillow and cried myself to sleep. I had only slept for a few hours when Lily and Rochelle came down the stairs, chatting loudly about the wild party they had been to. Rochelle talked like she was there as a guest, enjoying the food and free drinks. I pretended to be asleep, not wanting to talk.

CHAPTER 17

"What's this?" Lily asked the next morning, her voice thick with sleep. She unfolded a newspaper. I sat up quickly. Everyday was exactly the same. We never got the paper. "An article is circled," she told us. Wide-awake, I got out of bed and padded over, ignoring the cold floor on my bare feet.

The story didn't make the first page, but there was no mistaking the seriousness of the situation. A picture of Mario, minus the costume, looked up at me, under the headline MAN FOUND DEAD IN PARKING LOT.

"I don't get it," Lily said and tossed the paper to the side. She picked up a banana and began to peel it. "Why would we care about some dead guy?"

Nerves prickled my skin. I reached around her and grabbed the paper. "You wouldn't," I agreed. "But I would."

"Huh?" she asked with her mouth full.

"This guy ... he ... he was my client from last night."

"And you killed him?" Lily asked with an eyebrow raised. "What you do, fuck him to death?"

I shook my head and skimmed the article, too freaked out to slow down and read the entire thing. "No, Zane did," I breathed.

"Huh?" Lily repeated.

My hands began to shake. "This guy," I said and tapped the picture. "He knew who I was."

Lily took another bite of her banana and shrugged. "So?" She eyed the paper before it dawned on her. "Oh! Like he *knew* you were Adeline Miller, this missing girl."

"Yes. He said he recognized me from being on the news. He wanted to turn me in for reward money or get paid to keep quiet." I closed my eyes in a long blink. "He's quiet now."

"What if Zane gets caught?" Lily asked, and I thought I heard genuine concern in her voice.

"I hope he does get caught," I stated. "I'd love to see him in an orange jumpsuit put in with general population."

Rochelle sat up and rubbed her eyes, smearing electric blue eye shadow. "What are you guys talking about?" she groaned.

"Zane killed someone for Addie!" Lily exclaimed.

That caught Rochelle's immediate attention. "What?" she asked, her voice too shrill for someone who just woke up.

"He didn't kill *for* me," I explained. "He killed someone to save his own ass."

Rochelle scrambled up, her feet catching in the blankets. She flailed to untangle them and rushed over to the table. "What?" she repeated.

It felt like everything had just happened. I remembered the chilly night air, the trick-or-treaters running up and down the streets, the way I could see the false eyelashes every time I blinked. I remembered how hopeless I felt, how I didn't see a way out. And then I heard my name.

"Addie!" Rochelle yelled.

"Quiet!" I told her. "You'll wake Phoebe."

"I don't give a fuck about Phoebe," she spat. "What the hell happened to Zane?" Her eyebrows pushed together and I could see her clenching her jaw.

"Along with being a sadistic, chauvinistic dick, he's now a murderer."

"Don't talk about him like that!" Rochelle said, her brown eyes flashing with anger. "What did you do?"

"What did *I* do?" I questioned.

"Yes," she spat. "What the hell did you do? You must have fucked up, big time."

"I didn't do anything!" I shouted, forgetting about wanting to keep quiet. "Oh, wait, never mind. *I* got kidnapped. *I* am being forced to stay here, forced to have men pin me down and do whatever they want to me. All I want to do is go home, but I can't because that psychotic, twisted, creep has made it impossible to do so!"

Rochelle recoiled from my words. "Don't say that!" she snarled.

My hands flew up. "What is *wrong* with you?" Exasperated, I shook my head, mouth open as I panted with rage. "You're just as much of a victim as I am!"

"I'm not a victim," she retorted, looking just a bit perplexed.

"Yes you are," I cried, tears of frustration blurring my vision. "Why can't you see that?" I put my head in my hands. "I was so close," I muttered. "He knew who I was. He knew me, he knew me," I repeated and began crying.

Lily made a move to console me but Rochelle grabbed her shoulder. "No," she told her sharply and took a step toward me. "Listen, *Addison*," she said pointedly. "If anything happens to Zane, you're gonna be sorry."

"My name is Adeline," I corrected and composed myself. I had to keep it together. "My name is Adeline Miller. And people are still looking for me."

"Oh my God!" Rochelle huffed and threw back her head. "Will you stop? We get it, okay? People are looking for you, you have a family, they miss you, blah, blah, blah," she spat, her tone mocking. "I am so sick of hearing about it! When will you give it a rest?"

"When I'm out of here," I told her.

"I say we let them have you. Maybe they can put up with the constant whining better than we can." She heavily exhaled and strode to the shower. I watched her check herself out in the mirror and felt truly sorry for her. She was so broken and she didn't even realize it.

The basement door opened. His heavy footfalls gave his identity away. Apparently not caring if Jackson saw her naked, Rochelle stripped out of her clothes and stepped into the cold shower.

"I'm supposed to take the newspaper," Jackson told me. He gave me a small half smile that I returned with a glare. "Nate doesn't want you reading anything." His words were defeating. "Okay," I said simply and extended the paper to him.

"That's my favorite," he said, his eyes on my wrist.

"Huh?" I asked then realized he was looking at my tattoo.

"I love all the Harry Potter books," he said shyly. "But the Deathly Hallows was my favorite." He gave me a small smile. "Though I kinda hated it for being the last one."

I stared at him, open-mouthed before stammering, "Yeah. Me too." I blinked, shaking my head.

"I think I read it over a dozen times," he confessed.

My lips pulled up into a half smile. "I read it a few times too. And cried every time." Talking about books with fellow fans came natural to me. It was the next best thing to reading them.

I looked at Jackson, studying the bruises on his face. Did he like to fight? He had to do the grunt work for Zane, roughing up customers who didn't pay. It didn't seem fitting. Jackson was free to come and go as he pleased, right? He had to work for Nate just like Zane did. I blinked, casting my eyes down, slowly tracing his body. I hadn't acknowledged how firmly built he was until now.

"The movies are good too. One of the rare instances where the book to film conversion wasn't butchered."

"I haven't seen them all."

"Seriously?"

"Yes," he said meekly.

"Oh. Well … you should." I shrugged, not knowing what else to say. Jackson folded the newspaper in half and just stood there for a few uncomfortable seconds.

"I didn't want to read anything else after I finished that series," he said shyly.

I couldn't help but lean forward and agree. "Total book hangover."

"Book hangover?" he questioned, the words foreign.

I raised my eyebrows. "Yeah. You know, when you get hung up on a book."

"Oh, right." Then he smiled and almost looked happy. "I love that books can do that. Effect you so much, I mean."

"Yes," I gushed, my mind going into obsessive reader mode. "I do too. Books are dangerous. They pull you in and make you fall in love or totally destroy you. For the time being of course. Then you finish it and those feelings linger around in agony until you start another and the whole process happens again." I let out a breath and suddenly felt vulnerable in front of Jackson. I regretted being so open. Would he use it against me?

He bit his lip and diverted his eyes, blood rushing to his cheeks. I didn't want to admit that I found him sorta cute. He was a bad person, just like Zane. When he turned and went up the stairs, I found myself wishing he had stayed.

CHAPTER 18

I carefully scraped a perfect arch in the frost-covered window. The thin ice melted instantly when it met my skin. I watched thick snowflakes collect on the brown grass and thought about my dogs. Scarlet loved snow. Even in her old age, she would leap through snowdrifts like a puppy. I sighed, my breath clouding around my face. I hugged myself, rubbing my hands up and down on my arms.

"Why are you dressed like that?" I asked Phoebe as I stepped down from the chair and turned around. "You look like a candy cane."

She looked down at the red and white stripped spandex jumper she had on and raised an eyebrow. "That the point." Her expression saddened when she saw my confusion. "Addie," she said gently. "It two days before Christmas."

"Really?" I asked. I had just returned to the basement from the guest room. My wrists hurt from being tied up all day, and my arms were stiff, pulled unnaturally over my head. The muscles in my thigh quivered, sore as if I had worked out. Really, I tensed every time I was raped, fighting my rapist each and every time. When it was too much for them to handle, Zane tied my ankles to the bed. One time he held me down and watched the rape happen.

I knew Christmas was approaching, but I didn't realize it was *that* close. The house hadn't been decorated for the holiday.

Had two months really passed since I last stepped foot outside? "Oh."

Next to Halloween, Christmas was my second favorite holiday. It was my mother's favorite by far. She had always gone all out, decorating the house to the point of making me feel claustrophobic. She was good at finding everything and anything Christmas themed. One year she even found holiday printed toilet paper. I wondered if she even bothered to decorate this year. I hoped she had. I didn't want my family and friends to entirely move on and bury my memory, but I wanted them to be able to live their lives. Nate might have control over my life, but I didn't want him to have that effect on the people I care about.

"No wonder you've been so busy," I said quietly. I had a hard time keeping track of time. Everything blurred together. "What is wrong with people that they would want to celebrate Christmas with an underage prostitute?" I asked myself and shook my head. I closed my eyes for a few seconds, pushing away thoughts of my family. I wanted to wait until the girls were gone to have another breakdown.

The basement door opened and Jackson plodded down the stairs. He hadn't so much as said a word to me since we talked about books right after Halloween. I sometimes found myself wanting to discuss the topic again, but quickly reminded myself that he wasn't anyone I wanted to be friends with. Still … the topic of reading brought a sense of comfort. It reminded me of my life before being taken.

His right hand was wrapped in a bloody bandage, and he held his arm close to his body. He kept his eyes on the ground as if he refused to acknowledge my presence.

"Ready?" he asked, directing his question to no one in particular.

"Yeah," Lily said and stood. She put a knee length, red sweater over her tight jeans and a midriff showing white, fuzzy sweater.

I found it odd that Jackson was taking them instead of Zane. Even after I stopped going out, Zane came down to get the girls, and Jackson brought them back. I sat on the cot, feeling lonely and scared as soon as Lily and Phoebe left. Rochelle had disappeared with Zane the night before, and she hadn't been back since. I was certain she was too important, business-wise at least, to Nate for Zane to hurt her, but I couldn't help the sick feeling that curdled in my stomach when I thought of her being alone with him.

Feeling restless with fear, I sprang up off the cot and began pacing around the basement. It helped me stay warm, and it helped stop the fight-or-flight feeling from taking over. I slowly crept up the stairs and jiggled the knob, just in case. Of course it was locked.

The wonderful aroma of freshly baked apple pie wafted through the cracks in the doorframe. I stuck my face close to the door and inhaled. The smell immediately made my mouth water and brought up another family Christmas memory.

The floorboards creaked in the kitchen. I gasped in fear and scurried down the stairs just in time for the basement door to fly open.

"Adeline," Zane called.

"What?" I responded. Just the sound of his voice caused my hair to stand on end.

"What?" he scoffed. "I called you, come here," he stated, talking to me as if I was a dog.

I planted my sweaty palms on my thighs and stood before slowly walking to the base of the stairs.

"You're so fucking slow," he sighed.

I took as long as I could to climb up the steps. As soon as I was on the first floor, Zane shoved me forward and slammed the basement door closed. He took a hold of my arm and led me to the front door. He let go, put on a coat and gloves, and opened the door. He pushed me outside and stepped behind me.

I shivered as fluffy snowflakes landed on my skin. The wind had picked up, and the rate the snow was falling was increasing. Two cardboard boxes full of lights and garland sat to my right.

"Nate wants the house decorated," Zane told me. He pulled a silver flask from his pocket, put up his hood, and leaned against the side of the house. I didn't move. Zane jerked his head forward and widened his eyes. "What, are you fucking retarded?" he snarled. "Put up the decorations."

"I-I don't have shoes," I stuttered. "Or a coat. It's cold."

Zane shrugged. "That's your problem. I don't give a shit."

I stared at Zane in what should have been disbelief, but by then I knew anything was possible with him. He unscrewed the flask and took a sip. He reached behind him, trading the flask for something else.

"And feel free to run. I've been wanting to hit some targets," he growled and flashed his gun.

My hands were already shaking from cold. I eyed the weapon, taking in the long silencer, and swallowed my fear. I just moved my head up and down and reached into the box. Everything was tangled; it took fifteen minutes just to get the garland and lights unknotted. I moved to the other side of the wrap around porch, and Zane came with, keeping his gun in his hands and his eyes on me.

My fingers hurt from cold as I wrapped the garland around the railing of the porch. Before I was taken I enjoyed decorations so much better when someone else put them up. Even if I wasn't shivering uncontrollably, I would have had a hard time keeping the lights perfectly even with the garland.

"It's messed up there," Zane pointed out. "Fix it."

My teeth chattered, and my arms began to shake along with my hands. My fingers were numb and I couldn't get a grip on the strand of white lights.

"Fix it," Zane snarled again.

"I'm t-trying," I mumbled.

"Try harder," Zane said and pushed himself up off the rocking chair. He strode over and smacked the back of my head.

I knew I should have felt more pain that I did, though with the horrible stinging that plagued my feet, it was hard for new pain to register. I put my hands on the railing and pinched at the lights. My fingers were so numb, I couldn't tell if I really had it in my grasp or not.

"You are worthless," Zane said and shoved me to the side. He bit the tip of his glove and pulled it off with his mouth, then he picked up the lights and looped it around. "I'm going to freeze to death waiting for your slow ass," he complained.

"There," he said when he reached the end of the porch. "That wasn't so hard, was it?" he scoffed, ignoring the fact that he had only decorated the last four feet. I had done the rest. He pushed past me and went back into the house. I felt like my feet were going to crack and shatter as I walked, each step jarringly painful.

The best thing to do for frostbite was to submerge the frozen parts in warm water. Since that wasn't an option, I pulled the quilt off of Phoebe's bed and shakily sank down onto my cot, wrapping both quilts around my shivering body. I curled up in a little ball, tucking my feet as close to my legs as possible. I breathed on my hands and wiggled my fingers, trying to will the feeling back in and the cold out.

I was able to unclench my fists and flex my toes by the time Phoebe and Lily returned. I tossed Phoebe's quilt back and sat up.

"The house looks pretty," Lily said.

At first I thought she was trying to compliment my shitty job, but realized she had no idea I was the one who stood in the cold putting up the lights. I inspected my hands, looking for signs of damage. I wasn't sure if it was too soon to tell, but it looked like the damage done from my flesh freezing stopped at first-degree frostbite...or so I hoped.

"Is someone special coming?" she asked.

I shook my head. "I don't know. I'm assuming so. Why else would Nate want the house decorated?"

"Right." She sat at the card table and unzipped her boots. "I hate Christmas," she sighed. "Always have, always will."

"Why do you hate Christmas?" I asked, sensing her hidden sadness.

She shrugged. "It's a dumb holiday, that's all."

I just nodded, remembering her telling me about her bad family life. I didn't think Christmas morning was a joyful time in her house. I felt a stab of sadness in my heart when I imagined Lily waking up after falling asleep watching Christmas specials on TV. Her mom would be passed out and hung over if not still drunk and her step dad...I shuddered. I didn't want to think about what he might have done to her.

"I'm going to bed," Lily announced and changed into pajamas. Phoebe did the same. She crawled into bed rubbing her wrists.

"You okay?" I asked.

"Sore," she told me and held up her hands. The skin around her wrists was red and raw. It was something that had happened to me before.

"I hate being tied up," I said with empathy. "Want me to get you a washcloth?"

She shook her head. "Too tired." She gave me a feeble half smile and straightened out her quilt. "Night."

"Night," I responded and lay back down. I replayed my favorite Christmas memories over and over in my head, feeling more homesick than I had in a while.

Eventually I drifted to sleep and had a nightmare about Zane dressing up in a Santa suit and sneaking into my room. I woke the next morning with my heart racing and my forehead covered in a cold sweat.

My body was stiff from being so cold. Lily and Phoebe sat close together on a cot with a blanket draped over their shoulders.

"Want to sit with us?" Lily asked.

"Yeah," I said and got up. I quickly went to the bathroom and tore a leftover peanut butter and jelly sandwich in half. Lily lifted up the blanket. I sat down and wrapped it around myself, feeling instant warmth. Phoebe shuffled a deck of cards and dealt them out. We spent the morning playing Go Fish.

Sometime in the afternoon, the basement door opened. Lily had a moment of panic because she hadn't gotten dressed and ready for the day. My muscles tensed at the thought of Nate or Zane. Jackson's ungraceful footsteps offered just a smidge of relief.

His eyes met mine for a brief second the moment he stepped onto the concrete floor. Blood rushed to his cheeks and he looked away. It was odd, the way his embarrassment seemed so … so innocent. I watched him cross the basement, holding his arms close to his body. He couldn't be like Zane, could he? I bit the inside of my cheek as I thought about it.

It didn't matter. He was upstairs while we were trapped down here. He wasn't a good guy. He couldn't be.

"I need you to follow me," he blurted. "Dress warm," he added and crossed his arms over his chest. Phoebe and Lily got up and went to the selection of clothes, having a hard time finding something that provided warmth. "You too, Adeline."

CHAPTER 19

I was startled at the sound of my name. I looked at him in question. He frowned and gave a curt nod.

I stood, unease growing, and walked over to the dresser. I put knee-high black socks on and left on the blue pajama pants. I pulled a sheer, long sleeved black shirt over a pale yellow tank top. Lily eyed my mismatching outfit but withheld her comments. I stuffed my arms inside a jacket that was too big and zipped it up to my chin. Phoebe wore a red pea coat with a matching hat and gloves. Her hair was out of her face and tucked into the cap. She was one of those girls with a face so pretty that the unflattering winter hat enhanced her features. I looked like a swaddled skinny troll when only my face was showing. Not that I cared anymore anyway.

Jackson led us up the stairs. The kitchen was full of wonderful aromas. I stopped and did a double take at all the food that was spread out on the counter. It made the gargantuan feast my grandmother prepared look like a snack. The smell of sweet rolls was overwhelming. I reached out to take one. Phoebe grabbed my hand.

"Addie, no!" she whispered.

Jackson turned around. His brown eyes looked from me to the rolls and then to the floor. He grabbed his coat and opened the back door.

"Where are we going?" Lily asked. "I didn't think the path to the trailer was plowed."

"It's not," Jackson told her. Only about three inches of mushy snow had accumulated in the last two days. He stuck one of his arms through his coat, putting it on as he walked across the patio. Other than putting up the lights, it was the first time I had been outside since Halloween. Now that I wasn't worried about freezing to death, I took a deep breath and looked up at the cloud-covered sky. Then sun was setting, and an arctic wind caused goosebumps to rise on my skin.

Multi-colored lights had been strung up along the fence that surrounded the covered pool. One of the pine trees along the lawn's edge had even been decorated with big, shiny, red ornaments. I turned around and saw that the whole house was outlined in icicle lights. A big wreath rattled in the wind on the back door. The whole Stepford Wives vibe sent a chill down my spine.

We left the patio and walked several yards through the lawn until we reached a storage shed. Jackson spun the dial on the padlock and opened the door. He held out his arm, motioning for us to go inside.

I stopped dead in my tracks. "No," I said firmly.

"Nate wants us all to stay in here," Jackson told me, as if that explanation was enough to make me listen to him.

"I don't care," I spat. Phoebe reached behind her and took my hand. "I don't want to be locked in."

"You won't be locked in," Jackson said slowly. "I'll be in there with you."

I almost scoffed. Like that made it any better. Phoebe gave my hand a tug.

"Please, Addie. It cold out here. Don't get hurt," she begged. "Come in with me."

I pressed my lips together in a frown and stepped inside the shed. Jackson clicked on a flashlight and set it on a shelf. He moved out of the shed and began pushing snow around with his foot until he found the end of an extension cord. He shook the snow off, gave it a tug, and dragged it a few feet into the shed. The doors wouldn't shut all the way with the cord sticking out, but I was grateful for the small space heater it powered.

"You gonna tell us why we're out here?" Lily asked Jackson.

"Nate's sister and her family are in town," he began.

"They're coming over for Christmas dinner. He doesn't want us in the house."

The words were like a sucker punch to the face. Nate, who I considered the scum of the earth, got to spend Christmas Eve with his family, and I didn't. Suddenly, I decided that I wasn't going to feel sorry for myself anymore. A new kind of rage burned inside me, one that made me want to find the nearest pointy object and stab Nate repeatedly.

"That's fucking bullshit!" I spat. Jackson looked at me in surprise. I had barely spoken to him, let alone cursed in anger. "He gets to sit in there and act all normal and be warm and eat good food while we freeze our asses off huddled around a little heater in a shed!"

"Act normal?" Lily questioned, her blue eyes wide.

"Yeah, normal." I shook my head. "Or at least like a decent human being."

"What do you mean?" she asked, and a bit of innocence was visible on her young face again.

"His sister doesn't know what he does. If she did, he wouldn't have to hide us outside."

"Oh," Lily said. She looked down, her thoughts salient in her expressions. She knew everything about it was wrong, but she was so brainwashed, she was having a hard time figuring out just *why* it was wrong. "What he's doing is illegal," she concluded.

"And immoral, and degrading, and objectifying, and—"

I cut off when headlights illuminated the road in front of the house. A van pulled into the driveway, disappearing from view when it parked in front of the house. Then the back door opened, and Rochelle stepped out, looking behind her as she ran through the yard and joined us in the shed.

Everyone huddled around the space heater. I stayed by the door, watching the house through the crack in the door. We weren't far; I could easily get Nate's sister's attention. I could see them through the kitchen window. His sister was tall and blonde, just like him. I wondered if she had any idea just how sick and twisted her brother was.

I looked behind me. The four had their backs to me. They wouldn't notice if I slipped out. Slowly, I pushed the door open. I walked several feet toward the house and bent down, picking up a handful of snow. I balled it in my hands, ignoring the instant sting it brought my fingertips and waited for the surface to melt just enough to help the snowball hold its shape.

I focused on the kitchen window, pulled my arm back, and swung it forward. Right before the snowball left my fingers, Jackson grabbed me.

"What are you doing?" he cried and pulled me to him. The snowball flew through the air and smacked into the side of the house, missing the window by only a few inches.

"Let me go!" I screamed.

Jackson put his hand over my mouth and wrestled me to the ground. Someone rushed to look out the window and find the source of the noise. Jackson pressed his body over mine, pushing me down and out of the line of sight.

"Adeline!" he whispered. "Stop! You're going to get yourself hurt!"

I continued to struggle. The back of my pants felt wet already and snow found its way down the neckline of the jacket. I pushed against Jackson, realizing for the first time just how strong he was.

"Addie!" Phoebe yelled. "Stop!"

My body went still when I realized I was putting her in danger as well as myself. Jackson took advantage of it and scooped me up with ease. He hurried back into the shed and pushed the door shut. He gently set me down and brushed snow out of my hair. I jerked away from his touch.

"What the hell was that?" Rochelle spat and reached out, hitting my shoulder with her fingertips. "You want to get us all in trouble?"

"If trouble gets us out of here, then yes," I said slowly through clenched teeth.

"You look scary," Lily told me.

I moved my glare to her and softened my expression. I wasn't mad at Lily but I wasn't sure she could make the distinction. "I want to go home," I reminded her.

"You can't go home, dipshit!" Rochelle said. "We went over this, remember?"

"Fine," I spat just to shut her up. "I want out of here. I want to get us *all* out of here."

"Whatever," she replied and flicked her hand in my face. "If you're so high and mighty, make sure you tell Nate that *you* were the one who threw that snowball so only *your* ass gets beat."

I looked at Rochelle and nodded. Melted snow dripped down my back, making me uncomfortably cold. I took off the jacket and wiped away what I could. I moved closer to the space heater and turned around, wanting to dry the wet spot on my butt before the dampness sank into my bones and caused me to get sick.

No one dared to speak, let alone move, until the minivan disappeared down the driveway about five hours later. I was cold, stiff, and still angry, but I was also sad, tired, and scared. Very scared. I knew Nate would be beyond pissed, and part of me regretted throwing the snowball at the house.

Jackson walked into the house first. Nate and Zane were waiting for us in the kitchen. Jackson stepped to the side and stole a glance behind him. His eyes met mine, and he gave me a tiny nod. I wasn't sure what he was trying to tell me. Was he reminding me what I was in for?

Nate held his left out in front of him and removed a gold watch. He handed it to Zane and then rolled up the sleeves of his light blue button-up shirt.

"Who is the fucking idiot who hit the side of the house?" he began, the calmness that he usually carried was gone. The vein in his head was already prominent and pulsating. He eyed each and every one of us. My heart began beating faster and faster. Nate's hands moved to his waist and he unbuckled his belt.

Oh, God, not again. My stomach protested in fear, grumbling and churning. My cheeks grew red and sweat itched under my arms. I tried to open my mouth and failed.

"Oh, so none of you know what the hell happened out there?" Nate went on. "Very well," he said and whipped his belt through the loops in his pants. He folded it over and snapped it. The cracking of the leather echoed throughout the house. "You can all be equally punished."

There was no way I could let the others get punished because of me. I took a deep breath, ready to confess. But Jackson beat me to it.

"I did it," he said.

CHAPTER 20

"You?" Nate asked, disbelief in his voice.

"Yes, me." Jackson looked Nate right in the eye.

"Why?" Nate leaned forward and slightly narrowed his eyes.

Jackson's cheeks reddened. "I was knocking down icicles. I was bored." He shrugged.

"Well," Nate said, his unnerving calmness back. "That boredom cost you." He flicked his eyes over us. "I want this kitchen clean by the time I'm done," he ordered. "Come with me," he told Jackson.

I could feel my pulse bounding through every vein. A sick cold feeling washed over me as I watched Jackson slowly walk out of the room. Whatever they were going to do to him was going to be horrible.

Zane pulled out a chair in the breakfast nook and sat at the table. He scooted a plateful of snickerdoodles in front of him and stuffed two in his mouth. Despite his full mouth, he grinned, and I knew he was gloating in his ability to eat while we had to clean.

I turned to Phoebe, my expression pleading. She quickly shook her head. Lily's blue eyes conveyed the same don't-even-think-about-it stare. Rochelle tipped her head, looking at the spot Jackson had been standing in. She looked utterly perplexed, as is she couldn't understand why he took the blame.

And I couldn't either. Was he actually trying to help me? Or was he going to want something from me later? Zane smacked

Phoebe's butt hard when she picked up an empty gravy bowl from the table. A lump of fear formed in my throat. Jackson was going to expect me to pay him back, I was sure of it.

The sound of leather on skin resonated through the house. My stomach tightened. I turned my back, not wanting to look into the dining room and see Jackson getting the shit beat out of him. For covering for something I did. I clenched my jaw and took quick, sharp breaths through my nose. My feet were glued to the floor with fear.

Nate whipped him again. Lily flinched at the sound. Jackson grunted in pain when the belt cracked. My head fell to my chest. This shouldn't be happening. Not to Jackson. He was innocent. *I* was the one who should be getting the beating.

Phoebe turned on the sink, drowning out the noise. She walked past me, bumping into my arm. I caught her pleading stare and shook myself. With trembling hands, I picked up a plate and scraped the left overs into the garbage. Zane picked up another cookie before getting up and joining Nate. Unable to control myself, my eyes flicked to the dining room. Jackson was on the floor. I saw Zane kick him in the ribs. My entire body was on fire with fear. Were they going to kill Jackson right then and there? There was enough blood on the floor already.

Every punch, every kick, every time the leather belt cracked against Jackson's skin made it hard to breathe. Guilty tears stung the corners of my eyes.

"I have to go in there. I have to do something," I whispered to Phoebe.

"No!" she whispered back. "Addie, it be suicide! And Jackson get in more trouble for lying."

She was right. I sucked in my breath and shook my head. The world was spinning again and I was stuck on this nightmare of a ride. There was nothing I could do to stop it so I could get off. Phoebe nudged my arm and looked behind us, reminding me that we had to finish cleaning or else we would also feel the wrath of Nate. I picked up another plate and put it in the sink where Lily stood washing dishes.

I wanted to scream. I wanted to throw the glass serving trays against the wall and scream at Nate, telling him that he was a spineless psychopath who would get caught and arrested someday, and I hoped his cellmate was a large man named Bubba who would make Nate his bitch.

But I didn't.

I set the serving tray on the counter next to the sink and went back to the table to get another bowl. The cold mashed potatoes still smelled wonderful, but I felt too ill to even think about eating. I put the bowl down and grabbed the remaining dishes off the table, scraped the food from them into the trash, and put them on the counter next to the sink.

I wiped down the counters while Phoebe filled the dishwasher and Lily washed what wouldn't fit. Rochelle dried the dishes, carefully stacking them on the counter when she was done. When the counters were clean, I stood in the kitchen, not knowing what else to do. Crumbs littered the floor. If I had known where a broom, was I would have swept.

Before I could ask, Zane came back into the room. Blood had splattered across his white polo shirt. To say I was scared was an understatement. I backed up against the table, fear causing my skin to tingle. I wanted to run away and hide.

Then I saw the knife on the counter.

"Meet me upstairs in five minutes," he said to Rochelle and opened the fridge. He filled a cup with eggnog and took a long drink. I could smell the alcohol in it.

"Okay," Rochelle said, her voice breathy. She stared at Zane as if he had just slayed the dragon. She wiped her hands on a towel and immediately started fussing with her hair. Zane downed the rest of his drink, refilled the cup, and went upstairs.

I took a shaky breath and pushed off the table. I crossed the kitchen and wrapped my fingers around a butcher knife.

"Ever heard the expression 'don't bring a knife to a gun fight'?" Nate's voice came from behind me. I squeezed my fingers around the handle of the knife and whirled around. Nate leaned against the doorframe with one foot against the wall. He casually wiped blood off his hands. "Try it. We'll see who is faster." He took the knife from me and walked away, clicking his tongue. "Jackson, you know better than to leave the knives out. I guess I need to remind you." He held the knife up, light reflecting off the blade.

I imagined running at him, raising my arm, and driving the

knife down into his shoulder. Blood would spray in the air and splatter across my face. I'd bring the knife down again, this time hitting him in the spine. It would be a slow, painful death, and I would enjoy watching it.

I stood rooted in the spot, shaking with fear and anger. I watched as Nate stepped over Jackson, walking through the dining room, into the living room, and up the stairs. Rochelle brushed past me, practically skipping, and hurried up the stairs to get to Zane.

Lily scuttled to a closet and came back with a broom and a mop. I bit my lip and looked at Jackson. My heart began to flutter with nerves. Without a second thought, I left the kitchen and went into the dining room.

Jackson lay unmoving on the floor. Blood soaked through his shirt. For a split second, I thought he was dead. Then I saw him breathing. I took another step toward him. The floor creaked. I closed my eyes and winced before stealing a glance at the stairs. I let out a breath when no one on the second level left their rooms. Jackson tried to open his swollen eyes. His gaze met mine.

I knelt down next to him. "Why?" I whispered. "Why did you take the blame?"

He closed his eyes and flinched. "You're the only one," he mumbled and coughed. Blood dripped down the side of his mouth.

"The only one?" I questioned.

He tried to nod. "The only one who got stronger from being here. You're still you." He curled his knees to his chest, groaning in pain. "And you made it past the fence. I couldn't even do it," he wheezed. "And I tried five times."

"Why would you … Wait," I blurted as it dawned on me. "No …" I stood up, and shook my head. *No.* Jackson wouldn't try to escape. Why would he? He wasn't a victim like us. He couldn't be. He lived upstairs, with them. He couldn't … but it made sense. Cold shock washed over me. "You don't want to be here?" I finally asked.

"Of course not," he muttered.

The whole time I had thought of Jackson as an enemy. I backed up, looking at him in a whole new light, and hurried back into the kitchen. I picked up a clean bowl from the counter, filled it with warm water, and took the towel that was hanging on the handle of the oven.

"You shouldn't have lied for me," I said gently and knelt next to Jackson. His distant staring made sense now, and I felt guilty and stupid for not putting two and two together. I dipped the towel in the bowl of water and carefully pressed it to a cut an inch under Jackson's right eye. "I feel horrible. It's my fault."

"Don't." He squinted one eye open. He lifted his hand and gently took hold of my wrist, moving it away from him. "Don't feel bad, Adeline." He slowly moved his gaze to the living room. "And don't get yourself in trouble."

I pulled my hand back and shook my head. "I don't care." He still didn't let go of my wrist. I put my other hand over his and carefully pulled back his fingers. He grunted in pain. I slid my palm under his, blood smearing my skin, and looked at his hand. "I think your finger is broken," I said, noting the swelling of his index finger.

"Maybe," he said and wiggled his finger. "I can still move it."

I cringed at the thought of his bones snapping and laid his hand on his side. I dipped the towel in the water again. Both of Jackson's eyes were purple and puffy. Blood still dripped from his nose, and he had a large cut on the side of his mouth. I could see the teeth marks from where his own teeth had dug into it while being hit.

I moved my hand up his face and pushed his wavy dark hair out of his eyes. The strands caught in his wounds and painted a trail of red up his face. I wiped it away and ran my hand over his head, checking for more bleeding. He had a lump on the back of his head, probably from being kicked. I tucked his hair behind his ear and mopped up the blood that dripped from his broken nose.

The water in the bowl was red. I dipped the towel in and swirled it around, doing my best to clean it. I squeezed the extra water out and carefully pressed it to his mouth, wiping away the thick blood. It ran down into his ear and around his neck.

Bruises covered his arms, and the spots of blood that seeped through his shirt made me nervous. I put the towel in the bowl, wiped my wet hands on my pants and grabbed the hem of his shirt. Warm blood soaked through and stained my hands. I pulled the shirt up and gasped.

Scars covered Jackson's torso. Raised pink lines mapped years of abuse and torture. Cigarette burns and other patches of scar tissue trailed up his rib cage. I clenched my teeth together, trying to stay calm.

The blood was coming from a perfectly straight, large gash on his side. It confused me for a second since his shirt hadn't been cut. Then I realized that it was an older injury. The protective scab that had formed came off from the beating. I stared at it, horrified. It looked like someone had taken a vegetable peeler to him and removed a section of his flesh. The wound wasn't deep, but it was about an inch and a half wide and five inches long.

I felt dizzy. My ears rang and I wanted to throw up. I rocked back on my heels and sank onto my butt. Jackson feebly lifted his hand and touched my arm. His gesture of comfort caused a shiver to ripple over my body. I took a breath but felt like I got no air. I needed to compose myself.

I reached out next to me, feeling around until my fingers graced the side of the bowl. My vision was fuzzy; I wasn't exactly watching what I was doing. Water dripped on the floor as I moved the towel over to Jackson's body. I placed it over the cut and looked at Jackson's face. His eyes were closed again, and his eyebrows pushed together. I didn't want to think about the level of pain he was in.

When I moved the towel away, bright red blood pooled in the shallow wound. I pressed the towel to it, but the wet fabric did nothing to stop the bleeding.

"You need stitches," I whispered and tipped my head, examining the bruises on his ribcage. "And probably an X-ray. Your ribs could be broken." I traced my eyes over the rest of his exposed torso. He was lean and muscular, and I suddenly realized that all the yard work I had seen him doing wasn't by choice. Like us, he was forced to work. Just in a different way. How could I have been so blind to it before?

"I'll be okay," he tried to assure me. He took a ragged breath and slowly sat up. He reached for me, taking the towel from my hands. He pressed it against his nose and leaned back.

"You should tilt your head forward," I told him softly. "That way you won't swallow the blood." It took effort for him to bend over. "I'll get you another towel," I offered and began to stand.

"No," he said, his voice muffled by the towel. "It's okay."

I settled back down, hugging my knees to my chest. I ran my eyes over Jackson, taking in the strength of his arms and his broad chest. "Jackson?" I asked quietly. He tipped his head in my direction. "How come you didn't fight back?" I blurted.

He put his head back down again. "There were two of them and one of me," he began. "Zane is almost always carrying." He coughed and spit blood into the towel. "And I used to," he said and looked at me. "Fight back, I mean. The last time I did, I hit Zane in the mouth, knocked out one of his teeth in the front. He has a fake tooth now. You can't tell unless you're really close though," he muttered. "And Nate broke my arm. He made me wait nine days to get it casted."

I didn't know how to respond. I looked at him, wanting to apologize and nurse his wounds. I opened my mouth when the floor upstairs creaked.

"Go," Jackson told me. "Now!"

I scrambled to my feet, almost tripping over the bowl of water. I picked it up with such haste that I sloshed half of it out of the bowl. The unmistakable sound of liquid splashing onto the floor sent a jolt of terror through me.

"Go!" Jackson said again. He unwrapped the towel and planted a hand on the floor. He tossed the towel over the spilled water. "Adeline, get out of here!"

I scuttled into the kitchen and dumped the bloody water down the drain. I flicked on the sink and scrubbed at my hands, getting rid of all evidence of helping Jackson. I heard footsteps behind me. I took the towel and started wiping down the sink.

"Good enough," Nate spoke, causing me to jump, even though I knew he was behind me. He went to the basement door and waved us in. I set the towel down and stole one last look at Jackson before I went back into the cold, dark basement.

CHAPTER 21

Two weeks passed before I saw Jackson again. I was startled awake when I heard him plodding down the stairs. The bruises on his face had faded considerably. I opened my mouth only to snap it shut. I had no idea what to say to him. He looked at me before crossing to the table and setting our food down.

"Jackson," I said and sat up. "A-are you okay?" I stuttered.

He looked down at his body and shrugged. "I think so."

"Where have you been?" Zane had taken over the job of providing us with food and water. Instead of carrying it down the stairs like Jackson did, he threw it. The water bottles had burst open more than once, and we had to scrape our sandwiches off the dirty floor.

His eyes went to the floor, and he shook his head, not wanting to talk about it. He took a step back and turned around. "I can't stay down here," he told me and took another step.

I tossed the blanket back and got out of bed. "Thank you," I said quickly. "I never said thank you for what you did. I wish I could pay you back somehow."

"You don't owe me anything, Adeline." He gave me a small smile and went upstairs.

I ate breakfast and paced around the basement while Phoebe slept. Lily and Rochelle went to work at the club the night before and had yet to return. Phoebe didn't feel well again, and for three days, all she had done was sleep when she wasn't working.

I went to the table and shuffled the worn deck of cards. I

tried building a house, but the edges of the cards were too worn and bent to stay upright. I tossed them in the middle and leaned back in the chair, the hard metal pressing against my spine. I inhaled deeply and sighed, blowing loose strands of hair from my face.

The basement door creaked open and heels clicked on the wooden steps. Rochelle hurried to the vanity where she plugged in the curling iron and plopped onto the stool to fix her makeup. Lily went straight to her cot. Dark circles hung under her eyes, and lipstick was smeared across her face. She sank down on the mattress and flipped her head over, pulling her red locks into a bun on the top of her head. She stripped down to her undergarments and got under the quilt.

I stayed at the table, absentmindedly shuffling the cards while Rochelle primped and polished her already stunning face and Lily slept. When my feet began to fall asleep, I got up and paced around the basement.

"How do I look?" Rochelle asked me and stood from the stool.

"Beautiful." It was the truth.

"Great, thanks." She turned to inspect herself in the mirror one more time. "I hope Zane thinks so too." She changed her clothes and then skipped up the stairs. She knocked on the basement door and waited. About a minute later, the door opened just long enough for Rochelle to leave. Then it slammed shut, waking Lily.

"Is Phoebe working?" Lily rubbed her eyes and pushed herself up.

"No," I told her and pointed to the bed. "She hasn't gotten up yet."

Lily's young face muddled with worry. "Is she sick?"

I shook my head. "She has to be."

Lily bit her lip and looked concerned. "She's been sick on and off for so long now." She closed her eyes and shook her head. "Hey," she said suddenly. "Want to test me to see if I'm psychic?"

I blinked. "Uh, sure. How?"

She joined me at the table and shuffled the deck of cards. "You hold them up and I'll try to read your thoughts and say if it's red or black."

"And that can determine if you can see the future?"

"No, psychic," she said.

"Lily, you do know what being psychic means, right?"

"Yeah, duh. It means you, like, know things you can't explain."

I couldn't refute that. I got up, keeping my blanket close to my body, and joined Lily at the table. "If you can read my thoughts, you'd be telepathic, not psychic. Though I suppose telepathy is under the broad spectrum of 'psychic powers'." I shuffled the cards.

"How do you know that?"

I took a deep breath and sighed. "Books."

"Like witchcraft books?" she asked and leaned forward.

"Not quite. Fiction books, technically. About fantasy and magic. I used to read a lot."

"I don't like to read," she said casually. "It's boring."

"You sound like my sister," I said. I wanted to ask her how anything could be any more boring than being stuck in the basement but withheld my comment.

"What was her name again?"

"Arianna."

"Do you still miss her?"

"Of course," I said. "What do you mean 'still'?"

She shrugged. "I don't miss my family or friends anymore. I, like, never really missed my mom, and I definitely don't miss my asshole stepdad. I kinda missed my cousin at first. Then I stopped caring."

"That's sad, Lily."

She shrugged again. "They never cared about me, not really. But, like, whatever, right?" She closed her eyes. "Black?"

"Uh," I started. I hadn't even looked at the cards. "Red."

"Damn it." She closed her eyes. "Are you thinking? I'm not hearing anything."

I looked down at the black nine of clubs. "Why is Rochelle so obsessed with Zane?"

Lily shrugged. "He's nice to her, most of the time."

"I wouldn't care if he was nice to me all of the time, I know what kind of person he is. And I would *never* be obsessed with him."

"They used to, like, date."

"Date?" I shuffled the cards again.

"Yeah. Before Rochelle started working. That's, like, how they met." She bit her lip and thought. "I think at a street fair, or something like that."

I leaned in. "So she didn't know Zane was ... well, *Zane* then, right?"

She shrugged. "I doubt it. She told me that Zane swept her off her feet, they fell in love, and blah, blah, blah ... ya know, all that romantic shit that doesn't really happen."

"And it didn't happen."

She sighed. "Black."

"What?"

Her eyes widened and she shook her head. "The card, dummy."

"Oh, yeah. Uh, yes."

"Awesome!"

"So how did Rochelle end up down here?" I set the cards on the table.

"I don't really know." Lily brushed her strawberry blonde hair behind her shoulders. "Phoebe thinks it's so she can keep an eye on us or something. You know she'll tell Zane anything."

"That's ..." I trailed off, not knowing what to say.

"Creepy?" Lily offered.

"Among other things."

Lily stretched her arms above her head. "I'm tired." She stood and went back to her cot.

"Me too," I said, though I thought my sleepiness was brought on by boredom. I retreated to my uncomfortable cot and climbed under the covers. I closed my eyes and conjured up the comforting image of my family seated around the dining room table, eating and talking. I didn't realize I had even fallen asleep until I heard Jackson whisper my name.

"Adeline," Jackson repeated, speaking softly, pulling me from my sleep. I blinked open my eyes. "Sorry for waking you up."

I sat up and rubbed the sleep out of my eyes. "It's okay, but why are you?"

"Nate sent me down to get you." As soon as the words left his mouth, my body went rigid with fear. "He wants us to shovel the driveway."

"Really?"

Jackson nodded. "Several clients come on Tuesdays."

"Oh." I threw back the covers, stood, and realized that I didn't have any sort of winter gear. As if he could read my mind, Jackson motioned to the stairs.

"I have boots you can wear. They'll be big, but at least your feet will stay warm and dry."

"Thanks," I told him.

His dark eyes met mine. He looked at me with the same empty look that he always had, but I saw the real Jackson now. There was sorrow on his face, and it hurt. I now knew that the anger he held back was directed at Nate and Zane.

I put as many layers on as humanly possible and followed Jackson up the stairs. He was right. The boots were big, but I was thankful for them anyway. The sun was low in the gray, cloud-covered sky, and the wind had picked up. The shovels were already leaning against the house. I took one and started scraping snow off the porch steps while Jackson worked on the sidewalk.

"I can't believe you've never seen all the Harry Potter movies," I said, looking over my shoulder. My breath clouded around me.

Jackson's frown turned into a small smile. "I want to see them," he said. The smile disappeared. "I can't see movies though. Nate makes sure I don't watch TV or listen to the radio."

My stomach twisted with guilt. *Way to go, Addie. What a great topic to bring up.* The dejection in his voice hurt my heart.

"I went to the theme park two years ago. It was awesome. I got a wand," I said.

"I heard about that park. It sounds amazing." Jackson stopped shoveling and looked at me. A glimmer of hope sparkled in his dark eyes.

"It is," I said and went on to tell him about the park, only to get overcome with emotion since the memory involved my family and Lynn. I blinked back the tears, not wanting them to freeze as the streamed down my face. We went back to shoveling.

"Did you really want Zane to kill me?" I asked rather suddenly.

"Huh?" Jackson said and looked up.

I turned around to face him. "When he took me. You said there were other ways to handle it and Zane made it sound like you were suggesting he kill me."

Jackson shook his head and his wavy hair fell into his eyes. "No. I was hoping he'd beat the shit out of you and leave after the usual threats," he explained. I made a face, and he shook his head again. "Not that I wanted you to get the shit beaten out of you, but anything is better than this, isn't it?"

"That is very true."

"What were you doing at the parade?" he asked slowly. "Are you … ?" he trailed off and looked at the ground.

"Gay? No, I'm not. My friend Matt is, and he was in the parade. I went to watch and support him."

Jackson's face turned a little red, though it could have just been from the cold. "Were you there with anyone?"

I nodded. "My best friend and my sister."

"I'm really sorry, Adeline," he said and pushed the shovel forward, scraping the metal edge on the cobblestone.

"It's not your fault." I finished clearing off the porch and walked ahead of Jackson. I plunged the shovel into a snowdrift. The whirl of tires and the roar of an engine caught my attention, and I flicked my head up. A truck slowly trudged down the slippery road and passed the farmhouse.

"We could run away right now," I told him.

"We wouldn't get far in the snow," he spoke.

"Yes, we could. We'd just have to make it down the road. Someone would find us sooner or later."

"You're not going to, are you?" he asked, apprehension in his voice.

I shook my head and sighed as the logic set in. "Not now. It's too cold. I could freeze to death before I found help."

"Aren't you afraid of getting hurt?"

"Not really. I'm more afraid of my family getting hurt." I traced my eyes down the road, blinking away snowflakes that landed in my eyelashes. "I still think there's a way. Don't let fear keep you from dreaming, right?"

Jackson gave me the smallest of smiles. "Don't actually do it, okay? Not now at least. I don't want you to get hurt. Obviously," he added so quietly I could barely hear him.

"Why?" I asked and hoped he didn't think I was ungrateful. I just had to know why he thought I was worth it.

He shook his head and cast his eyes to the snow covered ground. "There's something so … so *alive* in you. You've been here for half a year, Addie, and you're even more determined to leave now than you were when we brought you here. You're not broken. You still hold onto who you are. I've never seen that before. Everyone ends up giving up. It's like they can't see any way out."

"Do you see any way out?" I asked slowly.

Jackson put both hands on the shovel and leaned on it. "I didn't, until recently," he admitted.

"What changed?"

He looked away. "Don't know. Sick of it?" he added quickly.

"Do you think about what life would be like if you weren't here?" I asked.

"Sometimes. I want to go to school. I want to study things, anything, I don't care what it is. But I should have started college three years ago, and Nate never let me finish high school." He shook his head and looked embarrassed. "It's just something to think about, I guess."

"No," I said and took a step closer to him. "It's more than just something to think about. It's what keeps you together isn't it? Keeps you from surrendering your hope. You have to hold onto it, want it, need it. Or … or else you'd have nothing."

Jackson's eyes moved from the ground to my face. His lips pulled into a smile, and some of the sadness began to disappear from his face. My heart skipped a beat, and I wanted to move closer to him, feel his body heat and start talking about Harry Potter and books again. We could forget about this nightmare for a few minutes.

"The driveway's not gonna shovel itself!" Zane yelled from inside the house.

Jackson's body stiffened, and a wave of fear washed over me. Jackson turned away so quickly, he slid on the snow-covered path. He recovered quickly and pushed his shovel forward, clearing away another few feet of snow.

I moved several yards away, taking big steps through the deep snow. I felt bad for Jackson. He seemed so sad, so defeated, and only a little sliver of his true self was left and was at risk of slipping away. I wanted to know just how long he'd been here and how he ended up here in the first place.

A north wind blasted through, spraying me with tiny shards of ice. I closed my eyes and braced myself. The frigid Iowa winters were nothing I wasn't used to, though I usually had proper attire on. I stole a glance behind me and saw Zane standing in the living room. He had closed the window but kept the curtain pulled back. He titled his head down when he saw me looking. His eyes narrowed, and the temperature felt like it dropped another ten degrees.

I pushed a shovelful of snow forward as fast as I could. I wanted to get away from the house and away from Zane. I worked feverishly, and in a matter of minutes my back and arms were tired. Jackson walked past me, already done with the section he had been working on. I watched him start on the driveway.

"Are we really going to do the whole thing?" I asked, feeling somewhat out of breath.

"Yeah," he replied, seemingly unfazed from the physical work. "There's a snow blower in the garage."

"Are you fucking kidding me?" I spat.

Jackson gave me a one-shoulder shrug. "I wish I was." He pushed aside more snow. "Zane is impatient. If I do something really slow, sometimes he lets me use a tool or something to speed it up."

"Oh," I said and remembered Zane pushing me out of the way when I tried to hang up the Christmas lights.

"And sometimes that just pisses him off and he punches me. I never really know." He let out a deep breath. "But today I'm guessing Nate will want the driveway cleared. So go slow. Don't strain yourself."

I nodded. "Okay." I took Jackson's advice to heart, mostly because I wasn't in shape enough to shovel the entire driveway without passing out. His words turned out to be true. About an hour later, Nate threw the snow blower's key into the snow. It took us nearly another hour to find them.

"Stay in here," Jackson told me when we went into the garage. "It's not warm but at least you're out of the wind."

I looked down the long driveway, which was in the shape of an 'L'. "It will still take you forever. I'll do the short part of the driveway by hand," I told him.

"I can do it," he told me.

"Really," I pressed. "Let me help." He still had to be hurting from the beating he took, especially if his bones had broken like I suspected.

"Okay," he said with a nod and fired up the snow blower. No sooner had he finished, a car turned down the driveway. Jackson exited the garage to direct whoever it was to the front door. I followed him. As soon as the car came into view, I froze.

"What's wrong?" Jackson asked me.

I shook my head. "I know that car."

Jackson gave it a second look. "Yeah, that's Travis—" he cut off. "Oh." Without another word, Jackson stepped in front of me, shielding me from Travis' line of sight. I moved closed to Jackson and cast my eyes to the ground. I didn't want to risk Travis seeing my face. Travis gave Jackson a small nod and continued on to the front porch.

"I bet you'd like to hit *him* with a car," Jackson said quietly, turning to me.

"You have no idea," I replied, looking up into his eyes. It was weird, feeling safe next to Jackson. Not that long ago I feared him. Now his presence brought me a little comfort. He had definitely proved that he cared about me by taking the fall. It wasn't that I wanted him to do it again, not at all. It was more like I felt like I had an ally.

Jackson turned around and studied my face. "We should probably shovel the sidewalk again," he said with a small grin. "Ya know, since it's been snowing this whole time."

"Yes," I said seriously and felt another ball of anxiety unwind. "I think that's a good idea. We should be thorough."

Jackson's grin turned into an actual smile. His eyes brightened, and for the first time, he looked like he wasn't wishing death on himself or someone else. I picked up my foot to take a step when the garage door opened.

"What the fuck is taking so long?" Zane barked.

"Snow's still falling," Jackson stated. "We need to re-shovel."

"You do it," Zane said. "Adeline has to work. Travis is waiting."

CHAPTER 22

"What?" I blurted.

"You're working. Get in the house," he said.

I felt like someone ripped out my heart and threw it into the snow. My body was too cold, too numb to move. I stood there shaking my head. "N-no," I stuttered.

"No?" Zane asked and raised an eyebrow. He laughed and sneered at me. "Get in the goddam house."

"Why?" Jackson asked. Zane actually looked surprised.

"What's it to you?" he retorted.

"He's Rochelle's client." Jackson took a step to the side, moving closer to me. I wanted grab his arm and hide behind him.

"Rochelle is busy," Zane snapped. "Adeline, get your ass in here before I come get you."

I knew my legs moved, but I had little feeling in my body. The floating feeling took over, the one I had become all too familiar with the last few months. I didn't want to be in my own skin anymore. I wanted to be anyone else, to be anywhere else but here.

I entered the house through a mudroom. I took off the oversized boots and unzipped my coat. Zane yelled at me again to hurry up and go upstairs. I let the coat fall to the floor and walked through the house.

Travis was waiting for me in the guest room. He had already started to remove his clothes. My brain checked out, and I went to the bed. I imagined I was somewhere else, somewhere not in my body, but no matter how hard I thought of warm sandy beaches or even my overcrowded English 101 class with Professor Fitz, who was always dripping with sweat and never wore deodorant, I couldn't block out the pain.

Travis pushed me down onto the mattress. I closed my eyes and took a breath, bracing myself for the initial overwhelming pain. I balled my fists and whimpered when he forced himself into me. I turned my head, not wanting to look the monster in the eyes.

Travis grabbed my chin and roughly forced my face straight. "Look at me," he said. I closed my eyes. "Look at me!" he said again and shook my head.

"I'd rather die," I said through clenched teeth.

Travis thrust into me as hard as he could, as if he was stabbing me. He was doing it on purpose, wanting to hurt me. "Look at me!" he said for the third time. His fingers dug into my face. I opened my eyes one at a time. "Now tell me how good this feels."

My brow furrowed as I tried not to cry. "So good," I whispered.

"Yeah, oh yeah," he groaned and started to thrust faster. He held my gaze as he finished. Panting, he collapsed onto me, making it hard for me to breathe. He lay there for a minute before he pushed himself off of me. I didn't move until he was dressed and out of the room. I sat up, swallowing the lump of sour vomit threatening to come up. Shakily, I got off the bed and redressed.

I used to like it rough. I wondered if I'd like it again. Not even rough sex … just sex in general. Would I even be able to have sex, enjoyable sex with someone I loved, again? Then again, who would want to be in a relationship with me even if I did get out?

I placed both hands on the dresser and bent over, taking a deep breath. I hated Zane. Hated him with everything inside of me. I had never been a violent person, but the thought of hitting Zane's head against a wall until blood oozed out brought me more joy than I was willing to admit.

I pushed off the dresser and stiffly walked downstairs. Zane was sitting on the couch, watching me come down the stairs. He tilted his head down and seductively bit his lip. His incredible good looks only made him all the more dangerous. I glowered at him and fought the urge to pick up the little glass statue of a bird that sat on the coffee table and hit him in the face with it. Jackson had said that Zane almost always had a gun on him. I didn't feel like getting shot today.

I hurried through the living room. I didn't want to go back into the dark hole that had become my home, but I didn't want to be anywhere near Zane.

Lily and Phoebe stood in front of the large mirror getting ready for tonight's work. Lily was chatting away, talking about working at the club over the weekend. She was excited and animated and seemed to be looking forward to it. I tried to give her the benefit of the doubt since I would rather strip and give lap dances with happy endings than go to the truck stops, but I knew deep down she was becoming exactly what Jackson was talking about: so broken she forgot she was a victim.

The girls left early that evening. I took a fast, icy shower and buried myself under blankets, trying to get warm. I was just beginning to drift to sleep when I thought I heard the basement door slowly creak open. I sat up, pulled the covers down from over my face, and blinked in the light. When I heard nothing, I lay back down and buried myself under the blankets again.

"Adeline?"

I shot up, heart racing.

"Sorry," Jackson said and took a step back.

"It's okay," I breathed, my eyes locking with his. I instantly felt a little safer. "I didn't hear you coming. I always hear you coming."

"I'm not supposed to be down here," he told me. "I … I wanted to see you."

I ran my hands over my damp hair. "Oh." It took me off guard, though at the same time a warm flutter ran through me. I like that feeling … I missed that feeling. I looked up at Jackson and noticed a new bruise overlapping one that was just starting to fade. I stood, keeping the blanket around my shoulders and gently touched his cheek. "What happened?"

Jackson put his hand over mine. The flutter turned into butterflies in my stomach at the feeling of his skin against mine. He looked away. "Zane hit me again."

"Why?"

"He saw me talking to you."

My eyebrows pushed together. "You can't talk to me?"

He frowned. "He said I wasted time by talking. Plus, I'm not supposed to do anything I enjoy while I'm working. Or ever," he added ruefully. "Not when he's around at least."

"You enjoy talking to me?" I couldn't help but smile when I asked.

His cheeks grew red. "Yeah, I do." The floor creaked above us. Jackson's dark brown eyes flicked to the stairs. "It's freezing down here."

I nodded. "It's awful." I pulled the blanket tighter around my shoulders. "I knew old houses were drafty, but this is just awful."

The floorboards creaked again. "I'll be back," he said and hurried up the stairs. I retreated to the lumpy mattress on my cot and hoped Jackson didn't get caught coming down to see me. I missed his company already. I tried to convince myself it was pointless to get to know him. Zane would make sure Jackson and I didn't have the chance to become friends.

Just a few minutes later, the door opened again.

Jackson emerged from the stairwell holding a ceramic mug. Steam billowed from it and the wonderful smell of hot chocolate filled the basement.

"Oh my God," I said when he extended the cup to me. "Oh my God," I repeated and inhaled the aroma. "Jackson …" I didn't know just what to say. I wrapped my cold hands around the mug. It was uncomfortably hot, and I knew I should set it down before I burned myself. I used a corner of one of the thin blankets to absorb the heat. "Thank you," I told him and looked him in the eye, noticing for the first time that a circle of dark brown outlined his pupils. "You shouldn't have, though. I don't want to see you get hurt. Again."

He shrugged. "No one will know as long as I take the mug upstairs before anyone sees it. Do you even like hot chocolate?" he asked shyly.

I nodded and blew on the beverage before taking a small sip. "Love it."

"Good," he said and smiled. "It's nothing special, just a mix."

"There's a way to make hot chocolate *not* from a mix?" I asked and took another sip. Jackson half smiled and nodded. "I didn't know that," I admitted. "Though I suppose years ago the little one-cup sized mixes didn't exist."

"Yeah," he agreed with another small smile. "I suppose."

I put the mug to my lips and sipped the hot liquid. I could feel Jackson watching me. I knew his shyness was genuine, so I pretended like I didn't notice him staring. There was more to Jackson than was visible on the surface, and I wanted to find out about it.

"It stopped snowing," he told me. "And it's supposed to be warmer tomorrow. The snow will probably melt by the weekend."

"Typical Iowa winter," I mumbled. "I hope it snows again soon so we can shovel. Not that it was the most fun thing to do, but being outside is better than this," I admitted. "I hate being locked down here."

"I hated it too," Jackson said, surprising me.

"You were locked down here?" I asked, the shock apparent in my voice. Jackson nodded and cast his eyes down. I got the feeling he didn't want to talk about it. "For how long?" I asked gently.

Jackson shuffled his feet and shrugged. "I don't really know."

I cupped my hands around the mug and brought it to my face, letting the steam warm me. I looked at the cot and then at Jackson. "Want to sit?"

"Yes," he said quietly. His body was stiff and he kept his arms close to himself. It seemed like he was afraid to be close to me. "Is this okay?" he asked and turned his head.

"Yes," I told him and realized that he was worried about me being afraid of him. I wasn't, not anymore. Being around Jackson was becoming more familiar and comforting. "So, are you from Iowa?" I asked.

He shook his head. "No. Illinois. You are, right?"

"Yeah. I was born in Pella and lived there for ten years. My parents always wanted to open an art gallery, so we moved closer to Des Moines for business when they finally had the money."

"And you were going to school?"

I nodded. "University of Iowa."

"Did you like it?"

My heart sank, and I felt like someone slapped me when I realized that a new semester had recently started. I wondered what classes Lynn was taking and who she had roomed with this year. "Yeah, I loved college," I told him.

The front door slammed shut, shaking the house. Jackson jumped up. "Zane's back," he told me. "I was supposed to get your laundry." He took the empty mug from me, hurried over to the overflowing hamper, and picked it up. "Night, Adeline," he said as he sped toward the stairs.

"Addie," I told him. "Call me Addie."

He looked back and gave me a small smile. "Okay. Night, Addie."

"Night, Jackson."

CHAPTER 23

Jackson was right. Three days later, the temperature went up to the mid-forties, and the snow melted. I was standing on a chair looking out the tiny window. Sunlight gleamed off the puddles. The grass was brown and matted down, making the day look bleak, despite the sun.

I had been alone all day. Lily was at the club with Rochelle, and Phoebe had been bought for an overnight bachelor party. I wished I could tell the bride-to-be she was marrying a disgusting piece of shit. I jumped off the chair.

"Maybe he doesn't know," I said out loud to myself. Maybe the groom's friends paid for Phoebe and it was all a surprise. Then I wondered if they even knew Phoebe was doing it against her will. Maybe they gave her the money and thought she went home to spend it on her shoe collection. They wouldn't assume the money would be ripped out of her hands and she would get shoved back down here.

"It doesn't make it right," I muttered and shook my head. I began pacing around the basement, doing laps around the card table. I paused at the base of the stairs to bend over and touch my toes. I had never been flexible. The stretching hurt when my fingertips brushed the tops of my feet.

The kitchen floor creaked. I quickly straightened myself and dashed behind the stairs, holding my breath. I heard the locks slip back and the knob turn. The first step creaked under someone's weight.

"Addie?" Jackson called. I felt instant relief and something else—that same warm flutter—at the sound of his voice. He clomped down the stairs. I went around and waited. Jackson stopped, standing a few feet in front of me. His eyes met mine, and he held my gaze for a couple seconds before he blinked and shook his head. "We have yard work to do."

"Yard work?" I echoed. "It's still winter."

He frowned and shrugged. "I know. I think that's the point; we'll have to do it over again."

"What are we doing?"

"I don't know. Nate just told me to get you."

I crossed the basement and grabbed a coat. "At least it gets me out of here," I mumbled. Jackson led the way up stairs, through the kitchen, and into the mudroom. I put on the oversized boots and followed Jackson into the garage. Nate stood in the driveway, looking as if he had just stepped off the set of an Armani photo shoot. His hair was exceptionally shiny in the sunlight, and his clothes were so well fitted, they had to be custom tailored. He waited for us to walk over.

"These bushes," he said and waved at the front of the house. "They have to go."

Jackson took a step forward, inspecting the row of boxwood bushes. "I just put those in this spring," he blurted.

"I don't care," Nate said calmly. "Get rid of them. I want something with flowers instead."

"It's too early to plant anything," I pointed out.

Nate turned to face me. "Do you think I'm stupid?" he asked, his intense eyes drilling into mine. I shook my head. "Good. I *know* it's too early. That doesn't matter." His eyes darted back to the bushes. "Get rid of the bushes. Level the ground. Take everything out back and burn it." His cold eyes flicked to my face. "Prove to me you're worth keeping." I stiffened and looked straight into his eyes. He turned his attention to Jackson. "I want it done by sunset."

Jackson's almond eyes widened, but he didn't say anything. I knew what he was thinking; there was no way we could get all of that done in just a few hours. "Yes, sir," he said. Nate extracted his phone from his pocket and briskly walked away. I trailed behind Jackson as he went into the shed to get tools.

I ran my hands over the smooth wooden handle of a shovel and looked at the house.

"You have a weird look in your eye," Jackson said to me. "What are you thinking?"

"I'm thinking about how nice it would be to beat Nate to death with a shovel. We could take him out and bury him in the backyard." I glanced at Jackson. "No, we should leave him in the house so when Zane comes back and sees the bloody and mangled body, he'll be shocked, and we can get him too."

Jackson seemed taken aback by my violence, but then he smiled. "Sounds good to me," he said and closed the shed, shovel and rake in hand.

"Seriously," I stated and turned around. The oversized boots clomped through the damp lawn. "Let's do it."

"Addie, we can't," he said.

"Why not?

"A bullet is faster than swinging a shovel."

"Oh," I said, feeling dejected. "Damn." We walked around to the front of the house.

"If I ever figure out the combination to get into his room at night, I'll slit his throat in his sleep," Jackson said very seriously.

"He has a combination lock on his bedroom door?" I asked.

Jackson nodded. "Zane too. Just like the ones on the exterior doors but with different codes."

"Do you know the combinations?"

Jackson nodded and stepped up to the bushes. He thrust the shovel into the ground. A thin layer of mud squished away. What was underneath it was frozen, and only the tip of the spade went in. He picked it up and shoved it down again, barely making a mark on the cold dirt. "Just the ones for the exterior doors. One-three-four-two," he told me. "For now."

"What do you mean 'for now?'" I moved in front of the bush next to Jackson.

"Nate randomly changes them. He's really paranoid." He chipped away at the ground. "I don't always know them, either, and if you get the combination wrong, an alarm goes off."

"Oh," I said and lifted the shovel a foot from the ground only to jam in into the solid dirt. We worked in silence for a few minutes, slowly chipping away at the frozen ground. My hands hurt from gripping the handle of the shovel, and my shoulders were sore already. I had barely made a dent when I checked out Jackson's progress, and was impressed to see he was much further along in digging up the bush than I was.

"What's your favorite book?" Jackson asked when he saw me looking.

"Oh gosh," I started. "I have like fifty books in my 'Top Ten Favorites' list." I shook my head. "That's a really hard question. I love so many. I will admit I'm biased toward paranormal or fantasy. There's just something about the worlds those books take place in. I used to say I'd give anything to live in a magical land but now …" I sighed. "People usually thought I was weird when I said that."

"I don't think it's weird," Jackson quickly agreed. "I'd give anything to be anywhere else."

I nodded and deeply inhaled the chilly air looking longingly at the street. I held my hand up to my forehead, shielding the bright sun from my eyes. Something moved by the mailbox. I squinted my eyes for a better look.

"Hey!" I said and dropped the shovel. "There's a dog!" Without a second thought I walked away from the house.

"Addie, no, Nate could see you!" Jackson said. I didn't heed his warning. "Addie!" he repeated. I heard a soft thud as his shovel hit the ground. "Adeline!" he called.

The dog saw me and froze. I knelt down and extended my hand. "Hey puppy," I said quietly. The dog tucked its tail between its back legs and sniffed. "It's okay, sweetie. I won't hurt you." It took a few steps forward.

"That's a Pitbull. Be careful it could bite you!" Jackson stated.

"Don't breed-stereotype," I said automatically. I made a kissing noise and wiggled my fingers. The dog slowly walked to me. "Hello beautiful," I said to the dog. It was brown and black brindle and very skinny. "You're a girl," I observed as she pressed her nose into my hand. "Are you lost?" Her tail began to wag.

"She seems friendly," Jackson said and knelt down next to me.

The dog cowered back. Jackson very slowly held out his

hand. After nervously eyeing him for a few seconds, the dog sniffed him. She turned her attention back to me, wagging her tail again. She moved closer, trying to lick my face.

"She likes you," Jackson said.

I smiled and gently put a hand on her back. Her tail wagged even more. "I think she used to be somebody's. She likes people." I opened my arms causing the dog's excitement to grow even more. Her whole body wiggled with delight. "Are you a lonely girl? Poor little thing, all alone," I said in a high-pitched voice. "You don't have to be lonely anymore. I'll take care of you."

Jackson rocked back on his heels but didn't say anything. We both knew there was no way I could take care of a dog, but for right now, I wanted to believe it. I could tell she had been on her own for a while, and I was sure as soon as we stood up and went back to the bushes, she would take off.

"I'll share my lunch with you," I told the dog and scratched her ears.

"We won't get food until we're done," Jackson said dryly. "Nate won't let us eat until this is finished."

I suddenly felt very hungry. I looked at Jackson, and he gave me that pitying stare and frowned. With a heavy sigh I stood. Jackson's knees cracked when he brought himself to his feet. We turned and walked together back to the house.

And the dog followed.

"Hey pretty lady," I cooed with a smile. "Are you gonna help us dig up the bushes? You can probably dig better than I can." I picked up the shovel and started stabbing at the ground. The dog pawed at my leg. I set the shovel down and turned. "You just want attention, huh?" I stepped over a row of dead hostas and sat on the cold, damp cobblestone. The dog left muddy paw prints on my pants as she climbed into my lap.

"You're a little big to be a lap dog," I laughed and hugged her. Jackson leaned on his shovel and watched. A tiny smile was present on his face. "You need a name, baby," I told the dog. She turned around for a back scratch. "How about Rosie? You look like a Rosie to me?" She whipped around and licked my face. Laughing, I pushed her away.

"Rosie wandered up to the right person," Jackson said. I looked up and smiled at him. He smiled back, causing some of the sadness to disappear from his bruised face. I turned my attention back to Rosie, baby talking to her. Out of corner of my eye, I saw Jackson start digging again.

"I'll help you in a minute," I promised.

"Don't worry about it," he said and chipped a chunk of frozen dirt up. "Play with Rosie while you can." He turned to the side and gave me another smile. I nodded and leaned forward, picking up a stick. I wiggled it in the air, watching Rosie's reaction before I threw it. She chased after it, caught it, chewed it, but didn't bring it back.

"Silly girl," I said when she trotted to me. I petted her again and jogged away to get the stick. I played with her for a few more minutes before going back to the bushes to help Jackson. Giving up on the tiny hole I had started, I moved next to Jackson and helped him work on the same bush.

Rosie stayed by our sides, rolling in the mud and chewing on her stick while we worked. The sun was beginning to sink by the time we got the first bush close to coming out of the ground. Jackson pulled it while I chopped the bottom with my shovel until the roots snapped and broke off.

"Well, it's not really out," he said and looked at the tangled mess of roots that remained. "The ground shouldn't be frozen that far down," he told me. "So it won't be as hard. I'll start the next one, and you can get the roots out."

"Okay," I said and leaned over to give Rosie another pet. We worked in silence, both of us taking breaks to play with and pet Rosie. The temperature continued to drop as the sun sank lower and lower in the sky. I was digging up the roots on bush number two when the front door opened.

Nate stepped onto the porch. He opened his mouth to bark an order at us but stopped when he saw Rosie.

"Where the hell did that thing come from?" he asked, his nostrils flaring with disgust.

"She just wandered here," Jackson stated his voice breathy from the constant digging.

"Make it go away."

Jackson threw his arms at Rosie. "Shoo," he said. Rosie stood and wagged her tail. Nate narrowed his eyes. Rosie dropped down on her front legs, her butt in the air, and yipped at Jackson, wanting to play. "Shhh," Jackson said, his eyes wide. "Rosie, be quiet!" he whispered. She barked again and ran through the dead flower garden.

"I don't want that thing hanging around," Nate stated. He stepped off the porch, reached inside his jacket, and pulled out a shiny metal handgun.

"No!" I shouted right away. "Don't shoot her!"

Nate leaned back and laughed. "I wasn't going to," he said and held the gun in the air, showing me that he was just going to shoot straight up to scare her away. "But now I have a better idea. Jackson," he said and pressed something on the gun. The clip slid out and he started removing bullets until just one remained. "Shoot the dog."

"What?" I blurted, my heart dropping into a bucket of ice. "No. She's innocent. Sh-she didn't do anything!"

"She'll leave on her own. Stray dogs don't stay in one place," he tried. His chest rose and fell rapidly. "She won't stay."

"That's beside the point," Nate said smugly. He walked down the cobblestone path. Rosie ran over, excited to greet a new person. He kicked her.

"Stop!" I cried at the same time Rosie yelped. She looked at Nate, trying to figure out what she had done to upset him. "Stop it! She's just an animal!" The shovel slipped from my hands, and I rushed over to Rosie, protectively wrapping my arms around her.

Nate grabbed a handful of my hair and pulled. Jackson raised his shovel. His body tensed and he jerked forward. Nate raised the gun, pointing it at Jackson.

"Drop the shovel, Jackson," Nate said so calmly his tone edged on boredom.

Jackson's eyes flew from the gun to me. Nate tightened his grip on my hair. I gritted my teeth against the pain. Looking defeated, Jackson let the shovel fall from his hands.

"Move over there," Nate said and used the gun to point to the path. Jackson stepped over the bushes and stopped on the cobblestone. "Get up, Adeline," he ordered.

I pushed myself up. Nate pressed the gun to the back of my neck. Terror paralyzed me. I looked at Jackson and felt tears well in my eyes. My breath clouded the air as I shakily exhaled. Nate reached inside his jacket and pulled something out. I heard a metallic click and. He stepped closer and removed the gun, only to place a cold metal blade against my neck.

"Jackson, shoot the dog." He extended his other hand, holding the gun by the barrel. "You so much as point the gun at me, I'll slit her throat."

My body shook. I was scared to breathe, afraid the slightest movement could cause the knife the cut open my skin. It would take less than a minute to die.

"Jackson!" Nate bellowed, causing me to jump. The sharp blade bit into my neck. Stiffly, Jackson walked over. He took the gun from Nate. "Her blood will be on your hands," Nate reminded him. "Shoot the dog and throw the body in the woods."

Jackson nodded, his mouth opening in horror. He blinked and turned to Rosie.

"Come here, girl," he said softly.

Hot tears slid down my cheeks. A knot formed in my chest, painfully squeezing my heart. How could Nate do this? Not only to Rosie but also to us. Rosie jumped at Jackson. She was so innocent. She did nothing wrong.

A tremble ran down my spine. I clenched my jaw, terrified of moving and having the cold sharp metal cut into my skin. Jackson took a step away from us. Rosie followed, tail wagging as if she was playing a game. All she had done was give me a few minutes of happiness, and now she was going to die.

Jackson's eyes met mine, pleading. I held his gaze, his face blurry through my tears. I wanted him to know it wasn't his fault, that I wouldn't blame him for what was going to happen. He turned his head down, his brow pushed together. He didn't want to do it. He didn't want to take away the one thing that had made me happy.

But he didn't want me to die, to watch the blood spray from my neck and my lifeless body crumble onto the cold hard ground. He swallowed, jaw quivering. He turned and cocked the gun. I closed my eyes, imagining where Jackson was, and began counting.

One, two, three …

CHAPTER 24

I knew it was coming, but my body flinched at the sound of the gunshot. My tense body pressed backward into Nate. Rosie's final yelp resonated, breaking my heart. Nate twisted the blade so the flat end was against my skin. He pressed it into my throat before slowly dragged it away. He suddenly released me, shoving me forward. I fell, my knees hitting the hard stone path.

Jackson stood frozen with horror, the smoking gun still raised in his hands. His body swayed, and I could hear his rapid breathing as he stared at Rosie's body. His arms faltered, and his hands dropped to his sides. Nate strode past, pushing me over. I fell onto my side.

I planted my hand against the ground and started to push myself up. The breath caught in my chest, and it hurt to breathe. Rosie was dead. Nate forced Jackson to murder a harmless animal. I looked up and Jackson. He was so dejected, so ashamed of himself. He still hadn't moved from where he had been standing. He turned, his mouth was slightly open in shock, and his brown eyes were misty.

Nate laughed, flipping the switchblade opened and closed. He walked over to Jackson and took the gun from his hands.

"Get back to work," he snarled.

Jackson blinked and snapped his hand back, recoiling from Nate's touch. Suddenly Jackson's demeanor went from despondent to angry. Very angry. Nate's smug face went blank. His eyes widened when Jackson pushed past him.

"Jackson!" Nate snapped. But Jackson didn't listen. He rushed to me, dropping to his knees. With tears in my eyes I turned my head up to him.

"Addie," he whispered, his voice trembling. "I'm sorry. I'm so sorry."

I opened my mouth to tell him it wasn't his fault, but my words twisted into a sob, and I pitched forward. Jackson put his hand on my arm, gently pushing me upright. Without even thinking about it, I threw my arms around him. His body stiffened, and he put his arms out by his sides, unsure of what to do. Cautiously, he bent his elbows and placed his palms on my back.

I buried my head into his shoulder, crying. He tightened his embrace. His arms around me were so comforting, so reassuring, so *needed*.

"I told you to get back to work!" Nate growled and stormed over. He grabbed a tangle of Jackson's hair and yanked. Not balanced, Jackson tumbled back off of his knees. I went with him and awkwardly landed on top of him. Nate reached down and grabbed my shoulders. He shoved me back.

It took a great amount of energy to pull myself to my feet. I turned and faced Nate. "You're a monster," I said through clenched teeth. As if he didn't even hear me, Nate walked back to the porch. He put his hand on the keypad, punched in the combination, and walked into the house.

"I'm really sorry, Addie," Jackson said again as he stood, unable to meet my eyes.

I wiped tears from my face. "It's not your fault," I sniffled. "Don't apologize." I shot a look at the house. I picked dry leaves from my hair and blotted my nose with the sleeve of the jacket. I took in a shaky breath. The cold air rushed through me, stinging my broken heart. I couldn't bring myself to look at the spot where Rosie lay.

Jackson took off his jacket and covered the dog. Then he picked up his shovel and walked to the side of the porch.

"What are you doing?" I asked.

"I'm going to bury her."

I nodded, blinking away the tears that were still coming, and picked up my shovel. Together, we silently dug a hole just deep enough to hold Rosie's body. I turned away when Jackson scooped her up.

"I'll finish it, Addie," he said gently. I didn't want to make him do all the work, but I couldn't turn around.

"It's done," he said when he had piled the dirt back into the hole. I turned around. Pain stabbed me when I looked at the fresh grave.

"Thank you," I said through chattering teeth.

"Are you cold?" he asked.

"I think so." I was sure I had to be cold. I was just too numb to be able to tell anything at that moment. "You have to be too." His coat was still on the ground.

"Digging warmed me up."

I nodded. "Should we finish?" I waved my hand at the bushes.

"Yeah. You don't have to. I'll do it."

No, I told myself and picked up the shovel. I rammed it into the hard ground, pretending it was Nate's abdomen. I wasn't going to give up and fall apart. I was going to escape and turn Nate in. I had to. I needed to.

Jackson let his shovel fall and bent over. He grabbed the bush and pulled. I snapped out of my dark reverie and moved over. Channeling my rage, I hacked at the roots, and the bush broke free. Jackson stumbled back, not expecting it to come loose so easily. He tossed the bush aside and picked up his shovel again.

The front door opened again. Nate stepped out. He was wearing a different outfit and looked just as well put together as before in a pristinely pressed black and gray suit with a satin blue tie. "Inside," he ordered and slammed the door shut.

Jackson took the shovel from me. I followed him around the house and into the shed, not speaking. I stepped aside and watched him lock the shed doors, then walked close to his side as we went back around the house.

We went into the garage and stomped the mud off of our boots. Jackson turned to me. Our eyes met, and suddenly I wanted him to wrap his arms around me in another comforting embrace. My heart sped up. He opened his mouth to say something else when a car pulled into the driveway, the bright lights illuminating the interior of the garage.

"Zane," he mumbled and punched in the code. He opened the door and held out his arm, signaling me to enter first. I hurried into the house, removing the gloves and jacket. Jackson followed me to the basement door.

"I'll bring food down later," he told me.

I nodded and looked into his eyes. I didn't want to go downstairs. I didn't want to be away from Jackson. The garage door slammed shut, reminding me that Zane was back. I didn't want to see him, either.

I walked down the stairs and collapsed onto my cot. I cried for a while before rolling over, thinking about the comfort Jackson's embrace had brought. I held onto the memory, remembering the warmth of his arms. I began to feel sleepy when the basement door opened. I sat up, expecting Jackson.

Instead, I saw one of the last things I expected: Rochelle coming down the stairs with three full shopping bags in each hand. The sound of female voices echoed down the stairs.

"I'll be right up!" Rochelle shouted over her shoulder. She bustled past me and threw the bags onto the card table.

"Who is that?" I asked, my eyes lingering on the stairwell.

"Friends," she said casually.

"You have friends?" I blurted.

She raised her eyebrows. "Of course I have friends," she snapped.

I pressed my lips together and nodded. Rochelle rubbed the red marks the heavy shopping bags had left on her arms and hurried back up the stairs. The basement door clicked shut. I waited for the locks to slide into place. When they didn't, I got up and crept up the stairs. I put my hand on the doorknob and twisted.

It was locked, but the deadbolts weren't. Had Rochelle forgotten, or did she not want her 'friends' seeing her lock the door? I shook my head and went back down the stairs. I moved to the card table and investigated the shopping bags. I picked up a white bag with black handles, recognizing the logo right away. Two expensive sweaters were neatly folded on top of a pair of jeans that cost as much as the two sweaters combined. I peered inside a brown bag next, which was full of t-shirts and tank tops.

STAY

A small, black bag had pretty multicolored gemstone necklaces wrapped in white and gold tissue paper, and the other three bags housed shoes.

I opened a pink shoebox and held up a neon green stiletto. I was about to drop it back into the box when I noticed it was a size five. None of us, not even petite Phoebe, wore shoes that small. I turned and looked at the stairs. Was this stuff bought for the girls Rochelle called her friends?

"Why?" I asked aloud. I set the shoes down and went back to my cot. I wrapped my arms around myself and wished Phoebe was here. I pulled the quilt around my shoulders and lay down. I drifted into a light sleep. I dreamed that Jackson took me around the farmhouse to the shed, saying he had a surprise for me. When he opened the shed doors, I was looking at my house.

"Addie," he said in the dream. I turned to look at him. "Addie," he repeated.

I startled awake and heard my name again, that time for real.

"Sorry," Jackson said and looked down. "Did I wake you?"

"Yeah," I said, seeing no sense in lying.

"Oh, sorry," he mumbled. "I hope you weren't having a good dream."

"Of course not," I said, lying that time. I knew Jackson would feel bad if I told him the truth. I sat up and ran my hands over my messy hair, pushing it out of my face. "Who are those girls upstairs?"

Jackson frowned. "Zane's newest recruits."

"Recruits?" I asked.

Jackson nodded and sat on the cot next to mine. "Every once in a while he goes out, usually to the mall, and sweet talks a few girls into working for him."

I shook my head. "Why would anyone fall for that?"

Jackson looked down. "Zane has a way with people. He's good at getting inside your head, making you feel special. He's so manipulative it's almost ... almost animalistic. In the end, you *want* to do things for him."

"I'm sorry, but I don't care how sweet someone is to me. I would never agree to have sex for money that I can't even keep!"

"It doesn't work like that, Addie," he explained. "Zane picks out girls who already have issues, family, self esteem ... that kind of thing. He builds them up and makes sure they depend on him. Then he'll start asking for favors, but they're small at first. He makes these girls think that he loves them ... " Jackson trailed off, shaking his head. "And a lot of them are young. They believe what he tells them. And they keep the money at first. He buys them stuff." He sighed, looking at the card table. "Plus, if you haven't noticed, Zane exceeds the definition of 'attractive.' You girls eat that shit up."

I gently kicked his foot. "Don't group me with 'those girls,'" I told him with a small smile.

"Sorry," he said, his eyes smiling back at me. "But you know what I mean."

"I do," I said and shook my head. I thought of Arianna and how impressionable she was. I didn't want to admit it, but I knew she could easily be lured to a party with alcohol, and even drugs. I hoped she was smart enough to see the red flag in Zane's 'favors.' I knew many females, not just young teenagers, were willing to turn a blind eye for a guy that showed them even minimal affection.

"What's going to happen to them?" I asked.

Jackson shook his head. "I don't really know. Not yet, at least. A lot of them end up running away from home. Zane takes them in and ..." he trailed off. "You know the rest."

I shivered and turned to the milk carton next to the cot. Jackson had placed my plate of food on it. I leaned over and picked up the peanut butter sandwich.

"What if I was allergic to peanuts?" I asked and then felt a little embarrassed at the dumb question.

"It happened before," he said, knowing exactly what I had meant. "Her name was Jackie. She didn't even eat it. Just being around peanuts made her throat swell up."

"What happened to her?"

"She went to the ER and got shots or something. I don't really know."

"Nate will let us go to the ER?" I asked.

Jackson tipped his head to the side. "Some girls. It depends on who, and they always use fake names."

"Oh," I said and felt a little sick. "So, Zane and Nate."

"What about them?"

"Nate seems to like Zane."

Jackson nodded. "Yeah, he does. I have no idea how that relationship started," he stated, answering my next question. "I always thought Nate liked Zane from the start because he had the looks to bring girls in. Now he has the personality too."

I moved my head up and down as I took another bite of the sandwich. Jackson yawned, and I noticed the dark circles under his eyes. They were covered up with a fading bruise. "What exactly do you do?"

"Work," he answered with no hesitation. "I clean, cook, do yard work, drop off and pick up girls, bartend at the club sometimes, work in the restaurant if someone calls off."

"And you never get paid?"

Jackson let out a snort of laughter. "Oh, sorry. You're serious?" he asked when he saw my face. "No. Never. That's not even an option." He sighed. "Basically, I do whatever Nate tells me to do."

"Like with Rosie," I said carefully, knowing that Nate forced Jackson to do things far more unpleasant than housework.

His eyes darted to the ground. "Yeah," he said quickly and changed the subject. "What kind of dogs do you have?"

"German shepherds," I answered, and thought of my two over-sized lap dogs.

"What are their names?"

"Scarlet and Rhett."

Jackson smiled. "You like *Gone with the Wind*?"

"Oh my god!" I exclaimed. "You're one of the very few people my own age who knows who Scarlet and Rhett are! I love that movie."

"I've never seen the movie," Jackson admitted. "Just read the book more than once."

"I haven't even read the book," I said and looked at Jackson with admiration. His eyes lit up. "Is it good?"

He nodded. "It's long."

"Do you like to read?" I asked and took another bite.

"I do. That's what I do whenever I'm not working."

"That's how I used to be. I always had a book with me."

He smiled at me. "I like the way books smell. Is that weird?"

"Not at all." I leaned forward. "I have like a million books on my e-reader that I really want to read, but I keep going for my hard copies first. I have a serious addiction to buying books. You should see my bookshelf. It's overflowing. Literally. Books won't even stay on it anymore."

"I would love that. You can never have too many books, right?"

"You are reading my mind."

The floor creaked above us, and the sound of laughter floated through the air vent. Jackson flicked his eyes to the ceiling. "I should go," he sighed but made no attempt at getting up. I looked into his eyes and wished he could stay with me.

"Where do you sleep?" I asked, the thought suddenly occurring to me.

"I have a room upstairs," he said. "I used to stay down here, but Zane thought some of the girls looked at me." He raised an eyebrow and shook his head as if he couldn't believe anyone would ever look at him the same way they looked at Zane. "There's not much—" he cut off and quickly turned his head to look at the stairs.

"What?" I asked, nerves prickling.

"Someone's in the kitchen."

I stood and waved my hands. "Go! Before you get in trouble!" I walked with him to the stairs. He turned, our eyes meeting again. He gave me one more small smile and jogged up the stairs.

CHAPTER 25

"Addie," Jackson's deep voice whispered, waking me up the next day. "Addie, wake up," he said again and set a basket full of clean laundry on the floor. "You're having another nightmare."

He came over to the cot and knelt down, putting his hand on my shoulder. I shot up, breathing heavy. Jackson jerked his hand back, but I caught it, lacing my fingers through his.

"Thanks," I panted and let go of his hand. I put my head in my hands and rubbed my eyes. I could hear Phoebe shuffling around near the shower. I sat up and blinked in the dim, late morning light. I noticed that Jackson looked absolutely ragged. "Are you okay?"

He slowly blinked, looking as if he was having a hard time keeping his eyes open. He nodded. "I'm really tired. Nate wouldn't let me sleep until those bushes were dug up."

"Oh," I said, not knowing what else to say. I slowly shook my head. "That's horrible!" I finally said. "Why didn't he make me go out and help you?"

Jackson shrugged. "He said he was punishing me for something I did. That, and I think he's afraid you'll try to run again. It's hard to find people in the dark."

"I will run again," I said with no hesitation. "The next chance I get." I bit my lip and looked at Jackson's tired face. I whipped around to face Phoebe. "We should leave. The three of us," I whispered. I turned back around and locked eyes with Jackson. "There's three of us and two of them. We can do it.

We can leave."

Jackson's jaw tightened, and he crossed his arms but something sparkled in his eyes, bringing his run-down face back to life.

"Addie," Phoebe said, her voice monotone. "There no way to leave. We all try, and we all get hurt. It better to stay."

My eyebrows furrowed. "No! I'm not for sale. You're not either. Phoebe, don't give up."

She gave me a feeble smile. "I no want to get hurt. Not anymore." The smile faded, and she shook her head. "We have no choice."

I stood up, my hands curling into fists. "Yes, we do! We always have a choice." I shook my head, causing my hair to fall into my eyes. "Okay, maybe we don't have a choice in what is done to us, but we can chose to not give up!"

Jackson took a deep breath and straightened his shoulders. Despite looking like he wanted to fall to the ground and sleep for twelve hours, he nodded. "I wish we could, Addie, but it's not that simple."

"All we need is a head start." I continued.

Jackson crossed his arms, deep in thought. "Maybe if we—"

"No!" Phoebe said suddenly. "It won't work. It never work! You try, I try, she try. We all caught!"

"If we have a plan," Jackson said, "it could potentially work."

The basement door slammed against the stairwell. We all jumped, wondering who opened the door so quickly. Rubber soles echoed as someone descended down the stairs. The door clicked shut behind him.

"What's going on?" Zane asked, his voice smooth and seductive.

Jackson tensed and picked up the laundry basket, taking a few steps toward the dresser. I hoped Zane would think Jackson was only down here to do laundry.

"Nothing," he mumbled.

"Really?" Zane questioned. He stopped at the bottom of the stairs. He was holding a white plastic bag. I recognized the logo to be that of a pet store I used to frequent. Scarlet loved when I took her inside. "Because it sounds like you were talking to the girls." He stepped closed to Jackson. "Did I say you could talk to the girls?"

Jackson's cheeks flushed as he shook his head. I sensed that he didn't like me seeing him submit to Zane.

"Good. Put those clothes away." Zane then turned to face me. "If I'm not mistaken, I believe I heard this one talking about running away. Again."

I squeezed my hands shut, digging my fingernails into my palms so hard it hurt. "I will run away," I said through gritted teeth. "And turn you in."

Zane laughed, dismissing my threat as if it was nothing. "Sure you will."

He brushed past me and set the bag on the card table. He pulled out two plastic dog bowls, making a show of slowly placing them on the floor. He opened a can of dog food and plopped it in one of the bowls. Then he pulled out a metal choke-chain and a brown leather leash.

"You," he said to Phoebe. "Fill this up with water." He pointed to one of the bowls on the floor.

Phoebe tipped her head down and walked over. She leaned away from Zane, trying to stay as far away from him as possible, and picked up the bowl. She pulled back the shower curtain, ready to turn on the water when Zane stopped her.

"No," he said. "From the toilet."

Her dark eyes twitched but she did what she was told. Jackson took several small, tentative steps toward me. Phoebe carried the full and dripping bowl back to Zane. I wanted her to throw it in his face. She set it on the floor and wiped her hands on her pants.

"Adeline," Zane said, drawing out my name. He clipped the leash to the chain. "I hear you like dogs." He looped the chain through itself, making a self-tightening circle. He flicked eyes up at me. I used to think demons only existed on the pages of fantasy books, but in that moment, I knew they were real. I looked into Zane's sky-blue eyes and saw into his dark, empty soul. A twisted smile pulled his lips up.

He pulled the chain, opening the loop. Then he lunged forward and grabbed my arm. His fingers dug into a sensitive spot behind my shoulder, and pain rippled through me, rendering my body useless. I felt my knees begin to buckle, and he pressed harder on the pressure point. He slipped the cold metal collar around my neck and pulled. I coughed, gasping for air. Using his foot, Zane shoved me forward and onto all fours.

"Good dog," he spat and yanked the leash. My hands flew to my neck and I tried to slip my fingers under the collar. Zane let the leash go slack and I could breath again. "Get a drink, dog," he said and used the toe of his shoe to strike me on the tailbone.

"Stop it!" Jackson said, rage taking over his broken demeanor. "Let her go!"

"Or what?" Zane laughed. He picked up his foot again, ready to kick me.

Then Jackson lunged at him. Zane fell back. The leash was still wrapped around his hand. The chain tightened, and I was yanked back.

"Get the hell off me!" Zane yelled.

I twisted around, trying to scramble closer to Zane so I could breathe. I couldn't see what was going on, but I heard the distinct sound of someone getting punched in the face. I could only hope it was Jackson doing the punching.

Zane moved his arm up, blocking Jackson's blows. As his arm raised, the chain tightened around my neck. My eyes bulged and I heaved forward. I couldn't breathe. It wouldn't take long before I would pass out. And then die.

I tried to stick my fingers behind the chain, but I only scraped away a layer of skin. The chain was too tight. Black dots speckled my vision. I needed air, I needed to breathe. I planted my feet and pushed myself toward Zane where I could see Jackson on top of him. Jackson raised his fist and brought it down, hitting Zane in the mouth. He grabbed the neck of Zane's shirt and lifted him up before shoving his head down against the ground. He scrambled up and kicked Zane hard in the ribs before scurrying to my side.

"Fuck," he breathed and shook his head. He grabbed the leash and yanked, making Zane slide forward. As soon as it was loose, Jackson unclipped it and pulled the collar over my head. I put my shaky hands against his chest and looked into his eyes. Jackson placed his hands on my arms and nodded, understanding my unspoken question. He stood and pulled me to my feet.

"Phoebe," I panted and looked behind me. "Come with us!"

With his hand still wrapped around mine, we ran up the stairs. My heart was pounding when I reached the door. The knob slipped from my grasp as I madly turned it. When I finally got my trembling under control, I threw the door open.

"What the hell is going on?" Nate demanded, standing in our way. The air slipped out of my lungs and I suddenly felt dizzy. My head swam as my choices buzzed through my brain. In a split second, I decided to push past Nate and run.

But he was faster.

His hands found my chest, and he shoved me backward. I tumbled into Jackson, who tried to catch me. Everything felt like it was happening in slow motion: Nate's startled expression, helplessly crashing into Jackson's body, the feeling of my feet leaving the wooden stairs. Then we were falling, and I felt each and every step on the way down.

Jackson protectively wrapped his arms around me, keeping me from whacking my head on the cement floor. He suddenly pushed me away and rolled on top of me, shielding me from one of Zane's blows.

"He attacked me!" Zane screamed. I heard Nate rush down the stairs. "He fucking attacked me!" Jackson hugged me tighter as Zane kicked him. I could feel the force of Zane's violence as Jackson flinched in pain.

"What?" Nate asked, his voice shrill. "Jackson doesn't fight back. He never has!"

Zane kicked Jackson again. "I'll make sure he doesn't do it again," he said through clenched teeth.

"Get him up," Nate said. The beating stopped. Nate and Zane grabbed onto Jackson's arms and tried to lift him up. Jackson released me from his protective embrace, but I clung on.

"It's okay, Addie," he panted.

"No!" I cried and pulled him toward me, refusing to let go of his hand. "No, stop!" Nate kicked me in the face, the ball of his foot smashing my nose. Horrible pain shot through me as the fragile bones cracked, and hot blood poured out.

"Jackson!" I called and pushed myself up off the floor.

Blood dripped down my throat. I reached for him.

"Don't give up," he said as Nate and Zane dragged him back. "Don't ever give up."

"I won't!" I promised. Zane hooked his arms under Jackson's and pulled him up the stairs. Jackson suddenly stopped struggling, making Zane stumble and almost lose his balance. Nate punched Jackson in the face. I rushed over, reaching for Jackson.

"Stop!" I screamed. Nate turned and slapped me. The added pain to my broken nose was too much. I crumbled to the ground.

Phoebe ran over and put her arm around me, both to offer comfort and to keep me from going after Jackson. I blinked back salty tears and carefully put my hand over my nose, trying to stop the blood. I looked up just in time to see Jackson's feet disappear. I heard his body clunk against each step and the basement door slam shut.

I spit out blood. My body shuddered as a sob bubbled out of my mouth. Phoebe wrapped both arms around my shoulders and pulled me close. The full extent of the pain was starting to register and I began to feel sick.

"Jackson…" I began but trailed off, hiccupping another sob.

The back door slammed shut so hard it shook the house. Phoebe ran her hand over my hair. "Shhh," she soothed but I began to cry even harder. My throat hurt with each ragged breath. Phoebe continued to stroke my hair until I got my breathing under control. I sniffled, inhaling blood. She gently pushed me away and got a towel. She pressed it to my face. I put my hand over hers and leaned forward, letting the blood drip out.

For the second time, a gunshot echoed across the frozen land.

CHAPTER 26

I startled awake. My heart hammered, and sweat dripped down my back. The smell of gunpowder hung in the air, and my ears were still ringing from the shot. I squeezed my eyes shut and took a ragged breath. I threw the quilt from my sweaty body and pressed my hands against the cot.

I was in the basement. A gun hadn't gone off. Not since several hours ago at least. I turned on my side and brought my legs to my chest, pressing against my broken heart.

"Addie?" Lily sat up. "Are you awake?"

"Yeah." I sniffled. "I am."

Her cot creaked. I listened to her bare feet smack against the basement floor as she walked over. "I miss him too." She sank down next to me and put her hand on my shoulder. "I took him for granted. Like he was just there, bringing us food and doing our laundry. I never really talked to him. And now he's gone."

I didn't bother to wipe away my tears. I repressed a sob and nodded. Gone. Jackson was gone. He died protecting me. Guilt wrapped around the heartache. I turned my face into my pillow and cried. Lily lay down next to me, her body squished against mine on the tiny cot.

"It's not your fault," she soothed.

"No." I sharply inhaled and sat up. "It's not my fault." Anger burned inside me. "It's their fault. *They* did it. They killed Jackson. And I swear, if it's the last thing I do, I will kill them too."

Lily's green eyes widened. She sat and bit her bottom lip. "Okay." She nodded.

I closed my puffy eyes, grateful she wasn't going to tell me I was being irrational with grief. She picked up my quilt from the floor and wrapped it around my shoulders.

"You should sleep," she yawned.

"I can't sleep. I'll have nightmares." I shook my head. "But you can sleep. I'll be okay."

"Are you sure?"

"Yeah. Phoebe should be back from work soon," I added to help convince her. As nice as it was to have her comforting me, I wanted to be alone.

"Okay." Her eyebrows pushed together and she nodded. "I'm sorry, Addie."

"Me too." I flopped back down and pulled the quilt over my head.

My throat hurt from the snot that dripped down it. I hated that my nose ran every time I cried. Jackson's eyes flashed in my mine. My face crumpled. Sobs up bubbled from deep within me. Jackson's life was full of pain and misery, and it had ended that way.

Had he suffered? Was he left to slowly bleed to death, alone out in the cold? Maybe he died instantly and was in a better place now, though I wasn't sure if I believed in a better place anymore. It was hard to believe in heaven when I was trapped in hell.

"Adeline. Get up." Zane's voice was sharp. Each word cracked against me like a whip. I opened my eyes, puffy and swollen from crying myself to sleep. "Adeline."

My mouth was dry, and my skin stuck together when I parted my lips. I sat up and looked at Zane. He had a black eye, and his bottom lip was split open. The long sleeved, black shirt he was wearing covered the rest of the bruises.

"Blue looks good on you." I stared at his face with no emotion.

Zane's eyes narrowed, and his nostrils flared. He stepped

off the stairs, arms out to his sides, and limped. He abruptly stopped as if he forgot he was injured. "Upstairs. Ten minutes. Look decent." He set his jaw and turned around. I noticed his hands were balled into fists, and his shoulders were stiff. I hoped he was in a world of pain.

I swung my legs over the cot and stretched my back, tight from being in the fetal position for most of the night. My hip hurt from tumbling down the stairs. I groaned and feebly walked to the vanity. Phoebe was stretched out on her cot, fast asleep. Lily had the covers pulled over her eyes, but I got the feeling she was really awake.

I turned on the shower and splashed cold water on my face. I knew I looked like a mess. But I didn't care. Jackson was dead, and I was being forced to work—again. I didn't give a crap if my eyes were red. My nose was bruised from Nate hitting me and dried blood crusted on my neck, which was red and bruised from the choke chain. I ran my hands over my hair instead of brushing it and put on a black dress and red high heels.

I went up the stairs and pushed on the door. Of course it was locked. I turned around and sat on the top step, waiting. More than ten minutes passed before Zane thrust the door open.

"You look horrible." He grimaced when I stood. "I'm going to have to pay Keith to fuck you."

I bit the inside of my cheek and kept my eyes on Zane's face, focusing on the bruise around his eye. It was the last trace of Jackson, the evidence of his existence fading away. I took a breath, lifting my heavy heart back into my chest.

I kept my face still. I remembered the look on Jackson's face when he lunged at Zane. He was so angry, so ready to finally end this shitty life. Only it hadn't ended in the way he had planned.

Zane took a hold of my arm and jerked me forward, both of us limping through the house. He let me go and shoved me forward when we reached the stairs. I went ahead of him, seeing out of the corner of my eye that he needed to grip the railing and hoist himself up each step.

I went into the guest room. The man Zane called Keith was already there. I'd had him as a client several times before, but never knew his name. He was a large man, usually sweaty and reeking of cigarettes.

"What happened to you?" he grunted. He wasn't really asking to get a response. He didn't really care. It was something said to someone who looked like hell, and I fit the definition of that to a T. He walked to me and picked up a handful of my hair, pulling it away from my battered neck. "Rode hard and put away wet, eh?" He let go of my hair. It fell in my face.

His hands settled on my hips. Pain seared through me. I must have had a nasty bruise on my side from falling. He turned me around and pushed me over onto the dresser. His fingers slipped under the hem of the dress and pulled it up, wasting no time yanking my underwear to my ankles. He pressed his cold hands to the back of my thighs and dragged them up.

I closed my eyes, took a deep breath, and started counting as I let the air slip out of me. It was going to hurt when Keith entered me. There was nothing I could do to stop the pain. I could only brace for it. Pretend it wasn't happening. Think of something else. But I couldn't really escape.

Don't give up. Jackson's face flashed before me. I opened my eyes and stared at my reflection.

"I won't," I promised.

"What you say, girl?" Keith's breath was hot on my neck. He tipped his head up and looked at me in the mirror.

"I won't give up."

I pushed up against the dresser and brought my arm back in a swift movement. My elbow rammed into Keith's stomach. He pitched forward, losing his grip on my waist. I scuttled out of the way and raced to the door. My fingers closed around the knob. Keith sputtered behind me, zipping up his pants.

I threw the door open and leapt into the hall. My heart sped up. I whipped my head to the side and looked down the hall. There was no one there. I looked to the other side. Still no one. The stairs loomed in front of me. Without a second thought, I ran toward them, grabbed the railing, and flew down the steps.

I skidded to a stop by the front door. My hand shook as I reached for the keypad. The floor above shook as Keith plundered out of the room. *Shit.* He was coming. He would say something. And Zane would— *No.* I didn't have time to think of the horrible things he would do to me. That he *wouldn't* do to me. I was escaping.

My fingers hovered above the keypad. I sucked in a breath and closed my eyes. Here goes nothing. Four beeps echoed throughout the house as I randomly punched in numbers. For a split second, nothing happened. Then an ear-piercing high-pitched alarm blared.

Dread flowed through me, weighting my feet. I was too scared to run. Frantic, I pushed in another combination with no avail.

Fuck. It was over.

A door slammed from inside the house. "What the hell is going on?" Nate yelled over the horrible screaming alarm.

I whirled around. The coat closet was right in front of me. The floorboards vibrated from Nate's footsteps. I wrapped my fingers around the doorknob and twisted. I opened the door and stepped inside. Keeping the knob turned, I silently closed the door and sank into the full rack of jackets.

I clasped my hands together and held my breath. A line of white light filtered in through the space between the door and the floor. More people ran around the house. The floor shuddered under their frantic footsteps. Someone shouted, but the alarm made their words indiscernible.

I crouched down, using my feet to shove the shoes that were underneath me to the side. I wanted to crack open the door and see what was going on, see if I had a chance to run, but there was no way I'd risk that. I squeezed my eyes shut. This was stupid. What was I thinking? That I could stay hidden in the coat closet forever? It wasn't like I could sneak out once Nate and Zane went to bed or anything. I knew for sure they wouldn't rest until they found me.

The alarm cut off. My ears rang from the sudden silence. I put my hands over my mouth and turned my head so my ear was closer to the door.

"She's still in the house," Zane said. "There's no way she could have gotten out."

Dark shadows moved in front of the door. My heart skipped a beat and cold fear flowed through me.

"This is all your fault." Nate's voice was full of venom. "*You* brought her here. *You* will take the fall for this if she gets out."

Holy shit. Nate was going to let Zane take all the heat without batting an eye. And I thought he liked Zane.

"She's still in the house," Zane repeated, his voice cracking. "She has to be. She doesn't know the codes."

"Then fucking find her!" Nate screamed.

I hoped he would get mad enough to shoot Zane too. I pulled my arms close to my body to keep my trembling limbs from giving away my location.

Just move, please.

Someone, presumably Nate, stomped away. I wished my silent pleading had actually worked. I'd beg Nate to stick a gun in his mouth and pull the trigger. Zane turned. The floor creaked under him.

No, please no. I closed my eyes again. *Don't open the door.*

"Mother fucker!" Zane hit the closet door. I jumped, sending a leather dress shoe tumbling. Zane had to have heard it. *This is it. It's over. For real, this time.*

But he didn't open the door. He stormed away. I stayed frozen in the same position, not daring to move. My chest began to hurt, and I realized that I was holding my breath. I slowly let it out. *Now what?* I couldn't leave the closet, not yet at least.

With painstakingly slow movements, I repositioned my tingling feet. I didn't want them to fall asleep and be useless if I got the chance to run. I flicked my eyes up to the ceiling. Someone was making their way through the house, slamming the door to each room they inspected.

"Adeline," Nate's voice cut into me. Terror rippled down my spine. My legs shook. "Come on out, deary." His shoes echoed through the house as he walked down the stairs. "Come out now, and we can pretend this never happened."

Yeah fucking right. I wasn't stupid. There was no way Nate would pretend this never happened. My fingers closed around a shoe. The leather was stiff and smooth. It wasn't the best weapon by any means, but it was all I had.

"This is your last chance, Adeline." Nate walked into the living room. "Come out." I didn't move. "Very well, then. Bring her up."

Bring who up? What was he doing? I sucked in a silent breath and listened. I guessed the footfalls to belong to Zane. They grew fainter as he exited the living room. Then, there was nothing. The house was quiet, and that scared me even more.

The familiar sound of the basement door slamming shut reverberated through the farmhouse. Two people joined Nate in the living room.

"This is only happening because of you, Adeline," Nate loudly stated. I subconsciously leaned closer to the door and flinched when something clamored to the floor. "Last chance, Adeline!"

Leather cracked against flesh, and someone cried out in pain. "Addie stay!" she cried. "No give up!"

Oh my God. Nate hit her again.

Phoebe. I couldn't do it. I couldn't stay hidden. I had to come out. I had to help Phoebe. Vomit burned in my throat when Nate hit her again. My breathing quickened. I grabbed the shoe and sprang up. My fingers wrapped around the knob. Phoebe's cries of pain were a dagger to my heart. I wasn't going to let her get hurt because of me.

I threw open the door and jumped out of the closet. "Stop!" Blinking in the bright light, I stumbled into the foyer. Nate and Zane stood in the threshold in between the dining room and living room. Phoebe lay on the floor with her arms wrapped protectively around her head.

"Well, well, well." Nate turned toward me and smiled. "That's where you were." He let his arm fall, his leather belt swinging at his side. Then his lips pulled into a sadistic smile. He brought his arm up and whipped Phoebe.

I didn't even think. Fueled by anger I ran through the living room. Nate's cold eyes flashed with shock. Zane looked up, his face blank. For a few seconds, both of them just stood there, dumbfounded. Seeing me racing toward them was the last thing they expected.

And it worked in my advantage. I jumped over the coffee table and dove at Nate. I collided with his side. He stepped back, throwing his arms out to try and keep his balance. My head hit his shoulder. Searing pain rippled across my forehead. Ignoring it completely, I lifted my hand and brought the shoe down as hard as I could. The heel clipped his face.

He stumbled back, backing into a chair. It loudly scooted across the wooden floor. Nate's arms flailed. I watched it happen in slow motion. His feet went out from underneath him. His eyes widened and he reached out, grasping at anything in front of him. I leaned out of the way just in time. The floor shook from the weight of his body falling onto it.

And then, Zane was on me. He pushed me face down against the floor. My chin hit, and I bit my tongue. Blood pooled in my mouth.

"Get her!" Nate yelled. "Get her!"

I thought he was talking about me, and Zane already had me. Then, out of the corner of my eye, I saw Phoebe get up. Zane pushed my face into the floor and yanked my hands behind my back. I couldn't see what was going on.

Phoebe yelled something in Vietnamese. Then the belt cracked, and Nate cried out in pain. Phoebe had it. She hit Nate. She was fighting back!

I struggled to get out of Zane's grip. He pushed me down and climbed on so that he was straddling me. I bent my legs and brought them up, kicking Zane in the back.

"Get her!" Nate repeated.

I felt Zane's muscles tighten. If he got up to get Phoebe, I could get free. Phoebe hit Nate again. Zane jumped up. I put my hands on the floor to push myself up, but Zane was faster. He kicked hard against my side. The pain shot through my ribs, rendering me useless for a few seconds.

It was just enough. Zane grabbed Phoebe and threw her aside as if she weighed nothing. He pulled Nate to his feet and stood in front of him like the good guard dog that he was. I scrambled up and crawled backwards to Phoebe. I threw my arms around her, ready to shield her from any more damage.

"This is unacceptable!" Nate bellowed. I swallowed hard. Nate picked up the leather belt, seething with anger. "Get them downstairs. Now!"

Zane grabbed my ankles and roughly yanked me away from Phoebe. I kicked my feet but was unable to break free from Zane's grasp. He dragged me into the dining room.

"Let me go!" I shouted and thrashed against him. I twisted and reached out, taking hold of a table leg. Zane kept pulling, but I didn't let go. The table moved along with me, scraping the polished wooden floor. I didn't see Nate coming until his foot came down on my elbow. I screamed and let go.

Zane jerked me into the kitchen. He dropped my ankles, and my feet crashed onto the floor. Sharp pain cracked against my heels. My hands flattened against the cold tile floor as I frantically attempted to get away. I flipped onto my belly and crawled forward. Zane grabbed me around the waist and scooped me up before harshly flipping me over his shoulder. I pounded my fists against his back and screamed.

"Shut the hell up, you motherfucking cunt!" He swiftly turned into the wall. My head cracked against it. Black dots floated in front of me. He moved away and rammed me into the wall one more time. Debilitating dizziness took over. My arms went slack, hanging uselessly down Zane's back. He opened the basement door and leaned forward.

Numb and on the verge of passing out, I had little control over my body. I slid down Zane's front. At the last minute, I regained strength in my hands, and I grabbed his shoulders, buffering my fall. He bent his knee up and hit me in the stomach. I crumbled onto the stairs.

It took everything in me to crawl down them before Zane could push me. I made it halfway when Phoebe stumbled through the doorway. She hurried down the steps and helped me the rest of the way. Everything was blurry, and I was nauseous, but somehow I made it to the cot.

I fell onto it, head pounding. Nate and Zane were shouting at each other upstairs. I tried to open my eyes and failed. My eyelids were just too heavy. I took a deep breath and pushed myself up, wavering. *Fuck.* My head throbbed.

Zane ran down the stairs, blue eyes flashing with rage. I pushed against the mattress and stood. My knees instantly buckled. I didn't have a chance to get up again. Zane was right there, over top of me. He slapped me hard across the face. I fell backwards, my head too heavy to hold up.

I didn't see the syringe in his hand, just felt the sting of the needle in my arm and the cold burn as the drug pushed into my muscles. My fingertips tingled. I lost sensation in my legs. My chest was heavy, and I struggled to breathe.

"Put her in the closet," Nate ordered. "Since she likes being in them so much."

I opened my mouth to protest but nothing came out. My entire body was heavy, as if it were made out of lead. There was nothing I could do to keep my eyes open anymore. They closed, shutting out everything that was going on. I was losing consciousness, fast.

I remembered Zane's hands taking a hold of me one more time, then smelling the stale air that wafted out of the closet. He harshly set me down and slammed the door.

My cheek rested against the gritty cement floor of the closet. The hard floor painfully pressed against my hipbones. I had horrible cramps in my legs, and my left arm was going numb from being tucked underneath my torso.

I couldn't move. I wasn't even able to open my mouth to scream. Breathing took effort. The weight of my own body was suffocating me.

Tears ran down my face, dripping into my ear. I tried to scream but only managed to get out a weak wheeze. The deadbolt shot into place. The paralysis was making its way into my mind, pulling me under. Jackson's face flashed before me.

I'm sorry, I thought to him. This is what not giving up had gotten me.

CHAPTER 27

My eyes fluttered open. I was lying on the bed upstairs in the guest room. Zane was above me. He unlocked a metal cuff from around my wrist and let my heavy hand fall onto my face. He snickered and got off the bed. It was sometime in March. Several weeks had passed since I hid in the coat closet.

"You reek." He wrinkled his nose and shuddered. "I should take you out back and hose you off." He bent over and picked up my dress. He twisted it in his hands and snapped it against my bare breasts. "I don't want to touch you. Get up."

"Mhh," I mumbled. My mind was stuck in a perpetual heavy fog. I sat up, so dizzy it was hard to smooth out the dress and slip it over my head. My eyes closed on their own accord. I swung my legs over the bed, pausing to collect my balance.

Inpatient, Zane took a hold of my hands and helped me to my feet with uncharacteristic gentleness. He wasn't being nice. His patience was learned, albeit it had taken him several weeks to learn it. I was too heavily drugged to walk on my own. If someone didn't escort me back into the basement, I wasn't able to get there until the drugs left my system.

He kept a steady hold on me as we walked down the stairs, through the first level of the house, and into the basement. He dropped me off at the bottom of the stairs. Phoebe and Lily stood in front of the mirror, getting ready for another night's work. I wobbled on my feet and leaned against the wall or support.

Phoebe set down the tube of lipstick she held and rushed over. She wrapped her arm around me and led me to my cot. I flopped down on it and fell backwards. Phoebe lifted my feet onto the mattress.

"You burning hot." She pressed her hand against my forehead. "Lily, bring me wet cloth."

Now that she had mentioned it, I did feel warm. "I'm okay," I slurred. I blinked. Or at least I thought that was all I had done, but when I opened my eyes, Lily stood over me, folding a dripping washcloth in half.

"I say damp, not soaking," Phoebe said.

"No, you said wet," Lily told her.

Phoebe shook her head and took the washcloth from Lily. She wrung it out on the floor and draped it over my forehead.

Lily knelt down and put her hand on my cheek. "Is she gonna be okay?"

"I not know." Phoebe smoothed back my hair. "She have fever."

Lily shook her head, causing a cascade of strawberry blonde curls to fall into her face. "It's been three weeks. They need to stop drugging her. It's, like, gonna damage her brain or something."

"Guys," I mumbled. "I'm fine."

"No," they said in unison. Phoebe cast her eyes to the ground. "Addie," she said gently. "You sick. You not feel it because of drugs."

I nodded. She was right, and I knew it made sense. After my failed attempt at running out of the house, Nate locked me in the closet for three days. If it wasn't for Lily and Phoebe sneaking me food and water, I might not have made it.

When Nate finally let me out, he strapped a house arrest anklet on me and shoved a pill down my throat. As the grainy pill disintegrated, he told me that the anklet would alert him if I tried to take it off, and it had GPS. Even if I got out of the house, they would find me. I had begun feeling fuzzy as he spoke. It wasn't long until I was pulled into a drug-induced haze. I was too out of it to protest. I was too weak to run.

That had become my new routine. For the last three weeks, I was drugged, dragged upstairs, and chained to the bed. Once my work was done, Zane brought me back down to the basement. If Lily or Phoebe were there, they would help me eat, shower, or lay down until the drugs wore off. Then I'd have a few hours of being sober until the day repeated.

"She's shivering." Lily pulled the quilt over me. "Should I get her water?"

"Addie, you thirsty?" Phoebe asked.

"I think so," I answered. My throat burned. Maybe. I couldn't really tell. I still felt numb. Lily scuttled away, returning with a cup of water. I struggled to push myself up onto my elbows.

"Ugh," I groaned. I hated not being able to easily move. Phoebe took the cup and put it to my lips, slowly tipping it so I could slurp down the cold water.

"You almost ready?" Rochelle called and clomped down the stairs.

Lily shot up and scrambled over to the vanity. Her green eyes widened with fear, looking like she just got caught doing something she wasn't supposed to be doing. "Yeah," she said right away.

"No you're not!" Rochelle stopped at the base of the stairs. "You don't have any makeup on."

"She doesn't need any," I mumbled.

Rochelle ignored me and strode past. She sat Lily down on the stool in front of the vanity and started caking foundation over Lily's flawless skin. "Come on, Pheebs." She cast a look over her shoulder. Phoebe set the cup down and hugged me.

"Rest as much as you can," she whispered. "We go on two day trip. See you later." I collapsed back onto the bed and closed my eyes. I tried staying awake by listening to the girls getting ready but it didn't work. When I woke up, they were gone.

But I wasn't alone. Nate and Zane stood next to the cot, both dressed in formal suits. They both looked handsome. Inhumanly handsome, at that. I wanted to vomit.

Nate narrowed his eyes and looked at his watch. "I have some business to attend to."

I blinked and swallowed. Yes, my throat was definitely sore. "And I care because?"

"It's out of town," Nate continued.

"I still don't care," I told him and wished my voice wasn't

so scratchy.

"You're not going."

"No shit, Sherlock," I spat and hid the fear. Nate was up to something, as always. Why else would he be downstairs?

Nate sighed. "You just won't break, will you?"

"I never will." I said each word slowly and stared Nate right in the eyes.

"You know what they do to horses that can't be broken?" He shook his head. "Never mind." He turned to Zane. "Put her in the closet."

"No!" I screamed. Not again, not in the dark. Not alone.

"Stop the antics," Nate said, sounding bored. "I'm not leaving you to your own devices while I'm away on business."

Zane picked me up. The drugs weren't as strong, but I wasn't at full strength, and even if I was, being sick put a damper on my ability to fight off anyone, let alone Zane. He carried me like a rag doll and flopped me down into the closet. He kicked me in the stomach for good measure and dashed out, slamming the door.

I didn't get up. What was the point? I hadn't been able to get out before, and now I was weak. Tears filled my eyes. Nate was lying. He had to be. He really wouldn't leave me all alone for two days, would he? My lip quivered. I had been in there for three days before, and Nate had no problem with it.

Yes, he had to be serious.

Zane and Nate went up the stairs and locked the basement door. I lay on my side, curled into a ball, and cried. It hurt my throat. I desperately wanted water. I took in a slow breath and thought about my family. I was sitting at the dining room table again. My mom handed me a steaming cup of lemon tea. It was her cure-all for colds.

I would have given anything to be home again. Though I tried not to cry, the tears began to fall again. I shivered and hugged my legs closer to me. My body ached. I wasn't sure I would make it two days.

I wasn't sure I wanted to.

CHAPTER 28

I drifted in and out of consciousness, unsure of how much time passed since I had been locked in the closet. Again.

Sweat dripped down my back, and I shivered. I felt like my head was in a vice that was continuously being tightened. It hurt to swallow, and my entire body was plagued with chills and aches.

I thought I heard something clatter to the floor on the first level. I opened my eyes and squinted at the hole in the door from the missing doorknob. I coughed and closed my eyes. The heat from my fever was horrible. I brought my knees to my chest. Was someone there? My mind was too hazy to get the words out and call for help. Besides, it was probably Nate or Zane anyway.

Consciousness left me again. Sharp metal clicks roused me. I tried to roll over and look at the door, but failed. I lifted my head up for a brief moment only to have it heavily fall onto the hard floor.

Then the door opened.

"Oh God," a deep voice spoke.

I tried to open my eyes. Something fluttered inside of me. I knew that voice.

"Shit," he whispered and bent down, his knees cracking. "Addie?" He pressed his hand against my cheek. "You're burning up."

My eyes fluttered open. "Jacks…" I mumbled, not able to say his whole name.

"Don't talk," Jackson said quietly. "How long have you been down here?"

I opened my eyes again. I was dreaming. I had to be dreaming. Or maybe I was dead.

Jackson shook his head and pushed his dark hair behind his ears. "It doesn't matter." His arms slid underneath me and he picked me up, pressing my body against his. He didn't speak as he carried me up the basement stairs.

I struggled to stay awake as he crossed the kitchen. *Is this really happening?* My head jolted against his shoulder when he hurried up a second flight of stairs.

"Am I dead?" I croaked.

Jackson opened a bedroom door. "No, you're not," he said gently.

"What is…you…you…" I tried to make sense of the situation.

"Don't worry about anything right now, Addie. You're really sick."

"Okay," I breathed.

Jackson carefully lay me down on a bed. He pulled back the covers, tucked me in, and said he'd be right back. I was too out of it to wonder where I was. My heavy eyelids remained closed until I heard Jackson come back into the room.

He sat next to me and hooked his arm around my shoulders. "Here," he said and pulled me up. He put a cup to my mouth, carefully tipping it. Warm liquid touched my lips. I opened my mouth just enough to sip the drink. "It tastes gross," he warned just a second too late. I coughed and recoiled.

"Mhh," I moaned and shook my head.

"It will help," he said quietly and tipped the cup again.

I let the beverage spill into my mouth. It burned on the way down. Jackson switched to water, taking his time to let me drink as much as I could. Then he gently lowered me back onto the pillows and pulled the blanket up to my chin. The mattress sank down near my feet. I tried once more to open my eyes and get a good look at Jackson. I was pulled into a black sleep in just seconds.

The shaking of a pill bottle woke me up. The room was dark, illuminated only by a small lamp on the dresser across from me. I opened my eyes and took a breath.

"Addie?" Jackson said and stood. He had been sitting on the floor, leaning against the dresser. He was holding a book in one hand and a bottle of Tylenol in the other.

I blinked the sleep away and traced my eyes over his face. The breath caught in my throat, and tears stung my dry eyes. I shook my head in disbelief. "You're alive," I whispered.

Jackson gave me a small smile. "Yeah. I am."

"But they shot you."

He pushed up the sleeve on his right arm. "They did. I can't decide if Zane's aim is really horrible or if he meant to just clip me all along." I took in the nasty scar on his bicep. I opened my mouth, only to close it again. "Don't worry about me right now. I'm worried about you." He set the book on the dresser and moved to the edge of the bed. "Do you think you can swallow pills? We need to bring your fever down."

I nodded, and Jackson picked up a glass of water. He poured two pills into his palm and held them out for me. I took them, put them in my mouth, and let him hold the cup to my lips. I drank the rest of the water and leaned back on the pillows.

"Where am I?" I asked as I looked around. We were in a small room. The walls were white, the bedspread was plain and gray, and there was no décor on the walls. Only the lamp sat on the white dresser and cardboard boxes of books were pushed up against the wall next to the closet.

"This is my room," Jackson replied. My eyes widened. "Nate brought me back the day he left. I thought you were with them, but then I thought I heard something in the basement and I found you locked in the closet."

"You found the key?"

"No. I picked the lock. It took almost half an hour. Didn't you hear it?"

I shook my head. "I don't remember. You shouldn't—"

"Addie, you could have died. There's a few scratches on the lock, but I don't think Zane will notice."

I nodded and closed my eyes for a few seconds. I remembered Nate telling me he was going out of town. He was gone, and Zane was with him. My eyes flew open. "We should run."

Jackson looked down and shook his head. "Nate changed

the combinations on the doors. I can't get out, and I have no idea where he put the keys to the Blazer. We would literally have to run. On foot … and you're really sick." His eyes flicked to the foot of the bed, looking at the covered-up ankle bracelet. "They'd find us. It would only be a matter of minutes before Nate sent someone this way."

Dejected, I only nodded and ran my eyes over Jackson once more. So many questions rushed through my head, adding to the dizziness. "Where were you?" I asked, deciding that was the most important.

"After I got shot, I was in the hospital for a week," he answered. "The wound got infected. Then Nate took me to a house he just bought upstate. I wasn't allowed to come back here until I was done doing renovations."

"Renovations?"

"Yeah. Nate owns a lot of houses."

"Full of girls, right?" I asked.

"Yeah. There are probably a dozen girls at the new house."

I bit my lip, not knowing what to say. I hated Nate with everything inside me. And he terrified me almost as much. He had the farmhouse, the club, the restaurant, *and* another house full of girls? I shivered again, but it wasn't from the fever. "Why are you back here?"

He shrugged. "I finished the work on the other house, and Nate won't admit it, but he can't function without me." Jackson gave me a lopsided smiled. "I guess he's used to having me do all his work. This place was a disaster when I came back." He sat at the foot of the bed. "I'm glad you're okay. He used you as a threat, said if I tried to tell anyone what happened he would hurt you."

His eyes met mine and I smiled. Then I started coughing again. Jackson got up and opened a door on the side of the room. I heard water running, letting me know that it was an attached bathroom. He refilled the cup and offered it to me. I drank half of it and leaned back.

"I'm so tired," I mumbled.

"You need more sleep," he said and I nodded in agreement. "I'll be right back," he told me and hurried out of the room. I turned, watching him leave. I was comfortable and didn't want to get up, but I had to pee, so I pushed myself up and shuffled into the bathroom. I flicked on the light only to shut it off again. It was still too bright for my eyes.

I had just made it back into bed when Jackson returned with a steaming mug. He extended it to me. "It's that gross stuff again," he explained. "It helps, trust me."

"I believe you," I said and took the mug. I grimaced and drank the warm liquid. Jackson placed the empty cup on the dresser, trading it for a bottle of water. He twisted off the cap and offered it to me. I took a few sips before giving it back.

"Get some sleep, Addie."

I nodded but kept my eyes on Jackson. "I can't believe you're alive," I whispered, feeling emotional again. "What you did for me. And ... and then ..." I trailed off, sniffling and coughing.

"Adeline," he said gently. "It's okay. I'm okay. I hate that you thought I was dead. The whole time I was gone, I wished I could get a message to you, to tell you what happened. I knew they would make you think the worst."

"But Lily saw Zane digging a hole." I wiped away tears.

"He really played it up," Jackson said to himself and shook his head. He closed his eyes for a few seconds. "Get some sleep. You need to rest."

"Okay. You too," I told him, knowing it was late.

"I will," he promised. He backed away from the bed and picked up his book. "I'm just not tired yet."

I didn't believe him, but I was too worn to tell him that. I leaned back against the pillows and closed my eyes. Despite the emotions that flooded my ill head, I fell asleep quickly and was out for the rest of the night.

CHAPTER 29

Waking up in Jackson's bed wasn't as awkward as I thought it would be. I pushed myself up just enough to get a drink of water and glanced around the dimly lit room in search of him. He was nowhere in sight. I laid back down feeling a lot better than I had the night before. Still, my body was exhausted. I thought about Jackson and how he put himself in danger—again—to take care of me. I wanted to know everything about him. I wanted to make that deep, painful sadness in his chocolate eyes go away. The gentle hum of the ceiling fan lulled me back to sleep with the image of Jackson's face still lingering in my mind.

I woke up several hours later needing to use the bathroom. Grey clouds muted the early morning sky, and the promise of rain was heavy on the breeze that came in through the open windows. I swung my feet over the bed and stepped on a leg. Startled, I jolted forward. My foot caught in a blanket and I lost my balance. I fell in slow motion, catching myself on my hands and knees. Jackson sat up, looked annoyed for a second, and then smiled.

"Are you okay?" he asked and moved over to me.

"What are you doing on the floor?" I replied and disentangled myself from his blanket. He stood and helped me to my feet.

"I didn't think you'd want me sleeping next to you," he confessed, looking almost embarrassed. "And I didn't want to leave you alone. Your breathing was kinda shallow. It, uh, made me nervous. You look better now. I mean sound. Sound better now."

A half smile formed on my face. "I feel a lot better. What was that nasty stuff you made me drink?"

Jackson smiled back at me. I hadn't let myself acknowledge how good he looked when he smiled before. It was such a small, simple expression, and yet it changed his face so much. The heavy sadness was momentarily gone, and he looked boyish and handsome at the same time. With his dark, wavy hair and his strong jaw line, he was actually a very attractive man. It was just hard to see past the pain and the bruises that almost always covered his face.

"You don't want to know," he said with a smile. "It's an old family recipe with a little bit of everything in it. My grandpa used to make it for me when I would get sick. He said it 'burned the fever' out of me, though I think the alcohol just made it worse."

I bit my lip and tried to smile back at him. That was the first time he had ever mentioned anything from his past. "Well, whatever it is, it helped," I said gratefully. "I don't feel like I'm going to burn up from the inside anymore."

He gently pressed the back of his hand to my forehead. "Not from the outside either." He let his hand fall and stepped back, his eyes locked with mine. My heart did that flutter thing again. I took a step closer. "Are you hungry?" he asked, blood rushing to his cheeks.

"Yeah." I coughed and ran my hands through my messy hair. "I haven't felt hungry in days."

"That's a good sign. I'll make breakfast," he offered and strode to his dresser. He opened it, revealing a very small selection of neatly folded clothes. He handed me a white T-shirt and a blue pair of loose fitting exercise shorts. "I'm assuming you want to shower and change."

I took the clothes from him and nervously eyed the attached bathroom. "I do."

"There are towels in the cabinet under the sink. I'll stay out until you're done. Take your time," he said before turning out of the room. He shut the door behind him. I heard the stairs creak as he descended them. My head was still foggy with sickness but not enough to make me leery of stripping down in Jackson's room. What if Nate or Zane came home? Jackson was sure that

EMILY GOODWIN

they wouldn't just yet, and I believed him.

I walked into the bathroom nonetheless. It was small and, like the rest of Jackson's room, very neat and tidy. It was also void of paint and decorations. I turned the shower on and looked at myself in the mirror. Instantly, a small amount of embarrassment rose and caused my cheeks to flush. My hair was a ratty mess, old makeup clung to the skin around my eyes, and my nose was red with dry skin. I looked awful.

I raked my fingers through my hair while I went to the bathroom and was pleasantly surprised when I stepped into the shower. The water was warm. I stood there with my hands out, feeling the heat for several minutes. A hot shower was something I had taken for granted. It was something I knew I could always have, just a normal part of life. Having that taken away and being forced to wash my abused body in icy cold water was just another way Nate proved he had control over us. Each droplet of warm water that splashed down my skin was almost like I was taking something back.

I showered quickly and toweled off even quicker. I dressed in Jackson's clothes and slowly cracked the door open. He hadn't returned yet, and the bedroom door was still closed. I flipped my head upside down and rubbed at my hair, trying to dry it as much as possible before getting back into bed.

A few minutes, after I tucked the blankets around myself, Jackson opened the door carrying a very full tray of wonderful smelling food. His face lit up when his eyes met mine, and I felt a rush of something I hadn't felt in a long time flash through my body.

"Do you like biscuits and gravy?" he asked. "I just assumed and made it. I can make you something else if you don't like it," he added quickly.

"I love it," I said truthfully and lunged forward to grab a bowl. Even if I hadn't liked it, eating something warm and fresh wasn't something I was about to pass up. I stuck a spoonful in my mouth. "It's delicious," I praised. "You're a good cook."

Jackson sat at the foot of the bed, keeping a careful distance. I wanted to tell him he didn't have to stay away, that I liked him being next to me. I didn't, though. What if he didn't like being close to me?

He raised an eyebrow incredulously. "I've never cooked for you before today."

I shook my head. "You brought me barbeque chicken and mashed potatoes."

"Oh, right. I forgot about that. Still, that's only two things."

I ate a few more spoonfuls before speaking. "I can always smell what you make." I tore apart the biscuit. "And it always smells good."

Jackson shrugged off the compliment. "Thanks. I like to cook. Everyone leaves me alone when I do."

"You know how messed up that is?" I said with my mouthful.

Jackson raised his eyebrows and sighed. "I know how messed up everything around here is." He tipped his head down and focused on his food.

I slowly chewed my last spoonful and stared at Jackson, madly trying to think of something to say. I hated seeing him looking so dejected.

"You have a lot of books," I commented. My eyes darted to the cardboard box of books that sat in the corner by his closet.

He nodded and waited until he was finished chewing to answer. "Nate lets me read. It keeps me quiet, I guess." He shook his head. "Reading is a good way to escape the hell we're in."

"I had just gotten an email from one of my favorite authors the day I was taken."

Suddenly, my happy thoughts shifted. I had never gotten to reply to that email. I wondered what that author thought…or what anyone who followed my blog thought. Two other people ran the blog with me. Surely by now Lori and Lindsay knew I had been taken and wasn't blowing them off. Had they written a post about my disappearance? Maybe Lynn or my sister took it upon themselves to email them.

"You okay?" Jackson asked.

"Yeah." I blinked back the tears. "Memories," I said shortly and pulled my lips over my teeth.

"What do—well, *did* you do for fun?" he asked after a few seconds, changing the subject.

"Read, but you know that," I answered. "I liked to train my dogs. Scarlet is certified to do therapy. In the summer, we'd go to nursing homes and this school by our house for disabled children. The kids love her. We used to do agility, but she's too old for that now. I was going to start working with Rhett over the summer." I paused and heavily exhaled. "And I like anything that has to do with the paranormal. Lynn, my best friend, and I go 'exploring' anywhere remotely creepy to try and find ghosts. I like to paint too, but I'm not very good at it. I *might* have an unhealthy obsession with *Dr. Who*. And sometimes I play video games." It felt weird to think about the activities I used to do just for fun. "Saying it all out loud makes me sound like a nerd," I added with a small smile.

"I don't think so. It all sounds fun," Jackson told me. "I don't believe in ghosts."

"Really?"

He nodded. "Really. I've never seen one."

"Not yet," I said with a smile. "Jackson?"

"Yeah?" he answered.

"How old are you?"

"Twenty-three."

"What's your last name?" I asked.

He paused, like it was difficult to recall. "Porter. My turn. What's your favorite movie?"

"Hocus Pocus."

"I've never seen it."

"Are you serious?" I asked.

"Yes."

I smiled. "Well, some day we will watch it together."

"I'd like that," he said. Our eyes met and my heart skipped a beat. I looked down at the empty bowl and yawned. "Tired?" he asked.

"Yeah," I said.

"Me too," he said and stood. He took my bowl and empty cup and set them back on the tray. "As creepy as this makes me sound, I stayed up to listen to your breathing. For a while it really sounded like you were struggling for air."

The small smile returned to my face. "I felt like it. I kinda still do, but I think I coughed a lot of it up in the shower."

"Nice," he grimaced and moved to the other side of the bed, looking at his pillow on the floor. "Wake me up if you need anything, Addie."

I nodded and pulled the blankets over me. "Jackson," I started as he bent down to the floor. "There is enough room for both of us." I eyed the bed. "You don't have to sleep on the floor."

"Are you sure Addie?" he asked slowly.

"Positive," I said with a cough. I scooted toward the edge and patted the mattress next to me. "It's more comfortable than the floor."

"That is true." He shook his head, and his dark hair fell over his eyes in a way that I found oddly charming, despite the fact that it made him look completely disheveled.

"Hang on." He hurried out of the room and returned with a long, skinny decorative pillow from the guest room. He put it between us as he sat down. "I won't touch you," he stated.

"I know you won't," I said with a small smile. Part of me was still nervous to be this close to a man. Jackson treated me like a human being, cared about me, and wanted me to be comfortable and well. Reminding myself of that eased some of the anxiety.

He smiled one of his rare, genuine smiles. "Good."

I made myself as comfortable as possible and closed my eyes. Rain began to pitter against the window, and the slight breeze turned into wind. Mist blew across the room, dampening my face. I pulled the blankets up over my head, thinking that if it began raining any harder I'd have to get up and close the windows. Jackson beat me to it. He left them open only about an inch, just enough to keep the fresh air coming in and to allow the cleansing scent of rain into the room.

"Are you cold?" he asked me.

"Not yet," I told him.

"Okay. I can close the windows if you get cold."

"You don't have to. The fresh air feels good."

"It does," he agreed and settled back down.

My mom used to get mad at me when I'd leave the windows open and it was cold. She would say I'd have to start paying the bill to run the heater." I smiled at the thought of her face. Then unwelcome tears spilled down my cheeks.

As if he was able to sense my sadness, Jackson put his hand on the pillow in a gesture of comfort. Slowly, I stuck mine out from under the blanket and let my fingertips touch his.

EMILY GOODWIN

Jackson curled his fingers around mine, his touch nothing but gentle. I pushed my hand forward until our fingers were linked. It hit me, just then, how lonely I'd been. I'd been around people, shoved onto mattresses, and manhandled since I got here. It wasn't the same. It wasn't this, being close to someone purely for comfort. There was nothing sexual, nothing threatening or domineering about Jackson. He slowly moved his thumb into the palm of my hand, reading my face to make sure his touch was okay. Then he rubbed small circles onto my skin, relaxing me.

I liked the heat of his skin, his steady breathing, the way he smelled like soap and laundry detergent. I liked the way he was taking care of me, making sure I was comfortable and well. No, this was nothing like what I was used to. And I liked it.

"Jackson?" I whispered.

"Yeah?"

"How did you end up here?" I carefully asked. I opened my eyes and looked at him. Something dark crossed his face. His jaw tightened and he swallowed hard.

"It's a long story."

"You don't have to tell me if you don't want to," I said and gave his hand a squeeze.

"I do." He squeezed my hand back. "My mom was sixteen when she had me," he started. "In the beginning she tried. She married my biological father when she turned eighteen. I remember living in this shit-hole of an apartment with them. My mom used to tell me that we were happy back then, but it was never true. Dad drank and Mom smoked, and she didn't limit herself to cigarettes. They fought, and the fights got physical. When my mom wasn't around to beat up, my dad took out his anger on me. I was in first grade when child services got involved.

"My parents got divorced, and that was the last I ever saw of my dad. My mom became depressed and started doing more drugs and got herself arrested. That didn't go too well for me, as you could have guessed, so I got taken away. I was in and out of foster homes for a year before my grandma, my Mom's mom, legally adopted me. Like mother like daughter. She still smoked and drank and life was hell. She'd blow her money on drugs and booze and forget to buy me food. And clothes. And toys—forget it. I didn't have anything the other kids in school had."

He stopped and took a breath, his dark eyes fixed on the ceiling above us. "But I knew how to mix cocktails," he said with a forced laugh. He shook his head, and I noticed his eyes were glossy. "I still don't think she ever met Nate. It was one of those friend-of-a-friend kinds of deals. When I was twelve, she sold me to him."

My chest tightened, but it wasn't from being ill. I clenched my jaw and braced myself for the rest of Jackson's story.

"Nate used me for a while, but the clients interested in males like them young. I was too old already," he spat, anger and disgust heavy on his voice. "So he put me to work in other ways. It was simple stuff at first, like cleaning and yard work. When I looked old enough, he made me work in the club, mixing drinks, serving food, like I do now. I guess I was helpful enough to keep around, since I'm still here."

His words cut into the air and hung there, the tragedy of it all weighing down on us. I opened my mouth but was at a loss for words. Even 'I'm sorry' didn't seem to cut it. I wanted to hug him, embrace him, comfort him like he had comforted me. Just the thought of that much physical contact made me nervous.

I pulled my fingers out of his and pushed my hand across the pillow until it rested on his bicep. He hesitated for just a moment then put his hand on my arm. He took in a deep breath and sighed. I traced my fingers up his arm, running them over the bullet wound.

Everything I had felt that day, the day I thought Jackson had been murdered, ran through me. Tears pricked the corners of my eyes, and my heart swelled with sadness then relief. I moved the pillow that divided the bed in half and wrapped my arms around Jackson, pressing my face into his muscular chest. He held his arms out, unsure for a few seconds before pulling me into an embrace. He rested the side of his face against my hair and let out a heavy sigh.

So many things rushed through me in that moment. I was aware of every physical sensation: my breasts crushing against his chest, the pounding of both our hearts, the rise and fall of his breathing, the way our legs touched. He had one hand on the back of my shoulders and the other tightly secured around my waist. His biceps were stiff as he clung onto me, pulling me in as if I was the only thing keeping him together.

Feeling the exact same way, I closed my eyes and relaxed. Being physically close to Jackson was comforting. I felt safe wrapped in his arms.

I sat up so I could look into his eyes. I gave him a crooked smile and pushed his hair back, letting my fingers run through its length. He met my gaze, his eyes holding back a terrified desperation. I took a breath and moved my hand to his left arm. Slowly, I pushed up the sleeve. A thin scar ran down his bicep. A small, slightly sunken circle of pink skin was in the middle. I carefully touched the bullet wound. I swallowed hard, biting back tears.

Then it hit me just how much I cared about Jackson. I blinked, causing the salty water to spill down my cheeks. Jackson leaned forward and gently wiped them away.

"Don't cry, Addie," he whispered, looking like he was fighting back his own emotions.

The gentleness in his voice only made it worse. I shook my head and closed my eyes, tears streaming down my cheeks.

He gently wiped them away. "It's okay," he soothed. "Somehow, it'll be okay."

I nodded and suppressed a cough, my body going rigid as I did so. Jackson sat up, resituating my pillow so I could lay down.

"Here," he said and handed me the box of tissues and the water bottle.

"Sorry," I said after I blew my nose. "I must look disgusting."

Jackson slightly smiled and shook his head. "You look sick, not disgusting."

"I feel sick," I muttered and grabbed another tissue.

"Go back to sleep," he suggested. He looked at the door and bit his lip as he thought.

"Jackson?" I asked before he could push himself off the bed. He turned to look at me. "Will you stay?"

His smile returned. "If you want me to."

I nodded as I spoke. "I do."

He reached for the long, skinny pillow and glanced at me. I shook my head. I didn't want to keep him away from me anymore. We resituated the pillows and lay down together so that my head was resting on his chest. My breath rattled every time I inhaled, and my throat felt like I was breathing in fire, but lying there with Jackson was the most content I had felt in a long, long time.

I sat on the edge of the bed and watched the sun set. A ball of golden light glowed behind dark storm clouds. The temperature had dropped as the sun sank lower in the sky. Misty wind blew through the open windows, making me shiver. Jackson perched on the mattress to my side, draping a blanket around me. I pulled it tightly around my body and looked at Jackson, smiling. After a few seconds of consideration, he took my hand in his. I closed my eyes and smiled. Something sparked inside of me. I closed my eyes and rested my head on his shoulder.

"Addie?" His voice was gentle.

"Yeah?" I answered, not opening my eyes.

"Do you remember when you said I don't seem dead inside?"

I opened my eyes and looked up at him. "I do."

"And I said that I had until recently?"

"I remember."

"Well," he began. I could feel his muscles tighten. "It was you. You brought me back to life." He let out a breath and turned to face me. "It was getting hard finding hope after all these years. I was so close to giving up. And then I met you."

I let go of the edges of the blanket and twisted toward him, taking his other hand. Warmth ran through my body, making my heart swell and nerves tingle.

"I hated myself for doing nothing," he confessed. "I should have stopped Zane and let you run away. But I didn't, and now..." he paused, taking a breath to prepare for what he was about to say. "Now I hate myself for being glad that I didn't do anything."

"What do you mean?" I asked softly.

"I never would have met you. Not if you had run away. I would have let myself die inside without you," he shyly blurted.

"You're so full of fire. You haven't lost hope. I've never met anyone who can hold onto who they are in such a horrible situation. You saved me, Adeline. And now I want to save you."

The warm tingles made their way down my body. I looked at Jackson. Our eyes locked, and he moved his face just an inch from mine. He closed his eyes. My heart skipped a beat. I wanted him to kiss me. I wanted to feel his lips gently press against mine. I wanted to feel the pleasurable feeling travel all the way through me. I wanted to feel everything a kiss could bring.

But I was scared. I was scared that the moment our lips touched, I would flinch away. I was scared I was too damaged to love, or be loved. I didn't want fear to ripple down my spine instead of desire. I slowly let out my breath and allowed my eyes to close. Jackson tightened his embrace and pressed his lips to my forehead. I instantly relaxed and melted into his arms.

He ran his hands over my hair and rested his head against mine. I slowly flattened my palms against his back, cautiously feeling his muscles. My heart began to beat faster as I let my hands drop to his waist. I stuck my fingers under the hem of his black t-shirt and soaked in the warmth of his skin. He deeply inhaled and pulled me closer.

I couldn't help it. I recoiled, pushing him away, heart racing. The blanket fell to the floor. Jackson looked at me, hurt.

"I'm sorry," I panted, leaning over to pick up the blanket. "It's not you," I stammered. "It's…it's…" I couldn't get the rest of the sentence out before I started crying.

"Addie," Jackson said gently. "It's okay. It was my fault. I didn't think about it." His brown eyes clouded with sadness. "Do you want me to go so you can get some rest?"

I shook my head. "No. I like being with you," I said. I took a deep breath and slowly let it out, waiting for my heart to stop racing. I sat back on the bed and motioned for Jackson to sit next to me.

"I want to be able to be close to you."

"Okay," he said with a half smile. "Take it slow." Jackson was careful not to touch me as he settled onto the bed. I angled my body toward his, eyeing him up and down. I leaned closer and closer to him until my shoulder brushed against his. My heart sped up. Jackson rubbed his fingers against my palm again. I closed my eyes and rested my head on his shoulder. He carefully twisted and put his arm around me, gently resting his hand on my arm.

Jackson moved his face back. "Is this okay?" he whispered.

"Yes," I whispered back. It was more than okay. His touch was different, gentle, enjoyable. My fear of not being able to love someone started to melt away. I looked into his dark eyes. Being there, tightly wrapped in Jackson's embrace felt so right, so *normal*. I forgot about our hellish reality. All I thought about, all I wanted, was Jackson. He was the knight I had been looking for. Instead of shining metal he was covered in scars, which if you ask me, is some of the toughest armor one could wear.

I took my hand from his and moved it up, hovering above his waist. My heart skipped a beat when I let it fall. It was nerve wrecking to be this close to a man when every male I had encountered over the last few months hurt me in some way.

Jackson was different, I reminded myself. He was a victim, like me. I closed my eyes, feeling his muscle contract as he nervously held me in an awkward embrace. I wondered if I'd ever feel desire again. Was it possible for sex to be enjoyable?

I opened my eyes and looked into Jackson's dark eyes, needing to make sure the man I was leaning against was really him and not one of my clients. Jackson gave me another smile, one that made me believe that there really might be hope for us to get out of here alive … and made me believe that yes, I could feel that desire again someday. I could *want* him.

The front door slammed shut, echoing up the stairs and startling me.

"Shit," Jackson swore, his eyes widening. "Zane's home."

CHAPTER 30

"What do we do?" I asked and my body went numb with fear.

Jackson looked at the door, at me, and the door again. He jumped out of bed and ran his hands over his hair. He clenched his jaw. "Stay here. H-he probably won't go downstairs right away."

"Probably." I knelt on the bed, twisting the sheets in my hands. I sharply inhaled, but the breath got caught in my chest. I gasped again.

"Adeline, stay calm. It's gonna be okay. It has to be," he added. He took a breath, stepped forward, and put his hand on the doorknob. "I'll come get you when I can. Just, uh, be quiet."

Jackson left the room, closing the door behind him. I held my breath and waited. I heard Jackson walk down the hall, the old floorboards creaking under him.

I scrambled off the bed when I realized that Zane would immediately see me if he opened the door. I tiptoed across the room and stood in the threshold of the bathroom. My hands trembled. I was terrified of what Zane would do to me if he found me in Jackson's room, but I was even more afraid of what he would do to Jackson. I wrapped my arms around myself and closed my eyes, trying to will myself not to panic.

I thought about Jackson, remembering the way his lips felt against mine. I wanted to feel it again. I was scared we would never get the chance. I let out a breath and opened my eyes, having avoided hyperventilating.

Voices floated up the stairs. I strained to hear what was being said, but the words were too muffled. Then they stopped talking. I put a hand on the doorframe and leaned out of the bathroom. Someone walked up the stairs, the click of hard-soled shoes echoing throughout the house. I stepped into the shadowy bathroom. Jackson was barefoot. It was Zane who was walking down the hall.

I jumped into the shower, hiding behind the curtain. There was nothing I could use as a weapon. I heard a soft click as the bedroom door opened. I put my hands over my mouth to silence my ragged breath.

"Addie?" Jackson whispered.

"Oh, thank God," I breathed.

"Where are you?" he quietly asked.

I carefully stepped out of the tub. "I was hiding in the bathroom."

"Oh," he said as I emerged into the bedroom. He turned around, looking down the hall. "You have to hurry. Zane is changing. Go, now!"

I dashed to the door. Jackson put his hand on the small of my back and ushered me forward. He went first to make sure Zane was still in his room. With a racing heart, I ran through the hall. My bare feet slapped against the polished wood when I skidded to a stop at the top of the stairs. I internally winced but didn't look back, knowing that Jackson was right behind me.

We frantically ran down the stairs, through the living room, and into the kitchen. I had to stop and unlock the basement door before I could throw it open and hurry down into the dungeon. When my feet hit the cold cement floor, I felt a small sense of relief.

"I've never been glad to be down here," I panted.

"Me neither," Jackson agreed. "That was close. Too close."

I nodded. "Yeah." We walked over to the closet and I opened the door. Dread pulled down on me. I didn't want to go back inside.

"You won't be in there for much longer," Jackson told me. I wanted to believe him but we both knew there was no way for him to really know that. He stepped close to me, gently slipping his fingers through mine. "I have to pick up the girls now."

I just nodded again, holding his gaze. I tightened my hold on his hand. I hated being alone in the basement, and I hated it even more when I had to go back into the closet. It was tempting to just sit on the cot and see if Zane would notice, but there was no way I'd risk Jackson like that.

"I don't want you to leave," I whispered.

He stepped closer so that our foreheads touched. "I don't want to leave either. Not without you."

Jackson's eyes met mine one last time before he turned around and hurried up the stairs. The locks clicked into place. I stood in the dim light, looking at the spot where Jackson had stood. A shiver ran through me, bringing my headache back. I blinked and walked into the closet not a moment too soon, pulling it shut behind me.

I sat on the floor as Zane came down the stairs. *Oh, shit.* I was wearing Jackson's clothes. Would Zane even notice? I shook my head. He might not ... if he didn't notice that the door wasn't actually locked first.

I pushed my foot against the door to keep it from swinging open and held my breath. The key slid into the lock. Please, please, just turn normally. My heart pounded against my chest. I pressed sweaty palms onto my thighs. There was a small click and Zane pushed open the door. I moved my foot back and blinked up at him.

"Son of a bitch. You're still alive." He shook his head. "Why do I have such bad luck?"

And then he turned and left. *Oh my God.* He didn't notice anything. I let out a sigh and stood, just then realizing that I was shaking. I paced around the basement for a while and settled on my cot. I pulled the blankets over me and tried to relax. A smile subconsciously settled on my face when I thought of Jackson. I wanted so badly to be back upstairs with him.

I rolled over. We could be somewhere, anywhere but here. Together.

I had just fallen asleep when Lily and Rochelle clomped down the stairs. I sat up, blinking when they turned on the bright lights. Phoebe trailed behind them. Her hair was a tangled mess, and she had dark circles under her eyes.

I looked at Rochelle. She gave me a tight smile and turned around, sitting at the card table to remove her hot pink heels. Lily went to the vanity and started removing the obnoxious amount of makeup she had on. I got up and followed Phoebe, who staggered her way to her bed.

"Phoebe?" I said quietly and sat next to her.

"Hi Addie," she replied flatly.

"Are you okay?"

She gave me a weak smile. "Very tired." She coughed and pulled back the quilt. I put my hand on her cheek. "You better now," she said quietly.

"Almost." I moved my face close to her ear. "Jackson took care of me."

Confusion muddled her face for a second. "Oh, yes. He alive."

I couldn't help but smile. "He is."

"You see him?"

"He took care of me," I repeated. "He brought me up into his room and nursed me back to health."

"You have sex?" she asked a little louder than a whisper. I winced and hoped no one else heard.

"No, of course not."

"Right," she sighed. "We talk later, okay? I sleep now."

"Okay. Night, Phoebe."

She heavily flopped onto her cot and was asleep in minutes. I stuck my feet under my own blankets and lay down, listening to Rochelle talk to Lily.

"How are you feeling?" Lily asked, eyeing me in the mirror.

"Better," I said honestly. "I just slept the whole time."

"Good. You looked awful." Her eyes flicked to Rochelle, who was still busy unclipping her hair extensions. "Jackson's alive," she said quietly.

I couldn't help the smile that formed on my face. "I know."

Lily whirled around. "How do you know?"

Shit. Was I not supposed to know? "He brought me food," I said quickly.

"Oh," Lily said and shook her head. "I forgot he does that. I thought I could like see spirits or something. I was so sure he was dead."

"Me too. He really did get shot."

Lily's eyebrows raised in surprise. "Really?"

I nodded. Lily scrunched her face and looked down. I knew she was internally battling the truth versus whatever the hell she had been brainwashed with.

"He wouldn't have gotten shot if he did what he was told," she said and sounded just like Rochelle.

I didn't want to argue. I knew there was no point. I just nodded and rolled over on the lumpy mattress, wondering how many years of therapy it would take to fix Lily and Rochelle.

I pulled the quilt over my head and listened to Rochelle talk to Lily. Lily told Rochelle that she was tired of working so much. Rochelle abruptly changed the subject and told Lily that her clients loved her. She was a lot more obvious than Zane in her attempt to manipulate, but she was getting good. About an hour later, Rochelle finally shut up.

My headache was feeling more and more like a migraine again. I needed to sleep it off. I forced my eyes shut and focused on taking slow, steady breaths while thinking about Jackson until I drifted to sleep.

CHAPTER 31

I was warm, almost to the point of being hot. I pushed the old quilt back, enjoying the coldness of the basement that for the first time all winter. Then my eyes flew open. Why wasn't I cold? I sat up and noticed that a thick fleece blanket had been draped over me. I ran my fingers over the blue fabric and smiled.

A plate of buttered toast, apple slices, and three sausage patties sat was waiting for me, along with a glass of milk. I grabbed it and devoured the sausage. It was slightly warmer than room temperature. I must have just missed Jackson. I looked around the room. Rochelle and Lily were gone, and Phoebe was still asleep.

I put the empty plate down, the ceramic clinking against the cement floor. Then I saw something sticking out from under the blue blanket. I pulled it back and found a black hooded sweatshirt. It was oddly folded with the sleeves tied together, creating a strange ball of material. I picked it up and realized something was tucked inside.

A smile immediately pulled up my face. I slowly opened the book. The binding was cracked, and the edges of the cover were worn from being read over and over. I closed it and ran my fingers over the title.

"Gone with the Wind," I whispered and smiled again. I pushed my pillow against the wall, wrapped the blue fleece blanket around my shoulders, and opened the book. I read each line as slow as I possibly could, savoring every second of reading

I was able to get.

I was so enthralled in the story that I didn't hear Phoebe get up until she coughed. I jerked my attention away from the book. Phoebe staggered out of bed, her gait unsteady.

"Phoebe?" I asked and set the book down. I slid it under my pillow just in case. "Are you okay?"

"Khoẻ, cảm ơn," she said in her native language.

"What?"

She repeated herself, looking confused as to why I wasn't responding.

"English, please," I said. My voice shook. Phoebe's olive complexion was pale, with large blotches on her cheeks and hands. She had deep bags under her eyes, and her lips were chapped.

I got up and rushed over to her side. "You probably have what I had," I said, though deep down I knew it was more than a mild case of the flu. "I'll tell Jackson. He'll bring you something."

Phoebe coughed again and put her hand out, needing help. Her skin was hot to the touch. I led her to the shower and turned on the water. She sank down on the stool in front of the vanity. I grabbed a rag, held it under the icy water, and wrung it out.

"This should help," I said, trying hard to keep my voice calm. I placed it on the back of her neck. "You need to drink lots of fluids too. Once the fever goes down you'll feel better. I did."

She just nodded and rested her head in her hands. After she went to the bathroom and took a fast shower, I tucked her back into bed and brought her a banana.

"If you run," she began and peeled the banana, "find my family. Tell them truth."

"I won't have to. You'll tell them because you'll run too."

"Too tired to run," she mumbled.

"Today," I said and tried to convince myself it was true. "Today you are." I shook my head. "And I don't have a good plan yet. I need to figure out how to take this damn ankle bracelet off without causing the alarm to sound."

"Yes," she said and ate the banana. She said she was tired and laid down again.

I paced around the basement for a few minutes wanting

to stretch my tight muscles. Being curled up in bed feeling sick caused my legs and back to become quite sore.

Satisfied that I stretched enough, I went back to my cot and slid *Gone with the Wind* out from under my pillow. I read another ten pages before the basement door opened. I shoved the book under the pillow so fast it bent the pages.

"It's me," Jackson said.

"Good," I breathed. A smile immediately pulled up my lips. My heart swelled, and I wanted to be close to him, feeling his heart beat next to mine. "Phoebe's sick."

"I noticed." He hurried down the stairs. "When I picked her up I could tell. She's not herself."

"Will Nate let her go to a doctor?"

Jackson cast his eyes down. He knew something, and he didn't want to tell me. He walked over and stopped by the cot, sitting next to me. I scooted over to him, my heart speeding up at the touch of his skin. He slipped his fingers through mine and gently tugged my arm in his direction. I let my body fall and rested my head on his shoulder.

"What aren't you telling me?" He heavily sighed and let go of my hand to shyly wrap his arm around me. His fingers hovered above my waist, waiting to see if I'd object before he placed his hand on me. I took a deep breath and closed my eyes, not wanting Jackson to tell me bad news anymore. I just wanted to sit like this.

"I told Nate she was sick." He shook his head.

"And?" I asked, apprehension growing.

"He said that she was easy to replace. H-he doesn't care. I'm sorry, Addie."

"It's not your fault," I reminded him. We sat in silence for a few minutes, listening to Phoebe's ragged breathing. "Thanks for the blanket and the book."

Jackson's hold on me tightened. "You're welcome."

I twisted toward him, looping my arm around his. "Can you stay down here with me?"

"I can." He moved my hair over my shoulder. "For just a few minutes though. Nate is in the shower." He looked up at the pipes that snaked along the ceiling. "You can tell when the water shuts off."

"I kinda picked up on that," I said with a yawn.

"Tired?"

"A little. I still feel kinda sick," I admitted.

"Do you want to lie down? I can leave."

"No," I blurted. "I don't want you to go."

Jackson smiled. "Then I'll stay." He lifted his hand, extended it towards me, pulled it back, and then reached out again. His fingers were shaking when he put his hand on my back. Fear jolted through me as I got a flash of a client shoving his hand down the back of my pants. I took a steadying breath, reminding myself I was with Jackson, not a client.

I closed my eyes and put my head against his chest, listening to his heart beat. I remembered what he had said about being too old for clients. Did that mean he had been raped too? I hooked my other hand on his shoulder, turning into him.

"You're worried about her, aren't you?" His breath was warm on the back of my neck.

"Yes," I answered and opened my eyes to look at Phoebe. "And not being able to do anything just makes it worse."

"It does," he agreed and hugged me tighter. His lips brushed against my skin and it didn't abhor me. I felt safe, like nothing bad could touch me when Jackson was holding me. "I wish I could make her better." He sighed. "I wish I could make *all* of this better." He cautiously tightened the hug. I got a flash of the day Rosie died, remembered the instant comfort his embrace brought me. I pulled him a little closer to me, feeling his pulse bound through is body.

My heart began to beat a little faster. I loosened my grip on Jackson and looked up, bringing my face to his. He bent his head down until our noses touched.

"I'd do anything for you," he whispered.

I put my hand over the bullet wound. "I know."

He rested his forehead against mine. One hand gently cupped my face while the other moved to the small of my back, bringing me closer. He paused, making sure it wasn't too much for me.

I curled my fingers, balling his shirt in my hand. "Jackson," I breathed. I felt so deeply for him right then. Everything he'd been through … we'd been through … everything he risked for me. Tears welled in my eyes and my face broke.

"Adeline," he whispered back, wiping away a renegade tear with his thumb. "Don't cry. I promise, somehow it'll be okay. Somehow, some way I'll get you out of here."

I just nodded, unable to help the tears that kept coming. I blinked them away, watching as they fell onto Jackson's shirt. I took in a shaky breath and looked into Jackson's eyes. He held my gaze, looking past the hurt and fear, past the damage until he saw me, the real me.

He closed his eyes and kissed me, his lips gently pressing against mine. Warmth flowed through me as his kiss not only touched my lips but my soul. It was right then that I knew I needed him, that we needed each other. I leaned forward, opening my mouth just a little. I could feel Jackson's heart race as he held me close.

"Are you sure this is okay?" he asked, pulling away a few inches

"Yes," I whispered and put my hand over his chest, feeling his fast pulse. "I am sure. Is it for you?"

Jackson smiled. "Yes."

My chest tightened. "I hope you don't get sick from me," I told him.

"It'd be worth it," he said with a smile. He put his arms back around me and leaned against the wall. I relaxed against him.

The pipe rattled from the shower shutting off.

We sat up. My brow furrowed as I looked at Jackson. He put his hand on my cheek. "I wish I could stay with you," he whispered.

I wrapped my hands around his shoulders. "Me too." I closed my eyes and tipped my head up to see into his eyes. "You should go before you get caught."

"I should." His lips brushed against mine as he spoke, and he made no attempt to leave.

"Jackson," I whispered. "Go. Before you get in trouble." I had yet to release him from my embrace. He nodded again and stood, his hands lingering on mine before he walked across the basement.

"I'll set medicine for Phoebe on the top step," he said quietly and hurried to the base of the stairs. He grabbed the railing and put one foot on the first stair. "I'll come back when I can."

I gave him a small smile. "I know."

I looked at the spot where he had just stood, heart aching already.

Several hours passed before the door opened. I knew right away it wasn't Jackson. I stashed the book under my pillow and waited for Nate to walk down the steps. His eyes scanned the dim room.

"Where is the China girl? She was supposed to be ready ten minutes ago."

"She's from Vietnam," I told him. Nate glared at me. "She's in bed because she's sick." I gathered my strength and stood. "She needs to see a doctor." I turned around, waving my hand at Phoebe. "All she needs is some antibiotics and she'll be good as new."

"Get her up," Nate said calmly and looked at his gold watch. "Now."

"Phoebe," I said gently, turning to her cot. "Pheebs, wake up."

Phoebe groggily sat up, rubbing her eyes.

Nate wrinkled his nose. "She looks awful. You'll do," he said to me. "Run a comb through your hair and come here."

I swallowed hard and didn't move.

"Now," Nate repeated. When I stood in the same spot, he crossed the basement. I knew he would hit me, but I didn't care.

My heart skipped a beat when he walked passed me. He stopped next to Phoebe's cot and grabbed a handful of her hair, yanking her head up. Phoebe cried out in pain.

"Now." He twisted his fingers.

Shaking with fear, I scurried to the vanity and picked up a brush. I raked it through my tangled hair as quickly as I could. I set it down and turned to Nate.

"Get dressed."

I hurried to the dresser and put on a pair of shiny leggings, black boots, and a body-hugging red dress.

"Go upstairs," he said and didn't let go of Phoebe until I was halfway up the stairs.

Zane was at the top of the stairs. He grabbed my wrist and ushered me into his black Camaro after getting a warning from Nate not to let me be seen. Just when I wondered why he was even letting me leave the house, Nate said this was a long standing and trusted client who wouldn't turn him in. I madly looked around for Jackson but didn't see him anywhere.

Zane seemed bored as soon as we left the driveway. He plugged in his iPod and scrolled through his playlist, swerving each time he took his eyes off the road. I held onto the seat, digging my fingers into the leather, and tried to convince myself that getting into an accident could actually work in my favor.

Zane didn't so much as look at me on the drive into Davenport. My heart raced with excited nerves. I was out of the house and in the city again. Could this be my chance? I could run, scream, do anything to make a fuss and get noticed.

We drove through downtown and ended up in a neighborhood full of townhouses, reminding me of the subdivision my grandparents lived in. Zane pulled into a driveway, put the car in park, and jumped out. He grabbed my hand and walked slowly to the door. If anyone saw us, they would assume we were a regular couple. I craned my neck, looking for someone to call out to, but there was no one around.

The front door flew open before Zane knocked. A tall man with silver hair stood in the threshold. He was wearing a white cardigan over a pale blue button up shirt that was tucked into mud-colored dress pants. He let his eyes run up and down my body before settling on my face.

"My, my," he said. His voice was high pitched and raspy. "This one has nice skin. Hasn't seen a lick of sunlight." He reached out to touch me. Zane yanked me back.

"Pay up," he ordered.

The silver haired man licked his lips. "Yes," he said, drawing out the word. He turned around and quickly paced into the house. He came back with his wallet. "Cash only, right?" He asked and Zane nodded. I watched him slowly count out the money. My fear increased every time he added another fifty to the stack. He was paying for a long time.

"No refunds," Zane said with a smirk and shoved me forward like he always did. I was ready for it and didn't so much as lose my balance. I hoped it pissed him off. The door slammed behind me. I gulped in air, feeling like I was suffocating.

"Come in, come in," the silver haired man said, like I had a choice. I was standing on a small section of white linoleum that gave way to the carpeted living room. A flower-printed couch complete with pink lace doilies covering the arms. A teddy bear with a large pale pink bow sat in the center of the couch. A hand painted picture of a white rabbit with a butterfly on its nose hung over the couch.

"I'm Jeremy," the silver haired man said.

I looked at him. Clients never introduced themselves. The few times I had been told names was when they wanted me to call it out during sex. Jeremy held out his hand. I stared at it for a few seconds before reaching out and taking it. He led me through the living room and down a hall. Every bedroom and bathroom door was open. Except for one.

His fingers tightened with excitement, hurting my hand. He pulled a key from his sweater pocket, unlocked the door, and pushed it open. My eyes widened in horror as my breath escaped my lungs. I locked my knees, not wanting to go into the room.

Jeremy let me go and clasped his hands together, smiling broadly. "Come on in, my dear. It's time for tea!"

CHAPTER 32

My head shook, and I put my hands on my elbows, pressing my arms into my stomach. A hundred glass eyes glared at me. My lip quivered as I looked over the shelves of porcelain dolls. A small table was set up in the middle of the room covered with a white lace tablecloth. A blue and white china tea set was on the center of the table.

Jeremy pranced into the room and put a needle down on a record player. Scratchy crackles gave way to a slow violin. Jeremy picked up a blue satin dress, holding it as if it was sacred.

"Put this on and then we'll do your hair and makeup!" he cooed. I still didn't move. "Come on, be a dear!" he said and waved me in.

I slowly shook my head.

Jeremy's eyes narrowed, and his lips curled over his teeth. "They said you'd play along!" he growled, his Mr. Rogers demeanor gone. I stepped into the room. Jeremy moved with more speed than someone his age should posses and shut the door.

I wanted to scream when I saw him lock it and pocket the key. I was locked in the room with a maniac. *Holy shit*. I was terrified. I fucking hated porcelain dolls. They creeped me out. He thrust the blue dress at me again. I closed my eyes, causing tears to stream down my cheeks. I just wanted it to be over with.

I took the dress and turned around. I removed my clothes, glaring at Jeremy. My hands trembled with fear, and I struggled with the zipper.

"There you go, my dear," Jeremy said and moved over. He lifted my hair off my back and pressed it to his nose, loudly inhaling before he slowly pulled up the zipper. "Oh, my! Look at this, Miss Molly!"

I wrapped my arms around myself and looked behind me.

"You match!" he cried with delight and hugged a doll. She too was wearing a blue satin dress with white lace trim. Terror caused my arms and legs to lock up as I watched the psychopath cuddle the doll.

"Come sit and get your hair done," he said to me and waved at a white vanity table next to a window. He set the doll down, fussing with the bow in her hair, and opened the top drawer of the vanity. My lungs expanded and I sucked in air, yet I felt like I couldn't breath. What exactly did this creep plan on doing with me?

I sat on a velvet-lined stool and eyed Miss Molly. One of her fake eyelids was stuck halfway closed. Her hair wasn't perfectly neat like the other dolls. Her brown curls were shiny, but not as shiny as the plastic hair most dolls had. And then I noticed the split ends.

Oh God. Her hair was real. My pulse pounded, and I felt instantly cold. I blinked. That didn't mean anything, right? Maybe she came that way. Maybe Jeremy *didn't* dress up another living girl, kill her, and cut off her hair.

Or maybe he had. I needed to get out of there before I became the next victim. Fear tingled along my spine.

"I'll start with your hair," Jeremy said and plugged in a curling iron.

I shivered with disgust when he picked my hair up off my back. He combed it with his fingers before running a Victorian style silver brush through it.

"The color is a bit lighter than Miss Molly's, but it will do," he said.

Jeremy parted my hair down the middle. Then he pulled it up into pigtails. He stepped back and misted my head with hairspray before he began curling it. He worked slowly and meticulously making sure each curl was perfect and even, humming along to the old-timey music.

"Beautiful," he breathed and set the hot iron down. "Now," he said and turned back to the vanity, opening another drawer. "Your complexion needs some work." He reached inside the drawer and extracted several bottles of foundation, holding each one up to my skin to find the best match.

The liquid makeup was cold and sticky on my skin. I sat as still as my trembling body allowed. Jeremy had turned me away from the mirror. His face was close to mine as he leaned in to blend the makeup. I refused to look at him. My eyes scanned the shelves of dolls. Most were wearing frilly dresses in pastel colors, and almost all had large bows and shiny ringlets of curls. I started counting. There were forty-two crammed onto the top shelf across from me. Fancy teacups and antique silver jewelry boxes were randomly squeezed in between the dolls. I was sure if I looked hard enough I would find hidden jars of formaldehyde with floating body parts as well.

I flinched when he came at me with a mascara wand, causing little black lines to smear on my skin. Jeremy licked his finger and wiped away the makeup. I forced my eyes wide and didn't blink until he was done. He curled my lashes, going back and forth with the metal device until they were perfectly even. Next came bright red lipstick and enough powder to cause me to cough.

"Perfect!" he squealed and put his hands up to his face. He picked up Miss Molly. "What do you think, my dear?" He looked at the doll. "You are right. She *could* use some more powder."

I swallowed hard, anticipating that his next move would be covering my mouth and nose with a chloroform soaked rag. Instead, he spun me around so I could inspect my reflection in the mirror. My face was a shade lighter than its natural color. All the powder caused my skin to look cakey and fake. My eyes appeared surprisingly large on my face, and the cherry red lipstick looked ridiculous.

"What do you think?" he asked me.

"Beautiful," I said right away, not missing a beat. I wadded up the hem of the dress to steady my hands.

"I know!" He twirled around with Miss Molly. "And to think, they said mortuary school was a waste of time." He laughed and glided over to the table. "Now, come on, it's time for tea!"

With timorous movements, I pushed myself off the stool

and went over to the table. Jeremy pulled out the chair for me before seating himself. He uncovered a tray of tiny cakes and cookies. As much as I didn't want to admit it, they looked good. Good, but sure to house some sort of hidden poison that would render me unconscious and paralyzed on the floor.

"I just made these this morning," he said and picked up an oatmeal cookie. He broke it in half, giving part to Miss Molly. He put the other half on his plate. "Go on, be a dear and eat!"

If he was eating the cookies, they probably *weren't* poisoned, right? I apprehensively reached out and took an oatmeal cookie as well.

Jeremy poured three cups of tea and nibbled on his cookie. He never took his eyes off me and seemed to get enjoyment watching me sip the hot beverage. My eyes flitted to the window; the sun was low in the sky, leaving me to believe that I had been here for at least two hours.

The moment I set my teacup down, Jeremy refilled it. He gave me a slice of strawberry cake. I picked up a small silver fork and cut off a tiny piece. Jeremy bit his lip and leaned in, watching as I put the cake in my mouth.

Lynn liked strawberries and anything strawberry flavored. Strawberry wine was her current obsession. The cake wasn't bad. The frosting was very sweet and it hurt my teeth, making me wish I had gotten the cavity in my back molar filled over spring break like my dad suggested.

I broke off another piece and put it in my mouth, forcing a smile. I inhaled a mouthful of sugarless tea, hoping the sooner I finished teatime, the sooner this creep would be done playing living dolls.

I was wrong.

I set down my empty teacup feeling sickly full, fearful, and had to pee. Jeremy popped out of his seat and flew over to the record player. He put a new record on and spun around. He threw his arms out at me.

"Time to dance!" he said.

I stiffly nodded and forced myself up. Goosebumps had broken out over my skin. The room was cold. Probably to keep the bodies fresh.

"Have you ever been ballroom dancing?" he asked.

"No," I said. My voice was small and weak; the sound barely left my throat.

"We practice every night, don't we Miss Molly?" He cast an endearing look at the lifeless doll. "I will teach you." He pulled me close to him and placed my hands around his neck. "Just follow my lead."

He ungracefully shuffled his feet around. I struggled to stay out of the way and not get stepped on. I was by no means a professional dancer, or any dancer at all, for that matter, but I had watched enough cheesy dance competition shows with Lynn to know that Jeremy had no idea what he was doing either.

Finally the record stopped. Jeremy pulled me into an embrace. His hand moved from my back to my waist and slowly trailed up to my chest.

"Oh my," he whispered when his finger traced my nipple. "My oh my." Then he suddenly moved away, picking up the doll. He set her on the floor then had me lie down next to her. He picked up my arm, moving it so it was positioned the same way as the doll's. He messed with my curls then retrieved an old Polaroid camera.

The doorbell rang just as he took the photo. I closed my eyes and let out a breath. *Thank God.* My eyes flew open, and a desperate giggle escaped my lips when I realized I was happy that Zane was back. Jeremy sighed and stomped his foot in frustration. I stared at him, taken aback by his childlike tantrum, though what else should I have expected from a grown man with a room full of dolls?

"Time to take off the dress," he whined. I hurried over to the corner where my clothes had been thrown. I pulled the zipper down so fast it caught on the material. I didn't care. I yanked it over my head, wincing when I heard a seam tear. I froze, waiting for Jeremy to freak out on me.

He was too busy with the door to notice. I slowly exhaled and let the blue dress fall to the floor. I got redressed with such haste that I didn't notice I had put my clothes on inside out. I didn't care. I just wanted out.

Jeremy led the way through the townhouse. The doorbell rang again. That might have been the only time I was thankful for Zane's impatience. When the door opened, I expected Zane to grab me and drag me to the car, then peel out of the quiet little subdivision and speed down the highway.

Zane stood on the stoop all right, but his arms were crossed and he leaned against the side of the house with a smirk on his face. His eyes glinted with wicked amusement as he studied the man next to him.

"Adeline!" Jackson exclaimed. His brown eyes opened in shock, and his face drained of color. For months, I hadn't left the house. I was the last person he expected to see. And I was the only person in the house he was willing to risk his life for. Zane's smirk turned into an evil grin, and suddenly I knew the real reason why Jackson was back.

CHAPTER 33

An entire week passed before I was able to talk to Jackson. I hadn't been forced to work in that time. There had to be a reason. It wasn't like Nate had forgotten about me. I was too grateful to question it. Even thinking about it made me fear that I would jinx it somehow and Nate would order me back to the guest room.

Jackson carried a tray with our food allowance for the day down the stairs and set it on the table. Lily and Rochelle were in front of the large mirror, fussing over each other's hair. I sat on Phoebe's cot, snapping a rubber hair tie that I had stretched between my thumb and index finger.

Jackson's eyes swept through the room and immediately found me. It was awful being in the same room with him and not being able to touch him. He pressed his lips together and eyed the girls, then set the tray down on the card table and picked up a very full laundry basket. He looked at Phoebe, then me, his eyes questioning. I shook my head, telling him that she hadn't gotten any better.

I got up and went to the table, slowly sorting through the food. Jackson walked back and deliberately dropped the basket. I bent down to help him pick up the clothes.

"Are you okay?" he whispered and grabbed a pair of fishnet tights. "I wasn't expecting to see you at that house."

"I know," I told him and reached out for his hand. I laced my fingers through his and squeezed his hand. Our eyes met, and my heart ached, wanting to be closer to Jackson. Even though he was right in front of me, I missed him. "Nate brought you back for more reasons than to do housework."

"What?"

"It hit me when I saw Zane's face when you guys picked me up. He knew it would upset you to see me. He knows that you like me, and he likes hurting you so…"

"I did wonder why he came with," he said and bent forward to scoop up more clothing.

I swallowed hard and shook my head. "He will use me against you."

"I know," he admitted. He looked up at me, giving me a small, hopeful smile. I pushed my hair away from my face. "You can't let them know you have feelings for me. No matter what. You can't let them have that advantage over you." We stood, and I noticed Rochelle watching us in the mirror. "I'll come back when I can," he whispered and hurried up the stairs.

I opened a container of yogurt and picked up a spoon. I went back to Phoebe's cot and tried to feed her. She ate about half before she let her eyes close. My lip quivered, and hot tears burned in my eyes. I set the yogurt down and took her hand in mine, pressing it to my forehead.

"You're gonna be okay," I soothed. "You have to be."

"I'm cold," she said hoarsely.

I got up and took the blue fleece blanket off my cot and tucked it around Phoebe. Something was familiar about her symptoms, but I couldn't recall what was causing it. The splotchy skin, the constant fatigue … I was sure it was some sort of sexually transmitted infection.

"Is she okay?" Lily asked, her blue eyes wide with fear. She was holding a makeup brush in one hand.

"She won't be for much longer," I admitted and felt a lump of vomit rise in my throat. "She needs to see a doctor."

Lily turned to Rochelle. "I told you. Please, Rochelle. *Please*," she begged.

Rochelle finished applying her eyeliner before she even acknowledged Lily. "He will never listen."

The brush dropped from Lily's hand. "You have to try again!" She stuck her hand out. "Look at her!"

Rochelle closed her eyes, causing fat tears to roll down her face, streaking the thick makeup she had layered on. "Okay. I'll ask."

I had a feeling I knew who she was talking about. "Zane?" I asked.

"Yes," Lily answered. "If she can just get him to get a prescription like he did for you, she'll be fine, right Addie?"

I narrowed my eyes. "Prescription?"

"From Dr. Jerry," Lily said as if I should know. When she saw my blank expression, she went on to explain. "He's the doc who gives Nate our birth control pills. He's one of Rochelle's clients."

"Oh," I said, at a loss for words. I let out a breath. "Do you think you can get something, anything, for Phoebe?"

"I'll try," Rochelle told us. Her voice was level, but I could see that just the thought of asking Zane something terrified her.

"Thank you," I said sincerely and turned my attention back to Phoebe. She slept while Lily and Rochelle finished getting ready. Rochelle's heels clicked on the wooden steps. She paused at the top and knocked on the door. A few seconds later, it opened, and she and Lily were ushered out of the basement to begin the day's work.

I did my routine of pacing around the basement and straightening my cot. My skin under the ankle bracelet was dry and itchy. I scratched at it until it became red.

I sat at the card table with my head in my hands, staring at the broom closet's door. It taunted me, reminding me of my first few days as a captive.

"Addie?" Phoebe croaked. I stood up so fast, the metal folding chair fell to the ground.

"Yes," I answered right away.

"Can you bring water?" she asked.

"Of course." I hurried to fill up a plastic cup with icy water and bring it to her. She took small sips but finished the entire thing. She ran her hands through her messy hair and sat up.

"Feel better now," she told me with a smile. "No worry."

"I do worry. You're my friend."

She patted my arm. "Friend."

"Yes," I said with a half smile.

She took a deep breath and looked around as if she just realized we were alone. "You like Jackson," she stated.

I didn't even try to deny it. "I do."

"I see how he look at you. He like you too."

I felt my heart skip a beat. "I think he does."

"You more than think," she teased and nudged me with her elbow. She swung her legs over the cot and stood. Her hand flew to her forehead and she moaned in pain. "Head hurt."

I stood. "This should help," I told her and hopped over the cot and reached under my pillow, extracting a handful of little white pills. I picked off a few pieces of fuzz and hair and gave her two. She put them in her mouth and swallowed them dry. I closed my eyes in a long blink and refused to think about how unhealthy she was.

CHAPTER 34

I was alone once again. Around the time the sun had set, Phoebe had been summoned upstairs to work. I was wearing Jackson's sweatshirt with the hood pulled up over my head. I couldn't stop thinking about him, and I missed him so much it hurt. I hated that we were in the same house, so close together but separated by one locked door and lots of threats.

He was in the kitchen, or at least I thought it was him. I was able to tell the difference in Nate, Zane, and Jackson's footsteps. Zane was a fast walker and often took his shoes off when he was in the house. Nate, on the other hand, kept his on. Usually dressed for business, his dress shoes clicked on the hardwood floors. Jackson shuffled his feet and moved slowly. I assumed it was his way of silently protesting being forced to work.

Whoever was in the kitchen clanked dishes around. I heard water running, and the pipes shook when the dishwasher started. It was definitely Jackson. I got up, holding my arms out in front of me and shaking my hands so that the long sleeves fell back, and crept toward the stairs. I was halfway up when someone unlocked the deadbolt.

I froze, heart pounding in my ears. I grabbed the railing. It was Jackson. It had to be. My fingers tightened around the splintering wood as the oval doorknob turned.

"Shit!" Jackson swore and jumped back, almost dropping the laundry basket full of clean clothes he was holding. He immediately winced. "I wasn't expecting that."

My heart continued to beat faster, but not from fear. "I knew it was you up there."

"Really?" Jackson asked and looked behind him before slipping down the stairs. "How?"

I ungracefully walked backwards down two steps before turning around and jogging down the rest of the way. "Who else washes dishes?" I asked ruefully.

"True," he agreed.

I stopped at the base of the stairs and turned around. "What happened?" I asked and felt a stab of sickness. I took the laundry basket from him, set it down, and carefully touched a tear in Jackson's gray shirt. The edges were soaked in blood.

"Zane," he huffed and shook his head.

"You're still bleeding." I brought my fingers away, showing him the blood.

He shrugged and winced again. I put my hand over the cut on his left shoulder. "It'll stop eventually."

I pressed my lips together and shook my head. "I hate this."

"It'll be okay," he promised me and took my hands in his. Blood smeared against his skin. "Somehow, it has to be okay."

"I almost believe that," I whispered and let my head rest against his chest. I wrapped my arms around his waist and closed my eyes. "At least let me wash the blood off," I said and pulled away from Jackson. He nodded and sat on the cot. I grabbed a clean washcloth and wet it from the shower. I pulled the neck of his long sleeved t-shirt down and gently blotted at the blood.

"Thanks," he said, unmoving.

I pressed the cloth over the wound. He had so many scars. I slipped my hand inside his shirt and ran my finger over a jagged pink line of scar tissue that ran across the right side of his chest. "What is this from?"

Jackson put his hand over mine, feeling the scar. The he curled his fingers through mine. "Broken glass. Five years ago."

I removed the washcloth from his shoulder and dropped it on the ground. "What about these?" I asked and pushed up his sleeve. I traced five straight scars on his right forearm.

"Razor blade. A few months ago."

"And this?" I asked, pressing my lips to another rough patch of healing skin on his neck. Jackson's arms wrapped around me.

"Fire poker," he whispered. "Right out of the fire."

I kept my lips against his skin and reached under his shirt, running my hand up the horrible, thick scar on his side. I had seen the particularly nasty mark the night I learned Jackson's true nature. Before I had the chance to ask about it, Jackson put one arm around me and used the other to cup my face. He gingerly turned it in and kissed me. I stopped thinking about scars and focused on how warm and wonderful Jackson's skin felt. I pulled myself closer to him, pressing my lips harder against his. I ran my fingers through his dark hair and leaned back, bringing him with.

"Are you sure?" he asked so quietly I could barely hear him.

"Yes," I breathed and pulled him close. He was so careful and gentle and I wasn't afraid. His eyes were wide and he trembled slightly. He was nervous. He exhaled and put his lips to mine, starting off slow. He opened his mouth and waiting, pulling back. I moved my hands to his face and brought him to me, deepening the kiss. Then he suddenly stopped kissing me.

"Adeline," he said and moved his face away just enough to be able to see me. There was a light in his dark eyes and he gazed down on me, looking as if he had just found the thing he had been searching for his entire life. "I think I love you."

The breath caught in my chest. My heart swelled, and I smiled. "I think I love you too."

Jackson's entire face lit up and he gave me one of his rare smiles, the kind that erased the years of sadness and torture from his eyes. I slowly ran my fingertips down his back. He put his lips back on mine and kissed me again. I wanted him closer, so close our hearts pounded against each other's. I hooked my arms under his and leaned back, letting him know what I wanted. He let me pull him onto me with ease, carefully keeping his hips off of mine so only the upper half of his body was against me.

Jackson froze. "Is this okay?" he asked, afraid he went too far too fast.

"Yes," I whispered and put my hands on the small of his back. "It's perfectly okay. I can't explain it, Jackson," I started. "But it's different with you," I said. "It just feels *right*. I want you. I want this."

"I do too," he said with a smile. My heart fluttered when he lightly put his lips to mine, giving me a soft kiss. I pulled him close, wanting more.

The floor creaked above us. We both froze. Jackson slowly turned his face towards the stairs, as if he was afraid he would see Nate or Zane standing there.

"You should go," I whispered.

"Yeah," he agreed but rolled to the side, wrapping his body around mine. I moved around on the small cot being careful not to accidentally push Jackson over the edge until I faced him. My head rested right under his. I hooked my leg over his and he pulled me into a tight embrace.

"I wish you could stay. I want to fall asleep in your arms," I whispered. "I feel safe when I'm with you."

"I'll do anything to keep you safe," he told me and kissed my forehead.

I carefully touched the wound on his shoulder. A sticky scab was starting to form. I traced my fingers down his shoulder and wrapped my hand around his bicep over the spot where a bullet ripped through his skin. "Does it hurt?" I asked.

"It feels weird," he said. "My muscles feel tight around it, and the skin is tingly but has no feeling at the same time. Weird."

I closed my eyes and listened to his heartbeat. "What would happen if they found you with me?"

I could feel Jackson shake his head. "Kill me. Seriously." I buried my head against his chest. Cold fear pulsed through me, causing my nerves to prickle. "But we won't get caught," he added, sensing the terror that plagued me.

He couldn't promise that, but I wanted to believe it.

"What if we do?" I pushed myself up onto my elbow. "Jackson," I said frantically. "No, we can't. You can't. I don't want you to die." I shook my head so quickly it caused my hair to fall into Jackson's face.

He reached up and gently tucked my hair behind my ear. "Addie, I'd rather live one day with you than a hundred without. You're the best thing that's ever happened to me."

Jackson put his hand on my shoulder and I was able to relax. I laid back down and let out a breath. "But then I'd be alone."

"You have Phoebe," he reminded me and began rubbing my back. "You'll be ok…somehow."

I pushed his hand away. "Stop it!"

"Stop touching you?" he asked, his face falling.

"No. Stop acting like you're going to die!"

"Addie," Jackson said, his tone clearly telling me that he thought it was all too possible.

"No!" I shook my head again and squeezed my eyes shut, forcing away tears. Jackson sat up, crossing his legs. He pulled me to him. "Don't say it."

The front door opened and closed, sending a rattle throughout the old house. Jackson tensed and quickly disentangled me from his arms and climbed off the cot. I groaned in frustration. I didn't want Jackson to leave.

"The basement door isn't locked," he told me. I nodded, knowing how important it was for him to rush upstairs. "I'll come back," he promised.

He turned to me, eyes locking for a few seconds. Then he pulled me close and gave me another lingering kiss before he hurried to the stairs, skidding to a stop. He turned around and sprinted over. He threw his arms around me and pulled me in for one more kiss before he disappeared upstairs.

CHAPTER 35

Phoebe came back downstairs several hours after the sun set. Her eyes were bloodshot, and she squinted in the dim light. She slowly walked to the shower and turned on the water.

"Where Jackson go?" she asked and took off her clothes. "I see him leave with suitcase."

My heart sank. A suitcase? Was it for him? I hoped not. Maybe he was carrying it for someone else. I didn't want to even think about not seeing him for a long time. The hour-long gaps between our visits were hard enough. "I don't know." I shook my head. "And I don't think he knew since he didn't say anything."

She took a breath and stepped into the shower. "Girls have hotel party. Maybe he take them."

"Hopefully that's all it is."

"Is everyone gone?" I asked, feeling a spark of hope.

"Don't know. Nate here maybe."

"Oh. Damn."

"Zane has new friend," she called, her teeth chattering from the freezing water. "Tall guy. Dark skin. Handsome and strong like Zane. And mean like Zane."

"Great," I mumbled. "Is he going to stay in the house?"

"Think so. I see him before today too."

I bit my lip. My stomach churned, not liking the thought of Jackson being alone upstairs with Zane, Nate, and the new guy. "Have you ever heard of *Gone with the Wind*?"

"Clark Gable?" she called and shut off the shower. The

faucet squeaked and water continued to drip.

"Yes! You've seen it?"

"I have," she said and wrapped a towel around herself. "Illegally on internet." She gave me a small smile and tiptoed across the dirty floor. She stopped at the dresser and quickly pulled out an oversized t-shirt. She put it on, letting the towel drop.

"It's based off of a book," I told her.

"I not know that," she said and leaned over to grab the towel. She wobbled and had to grab the dresser for support. I put my hand on the thin mattress, ready to spring up and help her. She straightened up and blinked several times before giving her head a shake as if she was trying to clear her vision. "You read it?"

I pulled the book out from under my pillow. "I've only gotten through the first couple chapters."

"Oh!" she said, her dark eyes opening in surprise. "Where you get that?"

"Jackson," I told her. "He brought it down. Do you want me to read it out loud?"

"Story time?" she said with a grin.

I raised an eyebrow and shrugged. "What else are we going to do?"

"I like that." She flipped her head upside down and rubbed her hair with the towel. "You talk in different voices for characters."

"Hah, I'll try." I repositioned my pillow and opened the book, flipping to the first page of chapter one. Phoebe tossed her towel near the shower and sat on her cot, combing her hair with her fingers.

"I expect accents!" she teased.

"You won't want me to keep reading if I do that. My friend Lynn and I used to talk in British accents and pretend to be here on vacation. It was fun, until we ran into someone we knew."

Phoebe smiled, pulling her face up and hiding some of her sickness. "Sometime I pretend to be American," she laughed.

"I have to hear that accent" I said and put the book down, using my finger as a bookmark. She turned to me. Suddenly, her smile disappeared. "Pheebs?" I asked.

Her body began to shake. I jumped up. The book clattered to the floor, falling face down and bending the pages. I ran over to her.

"Phoebe!" I screamed. The convulsions increased, and she fell forward. I heard her face smack against the cement before I had the chance to catch her. "Phoebe!" I dropped to my knees. Phoebe's body trembled violently.

"Phoebe!" I screamed again, though saying her name had no effect. I reached out to hold her, but stopped. I had no idea what to do. I was so scared. I shakily inhaled, tears blurring my vision. "Help me!" I screamed as loudly as I could. "Somebody help!"

Phoebe's head smacked against the floor as the seizure intensified. I flipped her over and put my hands on her shoulders, trying to keep her still. Her eyes were wide open, and a look of sheer terror was plastered on her face. Blood oozed from her nose, and I wasn't sure if it was caused by her falling face first onto the hard ground or if something had ruptured internally. I began to hysterically sob, crying her name over and over. I reached over her convulsing body and yanked the pillow off her cot.

I wanted to run away and hide. Seeing Phoebe like this shook me to my very core. "Help, please!" I screamed again as I tried to get the pillow under Phoebe's head. Her body was stiff and I couldn't get her neck to bend up. Then blood-tinged saliva dripped from her mouth, and she made a gurgling sound.

I screamed when I realized she was choking. Tears fell, dripping onto Phoebe's body as I frantically turned her on her side. Her arm got stuck underneath her body, making it hard to turn her. I leaned forward, using my body to keep her from rolling onto her back.

The convulsions slowed and became less violent. I sat up, keeping my hands on her shoulder and hip. My lip trembled, and I subconsciously held my breath. Slowly, I let her body rock back. Her eyes were open, the whites tinged with blood.

"Phoebe?" I called. The only response I got was a blank stare. "Phoebe!" I repeated. "Phoebe!" I shook her. "No, no, no," I cried. I let go and put my hands over my face, sobbing. I pulled at my hair and screamed for help again. The floor creaked.

I held by breath, waiting.

But no one came.

"Phoebe," I cried, barely able to get the word out. I pressed my fingers against her neck. There wasn't a pulse. "No," I whispered.

Terror paralyzed me. My ears rang and I felt dizzy. With my vision starting to black out, I pushed myself up onto my knees and placed my hands on Phoebe's chest. I was shaking so bad it was difficult to establish a good rhythm of compressions, and I lost count after twenty.

I moved to her face, tipping her head back. I pinched her nose shut and blew all of my air into her mouth and them moved back to her chest. Something cracked when I pressed down. I screamed and recoiled, falling backwards and away from Phoebe.

"I'm sorry. I'm sorry," I cried and scrambled up. "Phoebe, please! Please wake up!" I closed my eyes and started compressions again. I counted out thirty and moved to give her air. Then I put my fingers over her carotid artery.

Nothing.

I pressed harder, convincing myself that I would find a weak, thready pulse. Her head flopped to the side. There was no heartbeat. She was gone.

CHAPTER 36

I collapsed, wrapping my arms around Phoebe, and cried. I wasn't sure how long I lay on the floor next to her, but the next time I sat up, her skin was cold and stiff. My hands trembled as I wiped my face, wet with tears and snot. I looked at Phoebe. Her eyes were half closed and her jaw had relaxed, opening her mouth just a bit. She was lying in a puddle of urine and had blood on her face. I didn't want to leave her like that.

I took a few shallow breaths and pushed myself up. My throat hurt, and I was thirsty from crying uncontrollably, though I had no desire to fill up a cup and get a drink. I picked up the towel Phoebe had recently used. It was still damp.

I didn't cry as I cleaned her. I was too shocked, too numb for any more emotions to register. I threw the towel in the shower and turned the water on to wash away the smell of urine. I went back to Phoebe. Her cheeks were already sunken, and her beautiful, olive skin had a grayish tint. I ran my hand over her wet hair, smoothing it into place.

"You're free," I whispered. "Finally free."

The wall broke and I started crying again. I covered Phoebe's body with the blanket from her cot, leaving her face exposed. I stared at her for a few seconds. Her eyes were so lifeless, so haunting. I pulled the blanket over her head. I got up, standing over her. I was trembling, but not from the cold. I pressed the back of my hands against my cheeks, surprised to feel how hot they were. Shakily, I walked back to my cot. I pulled the hood of Jackson's black hoodie over my head and lay down, curling into a ball.

I felt like I was getting sucked backwards into a dark hole filled with cold, muddy water. I gasped for air, breathing in tears, and clutched at my chest. I turned my face into my pillow and cried. Being trapped in the basement with a body—even though she was my friend—scared me. My fingers curled around the blue fleece blanket, nails digging into the fabric.

My eyelids were puffy from crying by the time my legs were stiff and sore from being bent in the fetal position. I stretched out and looked at the window. It was still night. I took in a deep breath and pulled the blue blanket over myself. I closed my eyes, wanting dark sleep to take over and block out the pain.

I slipped in and out of consciousness until the sun rose. Luckily, I hadn't gotten to the point of a deep sleep, the kind with the most vivid dreams. That also meant that I had held onto my anger and sadness. The salient fact that there was a body on the floor haunted me.

I woke up having to pee, but I didn't want to get up. I didn't want to see the lifeless body hidden under a faded quilt on the dirty, cold floor. I waited until it was necessary to get up and rush to the toilet. I kept my eyes on my feet, not risking looking up, and dashed back to the cot once I was done.

My stomach grumbled, and my mouth was so dry. Just then I realized that by sitting there, paralyzed by grief, I was letting myself die too. I got up, took in a breath, and went to the card table. I couldn't bring myself to turn around. I still couldn't handle seeing her. I sorted through the wrappers. The only food that was left was Phoebe's half eaten Pop-tart. I picked it up, breaking off the part she had eaten, saving the untouched part for myself. I quickly ate it and then went to the shower to fill up an unwashed plastic cup with water.

I picked up *Gone with the Wind* and sat on the edge of my cot. I flicked my eyes to Phoebe's empty bed and cleared my throat. My voice trembled as I choked back a sob. "Chapter one." I swallowed the lump that formed in my throat. "Scarlet O'Hara was not beautiful," I read. "But men seldom realized it when caught by her charm as the Tarleton twins were." I didn't know what else to do. I just kept reading.

"Addie?" Jackson's voice came from the top of the stairs, causing me to jump. He hurried down the stairs, his heavy footsteps echoing throughout the basement. I put the book down and stood, suddenly feeling weak. My bottom lip trembled. "What's wrong?" he asked as soon as he saw my face.

I couldn't say the words. I just pointed to Phoebe's cot. Jackson rushed over, his face going white when he saw her. He dropped to the floor and checked her, making sure she was really dead. He stood, taking a few steps back. His head slowly moved to the side. Once his eyes met mine, he snapped himself back to reality.

"Fuck, Addie." He ran over to me. Tears pricked the corners of my eyes. He pulled me in a protective embrace. His arms were shaking. "I'm so sorry."

"I tried," I told him, my voice strained and high-pitched as I tried not to cry. "I tried but it didn't work. I couldn't get it to stop and then I broke something."

Jackson pulled my hair behind my shoulder and rubbed his fingers up and down my back. "What are you talking about?"

"She fell," I said as warm tears streamed down my face. "And had a seizure. Then she stopped breathing and I couldn't find her pulse."

"Shhh," Jackson soothed when I started crying again.

I remembered the sound of her sternum cracking and the way it felt crunching under my hands. My knees felt weak, and my legs began to buckle. Jackson scooped me up and sat on the cot, keeping me in his lap. I hooked my arms around his neck and took a deep breath. He smelled clean, like laundry detergent and soap. For some reason, the scent was calming. I buried my face against his skin and closed my eyes.

"I won't let this happen," he whispered. "Not anymore. I can't ... we can't. I hate seeing you get hurt." He shook his head. "Let's run."

His words sent a shock through my numb body. "Really?" I asked and lifted my head off his neck.

"Yes, really." He pulled me to him, our lips meeting for a fleeting kiss. I tangled my fingers in his hair and never wanted to let him go. I loved Jackson, needed him. I didn't want him to go upstairs and be left alone down here. I didn't want Nate and

Zane to hurt him. I wanted us to be together without fearing for our lives. Shoes echoed on the old wooden planks as someone walked down the stairs. Jackson stood so fast I almost fell to the floor.

"What the fuck are you doing down here?" Zane asked Jackson. His tone was angry, but excitement gleamed in his eyes. He wanted to catch Jackson doing something he wasn't supposed to. It gave Zane a reason to hurt him.

"Phoebe," Jackson stated and waved his hand in her direction. "She's dead."

"Shit," Zane swore and looked annoyed. "No wonder it smells like ass."

I bit my bottom lip and stared at the ground. Jackson crossed his arms. "I'll take the body," he said.

"How dead is she?" Zane asked and walked around the cot. He covered his nose with his arm and nudged Phoebe's body with the toe of his shoe. "She was supposed to work." He tipped his head and knelt down. "Maybe … " he shook his head. "No, not fresh enough."

I thought I was going to puke. My head turned up, and I stared at Zane in horror. He stood and caught my gaze. He eyed me up and down and frowned in disgust. He swiftly walked over, extending his arm. Jackson ran over, putting himself in front of me.

"Don't touch her," Jackson said. His hands curled into fists.

Zane laughed. "Get the fuck out of the way," he ordered. "Unless you want me to shoot you. Again." He reached behind him and extracted a small, black handgun. Using it as a pointer, her flicked his wrist. "Over there. Now," he said to Jackson.

"No," Jackson said.

"Very well," Zane said and flicked off the safety. His eyes moved to where Phoebe lay. He let out a heavy sigh. "I really don't feel like dealing with two bodies. Last chance. Move."

Not breathing, I stared at Jackson. *Move, please move.* I couldn't handle losing anyone else, especially him. Finally, his tense shoulders sagged and he stepped aside.

"Get dressed," Zane ordered me.

"What?" I asked, shaking my head.

"Are you deaf?" He leaned forward and I jumped. "Put

something else on." He recoiled, wrinkling his nose. "I don't want to be seen in public with you. When was the last time you showered?"

It hadn't been that long, but I didn't tell him that. I didn't say anything as I glared at him, heart thumping in my tight chest. Was I being put to work again? I stood there, in a tense stare off with Zane, until he growled and lunged forward, taking a hold of my wrist. He dragged me with him, up the stairs and into the kitchen, muttering about how slow I was

"Lou," Zane called.

The man Phoebe referred to as Zane's new friend lumbered into the room. I let my eyes trace over his body. He took up the entire doorframe and had to duck to get into the kitchen. He boasted large muscles that were shown off under a tight-fitting white t-shirt. His head had been shaved, and his dark skin was gleaming, looking as if he had recently rubbed oil over it. Tattoos covered most of his exposed skin. He looked like he belonged on the cover of a fitness magazine.

"Watch her," Zane said to Lou. "I have to talk to Nate."

Lou leaned against the counter and crossed his arms, purposely flexing his biceps. He looked me over, raised an eyebrow, and shook his head. My eyes had to be red and puffy from crying. I was wearing Jackson's clothes. My hair was a knotted mess around my face. I looked behind me at the basement door. It was ajar, and I could hear Jackson shuffling around with Phoebe's body.

I turned my attention back to Zane, who was in the living room talking to Nate. I heard him mention Phoebe's name and something about not having time to make me look presentable. Fuck. Fear prickled through me. I was being forced to work again.

Nate stood in the middle of the room, repeatedly checking his watch. He flicked his eyes to the kitchen, pressed his lips together, and shook his head.

"She'll have to get ready there. More trouble than she's worth," he scoffed, looking in my direction and moving a few steps closer. "There's no time to clean her up. She's your responsibility. I don't want her associated with me."

He was wearing another custom-tailored blue pinstriped

suit with a thin, black tie held in place by a silver tie clip. His dark blonde hair was perfectly tousled. He turned his wrist in again, shaking his head when he saw the time. I noticed that his nails were perfectly manicured. "She's your responsibility," he pressed to Zane, who responded by rolling his eyes. "Jackson!" Nate yelled. "If you put one toe over the property line, I will tie your precious Adeline to the bed and make you watch her get fucked over and over."

My blood ran cold, and my head spun. I wanted to shout out to Jackson that it was still worth the risk, that he still needed to try and leave. I pressed my lips together, knowing that saying it out loud wouldn't end well for either of us.

Nate punched a code into the keypad and opened the door. Zane, of course, shoved me forward. The warm, spring air surprised me. Had that much time really passed? Zane took a tangle of my hair and dragged me to a black Mercedes. I got into the backseat.

My breath clouded on the cold window. I clicked the seatbelt into place and stuck my hands under my legs. Nate waited a minute, allowing the engine to warm before putting the car into drive. I felt like I was drowning in darkness again. Icy hands gripped my heart, squeezing harder and harder as the tires spun. I frantically turned around and watched the old house disappear from view.

I had never been in the car with Nate before. Where were we going? My fingernails dug into the leather seat. What the hell was going on? Was he finally fed up with me and was taking me to some secluded place to dump my body? No…that couldn't be it. Zane wouldn't want me to get dressed nicely for that.

I clenched my jaw shut to keep my lip from quivering as I tried not to hyperventilate. I pulled the hood up, closed my eyes, and envisioned Jackson's face. I recalled the soothing sound of his voice when he told me he loved me. I replayed his words over and over in my head as the car moved down the country road.

Unlike Zane, Nate drove slowly, and I doubted he went over the speed limit as to not call any unwanted attention to himself. The spring landscape was a whirl of pastel and green as we accelerated down the highway. I stared at the passengers in the passing cars and wondered what sort of normal activities they were up to.

I knew where we were going just moments before we pulled into the parking lot of Paradise, Nate's strip club. The neon sign that read OPEN was turned off, and two bouncers stood outside the door. Unable to resist a chance to shove me around, Zane grabbed my arm when I climbed out of the car.

Apprehension grew until it was almost unbearable. I had to force my legs to keep moving as we neared the entrance of the club. The two guys who manned the door nodded at Nate, looking at him with admiration. I could feel their eyes on me when I passed by.

Two tables were set up in front of the stage, seating a dozen men. A large man with combed over blonde hair sat in the center. He turned around at the sound of the door closing. He stood and opened his arms in a gesture of welcome when he saw Nate.

Zane grabbed my arm and yanked me around the stage. My feet caught on the dark red carpet as we wove through tables with overturned chairs resting on their tops and walked through a dark doorway that led behind the stage. Zane pushed open the door to the dressing room.

I was immediately choked by the overpowering scent of a dozen different types of perfume. The white laminate flooring was scuffed and worn from being walked on by countless girls. Lockers and hooks for purses and coats lined the wall that housed the door. Almost directly across from us was another door with a black and white sign that read STAGE taped to the middle, right at eye level. Tables with illuminated mirrors were crammed in the middle of the small room. Chairs with cracking vinyl cushions were haphazardly crowded around the tables. Racks of clothing—all lingerie—took up a good portion of this small room. A sparkly green corset caught my attention. Light reflected off the sequins, displaying an array of greens and blues, reminding me of a peacock. Then I saw the crusty white stain along the bottom.

Five girls were in there, dressed in lingerie and sky-high heels. All had a number pinned to them. They stopped what they were doing and snapped their attention to us. The girl closest to me was wearing a red push up bra that matched her satin panties. A short, sheer bathrobe did little to cover her exposed body. The number 261 was pinned to her back. She wiped tears off her cheeks with the back of her hand.

Zane tightened his grip on my wrist and walked ahead. I hurried to catch up and not get dragged behind him. Again.

"Put something else on, and for God's sake, learn how to use a hairbrush," Zane sneered at me. I crossed my arms.

"No."

He gritted his teeth, talking under his breath about dealing with me once the other girls were on stage. He snatched my wrist and pulled me along with him.

"Get in a line," Zane ordered the other girls. There were a few seconds of chaotic clacking of heels as the girls shuffled into a line. Keeping me next to him, Zane walked up the line, smoothing hair and straightening hems.

Tendrils of tension wrapped around me. Two girls at the front of the line clasped hands, both crying. My hands trembled, and I felt my empty stomach bubble with nerves. Zane looked the girls over once more and nodded in approval. Fear prickled down my spine. What the hell was going on? We went to the front of the line. Zane put his hand on the knob of the door that led to the stage. I caught a glimpse of Nate. His eyes met mine, and he flashed an evil grin.

"Let the bidding begin," he spoke.

Zane let go of my wrist. I brought it to my chest, rubbing the sore spot where his fingers had twisted my flesh. He ushered the first girl onto the stage. She was tall and pretty, reminding me of Rochelle. Black curls cascaded down her back. She had on ivory colored lacy boy shorts with a matching demi-cup bra. A thin, silver chain was loosely wrapped around her tight stomach. Her legs wobbled, and she teetered on five-inch heels as she crossed the stage. The number 258 was pinned to the back of her bra.

Just how many girls had Nate sold? Had the numbers once started from zero? I shook my head. It couldn't be true.

"Why are they bidding?" I couldn't help but ask.

"To buy, dipshit," Zane answered without looking at me.

It didn't make sense. We were sold for sex all the time. It was never a fancy show. A few times Nate had a new customer see us before taking his pick, but it was informal and done at the house.

Another girl, numbered 259, took the stage. She was short and tan and was wearing a sheer black nightie. The stage lights caused her nipple piercings to sparkle. She stared straight ahead, appearing emotionless, and walked the catwalk. She stopped in the center and slowly turned around before taking a place next to 258 on the side of the stage.

The remaining three girls repeated the process and then lined up along the stage. Zane moved out of the dressing room and quietly closed the door behind us. We stood at the back of the stage, just behind the curtain. I could see the men get up from their seats to inspect the girls.

The large blonde man pointed to 261. She nodded and quickly got off the stage and went over to him. She held her arms out a little at her sides, giving him a view of her entire body. He cupped her breasts and jiggled them. He frowned and turned her around. He said something to the man next to him, speaking in a language that I didn't know. He had her bend over and inspected her rear end.

"How much is this one?" he asked in a thick Russian accent.

"She starts at $15,000," Nate told him. "They all do."

My eyes bulged. *$15,000? Holy shit, that's a lot of money! Since when did … oh.* The girls weren't being sold for just one night. They were being sold for good. I felt dizzy and suddenly cold, so cold. What were these men planning on doing? It wasn't like they could take home their new sex-slave and show her off as if it was a new puppy. No, she would have to stay hidden, locked away like I was, only coming out to do her deranged master's bidding.

The men bartered and haggled with Nate. A burly, black man in a gray suit asked if he could take number 260 to one of the private rooms for a 'test ride.' Nate quickly nodded, saying yes, but only if he paid. The man handed Nate a handful of cash. He licked his lips and whisked 260 away.

The large blonde man finished inspecting another girl. "They pretty, no?" he asked his companion, who nodded in agreement.

"Do you see one you like?" Nate asked, standing with his

hands behind his back. He gave the blonde man a pleasant smile and reminded me of a used car salesman who would do anything to make a quick buck. Only worse. Much, much worse.

"All pretty. Very pretty," he said.

"Yes, they all are," Nate replied with another smile. I wanted to slap it off of his handsome face. "Any one of them will make a great present for your son."

"But they are all same." He shook his head. "No spark."

Nate's smile momentarily faltered. "No spark is a good thing. These girls know their place. They will do what they are told."

The blonde man ran his hand over his thinning hair and said something that I couldn't hear. I took a tentative step forward. He turned and inspected the girls again. Then his eyes landed on me. I froze as fear sliced through me. Then anger took over, and I flashed him a look that I hoped conveyed my disgust.

"What the fuck are you doing?" Zane demanded and grabbed my wrist. I twisted my arm and pulled back. "You can't go out there looking like that!"

"Let me go, asshole," I spat. Zane yanked me behind the curtain. "Let me go!" I repeated and swatted at him. Zane blocked my blow and retaliated by hitting me across the face. I tumbled back, tripping over my own feet. I put my hands out as I fell and landed on the other side of the curtain.

"That one," the large blonde man excitedly spoke and pointed at me. "Show me that one."

CHAPTER 37

The smell of bleach hung heavy in the stagnant air, burning my nose and causing my eyes to water. I sat on the edge of the cot with my bare feet planted on the cold cement ground. My hands were folded in my lap, and I stared straight ahead, looking at the bottom of the basement stairs.

I slowly blinked; my eyelids threatened to shut. My stomach twisted with hunger. I was so thirsty that my lips were dry and sticking together. It had to be well past midnight, and I had been sitting on the edge of the cot ever since I returned from Paradise.

A sharp click came from the stairs. I didn't allow myself to feel anything. Another lock opened. Still nothing. The third lock shot back. I was empty inside. I imagined the oval knob slowly spinning as someone opened the door. The hinges creaked, and the wooden plank of the top step protested under someone's weight. Then the door clicked shut. My brain wouldn't allow me to process any emotions. It had switched into survival mode, and I couldn't handle anything else. Cold and numb, I kept my eyes on the base of the stairs.

"Addie?" Jackson called. A tiny wave of warmth flowed over me. "Addie are you awake?" He hurried down the stairs, his sock-covered feet not making a sound. Concern muddled his face when he saw my blank stare. "How are you holding up?"

He crossed the basement and sat next to me. I soaked in his heat and instantly felt alive. Tears pooled in my eyes. A shiver ran down my spine. Jackson turned toward me and gently placed his hand on my cheek. I closed my eyes, pushing the tears out. They rolled down my cheeks. Jackson used his thumb to wipe them away.

I took in a shaky breath and put my hands on his thighs. "Jackson," I started but my voice choked up. I had no idea how to say what I needed to tell him.

"It's okay, Addie," he replied and lightly put his lips on mine.

"Nate had an auction," I whispered, keeping my face close to Jackson's. I moved my hands up his thighs and around his waist.

"I know," he said back. "Zane and the new guy are passed out drunk. They were celebrating how much money they made today." He shook his head. "Nate has one every few years. He sells the girls who get too old to bring in clients."

I bit my quivering lip and pulled Jackson closer to me. I didn't want to tell him. The thought of hurting Jackson was unbearable. He didn't deserve this—any of this. I would do anything to make him happy, and it killed me knowing what this would do.

"I…" A sob began to form in the back of my throat.

Jackson wrapped his arms around me. My heart swelled, and the same flutter ran through me. I loved Jackson so much. I didn't want him to let me go. I rested my head against his chest and focused on his steady heartbeat. He kissed the top of my head and ran his hands over my hair.

"Jackson," I tried again and sniffled. I straightened up, blinking back tears. There was no way to say it and make it better. I took a breath and spit it out. "Nate sold me today."

Jackson shook his head. "No. No. Not you. H-he wouldn't. Not you. No," he stammered. "It's too risky. You were kidnapped. People are looking for you. Why would he? No, he wouldn't. Not you." He sucked in a breath, close to panicking.

"Yes," I said firmly. "Me." Jackson looked over my head and composed himself. "The man who bought me is from somewhere in Europe." My voice cracked at the end, and the sob I had been holding back bubbled out of my mouth. "Nate said it was perfect, and he should have thought of it sooner. No one will know who I am over there. That's why I haven't been working. He was just waiting until he could get rid of me."

"Addie…" he began. I could feel his pulse pounding, and his arms trembled as he clutched me. "If you leave the country, you will never be found." His words cut through me, the truth searing at my soul.

"I know," I whispered. "And I'll never see you again."

"Do you know when?" His voice was strained.

I moved my head up and down. "Three months. I'm his son's fucking graduation present. And," I paused, my gut twisting with disgust. I closed my eyes. "I'm staying under lock and key until then. Jackson," I cried. "I can't escape with you." I pushed myself up onto my knees and looked into his chocolate eyes. "You have to do it. Escape without me. Send help."

Jackson pulled me forward, I moved onto his lap, putting my legs around him. "Adeline, no," he said gently. "They could still hurt you. Once they realize I'm gone …" He trailed off and let out an exasperated sigh. "They can take you somewhere else or … or ship you out of the country. I promised you that I would do everything I can to keep you safe, and I intend on keeping that promise." His hands flattened against my back and he drew me in. "You have to be the one to escape."

"How can I?" I asked, feeling so defeated. I put a hand on Jackson's cheek, resting my forehead against his so that our noses brushed against each other.

Jackson kissed me. His lips were soft against mine, and his touch was so intimate, so gentle. The love I felt for him shed a ray of light on the dark cloud of fear I was in and made it all so much harder. I didn't want to go to Europe and be a personal sex slave, and I didn't want to leave Jackson.

"You run. You were right all along, Addie. If you just run, someone will find you. Run. Just run, and don't look back." His hand raked through my hair. "I'll distract them, create a diversion long enough for you to get a head start." He kissed me once more. "We should do it now while it's dark. Stay off the road. It'll be too easy for them to follow you."

"Distract them?" I echoed, feeling like I was covered in cold mist. "How are you going to distract them from the alarm going off when the ankle bracelet leaves the house? There's no way unless … no!" I said too loudly. "Jackson, no! I know what you're thinking."

"Adeline," he said calmly. His mind was made. "It's the only way you're going to get out of here. I love you. I always knew I would die here. I can't think of a better reason than to die so you can live."

"I don't want you to die here," I breathed. "There has to be another way!"

"I know how much girls go for at auctions," he spoke. "And I'm guessing Nate put a pretty high price on you. You're not going to be left alone. Someone will be here, making sure you don't escape, making sure I don't try to help you escape. Adeline, please. Please let me do this for you."

My heart pounded, and my chest rapidly rose and fell as I gulped in air. The fact that Jackson was willing to die for me only made me love him more. My emotions surged, and suddenly all I wanted was to feel. I wanted to feel Jackson's skin against mine. I wanted to feel his tongue in my mouth. I wanted to feel our bodies pressed together, naked and sweaty. I wanted to feel free.

In a flurry of passion, I pressed my lips to his. Immediately receptive to the kiss, Jackson slid his hands back to my waist. I tipped my head, running my fingers through his hair. I moved my mouth from his lips to his neck. Jackson let out a breath when I sucked at the skin on his neck.

I curled my fingers around the hem of his t-shirt and pulled it up. Jackson raised his arms over his head, and I removed his shirt. Carefully, I traced the ragged circle of scar tissue on his left bicep where the bullet had hit him. He cupped his fingers around my chin and gently tipped my head toward him.

And then we were kissing again. I leaned back onto the cot. Jackson moved on top of me, situating himself between my legs. I could feel his erection through his jeans, pressing against me and making my body ache for him, a feeling I hadn't felt in so long. A feeling I wasn't even sure I'd ever have again. But there it was, surging through my body. I wanted him as close as he could possibly be … physically and emotionally. I wanted to be together, to share something that could only be expressed in one way.

I moved my hands down, fingers settling on the button of his jeans, pulling it loose.

"Are you sure?" he whispered, his voice trembling.

"Yes," I whispered back and pulled down the zipper. I pushed his pants down as far as I could reach. He sat up and kicked them off. Then he gently moved back onto me. I shook with nerves, feeling like it was my first time all over again. My heart pounded, but the love I felt for Jackson kept the fear away.

His rough hands slipped under the sweatshirt I was wearing. Slowly, he pulled it over my head. His dark eyes drank in the sight of my breasts, barely covered in purple lace. He nervously bit his lip and lowered himself back onto me.

His tongue entered my mouth after he removed my pants. I kept my eyes open, needing to see him, needing to know that it was Jackson who was on top of me with only the thin layers of our undergarments keeping us apart. It wasn't hard to forget. He was gentle, careful. I could feel how much he loved me with each touch, each kiss.

Jackson kissed my neck again, slowly moving his hand down my stomach. I took a deep breath and let it out as he slipped his fingers inside my panties, reminding myself that I wanted this, that I wanted *him*. And only him.

But when he touched me, I panicked.

"Addie," he said, moving off me so fast he fell off the cot. "I'm sorry, I'm sorry," he repeated. I grabbed the blanket and pulled it over me, feeling embarrassed and stupid. "Are you okay? Do you want me to leave?"

"No," I said, heart still racing. "Please, no. I'm sorry." I curled my legs up, shaking my head. "Just … just give me a minute." I closed my eyes and focused on breathing, trying to steady myself. Jackson stayed at the foot of the cot, patiently waiting.

When I stopped shaking uncontrollably, I reached for him. "I want to try again."

Jackson stood but didn't move closer. "You don't have to, Addie," he said gently.

"I *want* to."

He climbed back onto the cot and laid down next to me, spooning his body around mine. "We will take it slow, as slow as you need," he whispered and put his hand on my hip.

I tensed, waiting for a flashback. When it didn't come, I

closed my eyes and relaxed against Jackson. "I think I'm more scared of the possibility of having a flashback than I am about having sex," I admitted.

"I know what you mean," he said. "So don't feel bad if you want to stop, okay?"

I nodded. Knowing that Jackson had been assaulted too made me feel more comfortable. He knew everything, knew exactly what I had gone through. There were no secrets. Everything was out on the table, and he loved me anyway.

I put my hand on top of his and guided it between my legs. Keeping my hand over his helped. It made me feel in control. With my hand still over his, he gently touched me.

Jackson continued to work his fingers. He bent his head down and kissed the back of my neck. I relaxed a little more. I pushed his hand against me a little harder.

"I love you," he whispered. I closed my eyes and felt my muscles loosen. I put my hand on Jackson's face, feeling his day-old stubble and a few scars.

"I love you too," I whispered back and moved his hand inside my underwear. I opened my eyes as I positioned his finger, trying to will my body not to tense. I had gotten myself to the point of being able to just lay there and take it when I was working, but I didn't want to feel like that with Jackson.

"Are you sure this is okay?" he asked again. I nodded, and the way he was so patient and gentle eased my anxiety. He put his finger inside of me and waited.

I pulled his face to mine and kissed him while he began to move his fingers, reading me the whole time. I didn't feel anything at first, but then his touch felt good, sending little pulses of pleasure down my thighs. I let go of another ball of stress and slipped my tongue in his mouth.

After several minutes, I longed for more. I put my hands on Jackson's waist and guided him onto me. He settled between my legs, every inch of him pressing against me. I wasn't scared. It was Jackson.

I tugged his boxers down and arched my back so he could take off my panties. He positioned himself to enter me and waited, wanting to make sure it was ok with me. I kissed him again and opened my eyes, needing to look at him when it happened. I gripped his arms and let out a steady breath. I nodded ever so slightly to Jackson. He put his lips against mine and entered me, only pushing himself in half way.

I took another breath and cupped my hands around his face. I felt my muscles relax. I reached down, putting my hands on the back of his thighs, and pulled him closer, pushing him all the way into me.

We took it slow. Jackson gently moved back and forth. He let out a soft moan of pleasure. I kept my hands on him, feeling him, guiding him on how fast or slow to go. Being in control was empowering. I was having sex on my own terms.

And I was starting to enjoy it.

"Adeline," he panted, eyes fluttering open. "Are you—"

"Yes," I answered before he could finish the question. "I … I am." Pleasure tingled between my legs. I forced myself to relax, thinking only of Jackson and how much I loved him. A jolt of desire shot through me, winding tight in my stomach.

My eyes closed and I threw my head back, breath quickening. I wrapped my arms around Jackson, pressing my lips to his neck. I got hit with another flashback, though this one was different. The image of my room flashed before my eyes, and suddenly I imaged the both of us there, in my own bed.

The tight coil in my stomach sprung free as I had an orgasm. I threw my head back, unable to help the soft moan of pleasure that escaped from my lips. Jackson, who had been waiting for me to come first, climaxed seconds after I did. He lowered himself on me, kissing my neck. He picked his head up and looked into my eyes.

I smiled, heart still pounding. "I wasn't sure if I would ever enjoy sex again," I panted.

"Did you enjoy that?" he asked shyly.

"Yes. I did." It had been healing. I had taken something back, a part of me that I was afraid was lost forever in the dark. "Did you?"

"Yes," he said definitely. "I'd never …" he started then buried his head in my shoulder. He slid out of me and rolled to his side, pulling me close. My legs trembled slightly. "That was my …" he started then diverted his eyes, shaking his head.

"What is it, Jackson?" I asked gently and kissed him.

"I'd never done it before without being forced," he blurted.

"Oh," I said, and ran my fingers up and down his arm, feeling a little sick.

"I'm glad it was with you," he said and tightened his arms around me. We stayed wrapped in each other's embrace until our hearts stopped racing.

"We should get dressed," Jackson said quietly. "In case …"

"I know," I groaned. I didn't want to get dressed. I didn't want to think about what could happen. I wanted to stay there, crammed on the tiny cot, on top of Jackson. I wanted to feel nothing but him but that wasn't going to happen.

CHAPTER 38

I rolled over on the cot, trying to get comfortable. I was exhausted but unable to sleep. Images of Phoebe's lifeless eyes haunted me. Several times I woke from the dark hands of a nightmare clutching at my heart expecting to see her. The pain hit all over again when the realization crashed down on me. She was gone.

Making love to Jackson was empowering, making me feel like me again, though it only lasted a few short minutes. But the confidence it had given quickly work off. I had a dream of being shipped to Europe in a coffin. Phoebe's dead body had been dumped on top of me to cover up the fact that a very alive person was inside the polished wooden box. I woke up with cheeks wet from crying.

It took over an hour to calm down. Once I did, I shot up in bed, worried about the stains on the quilt. Jackson did the laundry, but what if Lily or Rochelle noticed before he got the chance? They would know we had sex and Jackson would get beaten … or worse.

I tossed and turned until the sun started to creep up over the horizon. The golden light muted my fears, and I was able to drift into a light sleep, not waking until the basement door slammed shut. Sobs resonated off the dry walled staircase. I sat up and twisted around to see Lily emerge from the stairwell. She had her face in her hands, mopping away mascara streaked tears.

"Jackson told me," she cried. Her red eyes flicked to

Phoebe's bed. "She's really dead?" Her voice was strained.

"Yes," I said and felt my own eyes prickle with tears. I blinked them away.

"You were with her, right? She didn't die alone?"

"I was there until the end," I said, wanting to comfort Lily. I swung my legs over the side of the cot and patted the mattress next to me. Lily sank down and started crying. I put my arms around her and smoothed her hair, which was stiff with hairspray.

"Was it peaceful?"

"Yes," I soothed. The image of Phoebe violently convulsing on the floor while blood oozed from her mouth and nose flashed through my brain. The sound of her face smacking against the floor caused a shudder to ripple through me. "In her sleep." My jaw trembled, and I tried to block out the heartbreaking grief.

I failed. I hugged Lily and cried with her. I thought of Phoebe and wished I had a good, lighthearted memory of her to share, but I didn't. All I had was the comfort she had given me, the times when she had tended to my wounds after getting beaten by Zane and Nate, and the hope she instilled in me from the very beginning. I had no comforting words. I couldn't reflect on the good life Phoebe lived. I couldn't take consolation in knowing that each day was filled with happiness. She was living in hell on earth, and I could only hope that heaven was real and that was where she was.

And now she was gone without a trace. Even if her body was recovered from the woods, would anyone know who she was? She was illegally smuggled into the country. She had no last name, no passport, and no records of even existing.

"You guys okay?" Rochelle's voice came from across the room. I hadn't even heard her come down the stairs.

"No," Lily cried. Suddenly, she sprang up. "You should have gotten the pills! You didn't even try! You were too worried about upsetting Zane. And now she's dead. Dead, Rochelle! And never coming back!" Lily's hands balled into fists, and her arms shook. "I hate this place. I hate it! I want to leave." Her hands flew to her head, her fingers scrunching her hair, and she broke down in hysterical sobs.

"Don't say that!" Rochelle snapped. "It's not true."

"Yes, it is! Phoebe was right. This place is hell!"

I got up and put an arm around Lily. "She's right," I agreed.

"Stop it!" Rochelle yelled. "Both of you. Stop it!"

"Why should we?" I countered. "This place *is* hell, and you can't deny it. If there was a way out, I'd be the first one leaving!" I spat.

"And you will be," Zane's smooth voice floated down the stairs.

We all paused, waiting for him to reach the bottom. Dressed in dark washed jeans, black leather boots, and a long sleeved gray shirt under a motorcycle jacket, Zane reminded me of a raven. Sunlight gleaming off shiny black feathers, swooping down on his prey with gossamer wings, luring in victims with his grace and beauty, then razor sharp talons pierced through even the toughest of flesh, digging deep until they grasped the soul. By the time his true nature was found out, it was too late.

"Just three short months, and you'll be out of here."

"What is he talking about?" Lily asked, her eyebrows pinched together with worry.

"You didn't hear?" Zane spoke to her, but his eyes were focused on me. "Little Miss Adeline was the star of the auction. You should have seen the bidding war that went on." He crossed his arms and leaned against the wall. "It was a first for us. Who knew this little *spark* could be worth so much?"

"What?" Lily asked, the color draining from her already pale face.

"And to think," Zane continued, ignoring Lily. "Mr. Shevchenko paid twice the going rate for someone who has been nothing but a pain in my ass." He laughed. "You'll be his problem soon enough."

"What?" Lily repeated, her voice desperate. "What is going on?"

"They sold me at the auction," I said, my voice hollow. My breath whooshed out, leaving me feeling empty. Zane's eyes met mine, flashing sadistic enjoyment. Rage waved over me, and I desperately wanted to hurt him.

"You're a pathetic, psychotic loser," I sneered. "The only thing you have going for you is that pretty face. Someone's gonna enjoy making you their bitch in prison."

"Shut up," he retorted.

"I can see it now, the inmates fighting over who gets to stick it up your tight little ass."

"I said shut up!" He pushed off the wall.

"Maybe they'll take turns, and you'll finally know how it feels to be raped over and over again. I hope they pull you apart and make you bleed."

He lunged forward and took hold of the neck of my shirt. He raised his fist and stopped. "Can't damage the merchandise," he said through clenched teeth. Needing a release, he let me go, turned around, and hit Lily. She cried out and fell to the floor. "That was your fault," Zane told me, his voice thick with held back anger. With his lips pulled back in a snarl, he grabbed Rochelle by the arm. "Go upstairs. Wait in my room."

Rochelle nodded, doe-eyed, and reached out to touch Zane's face. He jerked out of the way and stormed over to me. I stood my ground, taking a deep breath. I didn't think he would hit me, not with so much money riding on my well-being and physical appearance. He grasped my shoulders, yanked me forward, and kneed me in the stomach. The wind got knocked out of me, and pain radiated, making me feel like I was going to throw up.

"It'll heal," he said mostly to himself. He turned on his heel following Rochelle up the stairs. I panted and pushed myself up.

"Lily," I said and rushed over to her. Droplets of blood splattered onto the floor.

She pressed her hand over her nose and gagged. Blood continued to seep through her fingers.

"Lean forward," I told her. "You're swallowing the blood." I put my hand on her shoulder.

She shook me off, narrowing her pretty green eyes. "Stop," she mumbled.

I recoiled, my feelings hurt. "I'm sorry," I apologized, though I didn't think I needed to. Zane hit Lily because he was bat-shit crazy. I didn't make him.

"Just leave me alone," she said, spitting out blood. "Yuck." She pinched her nose and tipped her head up, ignoring my advice, and struggled to her feet. She went over to the vanity. "Fuck. I'm supposed to work the streets tonight. Who's gonna want me now?" she muttered. She spoke low as if she was talking to herself, but I knew she was saying it aloud only to make me feel bad.

"Maybe you'll have the night off?" I offered.

"And lose money?" she scoffed.

I stared at her reflection. Where had the girl gone who, just a few minutes before, wanted to escape? Her mindset was changing. She was becoming more and more brainwashed, just like Rochelle. I retreated to my cot, wrapping the blue blanket around my shoulders. Lily showered and dressed in pajamas before working on her hair. I ground my teeth and fought back tears.

The whirl of the hairdryer drowned out the sound of the door opening. I didn't know Jackson had come down the stairs with our daily food until he set the tray down and came over to the bed. He touched my shoulder; I startled and jerked upright.

"Sorry," he said and backed away, nervously eyeing Lily, who had her head upside down, blasting it with hot air.

I nodded in understanding. Our eyes met. I wanted so badly to pull him to me, to wrap my arms around him. My heart ached and I longed to feel the heat of his skin against mine. It hurt, being this close to him without being able to touch him. Lily flipped her head up. Jackson turned around and went up the stairs. I got off the cot and grabbed a granola bar. I ate it slowly and lay back down.

After getting her hair stick straight, Lily climbed into bed to nap before tonight's work. A ring of purple circled her nose, but the bone was still straight, leading me to believe it hadn't been broken. I closed my eyes and imagined my house, letting my mind take over. I was sitting in the dining room, a room we rarely used, since sitting down for a family dinner wasn't an every day occurrence. Arianna sat, texting on her cell phone. Dad would scold her, damning technology. Mom would go into her rant about how she thought the constant usage of cell phones and tablets damaged family values. And I would smile and nod, pretending I agreed while I helped myself to a second piece of cornbread.

It wasn't the first time I created that same scenario in my mind, but this time something was different. There was another person at the table with us, enjoying dinner and putting up with my parents' crazy lectures. Jackson was deep in conversation with my father, talking about how important it was for children to read books instead of watch TV.

I smiled to myself, feeling warm and fuzzy inside. Then heartache crashed over me, tearing into my soul. As much as I wanted to believe that could happen, a nasty little thing called realism chipped away at my happy vision, reminding me that the chances of both Jackson and I getting out alive, let alone together, were slim to none.

I took a deep breath and focused on the dining room. I could almost smell the hot bowl of my dad's chili in front of me. Jackson put his hand on my thigh. His face was clean-shaven and bruise-free. The scars on his body had faded. I put my spoon down and put my hand over his.

Something glinted on my left hand. Involuntarily, I had put an engagement ring on my finger. My heart fluttered. It was stupid to think about rings and weddings. Deep down, I knew it was, but I needed a reprieve. I needed to think about shiny happy things.

My vision of a hall decorated with white and purple flowers started to darken and Nate stood in the shadows, holding a length of rusty chain. I opened my eyes and sat up, my hand flying to my chest. I took a breath and tried to slow my heart rate. I curled into the fetal position and pulled the blue blanket over my head.

When I couldn't stop the dark thoughts from taking over, I sat up and looked around the shabby basement. With a heavy sigh, I threw the blankets back and swung my legs over the side of the cot. I walked over to the vanity, picked up a bobby pin, and pulled the rubber off the end. I turned around, eyeing the stairwell before scurrying over. I scraped a thin line in the dry wall, starting my three-month count down to the day I'd be shipped off.

CHAPTER 39

Rochelle returned sometime after sunset. She showered and immediately began getting ready for the night. I watched as she braided extensions into her hair, studying her reflection in the mirror. Rochelle was gorgeous. She was tall and lean, sporting a naturally toned body, despite her lack of working out. Her dark skin was flawless, and her cheekbones were to die for. Her breasts were large enough to make me wonder if she had implants, and her brown eyes were big and bright.

Her smile lit up her entire face, giving off a glow of innocence. She looked like freaking Miss America. Yet there she was, nothing more than a prostitute. Only worse. She was stuck in this life with no choice in leaving, and had no idea that this wasn't what she wanted.

"I always wanted to go to Europe," she said, her eyes flicking to mine in the mirror.

"What?"

"Travel. I want to travel." She picked up another hair extension. "Maybe you're going about this being sold thing all wrong. You'll get to see Europe. How cool is that?"

I balked at her reflection. My mouth opened and closed several times, like a fish out of water. "There is nothing *cool* about being sold," I finally stammered. "I'm going to a family that buys humans for graduation presents."

"Yeah, but it's in Europe. You might end up in a castle, or next to the Eiffel Tower or something. There are tons of great places to shop in Paris."

"Right. Never mind being a forced sex slave in a foreign country or anything," I spat.

"You have such a bad attitude," she said and fluffed her hair.

"Can we stop talking about this?" I asked, squeezing my eyes shut. I felt dizzy again. It was a warning that the feeling of floating above my body was coming. I didn't want my mind to check out. I needed a plan. I needed to think.

"Whatever," Rochelle said.

I retreated under the blanket, shaking. I hadn't left Iowa in years, and had never even been out of the country. Then there was Jackson ... I closed my eyes before I started crying. My stomach twisted, and my head spun. I reached under my pillow and ran my fingers over the worn cover of *Gone with the Wind*, focusing on the way the old book felt.

I heard Lily get up. She complained about how the humid weather instantly caused her naturally curly hair to frizz, while Rochelle helped with her makeup, promising to almost eliminate the signs of her bruised face. I stayed hidden under the covers until Lily and Rochelle stomped up the basement stairs, leaving for another night's work.

A loud thud from upstairs made me jump. Nate shouted at someone, but no one replied. I held my breath and listened. He said something about a payment being late and threatened whomever he was talking to, but still no one fought back.

"He must be on the phone," I whispered to myself. He wasn't yelling at Jackson ... for now. I sighed and spun around, heading to the shower. I washed quickly, not wanting to be in the icy water for any longer than was necessary. I put on a pair or grey leggings, a black t-shirt, and Jackson's sweatshirt. I braided my hair and sat at the card table reading.

About an hour passed before an exterior door opened and closed. I looked up at the ceiling as if it would allow me to better hear what was going on. The distant hum of an engine came to life and gradually faded. Then the house fell silent.

I couldn't help the apprehension I felt when someone unlocked the door. I set the book down, sliding the tray over top of it.

"Addie," Jackson called from the landing. "It's me. Come

here," he whispered.

I jumped up from the table, grabbing the book. I shoved it under my pillow and rushed to the stairs. He waved me up. My sock-covered feet didn't make a sound as I jogged up the steps. Jackson grabbed my hand and guided me forward. He nervously looked around and shut the basement door.

He stepped close, locking his arms around me before he kissed me, his tongue opening my lips. He pressed against me so that my back pushed against the door. I wrapped my arms around him, my heart instantly fluttering. For a second, everything bad disappeared. Only Jackson existed. I breathed him in, feeling a warm tingle between my legs, which was a long forgotten but most welcome feeling. When Jackson finally pulled away, we were both breathless.

"Hello to you too," I panted.

His hands ran down my arms and into my hands. He pulled me forward. "Rochelle got arrested."

"Are you serious?" I asked.

He nodded and took a step forward. "Yeah. For prostitution. Nate just left. The new guy is still here though." We sneaked through the dark kitchen. "He's in Zane's room. I think he's watching porn," he added quietly.

I felt a prickle of nerves when the stairs came into view. Moonlight gleamed on the polished wood. I tightened my hold on Jackson's hand and followed him up to his room.

Since I had been less than aware the last time I was up here, I hadn't noticed the lock on the outside of his door. It was the kind that could only be accessed from one side. I swallowed hard, not wanting to think about Jackson being locked in his room. At least it was better than the basement.

"What's going to happen to Rochelle?" I asked once we were in the safety of Jackson's room.

He shrugged. "She'll get released. Eventually. This isn't the first time she's been arrested, either." Jackson pulled the covers back on his bed and moved the pillows so that they were straight against the headboard. "I don't know how the legalities of it work. She's usually home the next morning. I think Nate might pay someone off."

I sat on the bed and tucked my feet under the covers. "When

will they come home?"

"A few hours at least. Nate does the talking but I know Zane is there, waiting in the parking lot. He won't leave until she's out."

"What's up with them? Does Zane love her or something?"

"He has some sort of obsession with her, which isn't love. He loves the way she loves him, if that makes sense. He can get her to do anything. She'll fawn and fight over him just for a minute of his attention," he explained.

"What a creep," I mumbled. Unable to shake the chill, I looked around his room. It was just as I remembered it. As plain as possible, it housed only a bed and a dresser. There wasn't a mirror above the dresser. If it weren't for the boxes of books, the room would look like no one inhabited it. I got up and knelt down next to the books.

"You have an interesting variety," I noted and picked up a large textbook about anatomy and physiology. Behind it was another heavy book entirely written in Spanish.

Jackson shrugged again. "Since I didn't get to finish high school, I like to read whatever I can."

"You don't seem—" I started then stopped myself.

"Dumb?" he finished for me with a smile.

"That wasn't what I was going to say," I pointed out. "But no, you don't." I flipped through a calculus workbook, a little surprised to see answers to the problems. I peeked back into the first box. There were half a dozen Steven King novels, two well-known romance books that even I hadn't read, and a ton of fantasy books. The second box had more textbooks and just as many fiction books. "I'm surprised you're allowed to have books."

"I was too. Nate says it keeps me quiet." He sighed. "I want something new. But I shouldn't complain, right? I'm happy I at least have those, even though I've had exactly those for the last five years."

"You're too good," I said and stood up. I got into bed, snuggling close to Jackson. He enveloped me in his arms, rolling so that I rested on his chest. "How will we know when Nate and Zane come back?" I asked, trying my hardest to push the fear away and just enjoy being alone with Jackson while I could.

"I cracked the window," he said. "We'll hear the car coming down the driveway."

The knot in my stomach lessened a bit. "And Lou?"

"He hasn't bothered me …yet. I don't think he will come in unless he hears us, but given that I can literally hear the ass-smacking from whatever shitty film he's watching, I don't think will be a problem."

"Good," I said and draped my leg over his.

Jackson pressed a kiss to the top of my head and ran his fingertips up and down my back. "I love you," he whispered.

"I love you too," I whispered back and closed my eyes.

Jackson put his hands on my hips and flipped us over, resituating himself between my legs. He brushed a loose strand of hair out of my eyes before lightly kissing me, leaving me wanting more. I reach up and touched his face, running my hands back through his dark, wavy hair. A smile pulled up his lips.

"I've been a slave for over ten years, and I'd be a slave for ten more just to spend one more day with you," he said quietly.

I shook my head. "Why does that sound like a goodbye?"

Instead of answering, Jackson kissed me just as passionately as he did at the top of the basement stairs. The warmth of desire began to burn red hot. I turned my head to the side when he moved his lips to my neck. I slid my hands under his shirt.

"Are you sure?" he asked, not moving away.

"Yes," I breathed. "You don't have to ask me anymore."

"Are you—" He cut off and flashed a small smile. He took his time removing my clothing, giving me soft, passionate kisses. I forgot about everything bad in the world. My body began to hum with pleasure as our love physically manifested.

The floor creaked. We both froze, hearts already beating fast. Jackson leaned up, his dark eyes focused on the door. Then we heard a toilet flush. Jackson took a deep breath and moved over top of me. Fear had instantly killed the mood, causing me to tremble. I took several steady breaths then curled my legs up, allowing Jackson to enter me.

I wasn't scared of a flashback, but I wasn't able to get the fear of getting caught out of my head. It took effort to concentrate on how Jackson felt, moving in and out of me. I was able to relax. I ran my hands over his biceps, feeling his tight muscles as he held himself over me. My fingertips brushed the little mound of scar tissue from the bullet wound. I closed my eyes. It was starting to feel good. Really good.

I wrapped my arms around Jackson's torso, arching my back. He let out a moan and bent his head down to kiss me. I held on to Jackson and wrapped my legs around him, pulling him in. He buried his face into my neck, kissing me. A shiver made its way down my body and I opened my mouth, gasping in pleasure.

I pressed my lips together, not wanting to be heard. Jackson sped up his movements, and the bed creaked. We both froze. Panting, I put my hands on Jackson's shoulders and looked at him.

"Do you want to finish?" I asked then internally winced. Way to kill the mood.

Jackson nodded. "If you do."

"Yes," I said right away. I was getting close to coming. The buildup couldn't end now. I moved my hands to cup Jackson's face. I kissed him as we started again. My fingers tangled in his hair, my grip tightening more and more as I came closer and closer to coming.

Jackson's breath came out in a huff. I pressed my mouth against his shoulder to muffle the moan that escaped my lips as I climaxed. I let go of Jackson's hair, suddenly aware that I had been pulling it. I held onto him, breathing heavy as he finished.

Jackson rolled over, pulling me on top of him. He kissed the top of my head and held me against him for a minute before we got dressed. After using the bathroom, I cuddled back into Jackson's arms.

"Why did you say 'one more day?'" I asked, tracing my fingers over the contours of his bare shoulders.

"I was hoping you'd forget."

"Not a chance."

Jackson took a breath. "Nate and Zane are gone. This is as good a time as any for you to escape."

I pushed myself up so I could look him in the eyes. "And you too, right?"

Jackson frowned. "I don't know the codes right now. You'll have to go through a window."

"So?" I asked, feeling panic rising. "You can come with me." I shook my head. "Windows are quiet anyway. By the time I get out and the alarm goes off, we can be long gone."

"As soon as I unlock a window on the first floor, the alarm will go off. The only windows I have access to up here are straight drops. You could fall and hurt yourself, and then you wouldn't be able to run. And you're forgetting that the ankle bracelet has a GPS tracker. Lou can go after you and find you. I have to distract him."

"Jackson, no. Please!" My eyes filled with tears, and my palms began to sweat. I desperately shook my head. "No. I can't leave you. I *won't* leave you."

"You can send help."

"We both know that's a load of shit," I said. I blinked back tears. "You'll be dead by then."

"Adeline," he whispered and reached up to caress my face. "That's why I brought you up here. I wanted one more time with you. You've given me so much, more than I deserve. Now it's my turn to give you a chance. You can have your life back, start over. You don't need me."

"I don't want to start over without you." My voice quivered as tears slid down my face. "I need you. I need your arms around me, holding me, keeping me together. I need your lips to press against mine, to hear your heart beating, to feel the heat of your skin. I need you."

"You'll find somebody else, someone who can give you a better life than I could."

"Stop it!" I cried. "I don't want anyone else. I want you! I love *you*, Jackson. No one else."

"And I love you, Adeline. Enough to sacrifice myself for you. Please, Addie. Let me do this for you. Take this chance. My death will set you free."

I pushed his hand away. "No. Do not tell me goodbye. It didn't work last time, and it won't work now. There has to be another way. There *has* to be. I won't let you leave me."

"If there is, I can't think of it. Adeline, listen to me. You have to get out. You have to get help. You might not save me." He pushed my hair over my shoulder. "But you'll save so many others. Just think of all the girls Nate has now and all the girls he'll have in the future. He has to be stopped."

"You're right," I agreed, mad at him for being logical. My heart tore into ridged pieces just thinking about leaving him. Then something clicked. "Jackson!" I grabbed his arm. "You'll pick up Rochelle and Lily again, right?"

"I'm sure I will someday, why?"

"That's our key. That's how we will both get out."

"What are you getting at?"

"The next time you go out, get pulled over, steal from a gas station, I don't know, just get police attention."

"No, Addie, they will hurt—"

"No they won't," I interrupted. "Not severely at least. I'm too important to Nate right now. Monetarily that is."

Jackson smiled slightly. "I think you're right." His smile widened. "You are right. Nate won't let anything too bad happen to you. Still, there's a risk to you."

"It's more than worth it, Jackson. If it gets us *both* out of here, a little pain is more than fine."

He didn't look convinced. His eyes scanned mine, and finally he said, "I'd rather see you in a small amount of pain than see you shipped off to the other side of the world. There is a cop parked at a gas station on the way to the truck stop. He's there almost every Saturday night. I'll speed past. In a matter of days, we will be free." He wrapped his arms around me and planted a big kiss on my lips. "You're a genius."

"I don't know about that," I said and squeezed him back. My excitement started to morph into nerves. "Are we really doing this?"

"Yes," he said.

"As much as I want to leave I'm scared," I confessed. When the chains finally came off, we would be naked.

"It'll work out," he promised and lay back against the pillows. I yawned. "Get some sleep, Addie. I'll listen for the car."

"Okay," I said, not needing much convincing. I rolled onto my side, getting comfortable. Jackson's body curved around mine. Somehow, his presence kept the bad thoughts away, and I drifted to sleep in a matter of minutes.

CHAPTER 40

Roughly half an hour later, Jackson woke me up. "I think you're having a nightmare," he said quietly.

I sat up, blinking. "I was. I dreamed that Zane cut off my feet so I couldn't run away."

Jackson put his hand on my waist. "I won't let that happen."

"I know," I said and flopped back against the pillows. I was tired, so tired. As soon as my eyes closed, Jackson shot up, staring at the window.

"They're home."

My pulse instantly quickened. Jackson crept into the hall, making sure Lou was still stowed away in Zane's room. He waved for me to come out. I slinked after him, holding my breath when I passed Zane's door. I put my hand on the railing and dashed down the old, dark staircase. I was in the middle when the door opened.

"Hey," Lou called. "White boy. Come here."

"Go!" Jackson mouthed. "Run!"

I took off, tripping on the gold and scarlet rug at the bottom of the stairs. I caught myself before falling and scrambled through the living room and into the kitchen. I threw open the basement door, silently closed it, and ran to my cot, shaking.

Then I realized that the door wasn't locked. Rochelle would be brought down, probably straight away. Nate and Zane would see that someone had been down there with me, and it wouldn't be hard to figure out it was Jackson.

"Fuck," I muttered and grabbed my elbows. My teeth chattered with nerves. I got up and paced in front of the stairs. The floorboards in the kitchen groaned under foot. I paused, biting my lip. They moved closer. I ducked behind the dry wall. The sharp click of the deadbolt being shot into place was like a choir of freaking angels. My body relaxed. Jackson had gotten to the door in time.

I retreated back to my cot. The sudden, intense fear had caused a headache. I sat on the edge, waiting for the girls to come down. Lily came down first, looking more annoyed than anything. Rochelle followed. Her silver eye shadow was smeared, and eyeliner dripped down her cheeks.

"I fucked up, I fucked up," she muttered over and over.

"It's not your fault," Lily said in a tone that conveyed it wasn't the first time she had said that. "You had no idea."

"I should have known," Rochelle said. "I should have known!" Her legs threatened to buckle. Lily helped her to her cot.

"Hun," she soothed and brushed back Rochelle's tangled hair. "He was undercover. None of us would have known." Lily looked up at me. "Hey, Addie,"

"Hi," I said back.

"Interesting night." She rolled her eyes.

I pressed a smile and nodded, still listening to Rochelle crying about fucking up. Finally, Lily got her to take some sort of pill that took effect in just a few minutes. Lily tucked Rochelle under the covers and removed her own clothing, redressing in yoga pants and a tight tank top.

I looked at Phoebe's empty cot. The sting of grief washed over me, and I buried my face into my pillow. I knew I wouldn't be able to fall asleep, so I replayed the fantasy dinner scene over in my head until I passed out.

A full day passed before I was able to see Jackson again. Lily and Rochelle were in the basement with me that night when he brought down our food. His right eye was bruised and swollen shut, and he was limping. I got up from my cot and rushed over, taking the tray from him.

"What happened?" I asked.

He just shook his head, glancing at the girls. "Don't worry about me. Go back to your cot, Addie. Don't act like you care."

I set the tray down and took his hand in mine. "You look awful." I felt like crying or throwing up. Maybe I'd throw up, *then* cry.

"Nah, I've had worse." He nervously cast his eyes at Rochelle and Lily, his fingers tightening around mine.

"I know. You have." I stepped in toward him.

"Any day now," he reminded me and squeezed my fingers again. His eyes flicked behind me to the girls. "I should go," he whispered.

I let his hand fall from mine and nodded. I watched him go up the stairs, a hole forming in my heart as he left. I swallowed hard and turned around, blinking away any tears. He was right. I had to act like I didn't care. It was incredibly hard to do. I ran my hands over my face, trying to shake the feeling of heartache, and sat at the card table, picking apart a cereal bar.

"Is there something going on between you two?" Lily asked, joining me at the card table.

My heart stopped beating. A hot rush of blood turned my cheeks right. "No."

She pressed her lips together and opened a little carton of milk. "I know he likes you. He looks at you all googly-eyed."

"I've never noticed," I muttered.

"Sure," she said and rolled her eyes. "Addie, it doesn't matter to me. He's, like, kind of a lost cause, but Jackson's okay in my book. He's kinda cute, and I think he's nice ... maybe. He doesn't talk much. It's just that ..." she lowered her voice, blue eyes flashing to Rochelle. "We all know Jackson has feelings for you. You say you don't see it but it's *so* obvious. Hello? Remember Christmas?" She shook her head. "Zane wanted us to tell him if we noticed anything on your end, since no one knows how you feel. If he knows you like Jackson back, he won't let you guys be together. Like ever. I won't say anything of course but ..."

"Thank you," I told her. "But there's nothing going on. Like you said, he's nice but never talks to us. I don't know him, so I can't like him."

"Sure," she repeated with a wink. I ripped open a package of fruit snacks and leaned against the table. The door opened again. My eyes flitted to the stairs, hoping to see Jackson again.

"Adeline," Nate called. "Get dressed and come upstairs."

The hinges squeaked as the door slowly swung shut. I put on socks and struggled to get a pair of boots to fit over the clunky ankle bracelet. The girls watched me in wonder. I shrugged, telling them that I had no idea what Nate wanted.

Lou was waiting in the kitchen. He took me into the mudroom. As soon as I set foot near the door, the alarm went off blaring through the house. Lou grunted and punched in the code to open the garage door, silencing the alarm. His large body blocked the keypad from sight. We got into Zane's Camaro. Lou ushered me into the back, behind the passenger's seat, which he took. He scooted it back until it hit my already cramped legs. Then he pushed it back even more.

Zane got in, sighing dramatically, and cranked the music. A song I liked came on, and Zane changed the station. *Go fucking figure.* He sped down the country road and headed for the Quad Cities. I kept my mouth shut as confusion grew. I was almost sure I wasn't being put to work. It would go against the deal Nate had made.

I nervously fiddled with the hoodie strings and watched the city flash by. Zane made a sharp turn down a road I was completely unfamiliar with and slowed.

"There," Lou said, his voice gruff.

Zane revved the engine as he accelerated into the parking lot of a doctor's office. The car lurched forward, and I began to feel sick. Part of me wanted to get carsick and barf all over the nice leather seats, but another part didn't want to face an angry Zane ... and I just didn't want to throw up in general.

We parked behind a medical complex. Lou got out and flipped his seat up. He reached into the back, making me think that he was being polite and offering a hand to help me out. I was wrong. Like Zane, he liked to yank and drag me around. He marched us to an employee-only entrance. Zane knocked.

A few seconds later the door opened. A middle-aged man, as tall as Zane with salt and pepper hair, stood to the side, allowing us in.

"It's good to see you again," he said to Zane and shook his hand. He had on a white lab coat over dress pants and a button up shirt. Dr. L. Jerry, OB/GYN was embroidered on the breast of the lab coat. "This must be the one." He looked at me.

"Yeah," Zane said. "How long will this take?"

"Normally a few days, but for you I'll have the tests run immediately."

"Good." Zane put his fingers in the middle of my back and pushed me forward.

Dr. Jerry led me down a hall with exam rooms on both sides. He unlocked a bathroom door, handed me a plastic up, and said, "You know what to do. Put it through the window when you're done."

I just nodded and took the cup, unsure why he wanted a urine sample. I had to pee anyway, so I willingly went into the bathroom and shut the door behind me. There was a little metal door in the wall next to the toilet. I opened it and set the full cup inside, then flushed the toilet and washed my hands. Lou was waiting for me outside the door.

"This way," Lou said and took a hold of my wrist and pulled me down the hall. He hoisted me onto an exam table. "Take off your pants," he ordered.

"What?" I asked, my blood running cold.

"You heard me, bitch. Take off your pants." Lou narrowed his eyes.

"Please," Dr. Jerry said from the hall. "Let's be professional about this. Miss Miller, I am going to do a full pelvic exam. Everything off from the waist down." Lou huffed but left the room. Dr. Jerry closed the door halfway.

The room was cold. My hands shook and I looked around, spying a clock above the door. It was nearing eight, definitely after hours. There was no one else there. I stood and pulled down the pajama pants I was wearing. I removed my underwear, folding and sticking them inside the pants. Shivering, I sat back down on the hard foam bed. The protective paper covering crinkled underneath me.

Dr. Jerry came in. I noticed the needle in his hand right away. I had a horrible fear of needles. My ears started to ring and I felt dizzy. I didn't fight it. The ringing grew louder and louder until it was hard to hear what was being said around me. My mind checked out just in time. Dr. Jerry tied a rubber band around my arm and took a blood sample.

I felt like a rag doll. Dr. Jerry laid me back and put my feet up. I felt a cold metal tool get shoved inside me when he started the exam. Tears rolled down the sides of my face.

"Looks good, considering. There is some slight tearing but nothing that won't heal on its own," he said, loud enough for the guys to hear in the hall. He removed the tools, scooted his stool back, and opened the door. Everything was fuzzy. I sat up, but was too dizzy to get off the exam table without falling. "I'm going to check on those test results," he told Zane.

Zane said something in response, but it didn't register in my mind. I wrapped my arms around myself and took a deep breath, waiting for the world to stop spinning so I could put on my underwear. I edged myself off the table and stumbled. More than aware Zane and Lou were in the small exam room with me, I tried to gather my composure and get dressed.

I sat back on the exam table. I felt violated and exposed again along with being sore from the physical exam. I brought my knees to my chest and closed my eyes. I might have fallen asleep. Or maybe I was getting good at repressing what I didn't want to remember. All I knew is that I had no concept of time.

"All right," Dr. Jerry said. "Test results are back."

"And?" Zane asked.

"Nothing untreatable. Chlamydia is very common too. A week's worth of antibiotics will clear it up. It shouldn't cause any issues for the buyer. Once this is gone, she'll be clean." His voice was a distant echo. I felt like an expensive show dog going for a final vet check before my new owners took me home.

I had chlamydia, and if I had it, then Jackson did too. My heart sank to the floor. Dr. Jerry was still talking to Zane, asking him if he needed more birth pills. Zane said yes, though I wouldn't need it anymore, and the doctor left the room. He came back with the medicine.

"I'm allergic to macrolides," I said when I saw the white box of azithromycin.

"What happens?" he asked and set the antibiotics down.

"My throat swells," I lied. Really, it just made me itchy.

"I'll get something else," the Dr. Jerry stated. He left and came back again and asked me about another medication. I nodded, telling him it was okay for me to take. He put it in a bag along with the birth control pills. He went to the door. Lou and Zane followed.

The white box of antibiotics sat on the counter. I bit my lip and flicked my eyes to the men. When no one was looking, I reached out and snatched the medication, shoving it into the large pocket on the outside of the hoodie. I held my hands over my stomach, nervous that the pills would rattle and give away the fact that I took them.

I sat on the cold leather backseat of the Camaro, still dizzy. I rested my head against the side of the car and curled my legs up onto the seat and stayed that way until we pulled into the driveway of the farmhouse. My legs had fallen asleep from being tucked underneath me, and I wobbled my way inside.

Zane punched in the code to open the door, then entered a different one to stop the alarm that sounded from the ankle bracelet. He stepped aside, making sure I went willingly into the house. I crossed through the mudroom and into the kitchen, heading straight for the basement.

Something dark was smudged on the door, contrasting against the white paint. I narrowed my eyes, unable to discern exactly what it was in the dim light. Lou flicked the lights on. I blinked as my eyes adjusted and I recoiled when I realized the dark smudge was blood.

"What are you waiting for?" Lou grumbled.

"M-medicine," I stammered, not taking my eyes off the blood.

Lou grunted and called for Zane. He reached into the white bag and threw an orange bottle of pills at me. I didn't catch it; the pill bottle rolled across the floor. I deliberately moved slow as I bent to pick it up.

Zane rushed forward and grabbed my wrist. "You better take all of those," he sneered.

"Why the hell wouldn't I?" I quipped, my face twisting with rage. "It's not like I *want* to have chlamydia, idiot."

Zane raised his fist. Lou caught it. "Hey now," Lou said in a low voice. "She's not ours anymore."

"I was never yours," I snapped. Zane's sky-blue eyes flashed but he lowered his arm. He unlocked the basement door. I could tell it took a great deal of restraint for him to not push me down the stairs.

Little droplets of blood had splattered the wooden steps. The railing was stained scarlet where someone's bloody hand had clutched onto it as they struggled down the stairs. Apprehension built up, and I hurried down the stairs.

"Addie," Lily panted. Standing in front of a cot, her body blocking someone from view.

"Thank God." Rochelle sat on her bed, biting her lip and looking away. "I can't get the bleeding to stop."

Lily stood up, the front of her clothes red. "He's going to bleed out," she whispered. She swallowed hard, her eyes wide with terror.

"Who?" I asked, though I already knew. Lily took a step away from the cot. The orange pill bottle fell from my hand. Jackson sat on the edge of the cot with his hands pressed to his abdomen. Blood seeped from between his fingers and dripped onto the floor.

CHAPTER 41

"Hey Addie," he said through gritted teeth. I felt as if the floor gave out from under me and I dropped through blackness into freezing water. I was drowning. "It's not as bad as it looks," he said with a forced smile.

His dark eyes met mine, reminding me how to swim. I rushed over to him, dropping to my knees. My body trembled. I put my hands over his. "What happened?" I asked quietly, hardly able to get any volume to my quivering voice. I forgot to act like I didn't care. Even if I had, I couldn't hide my fear.

"I pissed off Nate," he grimaced.

"So he stabbed you?" I asked, heart racing.

"Not exactly." Jackson wrapped his bloody hands around mine. He closed his eyes in pain. "Sliced."

"What?" My voice was shrill and pinched with fear. I raised my hands up bringing Jackson's with me. The front of his gray t-shirt was saturated with blood. Terrified that I might see his intestines hanging out, I slowly peeled the wet shirt off his skin. "Oh God," I breathed.

Starting under his ribs and going diagonally down to his right hip, was a very fresh cut. It was straight and the edges were clean. I sucked in a shaky breath.

"How deep?"

"Not very. Barely got the muscle. I think."

"Think?"

"I can still move," Jackson theorized. "So it can't be that

bad."

"Right." I sniffled, unaware until now that tears were streaming down my face. "Lay back," I told him. "Lily, bring a towel."

Jackson winced but obliged. I rolled up the hem of his shirt and put my hand over the wound, gently pressing down.

"Hurry!" I called to Lily.

"It's okay, Addie," Jackson tried to soothe me. "I've had worse and lived."

"You're not helping," I told him.

"It's true."

I pushed both sides of the cut in, hoping that if I closed it off, the blood would clot and form a scab.

"Will this work?" Lily frantically asked. She held up a washcloth.

"Good enough," I told her. She ran over and handed me the washcloth. I folded it in half twice and laid it over the wound, then flattened my hand over that and applied pressure.

"How long 'til it stops bleeding?" Lily asked. She chewed on her nails, nervously shifting her weight. "I've never seen this much blood before. I didn't know it had a smell to it. It smells like pennies," she rambled.

"I don't know," I answered. "Soon, I hope." I could feel Jackson's abs flex as he started to get up. "No," I told him. "Do not move. You're going to make it bleed more. No moving until it stops."

He grunted in response but didn't attempt to get up. My hands shook, and more tears spilled. Bloody fingers caressed my cheek. I turned my head to look at Jackson. His eyes locked with mine. His already beaten face had a few more bruises. There was a fresh cut next to his right eye. Blood was crusted on his chin, and the skin on his neck was red and irritated, as if something had been wrapped around it.

I tipped my head into his hand, comforted by his touch. I closed my eyes and felt myself relax a bit. Then I turned my attention back to his bleeding stomach.

"What can I do?" Lily asked.

I swallowed hard and looked up at her. "Is there any rubbing alcohol left?" I asked her.

"Maybe. I'll check."

"Okay. Bring it."

"Sorry, Jackson, that's gonna hurt." Lily hurried away.

He made a face but shook his head. "It'll be fine."

"Liar," I teased and gave a half smile, easing some of the tension. My heart was beating a million miles an hour, and my stomach twisted in knots.

"It's going to be okay," he repeated so that only I heard him. "I promise you, Addie."

"I hope so," I whispered back.

Jackson put his hands over mine, pressing down on the cut. I slid my hand away and moved up toward his head. My knees screamed at me to stop kneeling on the cement. I ignored them and blotted at the dried blood on his face.

"What happened?" I asked.

"Got into it with Nate." Jackson turned his head so I could clean the crusty blood from inside his ear. "I didn't realize he had a taser on him. He hits me in the back, and the next thing I know, I'm on the floor being tied up." He weakly smiled. "I got him though, before he tased me. Punched him right in the jaw. He'll have a nice bruise in the morning."

"Good," I whispered and folded the rag to use the clean side. "But why are you down here?" I brushed his hair back.

"Nate likes Lou and wants him to stay. He'll take over what I did when it comes to the girls. And Zane won't share a room."

"Oh, so they kicked you out of your room and back down here?" I looked into Jackson's eyes, wishing so badly that I could kiss him, comfort him, and ease his pain. I ran the rag over his forehead, wiping away tiny splatters of blood.

"Yes," he said gravely. "All my stuff is over there." He pointed to the table. I turned, seeing a torn box of books and a pile of clothes.

"At least we're down here together," I said with a weak smile. Jackson's sad eyes said otherwise. Then it hit me. Together.

Shit. *Together*. We were both trapped in this hell-forsaken basement. Jackson would not be picking up the girls anymore. Our plan of escape would not be executed. We would not be free.

CHAPTER 42

Thunder shook the house, causing me to stir from my sleep. I sat up and pushed my damp hair out of my eyes. Jackson's arm was draped around me, and his leg was hooked over my body. Careful not to wake him, I slid out of his embrace, awkwardly lowering myself onto the cold cement floor.

I stood and flicked my eyes around the basement. Thankfully, we were still alone. I was supposed to stay awake and keep watch, but that obviously hadn't worked. As soon as the girls left for work, Jackson and I stayed close together, cuddling. One of us always kept watch while the other rested so we could break apart before we got caught. Without Jackson's warmth, the already cold basement felt even colder. I shivered and turned around, pulling the blue fleece blanket up to Jackson's chin.

I picked up a mangled bobby pin that I had twisted around the milk crate and crossed the basement. I pinched the Bobby pin in between my thumb and index finger and scraped another line in the drywall that encased the stairs. I stepped back and looked at the countdown. There were four rows, each with seven lines. Jackson had been down here for a month, which meant I only had two left until I would be shipped off to Europe.

It had taken a week for Jackson to recover from having his abdomen slashed. While he had not come close to bleeding to death, losing that much blood caused him to become dehydrated and weak. I was even more thankful that I had snagged the extra antibiotics for him and hoped that, along with curing the disease

I might have given him, it would keep his wound from becoming infected.

Those seven days had passed slowly. Every day was full of fear that Jackson would spike a fever, and I would wake up and realize his cut was grossly infected. I did my best to keep it clean. I washed it with soap and water every morning, even though the flower-scented bar of soap that we had was probably not antibacterial. Every night I used what little rubbing alcohol we had left dabbing at the skin around the cut. Though it wasn't ideal, it seemed to have worked.

Once Jackson was out of the woods, the days started to go by quickly since I was dreading the end of the three months. When Rochelle and Lily were here, Jackson and I kept a friendly distance. We talked, played cards, and sat on separate cots reading but didn't dare let it go further than that. A few times Lily caught us standing a little too close or looking into each other's eyes a little too long. She had raised her eyebrows and smirked, but didn't say anything. I was so incredibly grateful.

It was agony to be in the same room without being able to touch each other. He was so close I could feel his body heat, and I desperately wanted to throw my arms around him and feel my skin against his, to have our hearts beating against each other's. Instead, I turned away, pretending that I didn't love him.

Several times Nate had called Jackson upstairs and put him to work. He was gone most of the day and returned exhausted. Just the day before, Nate had him outside doing yard work. Jackson left right as the sun came up and didn't come back until after dark. He was tired and sore and fell asleep as soon as he got in bed.

The lights flickered. I looked up at the single bulb that hung at the base of the stairs. Heavy rain pelted against the small window and water dripped down the wall. Lightning flashed, and the power went out for a few seconds.

"The alarm system stops working when the power goes out. The electronic locks too," Jackson said, his voice thick with sleep.

I whirled around. "Go fucking figure," I huffed and shook my head. I went back over to the cot, set the bobby pin down, and sat next to Jackson. He took a deep breath and snaked his arm around my stomach. "Go back to sleep," I urged, twisting so that I was facing him. I ran my fingers through his hair.

"That feels good," he mumbled, already falling asleep.

I continued combing my fingers through his hair until his breathing slowed, steady and even. Wind pressed into the old house. Fear flickered through me. It was an old fear, one I've had since I was a child: tornadoes. My eyes focused on the small window. Now I hoped one would rip through the house, pulling apart the frame, leaving nothing but the foundation. Jackson and I would crawl out of the rubble and run to safety.

A boom of thunder made me jump. Lightning followed just seconds later. The worst was nearing.

"Lay down," Jackson spoke softly.

I nodded and stuck my feet under the blanket, snuggling next to him. It was an uncomfortably tight fit on the cot. I felt like I was going to fall off if I moved just an inch.

Jackson pulled me on top of him, solving that problem. "Don't like storms?"

"Storms are fine," I answered. "I don't like tornadoes. Though right now, I honestly hope one rips this house apart or knocks down a power line and catches the house on fire."

"We're trapped in the basement," Jackson reminded me.

"I know. Maybe the fire department would get here before we die of smoke inhalation."

"I'm not willing to risk that." He began rubbing my back. "We'll get out of here, Addie. Don't give up," he said.

"I'm trying." I rested my cheek against his chest. "I would have given up if I didn't have you. After Phoebe died ... I couldn't have done it on my own."

"Yes, you could. You're one of the strongest people I know."

"I don't feel like it."

He slid his hands under my shirt and traced little circles with his fingernails on my skin. "I think that's part of what makes you strong. You don't try to be strong, you just are." The lights flickered again. "If *I* didn't have *you* ..." he trailed off. "When I told you before that I was close to giving up, I meant it. I'd put a lot of thought into killing myself, not because I wanted to commit suicide, but because I wanted to die on my own terms, not Nate's. I didn't want to give him the satisfaction of watching me slowly die."

"I'm glad you didn't."

"Me too."

I raised my head and kissed him. Warmth tingled between my legs as I pushed my tongue past his lips, drinking him in.

"I am sure," I whispered before he had the chance to ask. "I love you, Jackson, so much."

"I love you too, Addie." A gust of wind hit the house, which creaked and groaned in protest. Fully knowing what we were risking, I slipped my fingers along the hem of Jackson's pants. Not only did making love to Jackson feel good, it felt *right*. And it made me feel like I was putting a piece of myself back together, and no one could take it away.

I scratched another line in the dry wall, completing the eighth row. Another month had passed and I only had roughly thirty days left. I had been slightly nauseous the last couple days, and seeing that I was getting closer to being shipped overseas made a lump of vomit burn in my throat.

I retreated to the cot, thinking about the girl numbered 261. I wondered what happened to her and where she was. Did the man who bought her use her exclusively himself? Or did he see her as a business investment and put her to work?

Then I thought about Nate. Usually when I thought about him, all I imagined was shoving something sharp and pointy into his chest, but at that moment, I wondered how he became the way he was. Were people born evil? When did he decide he wanted to get into this?

"I don't want you to go," Lily said.

I snapped back to reality. "I don't want to either. As fucked up as it is, I'd rather stay in this basement."

She looked at me in the mirror and picked up the curling iron. She ran a comb through her red hair and took a small section to wrap around the hot metal. "Your skin looks nice," she said suddenly.

"Uh, thanks?" I raised an eyebrow. "I don't know why it

would. I'm as pale as a ghost. I haven't seen the sun in weeks." I sighed. "It's depressing."

"It's chilly today," she said as if it was a consolation. "And windy. I don't know why I'm even bothering to curl my hair."

"It looks pretty," I complimented. I sat back, leaning on the wall. I could hear Jackson moving around upstairs as he cleaned the house. I knew it would take him all day.

"Thanks. I think I look older when I curl it. Don't you?"

"Yeah," I agreed and was reminded just how young Lily was. Legally, she couldn't even drive.

My stomach flip-flopped, and I felt like I might throw up. I begrudgingly got off the cot to get a bottle of water. I drank the entire thing and felt almost instantly better. I picked up Jackson's anatomy textbook and sat at the card table, flipping through the pages.

"Isn't that boring?" Lily asked.

"Kinda. I just like the pictures."

"Gross," she said with a smile.

I shrugged and looked at a page full of colorful pictures of body slices. I flipped back to the beginning and started reading. When I was in school, I hated reading textbooks. I rarely did, actually. Lynn and I discovered that we didn't have to actually read the whole thing, just skim through it and pay attention to anything in bold. Now I had nothing else to do other than obsessively worry and stress. I was pretty sure it had given me an ulcer, which was why I didn't feel well.

"How does it look?" Lily asked when she was finished curling her hair.

I looked up from a chapter on cell growth. "It's pretty."

"Do I look eighteen?"

I internally cringed at the hidden implications of her question. "Seventeen and a half," I answered. Lily made a face but smiled. She moved to the wall of clothes and put on a skintight hot pink dress and a silver jacket over top. She grabbed a pair of silver shoes and sat on her cot, waiting. All Zane had to do was open the basement door and she would get up and rush up the stairs. It reminded me of my dogs. The pantry door squeaked when it was opened. Knowing that their treats were stashed inside, both dogs would come running and sit patiently next to the pantry and wait for someone to give them a treat. And someone *always* gave them treats.

My head hurt again. It had been hurting off and on for the last few days. I went to the bathroom and then lay down on my cot, pulling the blue blanket over my legs. The eight rows of little scratches in the dry wall flashed before my eyes when I closed them. The tally marks were haunting, reminding me of how little time I had left. It was the longest I had gone without working, though, which was disturbing in its own way.

I rolled over and tried to fall asleep. The sun had only just set, but I was tired already. It wasn't like I had a well-defined sleeping schedule anymore. I pictured the dining room again. This time it was Thanksgiving. My grandparents, Aunt Gina, Uncle Henry, and their two kids crowded in with us. Jackson took his spot next to me. Arianna was still on her phone. The turkey was over done, and the mashed potatoes were lumpy. It was perfect.

My eyes opened and I sharply inhaled as a thought occurred to me. This was the longest I had gone without working … and it was the longest I had gone without something else. Sweat immediately broke out on my forehead. I was wrong, I had to be. I sat up, thinking back. Time had become ambiguous, and I wasn't sure just how long it had really been since I had it last, which meant it had probably been longer than I thought. I flew out of bed and darted to the vanity. I bent down, shuffling through a white plastic box that housed tampons.

"I know you're in here," I muttered. I had seen it before. It had to be in there, just buried at the bottom. "Yes," I said and grabbed it, ripping open the box. I sat on the toilet and unfolded the little instruction paper that came with the pregnancy test. I positioned the stick between my legs, making sure the end got saturated with enough urine.

My legs were shaking when I stuck the clear plastic cap over the pee-soaked end. The paper said to wait three minutes. I closed my eyes and started counting. I made it twelve seconds. The blue control line popped up right away. I brought the test close to my face and squinted, examining the spot where the second line would appear.

It was too dim on the toilet. Not looking away from the test,

I wiped, flushed, and moved to the vanity. I flicked on the bright lights and set the test down. I took a step back, telling myself that I would wait the full three minutes and then look.

That didn't work either. I put my hands on the counter and leaned down, glaring at the test. I still didn't see a second line. I blinked. Or did I? "No," I said to myself and looked at my reflection. "You're imagining it." I squeezed my eyes shut and took a breath. Then I looked at the test again.

The basement door opened and shut. The locks slid into place and Jackson clomped down the stairs. "My back fucking hurts," he complained. "Addie?" he said when I didn't move. "You okay?"

I turned around with tears in my eyes. My heart was pounding and I felt like I was going to pass out. I shook my head. "I'm pregnant."

CHAPTER 43

Jackson's face turned white. "What?"

I held up the pregnancy test. I felt like I was going to throw up again, though this time I thought it was from nerves. "I'm pregnant," I repeated. A mangled laugh erupted from deep inside of me, twisting into a sob. My knees felt weak, and I was dizzy. Jackson ran over and put his arm around me.

"It'll be okay," he said automatically.

"How?" I asked and turned into him. I wrapped my arms around his neck, still holding onto the pregnancy test. Everything felt surreal. *This isn't happening.* "They'll kill you," I rushed out. My entire body trembled. "They really will. Oh God," I sucked in air and exhaled quickly. "Jackson. They'll kill you and make me watch. And then, and then …" I couldn't finish talking.

"Addie calm down," Jackson said, but his voice broke. He pulled me close. I could feel his arms shaking.

A million thoughts raced through my head. There was no way out. "They will kill you," I stammered. "And then take it away from me." My hand flew to my abdomen, and I suddenly felt very protective of the little life that was growing inside of me. I broke down in sobs.

Jackson scooped me up and carried me to the cot. He sat, keeping me in his lap. "No they won't," he told me, sounding like he actually believed it. "No one will find out."

"Even if they don't." Tears quickly soaked the front of Jackson's shirt. "Then what? I'll be shipped off to Europe. I can't hide being pregnant for long. And what will happen to the …" I couldn't bring myself to say the word.

"Nothing will happen." He put his hand over mine. "We're getting out of here."

"We've been saying that for the last two months," I hoarsely reminded him. "And we're still here."

Jackson's heart raced, his pulse thumping so hard I could feel it in his arms that held me together. He was trying hard to remain calm for my sake, and that made me feel even more emotional.

"I'll think of something," he promised. "I have to. *We* have to. You are right, Addie. They *will* kill me, and I don't know what will happen to you." He let out a shaky breath and squeezed me against him. "You can't really be passed off as a born-again virgin anymore."

"They'll kill us both."

Jackson bent his head down so that his cheek rested on mine. "I won't let that happen."

I nodded. I wanted to believe him so much it hurt. "What if someone notices before we leave?"

"They won't. You don't look pregnant."

I gasped and pushed away from Jackson. "Yes, I do!" I put my hands on my cheeks. "My skin!"

"What?"

"Lily said my skin looked nice." I was on the verge of panicking again.

Jackson raised an eyebrow. "That means you look pregnant?"

"The pregnancy glow!" I told him.

Jackson closed his eyes for a few seconds, steadying his nerves. "I honestly don't think anyone will come to that conclusion."

"How can you be sure?"

"I'm not," he said nervously. "It's what I want, though."

"Me too."

Jackson took the test out of my hand and inspected it. "Yeah … there is no mistaking that."

"I know."

He rested his head against mine, holding me tight. Neither of us spoke. I thought back, wondering how far along I could possibly be. I knew for certain that I wasn't pregnant the time of the doctor visit.

"I'm so stupid." I whispered. "I stopped taking birth control pills. I … I just didn't think about it. And we only did it once since then. I didn't think," I stammered.

"You're not stupid, not at all. Neither of us thought about it," Jackson soothed. "We're going to get through this. Alive. Both of us." He smoothed my hair. "All three of us," he added softly.

"I love you," I whispered between sobs.

Jackson pressed a kiss on my forehead. "I love you too."

The distant groan of the garage door opening hummed throughout the house. I sat up, moving off of Jackson. His arms lingered around my waist, not wanting to let me go. I wasn't sure if I could function without him. I needed him to hold me, to tell me he loved me, and that we would be okay.

He stood, looked at the stairs, then down at the pregnancy test. He snapped it in half and quickly walked to the toilet. He broke into small pieces and dropped it in, flushing them away. I stuck my feet under the blanket and pulled it up over my head. Jackson picked up a book and sat at the card table, pretending to read.

It was horrible, lying in bed, acting like I was asleep. Lily and Rochelle moved about the basement, making small talk with each other while they freshened up for their next job. It would only be a matter of minutes before Zane came down to get them.

I had both hands over my stomach. *I'm so sorry*, I silently spoke to our unborn child. *I don't want you to be born into this*. Tears streamed down my face, soaking my pillow. I bit my quivering lip. *If there is a way out of this, we will find it. I want you to have a good life.* I turned my face in, struggling not to cry.

The girls wouldn't think much of me crying. I had done a lot of it. I knew it would kill Jackson to hear me cry and not be able to comfort me. A twist of nausea gripped me. I flipped over and peered under the blanket at Jackson.

He sat at the table, holding the book close to his face. At a glance, he appeared calm and collected, but if any of the girls stopped to watch him, they would notice he was bouncing his leg and flipping through the pages of his book way faster than anyone could read.

I closed my eyes, and the stupid vision of the dining room flashed through my head. Though this time a highchair was added to the table. *Don't cry.* My chest tightened. *Don't cry.* I yelled it in my head. *Don't cry, don't cry.*

Fuck.

I pulled the pillow around my face trying to muffle the sobs. I curled my legs up to my chest and tried to take a deep breath.

"I miss her too," Lily said.

I sniffled and nodded, knowing she couldn't see me under the blanket. Thinking of Phoebe sent an instant stab of pain to my heart. It also gave me the strength to find my composure. I sat up, wiped my eyes and nodded again so that Lily could see.

"I don't believe in God," she said and picked up the curling iron. "But I still think she's in a better place."

"Anywhere is better than here," I mumbled, still struggling to keep my voice level.

Lily bit her lip and looked down, not wanting to agree with me when Rochelle was right next to her. She picked up a loose curl and wrapped it around the hot iron.

"Ah!" she said and jerked her hand away. She stuck her index finger in her mouth. "Son of a bitch, I burned myself."

"How bad?" I asked.

Lily held out her finger. "Not too bad. Enough to hurt like hell though."

"You'll live," Rochelle told her and leaned close to the mirror. She reached inside her bra and pulled her breasts up, making them look even larger. "Almost ready?"

"Yeah," she answered. "How do the curls look in the back?"

Rochelle stepped behind her and took the curling iron. "You have it set too high. You're gonna scorch your hair." I watched her turn down the dial and fix a few more curls before misting Lily's head with so much hair spray I could taste it from across the room. I felt even more nauseous.

The girls put their high heels back on and sat on their cots, waiting for Zane. My eyes flicked to the curling iron. Rochelle had left it plugged in. I opened my mouth to tell her she was going to get us killed when a plan came to me.

CHAPTER 44

It took all I had not to throw the covers back and race over to Jackson. I stopped by the vanity first, surreptitiously turning the dial on the curling iron up as far as it could go. I filled a cup with water from the shower and sat at the card table across from Jackson. I picked a book up from the stack in the center and flipped through it.

"I have a plan," I murmured. Jackson flicked his eyes up for a millisecond. "Well, part of one."

Jackson nodded and stood, leaning over the table as he sorted through the books. It appeared that he was looking for something new to read. I quickly whispered my plan.

"It'll work." He sat down, opening a book. He didn't realize it was upside down. "And if Zane doesn't come down today, he will eventually." He absent-mindedly flipped the page. "You should get ready just in case."

My hands began to tremble. I placed them on the table and pushed myself up. My heart thumped in my chest, and I took short, shallow breaths. I went to the vanity and ran a brush through my hair, watching the girls in the mirror.

Lily was picking at her nail polish. Rochelle sat perfectly still, perched on the edge of the cot, looking beautiful and bored.

I flipped my head upside down and raked it into a ponytail. Then I went to the dresser and pulled out a pair of black leggings, trading them for the baggy pajama pants I was wearing. I looked over the shoes next. There weren't any in my size that didn't have heels. Going with a pair of brown boots with a wide, two-inch heel, I snatched them and sat on the cot.

Rochelle was watching me. I could feel her eyes on me as I zipped up the boots, yanking it over the ankle bracelet. My hands started shaking uncontrollably, and the smell of melting plastic permeated the air. Sweat beaded at my forehead. I forced myself to lie back against the pillow.

I heard the metal folding chair scrape against the basement floor when Jackson stood. He walked over to his cot and put his shoes on. My stomach churned, nerves increasing the nausea three fold. I started counting, imagining Jackson pulling a sweatshirt over his head. I could feel his body heat when he walked over, then I felt the cot sink down.

I felt a shade better just knowing he was next to me. I sat up, grinding my teeth, heart pounding.

"We can do this," he whispered.

"Yes," I agreed, voice breaking. I put my hand on his thigh. Jackson put his hand on the mattress behind me, leaning back so that his body brushed against mine. I reached over him, making sure my chest smashed into his stomach and grabbed a book that he had placed on the foot of the bed.

I heard the coils of Rochelle's cot squeak. *Please, please work.* I sat up, twisting so I was angled toward Jackson. He slid his hand in a bit. Our bodies touched innocently, but it was enough to raise suspicions.

"This part always makes me sad," I spoke. I cleared my throat. "When Scarlet falls down the stairs."

"Yeah," Jackson agreed and read the passage out loud. The basement door opened. Trepidation flooded my veins, and I suddenly had second thoughts. "You can do this," Jackson whispered.

"I don't know," I said back, my voice quaking with every word.

"Yes," he pressed.

"Okay." I moved my head quickly and nodded. The girls got up and moved to the base of the stairs.

"Rochelle, no," I heard Lily whisper.

We pretended not to hear. Jackson inched his fingers across my back until his hand rested on the curve of my hip. I tipped my head to the side, letting it fall on his shoulder.

"Just…no," Lily begged. "It's nothing. He's trying to make her feel better. You saw her crying over Phoebe. She doesn't like him like that." Her dangly earrings jangled as she shook her head. I closed my eyes and tried to telepathically tell her to calm down. If all went as planned, she'd be free too.

Despite our practice with the cards, Lily did not get my message. I could almost feel her panic from across the room. Adrenaline surged through me. Two sets of heeled feet climbed the stairs. Jackson put the book down and took my hand. We looked at each other for a fleeting moment.

Then I sprung up and went to the vanity. I unplugged the curling iron and wrapped up the cord as fast as I could. Jackson moved to the side of the staircase, pressing his body against the wall, concealed by shadows. I turned on the shower and scrambled back to the cot, sitting with my back to the stairs. I held the hot metal iron away from my legs and out of sight.

Zane rushed down the stairs, his shoes echoing with each heavy step. He came to a halt.

"Where's Jackson?" he demanded.

Right behind you, dipshit. "Shower," I answered and didn't turn around.

"I heard something interesting," Zane said and strode over to the shower. He had a gun tucked into the back of his pants. I thought my heart was going to explode. Part of my brain screamed at me not to follow through.

I felt a flutter in my stomach. I had to. *We* had to. The flutter turned into a spike of adrenaline. I rose from the cot, gripping the curling iron. An evil smirk twisted Zane's pretty face. He stuck his hand out, slowly moving it toward the shower curtain. I moved just as slow, sneaking up behind him.

Like a snake striking prey, he grabbed the curtain and yanked it back. "You're dead—" he began to threaten and cut off when he saw nothing but an empty shower. He whirled around, seething. "What the—"

He didn't get a chance to finish his question. I struck just as fast. I leaned back and brought my hand up, pressing the hot metal into his cheek. Zane cried out in pain. I shoved my hand forward, pushing against him. The smell of burning flesh choked me. When I pulled my hand back, bits of burned flesh stuck to the curling iron and peeled off his face.

Zane's hands flew to the burn. He fell to his knees, screaming. Jackson struck next, kicking Zane in between his shoulder blades.

"My face!" Zane cried. Jackson kicked him again. He grabbed the gun and tossed it to me. "Look at what she did to my face!"

Jackson wrestled him to the ground. He pulled Zane's arms back and shoved him face first onto the floor. "Do it Addie. Now!"

I raised the gun. My arms shook. I moved the barrel so that it was pointed at Zane's head. Jackson leaned back, moving out of the line of fire. Zane's malevolent blue eyes flashed to mine. His glare was full of nothing but wickedness. Even though he was staring down the barrel of a gun, there was no pleading, no regrets. There was just hate.

I looked right into those malicious eyes and pulled the trigger. And nothing happened. Shit. I didn't know how to use the gun. I turned it to the side, frantically looking for the safety. Zane struggled against Jackson.

"Cock it," Jackson called out.

Before I had a chance to even contemplate how to do that, Rochelle hurled her body through the air. She landed on top of me, knocking me over. The gun flew from my hands and skidded under a cot.

"You bitch!" she screamed and moved over me.

I bent my legs up, instinctively protecting my abdomen. Rochelle's hands gripped my shoulders as she wrestled me to the ground. Her acrylic nails dug into my skin.

"Addie!" Jackson called out, looking up from Zane.

Zane used the distraction to his advantage. He brought his foot up, whacking Jackson, who fell forward. Jackson recovered quickly, fueled by rage. He ducked out of the way, narrowly missing Zane's fist. Jackson pushed himself up onto his feet, spun and kicked Zane in the stomach.

I blindly extended my right hand, slapping at the ground as I desperately searched for a weapon. My fingers brushed the cold, flexible plastic of the curling iron cord. I didn't want to hurt Rochelle. I didn't even blame her for what she was doing.

But I had no choice.

I yanked the cord and gripped the handle of the curling iron, which was sticky from hairspray. I brought my arm up and struck Rochelle on the back of the head, hoping her hair would buffer most of the heat. She screamed and let go of my shoulder, raising her hand to strike me across the face. I twisted around, breaking out of her grasp and crawled forward on my elbows.

Rochelle caught my ankle. She dragged me back, knocking me off balance. My hands slipped out from under me and my chin smacked the floor, forcing my teeth down on my lip. I instantly tasted blood. I pushed myself forward, thrashing my legs. My heel clipped Rochelle in the face, and she fell back, her hands flying to her nose.

Hands grabbed at my arm. I jerked away before realizing it was Jackson. He pulled me to my feet. Zane staggered up from where he was slumped on the floor. I took a step back, looking for the gun. Jackson tugged my hand forward. If I went back for it, Zane could tackle me to the ground. There was no time.

We raced around the card table. Jackson skidded to a stop at the bottom of the stairs, wanting me to go up first. I grasped the railing and took the stairs two at a time. I felt like my legs couldn't move fast enough, and the tops of my thighs burned from desperate excursion. I flung myself onto the landing. Jackson was right behind me. He slammed the door and shot the deadbolt into place.

Chest heaving, I looked into his eyes for a second before running into the mudroom. I squinted in the dark, running my hand up and down the wall in search of the light.

"Come on, come on," I mumbled, my entire body alive with adrenaline. The light flicked on, and I raced over to the door. Hanging on the wall next to it was a key hook. I snatched the keys to the Blazer and raced back into the kitchen. Jackson stood in the breakfast nook, holding a chair above his head.

"What the hell is going on?" Lily asked. She was standing in the middle of the kitchen, looking terrified.

"We're getting out of here," I said and stood a few feet from Jackson. He turned his head and closed his eyes. "Come with us."

Jackson threw the chair through the window. The high-pitched, blaring alarm sounded. The floor vibrated as Lou raced out of his room. Lily didn't move. She stayed rooted in the spot, staring at me.

"Come!" I yelled over the alarm an extended my hand.

Lily looked at my fingers and then into my eyes. She wrapped her arms around herself and shook her head.

"Lily!" I cried.

Jackson took my hand. "We don't have time." He pulled me forward. "She made her choice." He used his elbow to clear away the shards of broken glass that clung to the window frame. He ducked through, jumping down onto the deck, and held his arms out for me.

"I'll send help!" I promised Lily.

Rochelle banged on the basement door, screaming for Lily to open it. I took Jackson's hands and climbed out the window. We sprinted around the house to the driveway. I fumbled with the keys and screamed in frustration when they fell from my shaking hands. I dropped to my knees and scooped them up.

I unlocked the Blazer and climbed inside. Jackson slid into the passenger seat. "Go!" he shouted, turning around to look at the house. I couldn't steady my hands enough to get the keys in the ignition. Jackson reached over and wrapped his fingers around my hand, steadying me. Together, we started the SUV. I threw it in reverse and stomped on the gas. The Blazer jolted back. It was still moving when I shoved the gear into drive.

The engine revved and we peeled down the driveway. I didn't even think about a destination. I yanked the wheel and sped down the street.

"He's following us," Jackson told me. His voice was tight with fear. We had only been driving for a few minutes.

"Who?"

"Zane or Lou. I don't know, maybe both. Step on it, Addie. Their car is faster."

I pushed the pedal down as far as it could go. The Blazer lurched forward, engine squealing. "Which way?"

"Straight. I'll tell you when to turn." I gripped the steering wheel and turned around. The SUV swerved. "Put your seat belt on," Jackson told me and clicked his into place. I reached over and pulled it halfway across my body. Jackson took it from me, knowing my shaky hands weren't functioning very well. It was taking all I had to keep the car on the road.

A gunshot echoed across the dark field from down the road. I screamed. Headlights grew brighter and brighter behind us. Jackson put his hand on my seat and twisted, watching the Camaro gaining on us. I stepped harder on the gas, pushing the old SUV past its limit. The entire thing started to shake as we took on more speed than it could handle.

"There's a turn up ahead," Jackson told me. "Go to the right!"

I let off the gas, my eyes scanning the unfamiliar road. I almost missed the green and white sign. Light bounced off the reflective numbers, and I slammed on the brakes. The SUV shuddered, but made the turn. I pressed the pedal down again, and the engine groaned in protest. My eyes flicked to the gauges; the engine was threatening to overheat. I couldn't let up. We barreled down the road. I wasn't aware that I had been holding my breath until my lungs begged for air. I opened my mouth and inhaled.

"They missed the turn," Jackson said. I risked a glance in the rearview mirror and saw the Camaro back up and whirl around before accelerating down the road. It bought us some much-needed time.

"They're going to catch up!" I cried. My fingers were going numb from grasping the steering wheel so hard. Jackson didn't respond. He knew I was right. "Should we get out and run?"

"No," he finally said. "There is a state road just ahead. You can't see it past the trees."

"What does that have to do with anything?"

"It's busy. Zane might not—" he cut off when a bullet hit the back window, shattering the glass. I screamed again, and the SUV dangerously swerved to the right. The tires caught on the rough side of the road. I yanked the wheel, over correcting and almost tipping the SUV over.

"Are you okay?" Jackson rushed out.

"I think so. You?"

"Yeah." He turned around. "Fuck." I looked at him, fear

closing around my heart. "Eyes on the road, Addie!"

I shook myself and watched the dark street disappear. Rapid gunfire rang out. The gas pedal was against the floor. The old Blazer would not go any faster, and the Camaro was just yards behind us. My chest felt too small for my racing heart.

Streaks of yellow light flickered through the trees ahead. Hope painfully flowed through me, prickling my skin. I stomped my foot down fully knowing it would do no good. I wanted to reach the busy road so bad it hurt. My breath came out in huffs. I clenched my jaw and leaned forward.

More shots rang out, pinging off the tailgate. Something splattered on the windshield. For a split second I thought we had hit something. Then I realized the blood was on the *inside* of the SUV.

"Jackson," I screamed and twisted my body.

His eyes were wide with shock. He leaned forward. Then the pain set in. His hand flew to his left shoulder, pressing on the bullet wound. Lights grew brighter in front of us. A car honked. I turned back around and saw that we were just feet from the intersection.

Everything slowed down in that second. The metallic smell of Jackson's blood filled the air. The brake pedal squeaked when I pressed it down and the tires squealed. The back end of the SUV fishtailed. The lights to my right were so bright. I closed my eyes and could hear my heart pounding in my head.

And then we crashed.

CHAPTER 45

The Blazer continued forward, diving down a ditch. The front smashed into the ground, deploying the airbags. It covered my face and felt like I was suffocating. The SUV tipped to the side. My head cracked on the window. An instant wave of nausea gripped me, and my ears rang.

Powder from the airbag burned my nose, choking me. Pain radiated along my temple. I felt a warm tingle run down my spine. My eyes were too heavy to keep open. They closed on their own accord, and I lost consciousness.

The heavy smell of gasoline brought me back. The SUV was lying on its side. I struggled to shove the airbag away. "Jackson," I cried. "Jackson!"

His body flopped over, held in place by the seat belt. Dark red blood dripped down his chest. His eyes were open, but he wasn't moving.

"Jackson!" I screamed again. I clawed at my seat belt. My fingers were numb, but I somehow managed to press the button and released the belt. "Jackson," I repeated. Tears blurred my already fuzzy vision. I reached out and touched his arm. He still didn't move.

Pain began to register in my brain. My head throbbed, and my legs hurt. I manically flailed about, trying to get my legs up from under the steering wheel. I twisted and grabbed onto the seat, using it to hoist my body up.

Glass crunched under my feet as I pushed off the driver's

side window. I needed to get out and pull Jackson to safety. The scent of gas was getting stronger. All it would take was one spark, and we'd be dead for sure.

"Hey!" someone shouted. "She's alive in there!"

The realization that other people had been involved in the crash weighed down on me. "Help!" I screamed. "Help him!"

There was a horrible screech of mangled metal. The SUV shook.

"The door's stuck!" the same voice yelled. Someone shouted back to them, their words far and indiscernible.

"It might be too late," a female voice spoke. "It smells like gas. Strong. Help me get them out!"

I clambered over the seat and pressed my hand to Jackson's wound. The bullet had struck in between his neck and his left shoulder. Blood pooled around my fingers. "You're gonna be okay," I frantically mumbled. "You have to be!" Sirens echoed, and red and blue lights danced across Jackson's bloodied face.

"Can you hear me?" a woman shouted. I jerked my head up, looking at the back of the Blazer. "You need to get out of there! Can you move?"

"Yeah," I answered automatically and turned my attention back to Jackson. My body violently trembled, rendering me useless. I shook my head. "Can't leave him," I said hoarsely. "Can't leave him." Jackson's blood dripped down my arms. Car doors slammed shut and multiple people shouted orders. I cupped a hand around Jackson's face. "Wake up!" I yelled. "Jackson, don't leave me!" Awkwardly contorted in the overturned Blazer, I slipped, crumpling down onto shards of broken glass.

The back passenger window broke. My mind flashed to Zane, and I thought he was here to finish us off. A low rumble of an engine shook the car. I scrambled back up, swaying when dizziness crashed down on me. My eyes threatened to close.

A horrible high-pitched sound filled the air when part of the SUV door was torn off. I looked up to see several firefighters working to cut away at the Blazer. They spoke to me, but their voices were a distant echo.

My knees gave out. I reached up, lacing my fingers through Jackson's. His arm was outstretched, unnaturally hanging to the side. I held onto him. I began to feel cold. The vision of Jackson and I sitting at the dining room table flashed before my eyes. It was the same as it always was, but this time everything was bathed in a bright white light.

Jackson's hand slipped from mine. I forced my eyes open and reached for him. He was lifted up, carefully moved out of the car. Then heavy hands landed on me, bringing me out to safety.

I was laid down on a gurney. I tried to sit up. The same firefighter who rescued me gently put her hands on my shoulders. "Stay," she said. "You were in a bad car accident," she reminded me as if I didn't remember.

"No," I protested and continued to fight against her. I looked up with a desperate fear in search of the black Camaro. Still down in the ditch, I wouldn't have been able to see the road even if the emergency vehicles weren't in the way. "Jackson," I mumbled. An EMT buckled a strap across my legs. "No!" I shouted. "Jackson!"

"He's okay," the EMT told me. "We're taking you both to the hospital."

"You …" I started and felt the dizziness sink its claws into me. "You don't understand."

The EMT put an oxygen mask over my face. I swatted it away.

"I might need some help over here!" he called and picked up the mask.

"No!" I mumbled again. "My name … my name is …" My eyes were pulled closed. Someone put my hands at my sides and buckled another strap around my chest. "Ad…e…line," I panted. "M-mill. Miller," I forced out.

It took an enormous amount of energy to turn my head. I opened my eyes briefly, but it was just enough to see Jackson being wheeled into an ambulance. Emergency workers surrounded him. One was pumping air into him, and another had hands on his chest. I wasn't sure if they were doing CPR or putting pressure on the bullet wound. My ears rang, and I felt the familiar feeling of my mind wanting to check out, unable to deal with what was happening.

"Adeline Miller?" someone questioned. Hearing my name jolted me to life. I tipped my head back and saw a police officer jogging over. "Did you say your name is Adeline Miller?"

"Yes," I said and strained against the safety straps. "My family. They said they'd go after my family."

The officer turned and said something into his radio. The EMTs pushed me forward and loaded me into a different ambulance than the one Jackson was in. The cop got in, staying in the back while the EMTs set to work on mending me.

"No," I said when one of them tore open a plastic case and held up a needle. My hands moved over my abdomen. "Don't hurt my ... my ...baby." Saying the word brought on all of the night's emotion.

"It's just for an IV, honey," the EMT spoke. Her auburn hair was pulled back in a messy bun and her brown eyes were kind. She picked up my hand, giving it a squeeze before extending my arm. "How far along are you?" she asked, wiped my skin with alcohol, and pressed at the skin inside my elbow, feeling for a vein.

"I don't know," I said. "Jackson," I mumbled. "I need to go to him."

"He's already on his way to the hospital," she soothed and unwrapped a needle. "You're gonna feel a little poke," she warned me.

The ambulance doors shut. I let my eyes close. Tears ran down the side of my face.

"Adeline," the cop said.

My teeth chattered as I tried to keep from crying. "Yeah."

"You're really Adeline Miller."

"Yes."

"You've been missing for over a year." My eyes opened. Had it been that long? "Are you able to tell me what happened?"

A chill made its way down my body. The memory of that day was still vivid. I could feel the sunlight on my skin. I remembered how excited I was when I checked my email and saw one of my favorite authors had sent me an advanced copy of her book.

"We were at the Gay Pride Parade."

"Yes, we know that," he said gently.

"I saw him." I stopped and swallowed hard. "I saw him doing something I wasn't supposed to see. So he took me."

"Who did you see, Adeline? Who took you?"

"Where's Jackson?" I asked and tried to sit up. "I need to find him."

"Who's Jackson?" the cop asked. "They guy who took you?"

"No." The EMT leaned over. "He's the guy who was in the car with her." She patted my hand. "Honey, your friend is on his way to the hospital. He'll be taken care of there. You can see him in just a little bit, okay?"

I blinked back tears and nodded.

"Adeline," the cop pressed. "Who took you?"

I didn't want to say his name. He was evil, and I worried that speaking his name would summon him like a demon. I closed my eyes again. "Zane. I don't know his last name." I shook my head.

"Do you know where he is now?" he asked patiently.

"No." The memory of Phoebe crumpled against the dumpster played out next. My heart broke all over again at the thought of her, and I started to cry.

"Maybe this should wait," the auburn haired EMT said under her breath.

Wait. The word reverberated in my head. Wait. It was exactly what I couldn't do.

"Please," I spoke with more clarity. "He said if I ever left he'd go after my family. And Lynn. My friend Lynn. You have to get somebody there!"

The cop nodded and spoke into his radio again. "Do you know where this guy, Zane, would go?"

"No. Maybe back at the house," I said and felt sick again. I wanted to be with Jackson. I wanted to hold his hand and tell him we made it, that we escaped. I wanted to press my lips to his and tell him I loved him.

"Where is the house?"

I sucked in air, on the verge of hyperventilating again. It didn't matter where the house was if Jackson didn't make it. Nothing mattered. I needed him. If it wasn't for Jackson, I would be leaving for another country in a few short weeks, never to be seen again. If it wasn't for Jackson, I would have given up.

"That's enough for now," the EMT said. She took my hand and talked me through quieting my breathing. I remembered what Jackson had said about saving the other girls.

"It's okay," I panted. I thought about the teeny-tiny little person growing inside of me and found a new type of strength. I took a long, shaky breath and looked at the police officer. And then I told him everything.

CHAPTER 46

Nerves twisted in my stomach. My abdomen tightened. I squeezed my eyes closed, and swallowed the lump of vomit that was rising in my throat. The ambulance stopped. The cop and the EMT got up, letting me know that we had arrived at the hospital.

"I need to see Jackson," I said.

"I know honey," the EMT said gently and grabbed one end of the gurney. I strained my neck, trying to sit up and look into the emergency room as I was wheeled in. Nurses and doctors buzzed about the busy hall.

"Where is he?"

"He's being taken care of," the EMT replied.

"I need to see him!" I said again, my voice rising. I struggled against the safety restraints, painfully twisting my very battered body.

"Calm down," the EMT said.

Calm down? She wanted me to calm down after what I had just been through? *No fucking way.* I thrust my weight to the side. The gurney came off balanced and almost fell. A nurse rushed over and put her hands on the foot of the gurney, steadying the little bed. I twisted again and yanked an arm up.

"We need assistance!" the nurse yelled over her shoulder.

I pushed up and pulled my other arm free. The IV line caught and ripped out of my arm. Pair seared through me, but that didn't matter. I needed to get to Jackson.

The nurse put her hands on my feet. "You have to stop moving," she said as she struggled to hold me down. "I don't want you to hurt yourself."

The EMT took one of my hands. "Adeline!" She stepped to my side. "Honey, stop it! You're already banged up. I'll find Jackson."

I jerked my head around. "Please do. Now. I need him!" I pulled my arm back, breaking free of the EMT's grip. "Jackson!" I kicked my feet. "Let me go! I have to find him!" He was okay, he had to be. We had come so far, risked so much…he was alive, and he would be okay.

My eyes flitted around the ER. Curtains were drawn around small rooms, and Jackson was in one of them. I had to get up, had to go to him. He needed me as much as I needed him. I swatted at another set of hands that tried to hold me down.

"Bring me IM Ativan!" a man shouted. He was standing to my side, pushing down on my shoulder. "Now!"

"She's pregnant," the nurse told him. "She can't have it."

"Jackson!" I called. All of my energy was draining fast. Everything hurt, but it didn't matter. I had to get up. I just had to. "Please! Let me see him," I cried.

A curtain across from me pulled back. Several nurses stood around a bed, working on a patient. I heard one of them say something about taking the patient into surgery. They pushed the bed forward. Then I saw dark, wavy hair. Bandages covered most of his face. An IV was strung from his arm.

"Jackson!" He didn't turn to look at me. He didn't even move at all. I shook my head. "No. No, no, no! Jackson!" I watched in horror as the bed rolled by, out of sight and the ER. "I have to go to him," I stammered as I fought against the hands that held me down. I curled my legs up.

"Adeline," the EMT grunted. "If you calm down we can talk about Jackson."

I stopped struggling. "Okay." I sniffled, becoming aware that tears were streaming down my face, and I wiped my runny nose. "Where are they taking him?"

"Into surgery," the man answered. I twisted to look at him. He was tall with dark skin and black hair. I couldn't pronounce the long name embroidered onto blue scrubs. His dark eyes were gentle. "You can go once he's out."

"Is he going to be okay?" My hand trembled as I pushed my hair behind my ear.

The doctor's face remained still. "We will know once he's out of surgery. Now you need to let us take care of you."

I nodded, agreeing. Then I was whisked into one of those small rooms and hooked up to several machines. I watched my rapid heart rate on the monitor that hung above the bed while the nurses and doctors worked on me.

I had a mild concussion and was dehydrated. I needed four stitches to the gash on my right shin, my left wrist was sprained, and my face and arms were scratched and bruised to all hell.

But I was okay. Technically, I didn't even need to be admitted. I was treated in the ER, and only time would heal the concussion and sprain. Medically, I was sound enough to be discharged. Mentally ... that was a whole other story. My brain hadn't allowed me to process anything. It was just too much. The words 'Jackson is in surgery' replayed over and over in my mind like a broken record.

I looked at the floor. Light reflected off the freshly waxed tile. I couldn't handle thinking about Jackson lying on a table under bright lights. I stared at the floor until my vision blurred and my eyes watered.

Dressed in only a hospital gown, I shivered. I rubbed my hands on my arms. The air was cold in the emergency room of Genesis Medical Center. I pulled my knees to my chest, watching the clock. Thirty-four minutes had gone by, and I hadn't heard anything about Jackson.

"Adeline?" the nurse called before she pulled back the curtain just enough to get into the room. "Hi, I'm Elyse." She smiled warmly. Her thick dark hair was pulled into a ponytail that swung when she walked. "The police would like to talk to you, but I told them they only could if it was all right with you."

"It's okay," I said automatically.

She moved over to the bed. "Are you sure? You don't have to do this now."

"No, it's okay. I just want to get it over with." I closed my eyes and exhaled. "I want this all over with."

"Okay." She gave me another sympathetic smile and left. A

few seconds later, a police officer and two detectives pulled back the curtain and came into the room. They had me tell them in great detail everything that happened to me over the last year. They didn't seem to believe me when I told them Jackson was the father of my baby. Almost as soon as I was done, two FBI agents came in and had me repeat everything again.

After they left, a tall and thin older man came into the room. He was carrying a sketchbook and a pencil. "Hello, Adeline," he said quietly.

Everyone seemed afraid to talk to me, like what I had been through made me too fragile to handle real life. I didn't want to waste the energy telling them they were wrong, that all the horrible shit I had been through only made me more of a fighter than I ever had been.

"I'm Ben." He pulled a rolling stool out from under the counter and sat, flipping open his notebook. "Do you think you can tell me what the guys that took you look like?"

I shifted my feet under the thin, white sheet. "Yeah, I can."

He nodded. "Good. You only have to describe the younger one. A few of the guys at the station are familiar with the other guy's ... uh, business ventures. They've seen him before. Ready to start?"

I nodded and closed my eyes, bringing the terrifying image of Zane's face to mind. I described his looks the best I could and hoped that the picture resembled Zane at least a little.

"Like this?" Ben asked when we were done. He held up the picture.

"His eyebrows are a little thicker," I said. I licked my dry lips and looked at the clock.

Ben turned the picture around and added to the sketch. "This?"

"Yes," I said, looking at the sketch of Zane. It was hauntingly lifelike. I felt as if the black and white eyes seared into me. I looked at the drawn-on burn and got a flash of pressing the curling iron to Zane's cheek. I could still smell the burning flesh.

Ben nodded and closed the notebook. At a loss for words, he only offered me a tight smile and a slight nod before he left, pulling back the curtain to exit the small room in the ER. The manhunt would begin, and the pencil drawing of Zane's face would be broadcast over the news.

I looked at the clock again. Two armed police officers stood outside the room. They told me that my family, as well as Lynn and even the dogs, had been moved into protective custody and would be brought to the hospital once it was safe. Several uniforms had gone directly to the farmhouse. Lily was still there. I asked what would happen to her and got a vague answer of her eventually finding a foster family. It took me a moment to remember that she was only fifteen

I lay on the bed, scraping my fingers along the sheet, and listened to the seconds tick by on the large, white-faced clock that hung over the door. Jackson had been in surgery for over an hour. I closed my eyes and thought of his handsome face. So badly I wanted to be with him, to hold him, to run my fingers along the many scars that covered his body.

The curtain pulled back. I opened my eyes and whipped my head up, which instantly caused me to feel sick. The same nurse, Elyse, stepped into the room.

"Are you doing all right, Adeline?" she asked carefully. She strode over to the computer in the corner and swiped her badge.

I didn't respond. It was a stupid question. I wanted to tell her so, but I could sense her concern and compassion. Besides, what else was she supposed to say?

"Are you in any pain?"

"Not really," I said.

"Your lab work is back," she said before I had a chance to ask about Jackson. "Your hCG levels suggest you're about seven weeks pregnant, which means you got pregnant about a month ago." She paused to let me absorb the information. "The doctor ordered an ultra sound."

"Jackson will want to be there," I told her and began to feel like I was getting sucked backwards. The room was spinning, and I slowly pitched forward. Elyse rushed over and helped me up.

"I can't imagine," she said softly and sat on the bed next to me. "I can't even begin to imagine what you went through. I'm so sorry." She shook her head. The phone that she carried in her scrub pocket rang. She stood to answer it. "He's in recovery," she told me and re-pocketed the phone.

My stomach flip-flopped and I nodded. "Can I go?" I pushed myself off the bed.

"Yes. But I'm taking you in this." She gripped the handles of a wheel chair.

"I can walk," I told her.

"I know you can, but you're my patient, and I want to take care of you," she said with a smile. "Plus it's hospital protocol." She wheeled the chair over. "Hang on. You're more than a little exposed in the back." She got a second gown and put it on me like a robe. "Better?"

"Yes. Thanks," I said quietly. She disconnected my IV and helped me into the wheelchair. I picked at the plastic hospital bracelet that was around my wrist as we went through the hall. The nurse hadn't told me anything about Jackson's condition, and I was afraid to ask.

There was a family in the OR waiting room. I knew that no scheduled surgeries were being done at this late hour.

"What happened to the people we hit?" I asked suddenly, afraid that the family belonged to the victim.

"Treated and released," the nurse said.

I internally sighed. Elyse pushed a button on the wall that opened double doors to a large room labeled PACU. A police officer stood outside that door as well. My heart began speeding up again.

There were several nurses standing around the very first bed we came up to. An older nurse with gray hair saw me and smiled.

"You have a visitor," she said softly to Jackson.

I got out of the wheelchair before Elyse came to a complete stop. The gray-haired nurse stepped aside. I flew to the bed. Tears stung the corners of my eyes.

"Jackson," I said and gently touched his hand. He was connected to a scary amount of tubes and wires going to various machines. One side of his body was covered in bandages, and his arm was precariously placed over his chest and propped with pillows. His eyes were closed, and his breathing was shallow. "Is he okay?" I asked, unable to keep the tears back.

"He's stable," the gray-haired nurse told me.

"Does that mean he's going to be okay?" I slipped my fingers through Jackson's. His eyes fluttered halfway open for a second before closing again.

"He has a long recovery ahead of him," she said, ominously avoiding my direct question.

I just nodded and rubbed the palm of his hand. Using my other hand, I wiped away the tears that streaked my face. Someone else joined the room. I could feel their presence behind me.

"You must be Adeline," a man with a heavily accented voice said.

I turned around. "Yeah," I said to the surgeon. His eyes were sympathetic and he looked at me as if he wasn't sure how to act. Deciding to just go with his professional norm, he began explaining Jackson's injuries to me.

The bullet shot right through Jackson's body, hitting his collarbone on its way out. The surgeon told me that the bullet missed his subclavian artery by just a hair. He said Jackson was lucky. Nevertheless, Jackson had lost enough blood to require a blood transfusion. He also sustained minor head trauma in the crash, and had a row of sutures above his right eye.

The surgeon's face paled when he told me that Jackson had multiple fractures to his ribs all in various stages of healing. He was concerned about the old gash on Jackson's abdomen and the indent of scar tissue along Jackson's side where his skin had been peeled off. Then the surgeon said something about Jackson's blood being infected, and that he put Jackson on a strong course of antibiotics.

I nodded, pretending to understand everything that was being told to me. After the doctor left, the nurses tended to Jackson and then stepped back, letting me have some time alone with him. Faye, the gray-haired nurse, told me that Jackson was most likely going to be very confused as he woke up. Having me there would help.

"Jackson," I whispered. "We made it. We got out." I rubbed my fingers in little circles on the inside of his hand. A monitor beeped along with his heart rate, slow but steady. I was slightly afraid it was a dream, and I was still in the basement. If it were a dream, Jackson wouldn't be injured. I blinked. *No, this is real.*

Jackson's fingers twitched. I leaned closed. "Jackson." I ran my hand over his hair, careful to avoid the stitches. "Jackson."

He opened his eyes and he took a deep breath. Then his eyes closed again. The pattern repeated a few times as he struggled to come out of the anesthetic.

"Addie," he mumbled.

"Yes, Jackson, I'm here."

He tried to sit up and groaned in pain. Faye hurried over.

"Hi Jackson," she spoke. "I'm your nurse. You just had surgery and need to stay laying down, okay?"

"Okay," Jackson agreed but tried to sit up again.

"Jackson you need to rest," I said, blinking back tears.

"I have to save you," he faintly murmured. He took another deep breath and opened his eyes all the way.

"You did," I whispered. "You did save me." I began crying again. I leaned over the bed, getting as close to Jackson as I dared without hurting him. He lifted his right arm, hugging me.

"Are you okay?" he asked me.

"I'm fine," I said right away. His hand fell back onto the bed. I leaned back and looked at him. His eyes were closed again. "Rest," I told him.

He mumbled something incoherent, but didn't object. Several minutes passed before he woke up again. He took his hand out of mine and put it over my stomach. I placed my hands over his and nodded, letting him know the baby was okay. His chocolate eyes met mine, and he smiled.

"Addie," he said. His voice was hoarse. "We did it. We're free."

EPILOGUE

"Can you pass the mashed potatoes?" Arianna asked.

"Yeah, here you go," Jackson told her and handed her the bowl. I spooned a heaping mound of mac and cheese onto my plate and passed the dish to Jackson, who plopped a spoonful onto his plate and passed the dish on to Lynn. Happy chatter buzzed around the dining room table as we passed plates and bowls of food back and forth.

Jackson looked at me and smiled. I put my hand on his thigh, giving him a reassuring squeeze. Even though he was familiar with my family and Lynn, being around everyone at once caused a bit of anxiety for him. I had told him we didn't have to go, that everyone would understand. He had just taken my hand and smiled, reminding me that he could do anything, as long as we were together. Plus, that dinner wasn't just a regular meal. It was a celebration.

The trial was finally over. Nate and Zane, along with a handful of their accomplices, were behind bars for good. It took four months for the police to catch them. It had been a long, nerve-wracking time for us, but I would never forget the look on their faces when Jackson and I walked into the courtroom to testify, hand in hand. I was seven months pregnant at the time. Zane had stared opened mouthed at my belly as if he couldn't understand what was happening. Then his eyes fastened on Jackson's fingers linked through mine and he exploded. We enjoyed watching him get shoved around by the police.

I picked up the platter of sliced ham, tossing pieces to Scarlet and Rhett, when a baby's cry came from the living room. I set the platter down. "Grace is awake," I said, though it was obvious, and started to stand. "That was a short nap."

"No, no," Mom said and sprang up. "Grandma will get her. You eat."

"Are you sure?" Jackson asked. "I can get her."

Arianna smiled. "You know she loves that baby. Let her," she said with a wink.

"As long as you don't mind," Jackson mumbled, shifting uncomfortably in his chair. Over a year and a half had passed since our escape, and he still had a hard time accepting help. I put my hand on his thigh and felt him relax.

"How's wedding planning going?" Dad asked Lynn.

She turned to her fiancé and smiled. "Good. Addie's been my lifesaver. She's kept me sane through all this. It's so fun!"

Luke rolled his eyes. "You two did it the right way," he said to Jackson and me.

I smiled and subconsciously twisted my wedding band around on my finger. Jackson and I had gotten married at the courthouse a few months before Grace was born. It was a bit of a sore subject for my mother. She insisted over and over that we wait until after I had the baby and could have the big wedding that I always had wanted.

It wasn't something Jackson could do. He had severe PTSD from being a slave for over a decade. When he was captive, he was able to slink throughout crowds unnoticed. Now that our story was out, we had become uncomfortably famous, in a weird way. The media had a fascination with our tale. We were constantly asked to do interviews or tell our story on TV. Neither of us spoke about our time at the farmhouse outside of the legal system, no matter how much money was offered.

I had my issues as well. I couldn't help but panic when I saw any male with dark hair and blue eyes. I had crippling crowd anxiety, feeling like I could get snatched away at any moment. Though I still wanted to wear a fancy gown and have my overly ostentatious reception, the thought of being the center of attention caused my heart to race. Jackson and I both regularly saw a therapist, but the nightmares hadn't stopped.

I was almost always scared. Scared Nate still had people out there that would come after Jackson or me—or worse, Grace—and scared I would run into another client, like what happened only a few weeks ago.

My parents took us out to dinner. Too afraid to take Grace into the ladies' room for a diaper change alone, my mom came with. On the way back to our table I froze, eyes landing on a familiar tattoo. I didn't know how Jackson knew but suddenly he was there, shielding me from Travis. As soon as he saw us, Travis froze like a deer in headlights. Then he got up to run.

Jackson stopped him, hitting him hard in the face then throwing him to the ground. I clung onto our daughter and broke down in hysterical tears. My mom ushered me away, and my dad rushed over to Jackson. Once he found out who Travis was, my dad threw in a couple punches before the fight was broken up.

It was one of my worst fears come true. Now Travis was in jail. Behind bars just like Nate and Zane. I tried to focus on that just like my therapist instructed.

Maybe someday Jackson and I could renew our vows and have the grand party. I looked at Jackson. I wasn't in rush. He was all I needed.

"No fuss, no wasting time looking at flowers, no missing Sunday night football because you're looking through book after book after boring book of invitations." Luke grinned at Lynn. "I suppose it's worth it."

"It better be," Lynn said with a grin.

"Ari, put your phone away," Dad scolded. Some things would never change.

"Sorry," she said and put her cell phone on her lap. "Rhia was asking me about the presentation tomorrow."

Dad's face softened. Arianna nodded. "All of my friends are coming, and I think all of their families too." She turned to me. "It's gonna be packed."

"I hope so," I told her, surprised I didn't feel nervous. "People need to hear this." For the first time, Jackson and I were speaking publicly about our time as slaves.

I started going to a local sex crime victim support group several months before Grace was born. It became apparent to me that without the love and support of a family and friends, it was hard for survivors to get on their feet and make a life for themselves. Though no one else in the group had been through what Jackson and I had, it was comforting to talk to other rape victims and know that I wasn't alone. Once Jackson and I started going, more and more victims came, saying our story of perseverance gave them the strength to come forward. I wasn't ready yet, and I had no idea when I would ever be, but I wanted to get more involved, offering help and support to those who didn't have it.

If it weren't for my family, Jackson and I would have nothing. My parents welcomed Jackson into their house with no hesitation, though it hadn't been easy for them to accept him. They wanted their daughter back, but had envisioned the old Adeline. My therapist still had to remind me of that too. I came back not only a changed person, but pregnant and with someone I wasn't willing to let out of my sight. It was a lot for my family to take in. Jackson had been my rock, my reason to keep fighting, and my freedom. He was just a stranger with a dark past to my family at first.

More than once my mother hinted that she wondered if I really loved him or had developed some sort of deep dependence on him while we were captive. There was never any doubt in my mind. I loved Jackson.

Our life wasn't ideal. I never thought I'd be married with a child and still living in my parents' house ... without even graduating. Jackson and I shared my old room, and the guest bedroom upstairs and been turned into a nursery.

Even if I hadn't suffered from crippling anxiety, I wasn't willing to leave Jackson and Grace and go back to school. I tried going to a local community college, but dropped out after just a few days, unable to deal with the questions and the whispers. Instead, Jackson and I both took online courses.

I didn't know if either of us would ever be able to get a job and support our family. I had cried over that many times. I wanted a normal life for us ... for Grace. We still talked about our dreams. I still wanted to be a nurse, and Jackson wanted to work in law enforcement, putting guys like Nate and Zane behind bars. If it didn't happen next year, then maybe the year after that. Someday, we'd both have jobs. Someday, we'd have our own house. Someday we would have that normal life. But for now we had each other. And that was enough.

Now that Grace was here, my parents didn't want us to leave. They loved their first grandchild almost as much as we did. It was hard for Jackson to adjust to being free *and* a father. Neither of us knew what we were doing. We read every baby book we could during the pregnancy, which did little to prepare us. I loved being a mother, and I loved my daughter more than I could ever thought possible. Jackson was wonderful. He was unsure of himself and nervous, but he was a great dad who loved his little girl.

"It's so scary," Luke said. "I had no idea that kind of stuff happened around here."

"Not a lot of people do," Jackson told him, unable to look him in the eye.

"You're so brave, Addie," Lynn said. "Both of you are. What you're doing is amazing."

I smiled. "Thanks."

Mom came back into the dining room with the baby in her arms. Grace caught sight of me and smiled. She had dark almond shaped eyes just like her father, and her wispy hair was brown with a slight curl to it. She was the perfect combination of the two of us.

"Hey there, pretty lady," Dad said and extended his arms. "Let Grandpa hold you."

"You had her before dinner," Mom told him. "It's my turn." She held Grace up in front of her and made a silly face, causing Grace to giggle. "Grandma loves her little angel, doesn't she?"

Jackson put his hand on top of mine. I turned to him, our eyes locking. I felt the familiar flutter in my stomach that had never gone away. Despite the horrors we had gone through, we were happy. We chose to be victors, not victims, going through hell and getting out of it not only alive, but also stronger … and together.

No matter what, *together* is how we would always stay.

ABOUT THE AUTHOR

Emily Goodwin is the New York Times and USA Today Bestselling author of over a dozen romantic titles. Emily writes the kind of books she likes to read, and is a sucker for a swoon-worthy bad boy and happily ever afters.

She lives in the Midwest with her husband and two daughters. When she's not writing, you can find her riding her horses, hiking, reading, or drinking wine with friends.

Emily is represented by Julie Gwinn of the Seymour Agency.

STALK ME

www.emilygoodwinbooks.com
www.facebook.com/emilygoodwinbooks
Instagram: authoremilygoodwin
Email: emily@emilygoodwinbooks